THE
CHILDREN
OF ASHGAROTH

By the same author

Quest for the Faradawn
Melvaig's Vision

THE
CHILDREN
OF ASHGAROTH

Richard Ford

GRAFTON BOOKS
A Division of the Collins Publishing Group

LONDON GLASGOW
TORONTO SYDNEY AUCKLAND

Grafton Books
A Division of the Collins Publishing Group
8 Grafton Street, London W1X 3LA

Published by Grafton Books 1986

British Library Cataloguing in Publication Data
Ford, Richard
The children of Ashgaroth.
I. Title
823'.914[F]   PR6056.O6636

ISBN 0-246-13054-7

Typeset by Columns of Reading
Printed in Great Britain by
Mackays of Chatham Ltd, Kent

To my parents

CHAPTER I

The warm spring rain fell gently onto Bracca's hair and trickled down his neck. As he walked, drops of water found their way between his tunic and his skin and made him itch, but he was too engrossed in his thoughts to notice. His bare arms and legs became shiny with the wet and seemed to glisten in the hazy white light of the sun. Under his feet, the path he was following grew muddy and little puddles formed in the hollows but he made no attempt to avoid them and his moccasins soon became soggy and uncomfortable.

Around him the forest was alive with the sounds of the rain as it tinkled and crashed its way from the highest branch of the tallest beech down through all the layers of foliage beneath until finally it reached the fresh green fronds of fern or bracken that littered the floor of the forest. The air seemed to vibrate with life, singing out a welcome to the drops, as they fell and washed away the dry dust of the recent past.

Yet despite the magical beauty of the green burgeoning life all around him and the exuberant singing of the birds that echoed and rang in the leafy cathedrals through which he moved, Bracca's heart was heavy and a dark shadow hung over his spirit.

The path turned a corner and Bracca came to the clearing

where most of the huts in the village stood. He walked past them, head down, and did not respond to the greetings that were called out by those few villagers who were not sheltering from the rain. At his lack of response they lowered their arms and stilled their voices and their distrust and dislike of this strange young man were further confirmed. Though he had lived among them since he had arrived as a young boy with his mother, Morven, and Melvaig, his father, they had never truly accepted him. There was something about him that set him apart and though outwardly they were friendly with the boy, inside their hearts were cold towards him.

Where had they come from, these three strangers who had suddenly, one summer's day a long time ago, walked out of the forest and appeared amongst them? Wild-eyed they had been then, as if they had seen and survived some great unnameable terror; something so terrible that simply to have lived through it had filled them with an exquisite and immeasurable sense of relief and joy. They had not said much at first but as their wounds began to heal and their bodies and spirits were refreshed with rest, so parts of their strange story started to unfold and the hearts of the villagers froze with horror at the words spoken by the strangers. Yet they could make no sense of what they heard and soon the members of the Stagg, the Council of Elders, had taken them away from the main village and they had heard no more until, a little later, the three were given a large hut a little way away from the rest. And now, when the villagers questioned them further, they would tell no more, only saying that they came from a land far off over the seas and that their boat had sunk near the shores of the village.

So time had passed but the terrible images conjured up by those first-revealed words refused to fade, and so the people were left with visions of a world where there were no trees and no grass, where the sky was always brown and the earth scorched, cracked and blistering under a relentless and constantly oppressive heat; where the only animals that lived were those reared by men for food and clothing and where plants had to be grown and worked for, not simply found and picked from the forest as they did. And the name of Xtlan lingered in the furthest reaches of their minds to strike fear into their hearts as they recalled the look of dread on the faces of the strangers when, in their first fever-ridden days among them, they had mouthed his name repeatedly in their delirious ramblings. And the knowledge of Xtlan became an ever-present cloud of darkness and evil which formed a constant threat to the peace and fruitfulness of the villagers' lives, yet all they knew of him was that he had ruled over the world that the strangers had come from.

The strangers were never really forgiven for the introduction of this shadow into the villagers' lives and their resentment was increased by the way that Melvaig, Morven, Bracca and the little girl, Shayll, born soon after their arrival in the village, lived apart from them, rarely mixing and spending most of their time either singly or with each other.

Their attitude to the wild creatures of the forest also set them apart; they treated them with respect and reverence which the villagers found impossible to comprehend and which irritated them immensely. They themselves, though prohibited from killing animals by the code of the Stagg, handed down from generation to generation, nevertheless saw nothing to worship or love in the animals and birds, the trees and the flowers, that filled the forest. Indeed this prohibition had begun to anger them; it was not always easy to gather enough from foraging, particularly in the winter, to keep hunger away. And yet there were animals and birds all around; many of them, they were certain, edible if they were allowed to kill them. Further, Melvaig had become a member of the Stagg, an honour accorded to very few of the villagers, and, to make matters worse, when he had retired recently through bad health, Bracca had been invited by the other elders to take his place. It was in fact, and the villagers who saw him guessed this, from a meeting of the Stagg that Bracca was now returning.

He came to a spot where the path on which he was travelling crossed another smaller one and he paused, as he always did here, to look up at the five stone statues that stood in the clearing at his side. No one knew who had carved them but they had existed for longer than any of the villagers could remember and it was said that they had been there ever since the village had been founded after the War. They were not large, not much bigger than lifesize, and yet they were possessed of a simple majesty which had enthralled Bracca from the time he had first seen them. Over the years he had noticed a decline in the care taken of them by the villagers so that now bracken and fern and moss crept over them, obscuring their feet and legs. Bracca had often been tempted to clear it away but he had refrained from doing so for fear of being accused of interference by the village. He also had a strange feeling that the statues themselves preferred it this way, shrouded in vegetation, looking out through leafy veils of oak and ash and birch. They stood in a small semi-circle; at one end the dog, Sam, and at the other Perryfoot the hare. Next to Sam stood the badger and at his side the boy called Nab and the girl, Beth. There was also Warrigal, a large owl, carved perching on the boy's shoulder. Their names, and the legendary story of their quest for the Faradawn, were as much a part of Bracca as the breath in his body, for Melvaig had told him of their epic struggle from the moment he had first been old enough to understand. In those days, when he was small, he used to love sitting with them, playing around them, talking to them as if they were real and then taking their parts and talking back to himself in their voices. So they were his friends; they knew all his secrets, his worries and his anxieties, when he was happy and when he was sad. They knew too of the turmoil in his spirit; the cold clamp of terror that encircled him at times for no reason, a legacy of his days as a child in the world of Xtlan and of his terrible ordeals during their escape from that world. They knew of the confusion he felt at his relationship with the other villagers; why had they never accepted him? Was it because he had not been born among them; or was it because of his love for the wild creatures in the forest, a love which they did not share or even seem to understand? Or was it because he enjoyed his own company, often going out by himself for long walks through the forest, learning about the animals, the insects and birds, discovering for himself their beauties, their mysteries and their behaviour? He had found within himself a deep and instinctive feeling for the whole of the natural world about him; a closeness and an empathy which never failed to delight and amaze him as he spent days wandering through the trees, listening to the birds, watching badgers in the twilight world of late evening or else laughing quietly to himself as he watched the antics of fox cubs playing outside their hole. Then was he truly content; then, as he sat under the flat, spreading branches of a huge beech tree and looked out over the valley into the dense, thick mosaic of greens, he found a peace which almost left him formless, forgetting who and what he was and becoming one with the forest.

He left the path now and walked slowly towards the statues through the young, green stems of bracken, letting the rich smell of the wet peaty earth wash around him and calm the anguish in his mind. He got to the figure of Brock and began to stroke the head, and in his imagination the rough stone became hair and the body became warm with life and breath.

He sat down on the small stone base of the statue and, with his arm around Brock's body, stared at the carpet of old dead bracken beneath his feet, dark with wetness. The rain continued to fall and the fronds of this year's bracken jerked and shuddered as the drops hit them so that Bracca was mesmerized as he became immersed in their uneven rhythms. Always, when he was among the statues, he found their presence a comfort and a consolation yet now the pain in his heart deepened for they were a tangible reminder of Melvaig's dream; the vision his father had pursued and eventually realized through all the horrors of the world of Xtlan, and the terrible words he had just heard spoken at the Stagg destroyed the security of that vision and sent the beauty

11

and truth of Melvaig's world crumbling into dust.

Bracca forced himself to think back just a short time to the scene at the Stagg. He remembered the walk to the cavern where the meetings were held. He could not have felt happier; the sun had shone and a warm breeze had bathed his face with all the fragrances of summer. Melvaig, Morven and his sister, Shayll, had left the hut at the same time to go for a walk through the forest; utterly content with themselves and with the beauty of the day. They would probably have returned by now, he thought bitterly, with their bags full of berries and fruits, eager to show him the treats they had found to eat. Through the village he had gone, even stopping and talking to one or two of the people he had passed, and then had begun the long climb up the hillside through the trees until he reached the cavern. He had stopped to rest for a while in the clearing outside the entrance and had looked across to the sea in the distance, sparkling and shimmering in the sunshine; its salty tang, carried on the breeze, evoking rich and poignant memories of the time Melvaig and Morven had taken himself and Shayll there to show them the beach where they had come ashore at the end of their escape from Xtlan. He remembered also the look of sadness on their faces as they showed himself and Shayll the place on the cliff-top where they had buried Shuinn. Shuinn, the giant, who he remembered with a rush of warmth even now, after all these years. Melvaig had often told him of their times together and of the part Shuinn had played in their terrible journey through Xtlan and, finally, of how the giant had died using his body to shield his, Bracca's, body from a great fire they had come through on the seas. He could just see now the great clump of oak trees on the edge of the headland under which was the cairn of stones that marked his grave. Yet always, when they talked of Shuinn, he could sense something that was not being told to him, some dark shadow over his memory which they would not reveal.

Then, his heart fluttering a little with apprehension as it always did before these meetings, he had passed the two old wizened oak trees at either side of the entrance and walked inside the cavern. There was a small narrow tunnel to go along first but then it opened out into a huge natural cave. Although at first, after being in the sunshine, it had seemed dark inside, he had soon got used to the gloom and he could see the shaft of light from a fissure high up in the wall illuminating the long stone table in the centre. The other members of the Stagg had just been settling down around it, pulling their wooden benches up to it and talking animatedly among themselves. It was cool inside the cavern, almost cold, even on a hot day like this, and he could smell and feel the dampness coming from the stone. Delicate little pale green fronds of fern grew out of the cracks and different sorts of moss adorned the walls. As the others saw him come in they fell silent and from one of the dark corners he could hear the sound of dripping water, steady and relentless as a pulse. He went forward and took his place.

At his side sat Stowna, old and grey. A small man even in his prime, he seemed to have shrunk with age yet his mind was still quick and his knowledge of herbs and plants unrivalled. His hair stood up from his head in a shock of long bristle and his eyebrows protruded like ledges. He had been on the Stagg for as long as anyone and of all the members he had been the most willing to accept Bracca. Yet now, strangely, the old man turned away as Bracca sat down, without offering him his usual greeting.

Across the table sat Barll and Nemm and they too avoided Bracca's eyes, looking down at the table intensely, as if to find there the answer to some difficult problem. Barll was the younger of the two and Bracca could remember when Barll had joined the council; called on to replace his father who had died suddenly and unexpectedly whilst out foraging in the forest with his son. The younger man had buried him where he fell, saying they had been too far from the village to bring the body back. There were some who wondered at this, suspecting that the father's death had been from other than natural causes, but they kept quiet for Barll had a quick temper and ready fists and now that he was on the Stagg he was in a position to make life uncomfortable for anyone he did not like. A big man, with an unruly mane of black hair and a thick black beard, he had always been antagonistic towards Bracca, arguing with him at meetings and ignoring him completely if they met or passed each other outside. Like his father before him, his special knowledge was in the weapons and techniques of fighting and warfare; skills that had never, to the recollection of anyone in the village, been needed, yet something in the collective consciousness of the people made it impossible to abandon this knowledge altogether and so for generations back Barll's family had had a seat on the Stagg. They guarded the instruments of battle in a place known only to themselves and always there had been a number of villagers, mostly men, who had been eager to spend time training with them. Both Bracca and Melvaig were certain, though they had not seen them, that in comparison with the awful ability of the warriors of Xtlan, Barll's weapons and skills were ridiculously inadequate but they said nothing, happy in the knowledge that they would never be needed; preferring to obliterate from their minds all memories of the terrible viciousness, cruelty and savagery that they had witnessed and endured in Xtlan. Yet despite Barll's pathetically ill-founded confidence in his military prowess there was something unsettling about him. He bristled with aggression as he strode around the village, his voice strident and harsh, relishing the respectful awe that he engendered among the villagers, the ripples of fear that spread out around him as he walked among them.

Next to Barll sat Nemm, as old as Stowna yet tall like a willow, so thin and frail that he looked liable to snap in the wind, his long strands of wispy grey hair floating like thistledown around his face and head. Like Stowna he had been on the Stagg for a long time, chosen in his youth for his exceptional intelligence which the village had utilized in many and varied ways; in the settling of disputes, in its organization and administration, in forecasting the weather.

14

He was also possessed of strange psychic gifts and the power of healing which he exercised by laying his hands on the afflicted. He could tell whether a person was lying by simply looking at their face, he could tell where a crop of berries or a particular herb was growing by closing his eyes and letting a picture of its location come into his head. He got in touch with those who had died and spoke from them to the living they had left behind. His attitude towards both Melvaig and Bracca had been ambivalent; neither welcoming them nor being unfriendly and this ambivalence was the result of fear that the arrival and continuing presence of the strangers, with their copy of the Book and their knowledge of Nab, Beth and the others, would disrupt the peaceful harmony of the village. Now, as Bracca sat down opposite him, he allowed a thin, nervous smile to flicker across his face but the grave disquiet he felt at what he knew was going to be announced at the meeting rendered him unable to meet Bracca's eyes.

Finally, at the head of the table, there stood Nabbeth, his cold grey eyes fixing upon Bracca with a piercing look as the young man took his place. Tall and straight he stood despite his age and his brilliant white hair glinted in the light as it flowed around his shoulders. His thin, elegant hands played absently with his long white beard as he looked around at each of them in turn, waiting for them to settle before the meeting began properly. As the head of the Stagg and the leader of the village he was entitled to wear the long green cloak reputed to have been worn by Nab himself in his last days and it fell about him now in deep folds as he went over to a wooden chest in the corner of the cave, opened the heavily carved lid and lifted out a small casket. Coming back to the table he placed the casket in front of him, laying both hands on it as he began to speak; his clear, imperious voice, deep and resonant, echoing around the high ceiling as he addressed them.

'As the direct descendant of Nab and Beth, as was my father before me and my father's father before him, and so on back and back to the very beginnings of our village; as

15

protector of their faith and as the guardian and vessel of their spirit, I welcome you to this meeting of the Stagg.' He paused and Bracca felt a tension in the air as silence hung heavily upon them. Nabbeth went on, his hands still resting upon the casket.

'What I have to say is neither easy nor pleasant for me and will of course be a matter for the Stagg to decide upon finally. Barll has informed me, and I have had word from the village, that our sources of food are dwindling; we have to forage further and further away to find berries and fruits enough to sustain ourselves. The problem is made worse by the fact that we are growing in number; every season that passes sees the addition of a handful more infants whose bellies need filling and who need clothing. We have tried; Nab knows how we have tried! The transplanting of roots to the village, the cultivation of fungus, yet it has not worked. The crop has lasted a season or two and then the birds have found them or they have been taken by the wild creatures that we love. It cannot go on. Our people are tired of nettles and chickweed; they are sick of leaves! They crave new food; plentiful food, new tastes to send the blood surging in the veins. They crave freedom from the endless build up of stocks during the warm times in preparation for the long, cold, wet winters. All their time is taken with foraging; they have no time for play or sport, for times with their families. Their lives are a constant drudge. And yet all around them, while they are toiling to keep the pangs of hunger away, they see blackbirds and thrushes and pigeons, rabbits and wild pigs and deer; the forest teems with these and countless other birds and animals. And our people wonder...'

He stopped as if to let those who were listening to him come to their own inevitable conclusions and Bracca felt a sickness in his stomach.

'The decision I have come to has not been easy to make. Long is the time I have spent in deliberation; in calling upon the spirit of Nab to guide me and in communication with the Book which, though its written words are lost to us, we know

16

through its pictures and from the spoken words of Melvaig, who brought it to us.' He looked down at the casket on the table in front of him and his fingers spread over the carvings on its surface as if in reverence for the Book that lay inside. 'From the beginnings our people, the people of the Land of Haark, have lived in the light of Nab, according to his beliefs and to his great faith handed down to us from generation to generation; the warmth of his love for all things being kept alive by the direct line of his descendants and by the wise men, the men of the Stagg, who have judged and governed and ordered our world even as he would have done. And so, as you well know, we have never killed any of the animals or birds or insects that share our home with us nor have we tasted of their flesh. Neither have we taken or destroyed their homes, living instead in harmony with them, and our lives have been peaceful and joyous. Yet now the people are restless and life has become difficult and there must be a change. I have prayed and communed with Ashgaroth the Lord of Light and I have invited Nab into my heart and, with their guidance, I have come to a decision.'

He stopped again and, in the cold damp silence, Bracca heard his heart pounding and felt sweat break out on his brow. High up, in the darkest corners of the cavern, a pigeon cooed. Nabbeth frowned, as if annoyed by this reminder of the wild creatures whose fate he was about to pronounce upon. Then, looking up at a spot on the far wall, he spoke, and his voice quavered slightly as though it was having difficulty in coming from his throat.

'It will no longer be forbidden to kill the animals or the birds for food. Further it will be permissible to clear space in the forest for the growing of our crops; to cut down the trees and to pull up the vegetation to create areas near our homes where we may tend our harvest. And if any animal or bird or insect comes into these cleared areas and threatens our crops then it may be killed also, to preserve our food. It may even be possible to capture some of the creatures alive, perhaps the rabbits or deer or the wild fowl, and to breed

17

from them, killing and eating their offspring. That way we would not need to waste time hunting in the forest, for our food would be all around us.

'But this I say to you; there must be moderation and gentleness in all things. No more land may be cleared than is needed; creatures may only be killed where necessary for food or preservation of food and with as little suffering as is possible. Our captive animals must be treated with respect and dignity. Where the killing is to conserve our crops then we must be certain there is no other way. Barll will teach us the ways of killing; the handling of the weapons he and his forebears have looked after for so long. He will show us how to make more weapons; bows and arrows, spears and clubs. And if...'

'No! Stop! You're wrong.' Bracca had leapt to his feet, interrupting Nabbeth and shouting out angrily at the top of his voice. The turmoil in his head had raged in silence for too long while Nabbeth was speaking and it had become too much to bear. Now, to his horror, he suddenly found all eyes upon him, staring at him in astonishment and contempt. For a few terrible moments silence hung in the air like a thunderclap while Bracca's mind raced furiously to put together all the thoughts and arguments and feelings that had filled his head while Nabbeth's words dragged his spirit into darkness. And then he went on, the blood racing in his veins, the faces around the table a blur.

'It is against everything Nab stood for and struggled and fought for. You could never imagine he would approve of this. We cannot decide to kill the animals any more than they can decide to kill us; they do not deliberately set out to kill us for food and neither can we kill them. They have as much right as we have to live, to share the forest with us...'

'Sit!' Nabbeth's voice, clear, sharp and strident with fury, cut into Bracca's tirade and he stopped and looked at the old man. Nabbeth's grey eyes, as cold and hard as stone, bore into him, paralysing him with the intensity of their awesome and majestic power.

18

'Sit,' he repeated, and Bracca felt himself responding to the command and succumbing to Nabbeth's will. As he sat down again he felt the force of the old man's anger as a blow to his stomach and from the others round the table he felt such a wave of animosity that his body prickled and tingled with discomfort. Nabbeth's voice grew quiet, his features drawn into an expression of disgust.

'You presume,' he said, 'to tell me how Nab would feel about such things. You know the faith better than I? How dare you! Am I not his descendant; the guardian of his faith? Have not my ancestors interpreted his spirit for generations past? Do you think these are decisions I have come to lightly without seasons of silent prayer and communion with him and with Ashgaroth? You! You, who have been with us for so short a time; a stranger, who is only in the Stagg because of his father's great courage and heroism and the knowledge of our faith which he brought to us. In your little time here you have shown yourself to be awkward, recalcitrant. Though only small when you arrived among us, you have grown up apart from the village, following your own ways; independent and separate. We have only born all this out of deference and respect for your father; do not imagine you are here for your own sake. While he was on the Stagg with us, he did not spurn our kindness and our generosity by arguing or criticizing. No! He was grateful to us, grateful to be among us. Simply to be here was, for him, enough. And so, Bracca, I will not argue with you; it has been discussed and decided by the rest of us. I will say simply this and it must suffice. Is not man superior to the animals? Was it not a man and a woman, Nab and the girl Beth, who led the animals to salvation as written in the Book? Why else was man given the power to think, to reason, if not to ensure his own self-preservation?'

Bracca had quailed beneath the first onslaught of Nabbeth's tongue and the power of his authority yet now, hearing the nauseating arrogance of the old man, he found a well of confidence and strength within himself enough to give him the will to stand up again and face Nabbeth. Then, as if from afar, he heard himself speak.

'And I am powerless to argue with you; it seems to have already been decided. Now, at least, I know my place among you. You are wrong, Nabbeth; of that I am certain. Something has happened today that marks the beginning of the end, for once you start down this path it will be impossible to stop. You do not know the frailty of the world you live in; its fragile delicacy is lost to you – you who have always lived amongst the beauty of its miracles. You say you live according to the will and spirit of Nab and the five other travellers from Silver Wood yet to you these are only ideas to which you pay token homage. You do not feel it deep within you, to the very marrow of your bones, as I do, for I have seen the other world; the dead, barren, desolate world of Xtlan. You speak patronizingly of my father, Melvaig, who brought you the Book you clasp in your hands and pretend to follow, who lived with the promise of its dreams and pursued the vision of its reality through all the horrors of Xtlan. The terrors of that epic journey have left him drained of any will to fight again; he has found his salvation and he has fought enough. Ashgaroth has rewarded him for the strength and endurance of his faith. But I, I am not drained, Nabbeth, and I will not let the truth and sanctity of his vision be destroyed; I will not stand by and watch it crumble and fade because of your mistakes. Who gave you the right to judge, to decide which creatures will live and which will die, to assume your life is more valuable than theirs? If you feel able to do this with the animals and the birds today, tomorrow you will start with the people.'

'Enough,' Nabbeth shouted, his voice echoing round the walls, but Bracca was already on his way out of the cavern and away from the meeting. As he walked his knees started to feel weak and the pounding of his heart sent the blood roaring in his ears. An image of the Stagg hovered before his eyes like a great dark shadow and, even as he walked out into the daylight and felt the first drops of rain on his face, he could still hear Nabbeth's furious shouts behind him.

20

Now, as he sat on the stone base of the statue of Brock and watched the rain form puddles on the soft earth, the recollection of those awful moments in the cavern set his stomach churning again yet he also felt a degree of pride and satisfaction that he had found the courage to speak out against Nabbeth. How would Melvaig and Morven react when he told them? Had he been right in what he said? What would the future hold now? What could he do to stop Nabbeth's terrible pronouncement from being carried through? A sudden wave of loneliness, as cruel and desolate as a plague, swept over him as the realization of being utterly and completely by himself engulfed him. He raised his head and saw a squirrel racing up the trunk of a large beech tree, a blackbird singing from somewhere behind him and, just to the side, the sound of the rain was shattered by the sudden rhythmic tapping of a woodpecker. A rabbit hopped into the clearing in front of him and, having nibbled at the grass for a few moments, suddenly saw him and dashed back into the undergrowth. All this, that had seemed so permanent, so inviolate, so reassuring in its constancy, was now under threat; the sanctity of its existence had suddenly become painfully vulnerable and he found the thought so unbearable that he felt tears start to well up behind his eyes and he buried his face in his hands. And then, through his darkness, he seemed to hear a voice. It came to him clearly and distinctly, in a tone that was soft and gentle and comforting.

'Be still,' it said, 'and do not be afraid. The mantle of my light is now upon you and my strength is within you. The time is now come when the jewel of my creation will be restored to its former glory and the earth will once again shine with peace and innocence and love. The final struggle against the darkness is at hand and you, Bracca, will be at the forefront; you will play a part that in the aeons of time to come will be regarded as the Beginning. Have patience and know that I am with you. When the time is right, then shall you be told all.'

The voice stopped, yet still Bracca held his breath, unable

to believe or comprehend what he had just heard and fearful that there might be more which he would miss if he opened his eyes and broke the cocoon of darkness within which the voice had come to him. But as the moments ebbed away and the voice did not return, he slowly took his hands from his face and looked out into the green forest.

Ashgaroth had spoken to him! Ashgaroth the Lord of Good who had made the world and who had chosen Nab to save his creation from the darkness of Dréagg, Ruler of Evil. Ashgaroth, who had come to Melvaig as a silver light and guided him through his terrible struggle to escape from Xtlan, Dréagg's disciple on earth. And now he, Bracca, had been chosen to banish the shadow of Dréagg forever.

For an instant, doubt came to him but then it vanished like a spangle of frost beneath the sun and in its place there took root in his spirit a feeling of supreme confidence and certainty; he felt himself to be growing out of the confines of his body, soaring up into the treetops and beyond them to the sky and at the same time embracing and absorbing all the green growing things of the forest, the creatures who dwelt there and in the skies and in the seas, so that he became as one with them all; he was in them and they were in him. For one fantastic moment he saw the whole of creation spread out before him like a carpet and the power and strength and magic of its beauty were unconquerable for love and harmony reigned over all and there was no pain or suffering, no illness or death; no creature lived off the flesh of any other and neither did they squabble or fight. Truly this was the world of Ashgaroth; and though the moment passed, the sparkling crystal clarity of the vision remained with him. Slowly he got up from his seat at the stone feet of Brock's statue and putting his hand on the badger's head looked round at the others. For an instant he imagined them alive, vibrant with energy, their eyes flickering over the clearing and their bodies shimmering with breath. They looked back at him and it was as if he were one of them, about to start out together through the forest on the final epic journey to fulfil the prophecy of Ashgaroth and rid the world of the dark shadow of Dréagg forever. He kissed the cold wet stone of the badger's nose and then, his body tingling with excitement, made his way back to the path and away from the clearing to his home with Melvaig, Morven and Shayll.

CHAPTER II

The rain had stopped by the time that Bracca came round the bend and saw the hut ahead of him. Built into the hillside which rose up from the forest floor, the back wall consisted of a large slab of natural rock, while the rest of the walls and the roof were of timber; small trees cut down with the stone axes used by the villagers and lashed together with thin young boughs. The gaps were filled with mud and clay and the floor was made of pieces of flat stone covered with bracken or heather or fern, renewed and replaced whenever necessary. There was a small round clearing at the front of the hut but the overhanging branches of the silver birch and ash and oak trees that grew around the outside came together to form a high leafy canopy through which the sun was now shining. The golden light sparkled off the raindrops on the leaves and sent dapples of light floating over the fresh green grasses on the floor.

Bracca stood still for a moment in the shadow of a large beech at the entrance to the clearing. The branches hung low around him and he could see the delicate bright green leaves starting to unfurl from their sticky, brown chrysalis-like casing. The heady scent of the damp rain-soaked earth and the wet leaves filled his nostrils and he gazed, as he had so often done before, at Melvaig, Morven and Shayll as they busied themselves around the hut; his heart full of love for his family. For Melvaig and Morven there was, in addition, admiration, respect and even awe at their escape from Xtlan and the bravery, courage and faith they had shown throughout their terrible ordeals.

He could see Melvaig now, sitting on an old log at the side of the doorway to the hut. On his knees lay a length of birch bark which Bracca guessed he was making into a new pair of moccasins; cutting the bark into shape with the edge of a sharp stone and threading it with bramble briars. A large boulder with a flat top stood just in front of the log and Melvaig was using it as a table to work on. His hair was grey now and long and, although he was not really old, his face was heavily lined and wrinkled. Xtlan had taken his toll, sapping Melvaig of his energy and strength and leaving him only a shadow of the brave young man who had set out so long ago from Ruann on his epic journey through the holocaust of the other world to find Morven and Bracca and finally to escape in the pursuit of his vision. And now he was living out the essence of that vision; content to be alive and to be amongst the green growing things and the animals of the forest, to be with Morven, Shayll and Bracca and to be at peace. Bracca looked at the quiet strength of his father's gentle features and the weight of the love he bore for the old man threatened to overwhelm him. How could he tell Melvaig what he had just heard from the mouth of Nabbeth? What would it do to him to destroy the purity of his vision? Bracca's mind baulked in horror as he imagined the old man's reaction.

Suddenly Melvaig looked up as Shayll came out of the hut, gave him a kiss on the cheek and sat down at his feet. She had with her a carved wooden bowl full of leaves and berries which she was sorting ready for their meal. He still felt a fierce surge of pride whenever he saw her; pride and wonder at the beauty of this girl, his sister. Now in the full bloom of her youth, she had the grace of a deer and the innocence of a baby rabbit. The sensuousness of her full

25

mouth and the voluptuous contours of her body contrasted strikingly with the fawn-like delicacy of her eyes. Now as she sat in the glade with her head bent over the bowl, the sun shining on her deep red hair seemed to strike ribbons of flame from her which filled the clearing. Yet as he looked at her sickening memories of the incident at the Stagg came back to him; images of Nabbeth's face and the echoes of his voice reverberated around his head and he forced himself to banish from his mind the awful recollection of the rumours that Nabbeth desired her for his woman. He had never liked the idea before; the man was too old and was lacking in the qualities that Bracca admired; gentleness, humility, perception and love for the world around him. Now though, after the Stagg, the thought was so obnoxious to him that his stomach tightened and his limbs grew weak with a terrible impotent rage. 'Never,' he vowed to himself, and then again, quietly under his breath, 'Never, to him.' Yet even as his resolve stiffened, a tremor of doubt as to the motive for his determination swept over him. Was it blind, selfish jealousy? A refusal to share the girl with anyone – his sister, with whom he had shared all his secrets and who, in turn, had told him hers; this girl, who knew him better than anyone else did, who he had lived with, walked, talked, played and laughed with, for almost as long as he could remember and who he found it almost impossible to conceive of as being an entity apart from himself, able to exist and live a life without his constant presence. Or was it something different? A revulsion against Nabbeth, a distrust of the man for what he was about to do to the world Bracca loved so dearly and for the arrogance he had displayed towards himself and Melvaig? Or, again, was it envy, simply envy of anyone who threatened to take her away? Would it be wrong of him to stand in her way if she was willing to go with Nabbeth? She would be well regarded then, a figure of respect, looked after with the best of everything. He thought back to when they had both been young together, during the first days in Haark. He remembered the long balmy summer evenings, sitting outside at

Melvaig's feet in the clearing in front of the hut while he told them stories of his legendary journey through Xtlan. They listened spellbound as the sun slowly sank behind the trees while they relived, with him, the grim horrors of the Gurrtslagg or the cruel and terrible majesty of the Blaggvald; the revulsion of the Dammfenn or the savage splendour of the city itself, the capital of Xtlan. And they heard about Jarrah, their grandfather, in the village where Melvaig and Morven had been born and brought up, and of Arkron the Hebbdril, the wise old man who had read the Book to Melvaig as they were taken across the desert of Molobb by their captors, the three scavenging Mengoy. But it was when he spoke of Shuinn, the Mengoy who had become Melvaig's closest friend and travelling companion and without whom he could never have survived the terrors of the journey, that their father's eyes shone wth love and his words were as magic, creating a picture of the red-haired giant so real and so vivid that he seemed to be a tangible physical presence sitting with them and when Melvaig stopped talking the giant stayed with them for some time after, next to them, the glow of his warmth washing over them. For Bracca, who had known both Arkron and Shuinn and who had seen many of the places his father described, Melvaig's words rekindled his childhood memories and helped him to sort out, analyse and absorb the desperate confusion that swam around in his head when he tried to think about those times; the times before Haark. For Shayll, born not many weeks after their arrival in Haark, it was the creation of a new and different world, frightening and terrible in its adversity, yet giving her a sense of her own roots and an awareness of her origins as well as enabling her to see Melvaig and Morven as they had been so that her parents were complete people, existing in the past as well as the present.

Later when she was old enough to walk properly, Melvaig and Morven had taken them both through the forest, teaching them about the animals and the plants. Much of this Bracca later learned had been taught to Melvaig by Stowna;

27

for Xtlan had been, for the most part, so barren and desolate that not much vegetation had grown there and there had been few wild creatures so Melvaig had known very little. With Stowna as his teacher though, he had learnt quickly and the old man had been surprised at his pupil's natural aptitude; his affinity with, and instinct for, the world of plants. And Melvaig had in turn taken great delight in bestowing the treasure of his new knowledge on his family, showing them where the elder tree grew and listing its many uses enthusiastically; the leaves turned into an ointment to reduce bruising, the delicate fronds of creamy flowers to cure illnesses of the skin and the berries to help relieve coughs and colds. The branches he hollowed out, cut and shaped so as to make flutes and pipes which one of the villagers, Magg, was teaching them to play. He took them to the part of the forest where pine trees grew and there they would gather pine needles to take back and use for kindling the fire. While there they would cut the bark of some of the trees with a sharp stone and gather the golden yellow syrup of the resin in their shell bowls to help in healing wounds. At other times they would go to the river and cut bundles of young, slender willow branches to use for weaving baskets and water carriers, or gather rushes and reeds for the same purpose. Many of the things they needed grew either in the river or on the bank, mint to add flavour and variety to the toadstools and mushrooms, watercress with its slightly sharp yet satisfying taste, meadowsweet to strew down with rushes on the earth floor of the hut to release its delicate scent when walked on, soapwort whose leaves they boiled in water to produce a liquid for washing with, and bog myrtle which, again when boiled in a large shell with water, released a scummy waxy liquid that they used to make candles out of. When Shayll had been a baby, Melvaig had, on Stowna's instructions, gathered marshmallows, and sucking the roots had seemed to have the effect of relieving her teething pains. At one spot along the river there was a large bog and if ever any of them cut themselves Melvaig would gather a clump of

28

the sodden green moss to hold against the wound as Stowna had shown him.

And so some of Bracca's most cherished memories of those early springs, summers and autumns were of wandering amongst the trees in the afternoons or evenings, picking bilberries or blackberries or raspberries, nibbling at young fresh leaves and shoots, enjoying the sweet taste of the beech or the vaguely smoky flavour of hawthorn; collecting toadstools carefully and putting them in the wooden gathering basket where they lay next to each other, golds, yellows and browns glimmering and shiny with moisture like fat, round, smooth pebbles at the sea's edge. At other times they would go nut-gathering, walking to the river over the bank where hazel, beech and chestnut grew and returning home laden with beechmast, sweet, fragrant hazelnuts and the burnished brown cobs of chestnuts, ready to roast on a big flat stone which was placed on one side of the fire.

He remembered the smells from those early days. Autumn; the sweet scent of hot chestnuts, the heavy musk of damp brown leaves as they lay mouldering on the ground, the woodsmoke hanging above the village and mingling with the chill mists. Spring; bluebells, wild garlic, the air full of an awakening freshness as all the new green leaves unfurled to catch the sun for the first time. Summer was very often dusty; little clouds of dry earth spurting up from the tracks as feet scuffed along them; in the air a rich mixture of sun-baked ground, warm green bracken and shimmering vegetation. And winter, with the sharp tang of frost, the crisp, frozen leaves yielding up a unique, heady fragrance as they were crushed underfoot. In the hut, the perpetual smell of woodsmoke permeating everything, clothes, hair and skin; sickly and cloying now that it was indoors and there was no respite from it; the heady aroma of his damp clothing as the bark dried out by the fire and the scent of the dried toadstools as they warmed in the heat of the flames. And, mingling with the smoke and the drying bark, was the deliciously piney smell of balsam resin as, infusing in hot water, it gave off its warm spicy vapours and those of them with colds or coughs took it in turns to sit over the steam and take deep cleansing breaths.

And so, as Bracca lingered in the sun-dappled shade of the beech, with drops of water from the recent rains dropping loudly on to the ground around his feet, his mind lingered in old memories, wandering through the pathways of his youth in a welter of nostalgia for the innocence and peace of those seemingly far-off days; a nostalgia born as a result of the momentous events of today which had, he now realized, started a new era in his life and sealed him off from his past forever. His reverie was rudely shaken by a sudden shout from inside the hut.

'Melvaig! Any sign of your son yet?'

It was Morven's voice, speaking in the language of Ruann as they always did amongst themselves. His gaze moved to the doorway and then beyond, into the dark gloom inside. He could see her busying herself on the floor with something and then, putting on one side whatever it was she had been doing, she slowly emerged into the bright sunshine, squinting a little in the dazzling light and stretching her back slightly as if she had been bent over for some time. As she came out both Melvaig and Shayll looked up at her and Melvaig spoke.

'No,' he said, and the tone of his voice was light and cheerful, resonant with happiness and contentment so that Bracca's heart ached with pain at the thought of what he would have to tell his father, if not today then at the latest tomorrow, about the events at the Stagg. How would Melvaig react? How could he, Bracca, contemplate causing him so much hurt? Better perhaps to say nothing. And yet, though perhaps that would be better, Bracca knew that he would have to share the turmoil in his spirit with someone and knew also that Melvaig was the person best able to help him, talk to him and advise him because of his past knowledge of, and experience with, the Stagg and the great depth of his understanding about the Book.

'Well, how long do you think he'll be?' Again it was Morven and as she stood at Melvaig's side, gazing around at the clearing, Bracca looked at her and thought, as he had so often done, how remarkable it was that through all the horrors of her time in Xtlan she had managed to retain so much of her beauty. The years had streaked the cascades of her golden hair with grey tints and at the corners of her eyes and the edges of her mouth, lines had started to appear but she was still startlingly lovely, the perfect oval of her face and her high cheek-bones giving her a quality that seemed to combine majesty with humility, command with submission and sensuality with innocence. Her blue eyes still shone with energy and a thirst for life and she laughed often and easily, lifting the heart of any who heard her so that misery and depression were difficult to sustain in her presence. She seemed totally, utterly contented; loving Melvaig as much as she had ever done and blissfully happy with Bracca and Shayll. The pain of her ordeals in Xtlan had receded into the distant past and only very occasionally would he notice the shadow of a cloud pass across her eyes.

And yet neither she nor Shayll were either liked or accepted by the other women in the village; partly because the strangers were not really trusted and partly because of their beauty. The women of Haark were dark; their complexions sallow and their demeanour shadowy and secretive, often glowering. They were well aware of how their men regarded the two fair-featured intruders, the longing that burned within them whenever Morven or Shayll passed near; the hunger that glimmered in their eyes. And there was much resentment that Nabbeth had, it seemed, chosen Shayll above all the women of his own kind to honour by making her his bride. So envy and jealousy kept Bracca's mother and sister largely within the company of their own family. Only when Shayll was being born, and Morven's screams were echoing around the hills and through the trees, sending the birds crashing out of their roosts and into the night sky, did any of the women ever offer any help.

And then it was only old Snargg, Stowna's wife, dead now for many seasons, who came scuttling through the village and out to the strangers' hut, bringing her strange concoctions and her well-tried advice, giving orders to Melvaig and Bracca with firmness and confidence until at last the little baby girl was born, with its shock of red hair immediately recognizable to Melvaig and sending a shiver of remembered pain through his guts as the baby's features thrust home the awful awareness that the child was not his, and he tried to calm his whirling emotions. But his anguished confusion was quickly forgotten beneath the pressures of the immediate demands of caring for Morven who after the terrible birth now lay drained, sweat-soaked and bloody amongst the soiled bed of bracken and meadowsweet. And still Snargg issued her commands; take out the old bedding and bring in new, clean the mother up, remove the piece of ash on which she had bitten during her labour so that there would be no memories of the pain if she saw it. Bracca, rapt and fascinated, had carried the wood out of the hut, marvelling at the depth of the indentations and the perfect pattern of the teeth. And he had hidden it, unable to throw away this tangible symbol of the miracle he had just witnessed. Many years later he had shown it to Shayll, describing to her every detail of what he had seen that night, as clearly etched in his head then as it had been at the time, and she had run home to Morven, crying and sobbing. Eventually, after what seemed an age closeted alone with her mother, the two of them had emerged and Shayll had seemed, somehow, magically different.

Then Snargg had taken the baby and laid it against Morven's breast, its red hair stark against the creamy white, and had helped the infant's questing mouth to find a nipple for Morven herself was barely conscious. Greedily then it had sucked, its little eyes shut, and despite himself Melvaig had looked away for the face he had seen pressed into Morven's ripeness had been that of Shuinn. The old woman had gone then, scuttling away through the trees as the morning sun

32

had appeared over the mountains, and Melvaig had gone after her to give her his thanks and to extend a welcome to her whenever she wished. And she had accepted his hospitality, returning frequently to see how mother and child were faring, doting on the little girl and bringing her gifts; carved wooden dolls, rushes intricately woven into the shapes of animals and birds. She never stayed very long or said very much yet they all got to know and like her and to feel more at home in the village, to have a link with it, because of her. Then one bitter winter morning, when the ground was ridged and rutted with ice and frost held the forest in its iron grip, Stowna came and said she had died and they felt they had lost their only real friend. He brought with him a ring of a deep golden colour, set with a silver jewel which shone through the gold like mist on an autumn morning, and he gave it to Morven saying the old woman had wanted her to have it. Ancient, it was, he said; no one knew how old nor where it had come from but it was rumoured to have its origins way back in the beginning and some said it was even mentioned in the Book. And from the first moment Morven had put it on her middle finger she had never been parted from it, and all who saw it were mesmerized by its mystery and its beauty.

After Snargg's death they felt more than ever isolated from the village and even Stowna seemed to grow away from them and become less friendly. Then the gossip started; the strangers had bewitched the poor old woman, put her under some sort of evil spell and it was that which had caused her wasting sickness and, eventually, her death. So they were more than ever shunned by the villagers and the only real contact they had with them was when Melvaig went to the Stagg.

Suddenly a blackbird flew out of a branch just above Bracca's head, calling loudly, and his thoughts came back abruptly to the present. He involuntarily shook his head as if to free it of the images that still hung there and then he walked forward into the clearing to greet his family. As he did so, Morven turned her head to look at him.

'Ah,' she said. 'Good. Now you can eat with us. Come and give me some help with the fire.'

'He won't want to eat,' said Shayll, teasing. 'He's always full to bursting after all that food they give him at the Stagg. Look at him; he can hardly move!' Her eyes shone and her voice quivered with suppressed laughter. She was referring to the feasts that were always held among the Stagg members at the end of a meeting; a privilege of membership. He hesitated, wondering whether or not to tell them he had not stayed till the end, but then he decided to keep quiet about it for the moment.

'You can talk,' he said, taking up her challenge. 'I get thinner as you get fatter. Look at you; you're as round as a tree-tunk! If you get any bigger we shall have to roll you around. . .' but he stopped speaking as she sprang to her feet and came chasing towards him and he ran away, back through the trees and round the clearing, dodging and ducking among the trunks until finally, laughing together, she caught him and, wrestling, they tumbled over and over on the ground, the dead brown bracken crackling beneath them and this season's new green shoots sending sprays of rain water on to their faces as they knocked against them.

'Stop! I give in!' spluttered Bracca, in between his laughter, as Shayll, pinning him down on the ground with her knees on his chest, tickled him in his sides unmercifully.

'Come on! Say it! Say I'm not fat.'

'Yes,' he said, only just managing to get the words out. 'You're not fat! You're not fat!'

'You mean it? I'm not fat!'

'No! Stop it! Let me get up!'

And she did, pulling him up by the hand with a snort of mock contempt.

Then Shayll fetched a tightly woven willow carrier from the hut and went to the little brook that ran at the edge of the clearing to fetch some water while Bracca gathered the flint and some dried moss and pine needles for kindling from their dry spot under his sleeping heather. Then he went round to the wood shelter at the side of the hut, took some small logs out and carried them over to the stone fire place close to where Melvaig was sitting. As he carefully laid the kindling down and began striking the flints together to try and make a spark he could feel Melvaig's eyes on him and could sense his father's feeling of unease.

'The Stagg...' Melvaig hesitated, uncertain of what to say, idly turning a half-finished moccasin over in his hand. 'It didn't last long. Over quickly. Was there anything interesting discussed ... that I should know?'

He always asked; more, Bracca guessed out of a sense of duty than real interest. He had been pleased to relinquish his position in the Stagg to Bracca, to abdicate responsibility, and was happy to leave important decision-making to others for he had had more than enough of that during the escape from Xtlan. Yet now, Bracca felt, there was something other than dutiful curiosity in his father's question; his voice was coloured by a vague tremor of disquiet. Was now the time to tell him? No. No, he would leave it until perhaps tomorrow. Now was the wrong moment.

'There wasn't much to talk about,' he said. 'Just a few ideas to improve our food stocks; that's all.'

'What kind of ideas?'

'Oh, new ways of storage through the winter. Fairer ways of helping the old and the ill ... you know.' It was a rule that a proportion of the food each adult collected went into a central fund for distribution to those unable to forage for themselves. What proportion should be taken and to whom it should go was a matter of constant dispute.

Melvaig paused and then, just as a spark leaped from the edge of the flint, he spoke again. 'What ways?' he said, and Bracca, suddenly overwhelmed by all the trauma and tension of the day and immensely irritated by Melvaig's probing questions, snapped back at him furiously.

'Killing!' he said viciously. 'Killing the animals!' and then, as soon as the words were out, he wished with all his heart that

35

he could take them back; make them disappear, forget that
they had been said. But that was impossible, the words lay
between them like a wall and everything around them
seemed to stand still as if suddenly they were enclosed in a
vacuum. Then Bracca looked up and the familiar surroundings seemed to have altered their perspective, they appeared
somehow different to him and even the air he breathed felt
disturbed by the terrible echoing aftermath of what he had
said.

Melvaig said nothing. He merely sat, his expression rigid
and fixed, his eyes staring vacuously at Bracca in horror and
disbelief.

'No . . . I. . .' Bracca began but he stumbled over the words;
there was really nothing he could say and so, finally, in
exasperation at his stupidity and his impotence, he said,
'There's no time now. Tomorrow. We'll talk tomorrow.' And
then, finally, 'I'm sorry.'

He was just in time. From the corner of his eye he could
see Morven and Shayll approaching, talking and laughing
together as they made their way towards them across the
clearing.

'Melvaig.' Bracca's voice was urgent, desperate. 'Melvaig.
Say nothing. Act normally. Please.'

To Bracca's relief, he saw his father's mouth move and
heard his response.

'Yes,' the voice was quiet and timorous; as if Melvaig was
dazed. 'Yes. I'll try.'

'Still no fire!' It was Morven's voice, brimming with faked
indignation.

'Too busy talking,' said Shayll. 'It's all the men ever do.'

'Now they'll blame it on the kindling or the flints.' Again it
was Morven, gently teasing, hardly able to contain her
laughter; and somehow that made the trauma that Bracca and
Melvaig had just gone through seem even darker. It was
Melvaig who, with an effort that only Bracca could appreciate
and perceive, first responded to their taunts.

'If we didn't talk,' he said, raising his head and looking into

36

Morven's eyes, 'how could we ever work out what to tell you to do and how it should be done.'

Morven and Shayll grunted in contempt.

'Rubbish,' said Shayll. 'If we had more of a share in the running of the village, we'd all be a lot better off; life would be a lot easier.'

'There should be a woman on the Stagg.' Morven's tone was serious now; the joking was over. 'Bracca! You must put it to the other members again. Keep on at them. You may succeed where your father couldn't.'

Melvaig had tried more than once to get the Stagg to agree to having a woman on the council but to no avail. They saw no need, they said; governing was man's province. Women had babies, cooked food and tended home while men foraged, built, provided and ruled. It had always been the way; why change it?

'Yes, mother,' said Bracca, trying to regain the atmosphere of mock rivalry. 'Now if you'll keep quiet for a moment and let me concentrate, I'll try to get this fire lit.'

He banged the flints together and, as luck would have it, a spark leapt from them on to the moss and caused a tiny glow. Quickly he lowered his head and blew on it very gently from between pursed lips. To his relief and pleasure the ember spread and he placed a few of the pine needles carefully around so that they caught alight also. Then some twigs, going gradually up in size until it was time to put a number of the smaller logs on. Bracca never failed to get satisfaction from the creation of a fire; it was like magic to him, the conjuring up of this flickering living flame from nothing and as he watched the logs start to smoulder red now, he became for a moment so immersed in the gently moving tongues of crimson spreading over the wood that he forgot the clouds hanging over him.

'Come on, Bracca. Move over. Let me get to it.' It took Morven's voice to shake him out of his trance and, a little wearily, he got up and sat down on the rock next to Melvaig. 'Are you all right?' she said, noticing the shadows tremble across his eyes.

'Yes,' he replied. 'Yes, thank you. Just a bit tired. And hungry, I suppose.'

'After your food at the Stagg!'

'I didn't have much. I wanted to get back.'

She said no more, busying herself instead with the preparation of the meal; a soup made from dried toadstools, flavoured and thickened with powdered dandelion root, mint and garlic. They ate it with some of the flat nut cake that she made, spread with honey; and after they had eaten, Shayll made them a drink, placing large deep shells on the hot stones round the fire, filling them with water, putting dried mint in and simmering for a time. When she judged the flavour to be right she took them off and they each had one, sipping the delicately flavoured liquid gently and in silence, buried in their own thoughts. Without saying a word, Bracca got up, walked across to the hut and went inside. There, hanging up on the wall next to the door were two elderwood pipes and a small brown pouch made from the skin of a rabbit that they had found dead while foraging some time ago. The familiar smell of the herbs, hanging in bunches from the ceiling, struck him as it always did with its unique mixture of scents; the sweet and the sharp, the pungent and the delicate. Mint, garlic, hawthorn and nettle; balm, camomile, rosemary, elderflower and wych-hazel; dandelion, fennel and garlic; blackthorn, chestnut and primrose. Each had its own particular virtue, its own method of preparation before use whether turned into an infusion for drinking by boiling in water or rendered down into an ointment. He lifted the pipes and the pouch down and took them outside with him, giving one pipe to Melvaig and keeping the other himself. Melvaig filled his pipe first, opening the bramble draw-string around the neck, taking pinches of the dark, rich, coltsfoot and honey smoking-mixture and packing it carefully in the bowl. When he had finished Bracca took it and filled his and then they both took an ember from the fire and lit up. They puffed away without speaking, feeling themselves relax under the regular rhythm of their breathing and the influence of the sweet smoke as it drifted around them.

It was evening now and the sky was clear; the clouds that had brought the afternoon's rain had all gone leaving a great empty void of dark blue nothingness above their heads, streaked with golds, purples and reds from the sun as it sank slowly down behind the hill at their side. Bracca emptied his mind of all thought, all feeling and emotion, banishing the sickening memory of the Stagg and the fantastic recollection of the voice that had spoken to him. Ashgaroth's voice? Had he really heard it or had it simply been his tortured imagination? Either way, he would have to tell Melvaig. The incident seemed an age away now; almost a product of a different era. Forget it; time enough to think of all that tomorrow. And so he drifted on a cloud of nothing; letting his breathing expand until it and his pipe seemed to be all that existed.

Then gradually he grew aware of a gentle intrusion into the oceans of silence in his head and slowly his consciousness returned until he was able to focus on the sound and then, suddenly, to realize what it was. He looked at Melvaig and saw him with his eyes closed, the pan pipes held against his lips and a look of utter peace on his face. The beautiful, clear notes soared up into the air in waterfalls of liquid sound and even the birds seemed to stop their singing to listen. Then the delicate crystal sounds returned to earth, bringing with them the very essence of the wilderness so that Bracca's heart lifted in a great surge of power and strength, the noise of the pipes taking hold of his spirit and filling it with a sense of omnipotence so real and so tangible he felt he could almost touch it. And then the notes would sound again and in them he could hear all the pain, the horror and the tragedy of the world of Xtlan; notes wrung by Melvaig from the deepest marrow of his soul, containing within their long-drawn-out cadences an evocation of all the sadness and sorrow he had ever witnessed – the creation of an infinitely heart-rending and elegiac anthem of mourning for all who

39

had ever suffered. Never had he heard Melvaig play like this before and it seemed to Bracca that the dreadful news of which his father was now aware had awakened in him all the memories which had for so long lain dormant, submerged beneath the halcyon existence of life in Haark.

Enraptured though he was by Melvaig's music, he turned his head slightly to look at Morven and Shayll and saw by their expressions that they too had been captivated by his playing. And so they sat for what seemed an age and let the sounds carry them where they would until eventually he stopped. No one spoke for a little while and then, with the sun having long since gone down and the night air grown damp and chill, Melvaig said simply, 'I'm tired,' and with one accord they all stood up and walked slowly across to the hut; going inside one by one, lying down on their beds of soft fragrant heather and falling fast asleep almost as soon as they closed their eyes.

CHAPTER III

'Now, tell me,' said Melvaig quietly.

It was the morning of the following day. Melvaig and Bracca had gone out foraging early, making their way up the hill at the back of the hut until they reached the top and then walking through the trees in the direction of the sea. It was a beautiful morning; the sound of bird song filled the air, echoing amongst the branches and the leaves and the bright spring sunshine poured out of a clear blue sky on to the forest. They had moved steadily, filling their foraging bags as they walked and saying very little to each other though the atmosphere between them was heavy with apprehension. And then, within sight of the sea, sparkling and flashing in the distance, they had come to a clearing with a river running through it and after having drunk their fill of the sweet, ice-cold water, had sat down on the ground with their backs against an old log.

Bracca's heart fluttered with nervousness as he began to relate the events of the previous day; the horror of the Stagg, the look on the face of Nabbeth, the bitterness and the raging anger. And then the walk back in the rain, his moments of solace with the statues and, finally, the ecstasy as the voice spoke to him; Ashgaroth's voice. Now, as he told Melvaig about it, he began to doubt again the reality of what he had heard and his speech was stumbling and hesitant, yet Melvaig's face remained downcast to the ground, his features impassive as if Bracca's words were floating over him leaving him unaffected and unconcerned. Yet Bracca knew that could not be the case; had his father locked himself away, withdrawn his emotions before the onslaught which his, Bracca's story was inflicting upon them? How would Melvaig react?

The story ended and there was silence except for the rushing of the river over the rocks, swollen and churning after yesterday's rain. Melvaig did not move; it was as if he was carved in stone. Bracca fidgeted nervously, unwilling to speak yet bursting with words; he cleared his throat, perhaps he had been wrong after all to tell Melvaig? Should he have discussed it first with Morven?

How long would it be before he spoke? The moments dragged themselves out interminably, unbearably, and still there was nothing. He could bear it no longer!

'Melvaig?' He paused, uncertain of his attitude; gently questioning yet fuelled by an aggressive impatience. Then his father looked up and there was a blankness in his eyes that struck Bracca to the very core of his heart; an emptiness that contained no trace of the familiar Melvaig. It was as if someone else, someone he did not know, was looking out from the old man's face. Bracca forced himself to meet Melvaig's gaze and, looking, eventually grew aware of the tremors of pain that swept across his expression and then, buried deep within the limpid pools of his eyes, he gradually perceived the terrible extent of the wound that his father had suffered and he grew suddenly shocked and horrified by what he had done. A great wave of pity and sympathy raged through him and he felt the hot sting of tears behind his eyes. Could he undo what he had done? No, and in any case the damage had been caused yesterday. This, today, was merely the confirmation of all that had been hinted at; of all that had haunted Melvaig's mind and tortured his soul since Bracca had first blurted it out.

And so Bracca, moved beyond measure by Melvaig's suffering, found a flood of tears pouring down his face and was, as if from afar, aware of himself wrapping his arms round his father and embracing him as he had not done since he was a child, his body shaking with sobs, his head cradled against Melvaig's chest. He sensed rather than felt the initial coldness, the withdrawal due to unfamiliarity but then, slowly, Melvaig responded and folded Bracca in his arms, patting his shoulder gently, consolingly. Over and over, in between the anguished sobs, the younger man repeated, 'I'm sorry, I'm sorry,' and Melvaig's hand came up and stroked the back of his son's head where it lay against his chest.

Suddenly Bracca grew aware of the situation for the first time, as if waking from a dream, and, feeling vaguely foolish and ashamed, he fought to stifle his sobs and to calm himself. Gradually the tears subsided and, as they did so, he felt Melvaig grasp him firmly by the shoulders and push him gently away so that his father was able to look him directly in the eyes. Around them the golden sunshine danced and played in the shadows of the leaves as they moved slowly in the breeze, while at their side, re-asserting its presence after the noise of the crying, the river gurgled and splashed on its way, unaware of the depth of the emotional drama being played out on its bank. Downstream, equally oblivious to the trauma that her husband and son were undergoing, Morven was washing herself in the icy water; her skin shimmering and tingling with the cold, her body revelling in the delicious sensuality of the experience.

'Look at me,' Melvaig's voice was pleading, urgent. 'What do you want me to do?' He spoke the words slowly, deliberately, in the form of a statement rather than a question; a statement of hopelessness and despair.

'What can I do?' he continued, and Bracca could almost hear Melvaig's unspoken thoughts: I am too old; I have been through too much. Have I not done enough, suffered enough? Leave me in peace; that's all I want, peace. Don't upset me now, don't disturb things; surely I've earned it.

Don't ruin it now, all that we struggled for, fought for, endured so much for; the vision, my vision. Then Melvaig spoke again and the reality of his voice chased away Bracca's imaginings.

'Perhaps. . .' he said, and his tone was thick and strange; clumsy and faltering. 'Perhaps they're right.'

There was a terrible silence. Through the tangled whirl of his emotions Bracca's mind froze; refusing to accept the awful significance of what he had heard. The look in Melvaig's eyes was guarded and defensive and Bracca's uncomprehending gaze, suddenly seething with anger and contempt, pierced him to the core. He shifted uncomfortably, averting his eyes, and tried to speak again.

'Perhaps . . . as long as there is as little pain, as little suffering as possible; if we only kill them when we really need to. Perhaps then . . . it's all right.' His voice grew stronger, gaining confidence from his own words. 'Is it right that we should suffer so much; from hunger, from the need to forage, from constant worry about food, when it could all be eased? There are so many of them, so many animals, all around us. As long as we didn't kill more than we had to. Is it so wrong? The animals kill each other; the owls, foxes, badgers. They do; why then shouldn't we?'

He stopped and looking up, tried to meet Bracca's look; to gauge the reaction of his words.

'When you first told me I thought, like you, it's the end. The collapse of everything that we fought to find; Ashgaroth's promise – betrayed. But then, as I thought it out, reasoned it out, I came to see it a different way; it's not that. . .'

'No, Melvaig,' Bracca's voice, interrupting, was soft and low as he fought to restrain the passions that were raging within. 'We both know the truth; we both know the spirit of Ashgaroth, you more than I. We are of the Eldron, who rejected the influence of Dréagg, the Lord of Darkness; who turned towards Ashgaroth and who abhor all cruelty as vile. We cannot live by killing; how would our spirits rest then? For we see the earth as the animals do and we are at one with them; we are blessed with the sight of magic in the mountains and the trees and the seas. You say that the other animals kill, why then shouldn't we? Yet they have no choice; they cannot reason out the difference between the light of Ashgaroth and the shadow of Dréagg. Do you not recall that when the Three Seeds of Logic were offered to the leaders of the animals, all those aeons of time ago in the deepest reaches of the great forests of Spath, they rejected them so that they might remain in the light of Ashgaroth. It is only man who has the capacity for evil; man, who was created by Dréagg as an instrument for revenge against the animals who spurned him, and upon whom Dréagg bestowed the gift of the Three Seeds of Logic. If you agree with what Nabbeth has decreed then you are following the ways of the Urkku, who dwell in the darkness; you are no better than Xtlan and his followers with their terrible capacity for cruelty, their vile and wicked appetites. The proclamation of Nabbeth is the beginning of the final end for here, in Haark, is the last enclave of Ashgaroth; the only place where Dréagg does not yet rule, the only place where the spirit of Nab still flickers and where some vestige of the splendour that Ashgaroth bestowed upon the earth, his chosen jewel, still remains. This is your vision; that burned bright for you through all the purgatory of Xtlan, that kept you alive when you should have been dead. You, Melvaig, above all people, know the terrible consequences when man chooses the path of the Urkku and elects to follow Dréagg. The Eldron do not survive by the suffering and exploitation of others, they do not live by death and destruction. Accept what Nabbeth has said and you betray Ashgaroth; you betray Nab and Brock and the others; you betray the spirit of the Book, but, most of all, Melvaig, you betray yourself.'

'Do not continue, Bracca. I grow weary... I cannot think. I am tired. Perhaps you're right; I don't know. I have been through too much; I don't have the strength any more. What you're saying ... that we are not yet at the finish of our journey ... the thought appals me! I can go no further. I

45

thought I had found the silver vision that beckoned to me from the pages of the Book, from the words that the wise old Hebbdril, Arkron, had read. I have been so content, so happy; and now you tell me it's over, after all this time. How do you know you're right? Are you really so certain? You say Ashgaroth spoke to you. Are you sure? Perhaps it was your imagination, wishful thinking. Why did he not speak to me?'

'Because you did not need him. You did not know of Nabbeth's decision till now. You were not suffering as I was. And because he does not come at will; you, of all men, should know that, father. But...'

Melvaig interrupted him, putting a hand on the trunk of the old tree they were leaning against and pulling himself slowly up onto his feet.

'Don't go on, Bracca. I cannot argue with you now. We'll talk about it later, when I'm less tired. I'm sorry.' He paused and looked at Bracca beseechingly, with eyes that almost begged for sympathy and understanding. But Bracca grew irritated and annoyed.

'No. We must talk about it now. We cannot leave it till later, it may be too late. You must see... You must! Sit down.'

'No, I ... I'm going back, back to the hut. Are you coming?'

'Father, listen...' but Melvaig interrupted him again.

'No? All right then, I'll go back alone,' and he slowly turned his back on Bracca and began walking back the way they had come.

'No! Come back, Melvaig ... please!' but it was no use, his words hung in the air uselessly as the old man made his way down the track, past a huge clump of rhododendron and then round a bend to disappear behind the trunk of an oak. A sudden crash in the undergrowth behind made Bracca turn to see a young deer running away up the hill and when he turned back Melvaig had vanished. He stifled the impulse to call out after him again and cursing violently, swung round and stormed off in the direction the deer had gone, his chest aching in a wild turmoil of frustration and anger against Melvaig and in guilt, remorse and doubt in himself at the pain he had caused his father and the awful barrier that had now sprung up between them; a great yawning chasm over which, Bracca thought with piercing sadness, he would never be able to cross to reach Melvaig again.

When Bracca was safely out of sight up the hill, a figure rose slowly and cautiously from amongst a heap of dead bracken a little way behind the spot where Melvaig and Bracca had been talking. He was smiling, for the news he had to report to Barll was good; the man could almost see the expression of satisfaction on his leader's face and hear the pleasure in his voice. Gradually, looking around him all the while and without making a sound, Straygoth the scout made his way back down the hill, pausing only to look from a distance at the strangers' hut and see Melvaig and Morven greet each other as the old man arrived back. He watched for a little while as they spoke together with some apparent consternation and then he slunk off around the back of the hill until he got to Barll's hut, situated on its own at the summit of a small hummock. As he moved he seemed almost to glide over the ground; his small thin body weaving through the undergrowth, while his pale face and his light brown hair blended perfectly with his surroundings. Barll called him Mouse with a mixture of contempt and amusement, for Straygoth's pointed face and general demeanour of timidity put all who saw him in mind of a rodent. The little creature was devoted to Barll, worshipping the big man's strength and aggression, wallowing vicariously in the fear that Barll inspired among the villagers. In this way his own life seemed to gain a purpose and identity for everyone knew him as Barll's man and they treated him with deference and respect for fear of displeasing the larger man. For his part Barll found the idea of a disciple immensely satisfying to his ego and he took great delight in tormenting the Mouse and pushing him to the point of tears, secure in the knowledge that Straygoth would never leave him no matter how degradingly he was treated. Indeed the more scorn and contempt that Barll

47

heaped upon him, the greater the degree of reverence that Straygoth gave back in return to his master. But above all, the Mouse had also proved invaluable as a spy; creeping around the village, lurking in the bushes or hiding behind huts, listening and gaining the information with which Barll was slowly and gradually building up the base of his power, sowing the seeds of discontent among the villagers, fermenting any restlessness he found and then relaying the 'mood of the people' to Nabbeth. And so it had been Barll who had been largely responsible for causing the unrest that had led Nabbeth to take his momentous decision; organizing his men to get to the food stocks first so they would take the best of the crop and leave barely enough for the rest and then slowly talking Nabbeth round into accepting the idea of killing the animals for food. It had taken time and infinite patience; Nabbeth was no fool and even Barll held him in some awe, yet by using all the guile and cunning he possessed, by implanting the ideas one by one and working on them steadily and patiently so that they grew in Nabbeth's mind, he had eventually been rewarded with success. He had let it be known secretly in the village that it was he, Barll, who had championed the cause of the villagers with Nabbeth and who had argued for a relaxation of the old rules. Now, it was he who would train them in the art of killing, the skills of using the weapons that only he had access to, buried deep beneath the ground in a hidden bunker at the place his family had always kept them. They would learn from him; he would be their teacher and their mentor and when they got used to killing, when the blood sang in their veins at the thought, then he would truly be ready to lead them into the glorious future that had so fired his imagination all those long years ago when the strangers had first arrived on the shore blurting out their garbled and incoherent images. As their words had slowly taken shape, causing such despair and horror among the other members of the Stagg, so in him there had taken shape a dream; a dream he had nurtured deep within his heart and for which he had worked and planned with inexhaustible and painstaking care until now he felt that, at last, he was on the threshold of making that dream a reality. An alliance with Xtlan! The idea even now, though it had been with him all these many years, still sent his pulse racing with visions of the power that would be his and the satisfaction of all the dark and forbidden appetites that had lain buried in his tortured spirit all his life.

He saw himself marching at the head of a great army, the army of Haark, their killing instincts unquenchable and their prowess with weapons skilful beyond measure from their practice on the animals; marching to meet Xtlan, to join this gargantuan figure of evil in his conquest of the world and his subjugation of all living things beneath the terrible yoke of Dréagg. He, Barll, would offer Xtlan Haark with its luxurious abundance of food, the purity of its air and water and the dazzling wealth of its beauty; the last enclave of the Lord of Light would then be gone forever and Ashgaroth would reign no more in the world. And in return all he would ask would be that he ride at Xtlan's side, as his second in command; a small price to pay, surely, for the handing over of the final victory. Yet he, Barll, would be as cunning as he imagined Xtlan to be. Lest Xtlan be tempted to claim Haark and its warriors for his own by killing its leader, the army would be trained in unswerving loyalty and devotion to one man and one man alone – himself, Barll. Fear and discipline would be the foundations of this army; it would be tiny in comparison to that of Xtlan yet it would be deadly – each man individually a master of the art of killing and every man welded together to fight as one in battle. Not for nothing had he and his family, for as far back as the time of Nab and beyond, guarded their secrets and studied the scriptures of war in the long wilderness when their skills were not needed; even scorned as useless and ridiculous. His chest swelled and the blood pumped in his ears as images of battle filled his head; all those aeons of time talking with his father and grandfather, thinking, planning and organizing; it was all now, finally, coming to fruition.

And so now, as Straygoth relayed to him the argument by the river between Melvaig and Bracca, Barll was indeed well pleased as the Mouse had known he would be. Opposition from Melvaig would have been difficult to ignore; Melvaig was still a figure who commanded a degree of respect and veneration from the village and, particularly, from the other members of the Stagg for his escape from Xtlan and his possession and knowledge of the Book. It would not have been as easy to argue against him, to ridicule and bombast him in front of Nabbeth and the others, as it was to defeat Bracca who was not held in anything like such high regard; some even despised him. Indeed, as it had turned out, he had not even had to speak in opposition to Bracca; Nabbeth had been so incensed by the young man's outburst that there had been no need. That had all gone according to plan; this though, Melvaig's siding with the proclamation of Nabbeth against the will of his son, was an unexpected, though very welcome, bonus.

'You have done well,' he said to Straygoth, and the Mouse glowed visibly with pride. 'It is good news; better than I dared to hope.' He paused and looked out for a moment at the village spread out in the valley beneath him basking in the bright midday sunshine. The air smelt fresh and sweet and a blackbird chattered loudly from the huge elm tree at his side. The future, with all its promise, beckoned him on with a strength so powerful it made him ache; he yearned with a ravening hunger for the triumphs that would be his in so short a time. He must control his impatience or it would be his downfall; he had waited for so long, now he must wait just a little while longer.

Suddenly he broke from his reverie and turning to Straygoth, he cuffed him hard across his ear. 'And you, my little mouse, deserve a reward. What do you want, eh?' He bent so that his eyes were on a level with Straygoth's and leered directly into the little man's face. 'Come on, tell me, what do you want? Don't be shy, go on.' But the Mouse simply looked down sheepishly. Barll began laughing uproariously; his loud guffaws echoing out in the still, clear air so that those in the village below who heard him, looked up and wondered.

'Come on then, you dirty little beast,' he said, and grabbing him by the ear he pulled him towards the entrance to the hut. He stopped outside for a moment and then, stepping back a pace and taking careful aim with his boot, he let fly. Straygoth was propelled forward into the darkness where he lay, spreadeagled, on the floor. Barll put his head inside and, addressing the two shocked-looking girls who were cowering half-naked against the back wall, he said in a voice that dripped with contempt, 'Now it's his turn. You know what he likes; make sure he gets it, all of it, or else you'll answer to me,' and laughing loudly again he walked away down the path towards the village.

CHAPTER IV

And so the killing started.

It was the night of the third full moon after the first hunt and Nabbeth was standing outside his cave high up on the hill next to the cavern where the Stagg held their meetings. His heart was heavy with pain as he looked down upon the village, shining in the silver moonlight. He could hear them now, the hunting party returning, and the sound of their shouting and laughter shattered the peace and stillness immediately around him. He saw the women start to emerge from the huts as they also heard the noise and then, when the first red embers of light became visible round a bend in the track, a huge cry went up; a cry of wild and delirious exultation that sent chills into Nabbeth's soul.

He could picture them now, their mouths slavering at the thought of that warm, bloody flesh; their eyes glazed and dancing with lust as they imagined themselves gorging on the soft, brown meat.

He had not thought it would be like this.

His mind went back to the first hunt. He had gone with them then, walking at the head with Barll; armed with spear, club, bow and arrow from Barll's secret arsenal. They had marched past Melvaig's hut and he had felt a quick spasm of guilt as he caught sight of Melvaig, Bracca, Morven and

Shayll, beautiful Shayll, staring at the procession from a corner of their clearing. 'The old man agreed with us; they had a row. It's only the young one, Bracca, who may cause trouble.' Barll's words had gone through his head and he had felt easier; relieved that Melvaig was not opposed to the decision. That awful decision; how he had agonized over it! Time and again he had refused to make it but in the end the pressure had been too great. 'The feeling in the village is overwhelming,' Barll had said. 'We cannot go on like this; they will rise against us.' And Nabbeth had feared that above all else; there must be no discord, there must be peace and harmony in this, his village, entrusted to him by his father and his father's father before him and so on back to the time of Nab himself. Was he, Nabbeth, to be the one who would preside over its collapse? No. He would not let that be so. Times had changed; Barll was right. The decision was right.

Up the hill they had climbed, their weapons in their hands, and all doubt had vanished from Nabbeth's mind. The spear felt easy in his hand as he carried it at the point of balance; the days spent training under Barll's supervision had engendered in him a hunger to use his new-found skills; to test his accuracy on real targets. He felt younger than he had in a long time; his eyes seemed to sparkle and his steps possessed a spring, an energy he recalled from his youth. The image of Shayll came into his mind and fired a passion that blazed deep within him; he would ask Melvaig after the hunt. She would be his! He had been too long without a woman, especially one as intensely desirable as Shayll. She raised in him feelings, yearnings that he had not felt since Brann was young. His beloved Brann who had died many years ago and whom he had loved dearer than his own life; who had been his strength through all the trials of his leadership. Would that she had been with him now, for the hardest decision of all!

Then, suddenly, they had seen the deer, ahead of them in a clearing a little further up. It was grazing on the long sweet spring grass, completely unaware of the humans watching it.

At its side was a fawn, nibbling at some leaves on a young sycamore; wobbling unsteadily on its long thin legs as it stretched its neck to reach the branches. The afternoon sun shone on its coat and burnished it with gold. Nabbeth looked at the mother and baby and marvelled at the exquisiteness of their limbs and the delicacy of their features; the great dark eyes, sparkling with innocence. The mother moved across and gently nuzzled the little one on its shoulder and then, as one, they both suddenly looked up and stared directly at the row of humans in the trees. It was at that moment that Nabbeth, with a rush of sickness, remembered why they were there. He looked at Barll whose hand was raised as an indication to them to be still. No one moved and the two creatures, which had not yet learnt to be afraid of man, turned away and carried on grazing.

Now Barll moved his hand slowly in a circle, and at either side the men began walking quietly around the outside of the clearing, keeping well hidden in the trees until the animals were surrounded. Nabbeth remembered the anguish he had felt at this moment; the torment that had twisted itself around in his soul. It was not yet too late. He could still stop it! He looked from the deer to the hunters with their spears raised and then, finally, at Barll. His mouth had turned dry and his heart beat so hard that his chest ached. Barll had his bow and arrow raised to his shoulder, the string taut and quivering with tension and the arrowhead aimed straight at its target. Next to Barll stood another man, Stigg, and he too was holding a loaded bow.

Suddenly, with a slight twang, the strings were released and almost at the same moment the arrows appeared, quivering, in the bodies of the deer. They staggered with the force of the blows and then started lurching about as if in some crazy dance, squealing with pain, the arrowshafts wobbling in the red flesh. Blood poured from the wounds, running over their brown skin in torrents of crimson, spreading over the whole of their bodies and flicking up in a spray as they flung themselves to and fro in their pain.

Nabbeth heard Barll's joyful shout, 'Now!' and watched as Barll and Stigg ran forward into the clearing towards the wounded creatures. Others came in from the other side, closing in on them, but there was a hesitancy about them and they moved slowly, reticently; on their faces a mixture of apprehension and bemusement. The animals dragged themselves desperately from one side of the clearing to the other, trying to get away from the men but to no avail; they were soon boxed in by a tight little circle of hunters. Now Barll began shouting at the others trying to get them to use their weapons; to overcome their reluctance. 'Kill,' he yelled, over and over, until his voice grew shrill and hoarse and then, in a blaze of temper, he pushed one of the men forward, took hold of the man's spear hand and, with the spear still in it, guided it into the neck of the baby deer. Thrashing wildly the little thing fell over on to the earth, a fountain of crimson gushing up into the air. Its mother then turned on the man and tried to charge him but the others, galvanized into action, fell upon it smashing down with their stone-headed clubs or stabbing with their spears. The terrible screaming of the animals mingled with the raucous shouting of the men and Nabbeth looked on in horror as the scene in the clearing developed into a frenzied orgy of killing, with the afternoon sun shining serenely down on the bloody mayhem that was taking place beneath its warmth. Each man was covered from head to toe in livid crimson gore and still the animals cried out their agony, still their limbs twitched and shivered with the last remnants of life. But the sound that chilled Nabbeth to the very marrow of his soul was the laughter that came from Barll as he stood to one side and watched; the laughter that first one and then another of the men took up as their blood lust swept over them, as the grotesque comedy of mortal agony was revealed to them in the wildly rolling eyes and frothing mouths of the deer.

Now Barll jumped in amongst them and raising his great sword, that had been with his family since the beginning, he swung it down once, twice, three times until he had severed the heads of the two deer. Then, giving the fawn's head to Stigg, he lifted the mother's up above his head and called out to them even as the blood cascaded down his arms and drenched him.

'Now, eat!' he said, and his teeth shone out white from the glistening crimson mask on his face. 'Taste of the flesh and drink of the juice of life. Feel its power and strength inside you.' He paused and his eyes roamed over the mob of hunters with a fierce gleam, a light born of darkness and madness. The men saw it and were mesmerized by its awesome strength; stunned at first into silence and then, as he shouted out to them, 'Are you with me?' they responded as one with a great roar. 'Yes,' they said.

'Who are you with?' he called.

'Barll, Barll,' they said, and the sound of their voices rang out through the trees, echoing in the forest and around the hills, and all the wild creatures who heard it were frozen with terror; snuggling down deeper into the grass or burying themselves further in the earth for they knew, deep within them, that it was the end of an era; the time of peace was behind them now: ahead, once more lay fear, pain, death and torture and their hearts grew cold and the marrow in their bones turned to water.

'Eat then, my friends. Eat!' he shouted, and bending down he ripped a piece of flesh from the baby deer and raising it to his mouth started tearing it with his teeth, chewing and swallowing, a thin trickle of blood running out of the corner of his mouth.

The men hesitated, doubtful; but Barll exhorted them again and, driven on by his haranging, first one and then another went forward and began pulling at the dead animals. They baulked at first, not used to the strange taste and texture, but Barll drove them on so that eating of the flesh became a mark of status, a sign of acceptance of the new way – the way of Barll. For some it was too much; the trauma of the kill and the rich warm taste of the meat were not for those with weak stomachs and they ran to the shelter of a tree to retch, hiding from the eyes of their fellows. And then they came back and with a coy smile tried again.

Nabbeth, watching the proceedings in a horrified trance, suddenly heard the sound of his name and became aware of a lull in the activity. All eyes had now turned towards him and there was a tense, awkward stillness in the air.

'Will you not joint us, Nabbeth? I should have offered you first choice; I apologize. But in the excitement ... you understand. Please, come forward now.'

Barll's voice was gently mocking; his tone deprecatory but barbed so sharply that Nabbeth felt afraid. The big man's eyes still shone with an awful yellow gleam; teasing and taunting his leader as if he knew, indeed had always known, what Nabbeth's reaction would be. 'You are finished; done! I have won.' Barll's eyes spoke to Nabbeth; daring him to come forward and try to reassert his authority.

It was a challenge the old man could not refuse. Slowly, his heart beating so fiercely that he felt the blood in his throat, he walked towards the men. They parted as he neared them, making a clear path through to the terrible heap of blood and mangled flesh on the grass. As he saw the hideous, unrecognizable mass before him an image flashed into Nabbeth's mind; a picture of the two deer, the mother and the baby, as they had been just a few moments ago, and he felt a tidal wave of repulsion well up from his bowels. Desperately he fought to control the nausea that threatened to snatch his legs from under him and to send him retching on the ground. And then, with his mind closed to what he knew he had to do, he bent down, terribly aware of all the eyes upon him, and scrabbling with his fingers among the slime and bone he tore a piece away. Then, as part of the same movement, so quickly that there was not time to think, he put his hand straight in his mouth and felt his tongue and teeth against something soft, warm and slippery. Not daring to pause he closed his lips and tried to bring his teeth together but, desperately though he fought against it, his stomach started heaving in revulsion, churning up into his mouth in

57

rebellion against what was about to be sent down to it. He felt the blood drain from his face and his head began to spin.

He had to swallow it! He felt Barll's eyes boring into him, willing him to give in and be sick. A thin veil of red began to dance before his eyes with the effort of concentration; the intense struggle between his willpower and his body almost sending him unconscious. And then, with a supreme effort, it was over; it had gone down, and the relief he felt outweighed the foul taste that lingered on in his mouth and the bilious rolling in his stomach.

He opened his eyes – he had not realized he had closed them – and looked out at the mass of faces before him. Barll was still gloating. And then, with a rush of despair, the awful realization came to him that it had not been enough. They had seen through him! The disgust had shown through too clearly on his face; the struggle had been too obvious. They expected him to be more like Barll; greater restraint and dignity than the younger man perhaps but still showing a measure of enjoyment and approval that would validate and sanctify what they had done. He could sense the feeling of antipathy and resentment that emanated out from them, disappointment merging into anger so that he felt threatened. Should he make an excuse? Say he was old; that it would take time to get used to it. No! That would make matters worse. Besides, he could not lie. His dignity and pride would not allow it. And so, summoning all his reserves of authority, he addressed them all in a voice that was as calm and imperious as he could make it.

'Come then,' he said. 'Let us return with our prize. We have done what we set out to do.'

'You do not wish to continue?' said Barll, and his tone danced with sarcasm.

'No,' replied Nabbeth, 'No, we have done enough for today.' Could they detect the lack of authority which he felt?

There was a long silence and the air was heavy with tension. Why didn't Barll answer him? Then he grew aware of a low undercurrent of murmurs and grumbling. They wanted to go on! To continue the hunt despite the fact that two deer would provide ample food for a day or two. They were not yet done with killing. But then, for some reason that Nabbeth could not guess at, Barll came to his rescue.

'Well then,' he said. 'Since you wish it, we will go back. There is tomorrow and all the days thereafter. Let us not be too greedy on this first time.' He turned to face the hunters, who had ceased their muttering and were listening to him intently. His voice was heavy with mock deference. 'After all, Nabbeth is our leader, the Chief Member of the Stagg. His desire is our command. Is it not so, men of Haark?' and raising his right arm high up in the air he called out a reply. 'Yes!' he shouted, but his was the only voice.

Nabbeth felt dizzy with anger and humiliation but he stood watching in grim silence; impotent before the cunning and strength of the younger man.

'Come my friends,' Barll went on, wallowing in his triumph. 'That is not good enough. I want to hear your support for our leader, the man who has led you away from the poverty and joylessness of a life led according to the Book, who has freed you from slavish obedience to the dictates of Nab. I will ask you again! His desire is our command. Is it not so?'

'Yes!' they shouted, but every man's voice tremored with laughter and a smirk of amusement played about their lips.

As the horror of that moment came back again to Nabbeth, standing outside his cave watching the return of the hunters, he felt sick and the sweat broke out on his forehead and his palms.

It seemed so long ago; so much had happened since that portentous first day. He had not gone with them again; that would have made matters worse as well as being too painful for him. He had agonized long and hard over the events of that day; in particular the behaviour of the men and his own reactions to the killing and the eating of the flesh, and the same question repeated itself over and over in his tortured brain; had he been wrong?

He watched again, in his mind's eye, all that had happened on the hunt; analysing, searching for excuses, looking for reasons, but through all the anguished sleepless nights and the restless pacing of his days, he came no nearer to finding an answer. The words of Bracca, harsh, strident and angry as he had spoken them in the Stagg, kept recurring over and over in his head like some grim refrain. Fragments of what the young man had said leapt out at him with a terrible force and haunted him in his torment. 'Once you start down this path it will be impossible to stop.' 'The beginning of the end.' 'Who gave you the right to judge ... to assume your life is more valuable than theirs.'

And just as Bracca's anger lived again in his memory, so did the viciousness of his, Nabbeth's, response and his heart shrank with shame. Why had he not listened; just listened! Had Bracca, after all been right? But no; so fragile had his decision been that he could tolerate no disagreement. And there was Barll; always Barll, with a word, an idea or a gesture, to steer his thinking along to its eventual conclusion. How stealthily Barll had played his hand and how bitter and damning the betrayal! Now, when he walked among the villagers they simply turned away or else hid, smirking, behind their huts as they watched him pass. There was in them an aggressive swagger, an arrogance, that had never been there before. Now that they were able to hunt for their furs instead of using only what they could find they vied with each other to kill the animals that were most rare so as to attain prestige among their fellows; they adorned themselves with feathers and teeth worn on strips of skin around their necks and arms, and everywhere they walked the putrid smell of rancid flesh followed them about.

The pattern of their lives had also changed. Whereas before they had spent the days foraging, now they went out hunting only once every third or fourth day, bringing back as much meat as they could carry, gorging themselves on it and then hanging around the village until hunger forced them

60

out again. During these times of idleness they had begun to fight; squabbling over women or else indulging in skirmishes over petty insults. These fights always ended in injury and even, on a number of occasions, death, as they all now carried a weapon of some sort made either of bone or antler. Life seemed to revolve around the feast-times when the freshly killed animals were brought back and, having been skinned, were roasted over the fires and eaten in a great orgy of gluttony, ending only when they were full to bursting and could eat no more; the frenzy of eating giving way to a torpor of lethargy. Then the sharp acrid stink of roasted flesh would linger in the valley, hanging over the village in a cloud, almost, thought Nabbeth, as if it were some tangible presence, a dark and brooding embodiment of evil.

Physically they seemed to change as well, though this might have been only Nabbeth's imagination. The lean angularity of their faces began to fill out into a new roundness; their cheeks looked puffy and their jowls grew heavier. They started to put on weight and many of them grew rotund. After the long years of frugality, the sudden abundance of flesh for their consumption could not fail to have a marked effect on them. The forest animals were easy targets; ready prey for the men with their rapidly improving skills under the tuition of Barll and his commanders. The animals had grown used to regarding man without fear and they rarely tried to run away. Indeed Barll had recently taken to employing some of the men in driving the animals up from the opposite direction to galvanize them into action and so provide more practice for the hunters in testing their prowess with weapons.

After the initial period of gluttony and idleness, Nabbeth saw that they had begun to clear certain areas around the village, cutting down the trees and dragging the undergrowth away before setting fire to what remained and leaving it a charred and blackened wasteland. The animals caught in these operations were either burnt alive, as in the case of an old fox that Nabbeth saw in this situation, to the great

61

amusement of the onlookers, or else were slaughtered in their desperate bid to escape. This land was then dug over and planted with fruit-bearing shrubs and bushes and the animals and birds were kept away by guards who were posted at the site, killing any creature they saw come on to the area.

And so the frontiers expanded and the wilderness was driven back; the birds stopped singing in the trees and the animals of the forest grew stealthy and furtive as they learnt to fear man. Barll had the order circulated among the villagers that any animal that threatened their food supplies was to be killed, from the smallest, berry-eating bird to the fox, the badger and the deer.

But as Nabbeth saw what was happening and his spirit fell ever more deeply into despair, so through the darkness came a single ray of hope and as the days grew darker he found himself clinging to it more and more. Bracca! Once again the words he had spoken on that fateful day in the Stagg rang out in Nabbeth's mind like a clarion call of salvation. 'I am not drained,' he had said, 'and I will not let the truth and sanctity of Melvaig's vision be destroyed. I will not stand by and watch it crumble and fade because of your mistakes.'

Then the words had goaded Nabbeth into a fury with their arrogance and the strength of their conviction. Now that same strength and purity of belief seemed to him to be all that stood before the final inexorable descent into the abyss.

So it was that, one sunny afternoon in the early summer when the sky was of the deepest blue and the leaves of the oak tree outside his cave were of the darkest green, Nabbeth set out on a little known path through the forest towards the home of the strangers to see Melvaig, Bracca, Morven and Shayll.

CHAPTER V

Melvaig watched Nabbeth make his way down the track through the tall green stems of bracken, and wondered; struggling to clear his mind of the clouds of confusion that had enveloped his thinking since that terrible day when Bracca had told him of the proclamation.

For a long time after the row with Bracca, Melvaig had refused to acknowledge what had happened; mentioning neither the conversation by the river nor Nabbeth's pronouncement. He had adopted an attitude of enforced gaiety and good humour which enraged Bracca and puzzled Morven and Shayll who still knew nothing. Whenever Melvaig and Bracca were together, there was an ugly awkwardness between them; the old man's false cheeriness grating against Bracca's surly silences. Nothing either of the women could say would induce father or son to reveal anything that would indicate the cause of the friction and Morven and Shayll grew exasperated by their recalcitrance; angry and depressed by the black atmosphere that hung over them all.

Then the killing had started and all Melvaig's will-power left him. The effort of sustaining his veneer of happy unconcern became too great in the face of the horrors that were taking place around him in the forest and his spirit seemed to crumple. He withdrew into himself, hardly speaking to anyone; sitting alone in a corner of their clearing, by the side of his favourite oak tree, for great long stretches of time. During these times he did not move; simply stared into space with a vacant expression on his face, a smile playing vaguely around his lips as if he were remembering something. Sometimes, during these sojourns, the hunters would pass by down the track from the mountain that led past the edge of the clearing. Then he would get up wearily and stand and watch them as the red glow from their torches disappeared into the darkness further down the valley. Morven would come to him then, put her arms around him and try to comfort him, knowing now of at least part of the reason for his anguish. It was no good; he seemed not to even be aware of her and eventually she would leave him there, her heart leaden with despair.

Bracca spent most of these times out foraging, wandering further and further from the village as he attempted to find some peace, some rest from the turmoil that raged within him. He ached for Melvaig's misery but felt powerless to help and he suffered with the creatures of the forest, feeling their fear and their pain even as they themselves did. The anger in him grew until it threatened to consume him beneath the enormity and depth of its power and at the same time he wept bitter tears of anguish when he saw the dead animals being carried carelessly back to the village by the hunters; the grace, power and beauty of their bodies reduced to an ungainly, dangling floppiness and their faces twisted into the grim tragi-comic mask of an agonizing death.

Often he sat with the statues, talking to them and feeling an uncanny empathy with them, so that, even more than before, he had to keep reminding himself that they were not alive. He felt that they alone knew what he was going through and could understand his sorrow and his rage. At times he grew muddled, confusing himself with Nab, and his mind would wander off into the legends of their epic quest for salvation against the dark forces of Dréagg. Then, when he came back to reality, he would cry out in desperation, 'Ashgaroth! Speak to me,' but, strain as he might to hear a voice in the rustling of the leaves and the sigh of the wind, no answer came and he grew to believe he had imagined it before.

When they began clearing the parts of the forest near the village, he found it unbearable to be anywhere within sight or sound of the activity and he would run far away so that he could not see them chopping down the trees, his trees that he knew and loved like friends, nor hear them crashing to the ground, nor smell the smoke as the undergrowth was razed with fire. Yet no matter how far he went, he seemed unable to escape completely; always there would be some scent of burning or crackle of flame or clamour of shouts carried on the breeze to remind him of the destruction.

For Morven, these times were difficult and painful. She had been happy and contented for so long that she did not, at first, recognize the dark shadow that had fallen over them. Relentlessly she tried to mediate between Melvaig and Bracca with Shayll also joining in, in an attempt to break down the walls that lay between them, joking, teasing and laughing, but their efforts went unrewarded. And then, when Morven saw the hunters and smelt the roasting flesh from the fires, she knew; knew the cause of the misery and guessed that the two men had argued. She tried to talk to Melvaig, to draw him out of the shell into which he had withdrawn but he was either unable or unwilling to discuss it and so she stopped trying and devoted herself to the ordinary everyday tasks that she had always done, finding in the constancy of the routine a solace and security which brought some comfort to her confused and troubled spirit.

It was not only Melvaig who saw Nabbeth walking down the hill towards the hut. Shayll was also watching and at the sight of the tall figure, his white hair shining in the sun and the green of his cloak merging with the bracken, she could feel her heart beat a little faster and her breath quicken. She was standing by an elder tree, collecting berries, and if he carried on along the path as he was doing he would be bound to pass right by her. The darkness of recent times had depressed her so much that life had become almost unbearable. Unable, like Morven, to bury herself in memories and routine and yet not wishing either to spend ages alone in the forest like Bracca, she found thoughts of the future bearing down upon her. What had she to look forward to? Treated as an outsider by the rest of the village there was little chance, she knew, of any of the men taking her as their woman. She was aware of the attraction she had for them from seeing the way they looked at her when she walked among them and the hunger in their eyes as she passed by, yet never had any of them approached her; not one of them had had the courage to defy the strictures of the village and become friendly with her. And so the burgeoning of her femininity had remained untested and untried; her tentative desires and curiosity unassuaged. For her the times ahead held promise of little else but a life spent living with, and then looking after, Melvaig and Morven, and despite her great love for both of them this prospect did not fill her with feelings of joy and satisfaction; it was not enough for her, she also needed the fulfilment of her sexuality.

Nabbeth had been a frequent visitor at their home when Melvaig had been a member of the Stagg. She had known him from when she was a little girl and he had brought her presents of delicately carved wooden figures that he had made. She remembered the long talks he used to have with Melvaig, on their own out in the clearing, and then, when the talking was finished, the way he used to come up to her, sit her on his knee and tell her stories about the wooden figures he had given her so that, for her, they became alive. He had no children of his own and intuitively she knew that he was giving her the love that would have gone to his own child.

Then when she grew older he stopped sitting her on his knee and she did not know why. He became distant and aloof and her puzzlement at his behaviour developed into anger but then, one day, her growing awareness of her body and the changes that were happening in her mind caused her perception of him to alter. She knew then the reason for his new attitude and she was glad for his reticence and remoteness for it spared her any embarrassment.

Somehow though, even through these awkward times, there was something between them that was precious, however hidden and tenuous that might be, and Shayll now knew that if she was to have anyone it could only be this tall, imperious, white-haired old man. Yet this knowledge was locked deep within her and in her confusion and uncertainty she became as distant and withdrawn from him as he was from her.

Then, when Melvaig made way for Bracca in the Stagg, Nabbeth stopped coming. He could have come to see Bracca but he did not. She knew, from Bracca, that he and the older man did not get on well and that, ostensibly, was the reason for his absence but surely, she thought, if he had felt anything for her at all he would have buried his feelings for Bracca in his wish to see her. And there was his friendship with Melvaig; that surely would have been an excuse to come to the hut and visit her. Was the animosity between himself and Bracca so strong that he had to sever all his connections with them? She found that hard to believe. No! The real reason, she thought, was that he did not want to see her again; the affection he had had for her as a child had come to an end now that she had grown up and he was avoiding her to spare her feelings.

She watched him through the leaves of the trees as he came to the corner of the path from which he would see her. Should she hide? It was too late. Suddenly he was there; stopped in his tracks at the sight of her, looking startled and surprised as if he had suddenly been woken up out of a deep sleep. For a few tense moments neither of them spoke, though their eyes met and struggled in the attempt to explore each other's thoughts. It was Nabbeth who broke the silence first, his voice hesitant and quivering with the effort of controlling his emotions.

'I did not expect to see you … here,' he said, and the beloved familiarity of his voice filled Shayll with the urge to rush up and embrace him.

'I'm collecting elderberries,' she paused. 'Were you coming to see us … to see Melvaig, or Bracca?'

'Both of them,' he answered, and as soon as the words were out of his mouth he regretted the clumsiness of what he had said. Should he have added '… and you'? Of course he had come to see her as well; she had rarely been out of his mind since the last time he had spoken to her; on the occasion that Melvaig had told him he wished Bracca to replace him on the Stagg. How often had he longed to come and see her, to talk to her, to tell her of his feelings for her. How many times had he imagined holding her, loving her; taking her back to live with him. And yet, despite his authority and his position and the knowledge that he could have any girl in the village simply by asking, he had not dared to give her any indication of the way he felt. If Shayll were ever to be his she would have to love him the way that Brann had loved him; for himself, not for the status he could bestow upon her. Nor could he take Shayll for his woman unless he knew she felt free to refuse him if she wished; she must not be afraid of him.

And so, because he was old and she was young and beautiful, because it would be presumptuous and arrogant of him to expect her to love him the way he loved her, because he must be certain she gave herself freely; for these and a myriad other reasons too numerous and complex to think of, he had never spoken to her of his feelings. And now, at last here he was; to speak to Melvaig and Bracca of the troubles but also to ask her to go back with him and to be his, if she would have him. He did not care to think how many long and sleepless nights he had spent in coming to his decision but in the end he had concluded that for his own peace of mind he had to at least ask her. And too, he was worried about her future in the village; about her safety in the kind of atmosphere that the ugly new mood of the people was

68

generating. Perhaps, in the face of this, he would be able to afford her more protection as his woman than she might otherwise have had.

'Will you walk down with me?' he said. 'It is a long time since we spoke ... since I saw you.'

Shayll was pleased and relieved at his invitation. She detected in him a new softer attitude towards her, a breach in the barriers he had built up between them, and she responded warmly with a smile that lit up Nabbeth's heart.

'Yes,' she said. 'I'd better show you the way. It's so long since you've been to see us that you'd probably get lost if I didn't.'

He smiled ruefully at her friendly rebuke.

'These are not easy times, Shayll. Bracca will have told you of my pronouncement – about the killing of forest creatures for food. We did not get on well before but that caused a terrible row between us. He walked out of the Stagg. We are both proud men – I could not come to see him. Do you understand?'

'No,' she replied, and had to use all her will to stop herself going on to say, 'you could have come to see me.'

Again Nabbeth smiled to himself at her friendly defiance of him.

'And since then,' he went on, 'things have been happening which I do not understand; a darkness has begun to spread over us which I have been struggling to make sense of. You must be aware of it yourself; have seen it around you. I have been ...' and he searched for the word, '... preoccupied, Shayll. But now my mind is clearing and I have come to Melvaig and Bracca – to talk to them and ask for their help.' He paused then and glanced up at her as she walked beside him; her eyes cast down to the ground, the mane of red hair flashing in the sunlight as it tossed around her shoulders, the easy grace of her limbs as she moved. 'And I came to see you,' he said, and though she showed no outward sign, Shayll's heart thrilled at the sound of his words.

It was early evening when Nabbeth and Shayll walked

69

together into the clearing. A blackbird sang sporadically from a nearby sycamore and in the sky the dying sun painted the clouds with gold and purple and deep, dark crimson. The dew was rising from the ground and the air was damp. Melvaig was sitting, waiting, on his boulder by the doorway and Bracca, who had just returned from foraging, was next to him. Morven was by the brook, collecting some water.

It was Shayll who spoke first, in an effort to dispel the tension that lay upon them like a fog.

'I found him wandering in the forest,' she said. 'Shall we give him a home?'

The three men ignored her attempt at levity. Melvaig rose and came forward while Bracca hung back, eyeing Nabbeth with a contemptuous scorn he did nothing to disguise. The two old men stood face to face, looked at each other for a moment or two and then Melvaig spoke.

'I bid you welcome,' he said, 'in the names of Ashgaroth and Nab. Many moons have waxed and waned since you last came to see us; we are pleased to have you.'

'Do not include me in your greeting, Melvaig. I am not pleased to see him.' Bracca's voice behind them was harsh with anger and Melvaig's eyes clouded over with embarrassment. Nabbeth ignored the outburst and spoke directly to Melvaig.

'I thank you for your greeting,' he said. 'I know now I should have come sooner but, as you know, Melvaig, these are difficult times and I have been embroiled in events which I do not comprehend. It is of these matters that I must speak with you and Bracca and Morven and Shayll. There is so much we have to discuss.'

'Yes. Yes, I know. Bracca and I, we have argued. And with you – he argued with you. I'm pleased you have come. Let us sit down and hear what you have to say.' He turned round. 'Bracca', he said. 'Come here. Please. We must talk.' The young man came forward to join them and as he did so Nabbeth turned to him.

'I understand your anger,' he said. 'I think now that you

are right. I am sorry; that's all I can say. I have come to you to ask for your help; to try and put right what has gone wrong. Please – can we not be friends?'

Faced with the old man's humility and the sincerity of his apologies, Bracca found it hard to maintain the degree of animosity he had previously felt for him. Gone was that awful air of arrogant superiority, the imperiousness that Bracca remembered from the last meeting of the Stagg. It would be ridiculous of him now not to listen to what Nabbeth had to say. And too, this was a chance to heal the rift with Melvaig.

'Morven!' Melvaig called her over from the bank of the stream where she sat with two full containers of water, watching Nabbeth with curiosity and apprehension about the reasons for his presence. When she had joined them and exchanged greetings with the visitor, Melvaig bade them all sit on the ground and they did so, gathering around Nabbeth automatically in a little circle. For a moment or two there was an awkward silence and then the guest began to speak. He recited nothing to them which they did not already know or had not previously guessed at, from the part played by Barll in Nabbeth's fateful decision to the general tenor of what had happened since; the killings, the new feeling in the village, the impossibility of ensuring obedience to the basic principles within which he had attempted to incarcerate the proclamation – that the killings only be committed when absolutely essential for food and that they be carried out with the minimum of suffering. Lastly he told them of his experience on that first hunt and, more importantly, of his reactions to it. For Melvaig, as he listened to Nabbeth's description, it seemed as if he himself was witnessing the horrible events of that day and his feelings were as those of Nabbeth; initial excitement turning into doubt and then finally to revulsion. And so, as with Nabbeth, the endless agony of uncertainty was resolved. Bracca had been right; and Melvaig found himself looking at his son, with a mixture of pride at the depth of his perception and regret at the rift that had sprung up between them. Bracca alone had had the purity of vision to interpret the spirit of Nab as it should be and he, Melvaig, had doubted it.

By the time that Nabbeth had finished speaking the moon had come out and the clearing was bathed in a white light which gilded the trees in silver and shadowed the faces of the little group with an eerie luminescence. Though they had learnt nothing new, they were glad for the clarity of Nabbeth's exposition and, when he had finished speaking, they sat for some time without saying anything, letting the full import of what they had heard run through their minds.

Then, when Nabbeth judged the time was right, he turned slowly to Melvaig and Bracca and began to address them in a voice that was resonant with emotion.

'So I turn to you, Melvaig, for your authority, and to you, Bracca, for the strength and passion of your beliefs. I ask you both to help me to put right my mistake; a mistake so terrible and far-reaching in its consequences that I fear for the entire future of our world, this last enclave of Ashgaroth, if we fail. It may, even now, be too late. The cancer, now it has taken root, may have spread too deeply and too far to be cut out.'

'What can we do?' It was Bracca who spoke and neither in his voice nor his eyes could Nabbeth detect any note of antipathy. 'What do you wish from us? We will do what we can.' Nabbeth's pulse raced with relief.

Melvaig looked first at Bracca, then at Nabbeth and, smiling at the old man, nodded his head in acknowledgement of what his son had said and agreement with it. Yet even as he did so, pledging all his strength and energy into defeating Barll and the evil that he was nurturing, so at the same time his spirit felt infinitely weary at the awful realization that the struggle to achieve his vision was not yet over. This was what he had fought so hard against believing when Bracca had spoken to him and what his mind had refused to accept. Now that Bracca had been proved right he was forced to accept the dreadful truth and the prospect of a renewed struggle left him feeling utterly exhausted.

'All we can do,' said Nabbeth, 'is to attempt to appeal to the people; to undermine the power of Barll. It will not be easy. They still have a respect for you, Melvaig; they find you a little awesome because of what you have been through – your knowledge of Xtlan – and your special relationship with the Book. We will call a meeting of the village. I am asking you to talk to them, Melvaig; to use all your authority and make them listen to you. Tell them of Xtlan; of the horrors of that world – a world where Ashgaroth does not exist. Use your eloquence to create a picture of that terrible place so vivid and real that it will lurk forever as a shadow in their minds. Tell them of cruelty and torture; of pain and humiliation, of greed and the lust for power. Explain what these things do to men where they are allowed to flourish unchecked by the hand of Ashgaroth. Spare no detail, however painful it may be to you to recall it. The world of Xtlan must be as real to them as it was to me when you first arrived on our shore and, in your fever, revealed snatches of the nightmare you had been through. Only the members of the Stagg heard your words and so dark and frightening were the images you gave birth to that we decided they should be kept hidden from the villagers. That is why you were kept separate from the others, as you have been. Now, Melvaig, I beg you to draw away that veil and warn them that the ways they have chosen, the ways in which Barll inspires them, can only lead to a world as dark and evil as that of Xtlan. You must warn them; make them believe that which Bracca told me and I did not believe – that once they start down this road it will be impossible to stop.'

He paused for a moment and, turning slightly, looked at Bracca.

'You see,' he said. 'I remember your words. They ring in my mind now even as they did then when you spoke them and I, in my arrogance, dismissed what you said. For my part,' he went on, 'I will stand before them and renounce my proclamation, revoke the decision. I shall admit my mistake and urge them to take heed of what they have heard from Melvaig. Yet . . .' there was a silence and his sentence hung, unfinished, in the air as he stared disconsolately at the ground. Then he continued, '... I fear they will not listen to me. Barll has captured their souls; they respond to what he gives them – they are already afflicted with a lust for violence and power which I cannot appease. The taste for flesh rages within them; the ritual of the kill has become an essential part of their lives. How could I satisfy that with talk of purity – of living in harmony with the other creatures of our world, of respect for their rights? No. Greed, the yearning for domination, arrogance – all these, that have lain dormant for so long in our people, have been re-awakened by Barll and grow daily more virulent. They have become voracious in their appetites; I can offer them nothing to take their place save ideas, vague concepts that they will find difficult to understand. Still, I will do what I can. You, Bracca; talk to the other members of the Stagg. Try and bring them round to our way. You may have some success with them; they are wiser than the rest of the village. And I, I too will speak to them and try and persuade them of the error of my decision – we may take Stowna and Nemm with us, I don't know; but with my authority and friendship and your fervour I have some hope, however small, that they will oppose Barll.'

So they arranged to call a secret meeting of the Stagg, without Barll, at which Nabbeth, Melvaig and Bracca would confront Stowna and Nemm and attempt to gain their support. Then later, when the time was right, Nabbeth would summon the whole village together.

Finally, when all this was settled, Nabbeth turned to Shayll and looked in her eyes with such tenderness that she knew instinctively, with a sudden rush of joy, what he was going to say before he began speaking.

'These should have been happier times,' he said, 'then I would have courted you as you deserve. Instead I have been distant – uncertain of your feelings for me; wary of rejection. But circumstances have forced me to discard any pretensions of modesty for I fear now that any moments left to us may be

74

precious. Shayll, I ask you now in front of your family, will you accept me as your man; to love you, guard you and protect you – to share your life with me whatever may befall us in the future.'

And Shayll, in a voice trembling with happiness, replied, 'Yes; I willingly accept you as my man and offer myself to you as your woman. And, if you wish it, I will return with you now for, as you say, our moments of happiness may be few and I would not let them slip by as leaves in the autumn air.'

Then, the formality of her reply completed, she turned to face him and, throwing her arms around his neck, pulled him to her and kissed him; at first tentatively and then, as her confidence grew, with mounting passion so that Melvaig, Morven and Bracca felt compelled to look away for fear of embarrassment. Melvaig and Morven were pleased for Shayll, for they both knew that this was what she wanted, yet they were also sad at the loss of their daughter whose laughter and spirit of fun had filled their lives with sunshine.

Then, as if reading their minds, she suddenly broke free of her embrace with Nabbeth and rushing over to her mother and father, hugged them tightly and said excitedly,

'I'll come back tomorrow ... and see you. I'm very happy. Thank you.'

Then she looked at Bracca who was sitting stony-faced, looking at the ground. She went up to him quietly and kneeling before him put her hands to his face and bent his head so that he was forced to look into her eyes.

'Don't,' she said, and her voice was soft and quiet. No one else could hear. 'For me, be happy. I love him. And you – he has apologized, told you you're right. You ...' but Bracca interrupted.

'I'm sorry,' he said 'It's just ... you know ... I'll miss you, being here, with us – with me. But, for you, yes, I'm pleased. And Nabbeth is a good man – I don't feel the way I did. Now go! You're keeping him waiting.'

So Shayll quickly went inside the hut and put a few of her belongings into a pouch, including a wooden owl Nabbeth had carved for her, a long time ago. Outside the others stood, a little awkwardly, until Melvaig called to her. 'You can get the rest in the morning!'

Yes, she thought. Yes, I can, so she hurried outside and with a last tearful embrace from Morven she took the hand that Nabbeth offered her and they set off together in the moonlight up the narrow winding path that led back to his cave. And somehow, despite the shadow that lay over them all, the joy that Nabbeth and Shayll had discovered in each other seemed to radiate out from them and leave a lingering aura of hope for the future. Then, with a last wave at a bend in the track, they were gone – swallowed up by the night.

A little later, when Melvaig, Morven and Bracca had gone inside their hut to sleep, a passing fox was startled by a slight rustle in the undergrowth on one side of the clearing. It was a man creeping furtively away; a slightly-built figure with light brown hair and a half-smile on his pale face at the thought of how pleased his leader would be when he reported back to him all that he had just seen and heard.

CHAPTER VI

During the rest of that summer and the early part of the autumn, Nabbeth and Shayll luxuriated in the pleasure of each other. With infinite gentleness and care he revealed the mysteries of love to her and she, rejoicing in the discovery of the magic of her body, responded to him rapturously, hungrily receiving the delights he gave her and then, when she was satiated, bestowing upon him in return such heights of blissful sensation that he felt he would explode with pleasure. Her innate capacity for sensuality was a source of constant amazement to him as, during the long hot nights of that time of year, their limbs slippery and glistening with sweat, they explored the mysteries of each other's body till they knew and worshipped every part: for her, his strong, lean muscularity, the hardness undimmed by age, and for him, her soft, white, rounded perfection at the sight of which, every intimate part exposed to his gaze, he often became so overwhelmed by her beauty that he felt tears come to his eyes, so great was the surge of desire that swept through him. At these moments he felt the need to possess all of her at once, to caress, nurture and cherish every fragile and delicate detail of her so that she would be a constant part of him – their sexuality forming a link between them that would remain forever. Only thus, he felt at these times, could he protect her from the evil that lurked outside the haven of their lovemaking.

During the days they often went for long walks together, meandering slowly amongst the trees, talking of their past. He told her of Brann; quietly, gently, building up a picture of the woman he had loved that Shayll could feel neither threatened by nor jealous of. He described the warmth of the life they had shared, their sadness as the seasons passed with no sign of children, the long discussions they had enjoyed in the evenings, under the stars, about the Book and all the other fables and legends of Haark. They had recited the tales in turn, embellishing and embroidering as they went along so that the stories, though well known, always seemed fresh in the telling. He told Shayll of the closeness between himself and Brann; the long silent oases of time when they would simply sit looking out over the forest or the sea and be completely at ease, their souls in perfect harmony as the magic of Ashgaroth's creations swept over them.

He told Shayll of his love for Brann, partly because he wanted to share that love with her and partly because, though he was reluctant to recognize it, he felt a little guilty – as if he was betraying the memory of his first love – and bringing her into his new relationship helped to expiate that guilt. Shayll understood all this and encouraged him to talk for she wanted to know everything about the man she loved and, as the myriad pieces of his past were gradually revealed to her, she found her love for him deepening and growing.

She learnt of Syrioll, his mother; warm, compassionate and gentle with an aura about her of stillness, an inner calm like the depths of a rock pool on a hot midsummer day. Nabbeth remembered her as being very tall and slender with a great cascade of golden hair that he would play with endlessly when little. She had died quietly when he was still young; causing hardly a ripple on the surface of the pool as she left. He had stayed with her for days then, unwilling to leave her, thinking she was just asleep, unable to comprehend the invisible barrier between life and death. 'Why doesn't she wake up?' he had asked, and his father had simply replied, to his bemusement, 'Because she has gone to join Ashgaroth.'

'But where has she gone?' he had persisted. 'Where is she?'

And his father had taken him by the shoulders and, leading him gently but firmly away from the body, had taken him to the cave entrance. Then, gesturing with his arm over the valley, he had said, quietly and proudly, 'She is there, amongst the trees, moving with the wind through the leaves. Listen! Can you hear her? And she is also in the sky playing amongst the stars at night and dodging sunbeams in the day. She is everywhere; all around us, all the time. When you speak she will hear you and when you cry she will comfort you. Your laughter will fill her with joy and your love will make her proud.'

Nabbeth had never forgotten these words; he had no need even to recall them for they were a part of him. He remembered the sadness disappearing as his father spoke; the mystery had been solved; there was no need for mourning. She was different, that was all; she had changed. She had left her body and gone out into the forest and the sky. She was everywhere! How wonderful!

Shayll, hearing Nabbeth repeat his father's words, had been overcome with emotion at their intense and poignant beauty. Tears had trickled out of the corners of her eyes and she had clung to him, finding comfort in the security of his arms, while an autumn breeze, heavy with the dankness of rotting vegetation, pulled the brown leaves off the trees and sent them drifting down around their feet.

On their way back, that same day, she had asked him about his father, also called Nabbeth as was the custom for the leader of the village. At first Shayll noticed a reluctance to talk of him, an awkward hesitancy, and she was sorry she had asked. And then, as he began speaking and a portrait of the father had begun to emerge, she became aware of a strange ambivalence in his attitude towards him. That he had loved his father greatly there was no doubt, yet she also detected regret, awe and even anger as he spoke. There had been, she surmised, a distance between them despite their occasional moments of deep warmth; a remoteness which, despite everything the younger man had tried to do to banish it, had nevertheless remained. Nabbeth described his father as a perfect figure; a man with no faults or blemishes, almost a god. Immensely strong in character, firm and resolute in judgement and commanding respect and loyalty from all who knew him. Yet it was this same perfection that formed the barrier between them for he never allowed his son to see any of the doubts and worries, the anger and the pain, the sorrow and the weakness which all men suffer. Emotion was never allowed freedom to affect his rock-like façade and so to his son, the young Nabbeth, shorn of his mother's warmth, he became unreal; a man who he was forever forbidden to know as a friend.

Shayll could hear the bitterness and pain in his voice as he told her of his longing to get close to his father; a longing that he slowly realized to be futile as every attempt to break through the shell to the reality of the man behind was frustrated by the other's implacability.

So the old Nabbeth brought up his son in his own image; austere, imperious, certain and versed to perfection in the story of the Book. Thus when the father died in the middle of a long, bitter winter the village accepted the son as the new leader. Trained to be impervious to emotion, still his father's death had left him sour with regret for the lost opportunities, gone now forever, to get to know him; a regret that was rendered almost unbearable by the occasional glimpses of softness he had shown, revealing a warm and gentle man underneath the hard exterior. It was these few moments of closeness that he clung on to; cherishing the memory of them so that the remembrance of his father should be suffused with an aura of love. The images that lingered then were the evenings spent storytelling by a fire, the shared sadness of Syrioll's death and the time spent on walks together when his father had taught him the secrets of the forest.

For her part Shayll had little to tell, for Nabbeth had known her all her life. Yet as she talked of Melvaig and Morven and Bracca he realized there was much he did not know. She told of the good times they had all shared together, particularly when she and Bracca had been younger; playing in the river, running, chasing and hiding, climbing trees, the excitement and fun of foraging together, and he felt pleased for her happiness as she laughed at the memories. He listened with particular interest as she spoke of their journeys to the sea; to the place on the cliffs where the giant, Shuinn, was buried and of the quietness that would descend upon Melvaig and Morven at these times as if they were too lost in memories to be aware of the present. Then they would walk down the cliff path to the beach to play in the sand and explore the rock pools when the tide was out, gathering armfuls of seaweed as they went, to take back and either dry for later use or boil to drink as soup that evening with some herbs.

So Nabbeth and Shayll basked in the idyll of their love and when they visited Melvaig, Morven and Bracca their happiness infected the others so that they all felt buoyed up on a wave of optimism. Gone was the awkwardness and tension of before; now they laughed and joked and made plans; their contentment with each other bolstering their confidence for the difficulties that lay ahead. They discussed the philosophy and reasoning behind what they were going to say, practising their speeches until they knew the words exactly and could concentrate on the manner of expression. The others interrupted, heckling and jeering to acclimatize the speaker to the response they expected to get from the village.

Their first test came when they approached the other members of the Stagg. It had to be done in secret; Barll must not know of what they were planning and so Nabbeth asked Stowna and Nemm to meet him at a spot high up on one of the ridges in the forest. It was known as the Gollstorr and in earlier times when the precepts of the Book were known and followed more closely, the belief was prevalent that it was one of the Scyttel, the places of power where the elves gathered for rejuvenation of their magic. And so Nabbeth had chosen it not only for its isolation and remoteness from the rest of the village but also because of the inspiration he hoped the place would give him and, perhaps, the influence on Stowna and Nemm of this link with the power of Ashgaroth. And so, on an afternoon in late autumn, when the mist was rising from the damp earth and the trees were bathed in an opaque golden aura, Nabbeth, Melvaig and Bracca walked up through the forest to meet Stowna and Nemm. When they arrived they found the two old men already there, sitting down behind one of the tall jagged outcrops of rock that stuck up out of the earth on this high and barren knoll. There was a gentle breeze and a slight chill in the air and the rock provided welcome shelter. Bracca loved this place; he often came, on his own, to sit and look out over the splendour of the forest as it curved away beneath him; to let his spirit feed on its strength. Now though, he felt nervous, his palms tingling with anticipation and his stomach fluttering with the weight of the responsibility he felt was on him. He watched the others greet Stowna and Nemm and then it was his turn. As he gripped their hands in the traditional welcome he felt their eyes turn away from him in embarrassment and confusion as the memory of their last meeting, in the Stagg, hung like a shadow over them.

They were all sitting down in the lee of the rock, in a little circle. Nabbeth spoke first, explaining why he had asked to meet them without Barll, here on the Gollstorr. They listened as he told them of Barll's influence on his ruling, unperceived by him at the time; his early doubts as to its correctness and then, after the hunt, the growing unease until eventually he became convinced of the error of the decision and the awful threat it represented to the village and to the rule of Ashgaroth over them. He stopped then and

Melvaig began speaking, telling them of the conflict he had felt within himself from the moment Bracca had related the Stagg's decision to him, the row with his son and then, his eventual realization, like Nabbeth, of the terrible consequences if it was not revoked.

Now it was Bracca's turn. While he spoke, small puffs of white cloud scudded through the dark blue sky and the breeze kept the clumps of heather around them in constant motion so that his words were accompanied by the sibilant whisper of the wind as it rushed through the foliage. He spoke gently and quietly, not mentioning the meeting of the Stagg but telling instead of his perception of Melvaig's vision and the world of Ashgaroth. And his words spun webs of magic around Stowna and Nemm so that they were spellbound by the pictures he created. He became mesmerized by his own images, as if they had come from somewhere else; the product of a gift for language bestowed upon him by some divine force. So powerful were his words that when eventually he stopped speaking there was no need even to mention the decision for in the world he had described, their world perceived through his eyes, it was so obviously wrong and its consequences so horrific that it would have been superfluous to state it.

There was silence now; only the distant call of an owl out hunting in the early evening broke the quietness. The strength of Bracca's eloquence had so swept them up that they now felt empty and drained of energy. His plea for the animals and the birds, for the forest and for the preservation of the life they had known had moved them deeply for they too, like Nabbeth and Melvaig, had grown dismayed as the consequences of the proclamation had appeared around them, spreading like some evil cancer into the fabric of their lives. They had watched in mounting horror as the familiar trees had been cut down and the land given over to the rearing of domestic creatures for food; wild goats the villagers had captured and were hoping to tame, rabbits and birds which they housed in small wooden sheds. Stowna and Nemm too

83

had witnessed the return of the hunting parties; the joys of the kill still shimmering in the hideous brightness of their eyes – the flopping bodies of their victims dripping a trail of blood onto the grass as they swung from the carrying poles. And, most disturbing of all, the two elders had watched Barll as his power had increased; seen the way the villagers looked to him now for guidance on the use of weapons and the ways of killing, the skilful way he fed their growing appetites so that they hung on his decisions. It was Barll who decided when and what they would hunt; Barll whose influence pervaded the debauchery of the feast days; and it was Barll's inner enclave that every villager yearned to enter, vying with each other in the provision of services or gifts so as to gain his pleasure and approval. Barll now, ever more confident and secure in his growing position of power, scorned the company of the two old Stagg members and they, freed from his influence, had grown to regret the decision they had made with Nabbeth at that fateful meeting of the Stagg.

It was Stowna who spoke, looking first at Bracca and then at Melvaig and Nabbeth, his dark eyes clouded with consternation under his great bushy eyebrows. The evening sun poured gold down one side of his face leaving the other half in shadow.

'It is good that we have spoken,' he said, his voice sounding weary and old. 'Our thoughts are the same. Nemm and I agree with you...' The other nodded, his long wispy hair framing his face in gossamers of gold. 'It was an ill-conceived decision, Nabbeth, I see that now. Yet at the time it did not seem so terrible. And you and Barll ... so certain.'

His words trailed off and he looked down at the ground, thinking back to the meeting. Then Nemm began to speak, his voice high and thin; his thin shoulders stooped and rounded with age. But still his eyes danced and flickered with energy; his mind even now wary and alert.

'But are we not too late?' he said. 'Too late; has it not gone too far? How can we stop it? We are too few. The villagers will never go back to the old ways. Never! What are your plans?'

It was Bracca who answered him.

'You are right, Nemm. It will not be easy. We may fail. But we have to try. We will address the whole village; gather them together and speak to them; all of us. Nabbeth, Melvaig, you, Stowna and me. The whole Stagg except Barll; convinced of the wrongness of the decision. Surely they must accept that...' But even as he said it a glowering shadow of doubt passed through him and his stomach turned over in dread.

'Why not just a meeting of the Stagg?' said Stowna. 'Barll would lose and the ruling to withdraw the decision could go down to the village in the usual way.'

'No,' said Nabbeth. 'We have discussed that. It would not work. The villagers would rebel against it; they would refuse to act on it. Barll has them on his side. That is why we must speak directly to them; it is our only hope.'

'Yes... Yes, I see that.' Stowna nodded his agreement and once again there was silence.

'How long ... when will the meeting be?' said Nemm. Already he felt nervous about it and he found difficulty in voicing the question.

'Soon,' Nabbeth replied. 'The longer we leave it, the harder it will be. Every day that passes, the villagers grow more used to their new life. Four days. In four days' time; at midday; by the stone statues. We'll talk to them from the rock behind; it's the traditional place. Will you spread the word around? Say nothing of what it is about. I will tell Barll, I shall tell him it's to find out if the villagers are pleased with the decision.'

The sun was almost gone now; disappearing down behind the far hills in a blaze of brilliant gold. Around them the great uneven columns of stone threw black shadows on the earth and down the slope; back towards the village, the trees were veiled in darkness. There was no more to be said and so, with Melvaig leading, they began to make their way together along the path that led down from the Gollstorr. As

85

they re-entered the forest a wall of dampness rose up to meet them, sending a chill through their bones as if it were the embodiment of some evil presence. A strange and disturbing feeling came over them, an inexplicable sense of alienation in this, their own familiar territory, that made them uneasy. The trees, usually so friendly, seemed to harbour a host of sounds, shapes and shadows that they did not recognize and could not identify. Was that an owl? And that a badger on his evening walk? Was it a fox that just snapped that twig? The mist drew itself into peculiar patterns that shifted and swayed as they walked past and the undergrowth seemed alive with rustlings.

Now the track divided. Stowna and Nemm set off back to their caves and Melvaig, Bracca and Nabbeth took the other path to the hut. Just behind them, a shadow flitted momentarily out from behind the trunk of an elm and, leaving both groups, made its way to where on the raised outcrop of rock outside his cave, Barll was waiting eagerly for news.

Later, when Straygoth had reported all that he'd overheard Barll spent the night rejoicing. He had never imagined it would be so easy. Four days! Just four more days and then the first part of his plan would be complete. The blood sang in his veins so that he could hardly contain his excitement; pacing the floor like a madman, pouring his energies into sport with the women, Hayllorn and Scrann, until they fell asleep, too exhausted to continue, and then gorging himself on vast quantities of freshly-killed deer, washed down with richly-honeyed mead. Wild images raced through his mind; he saw himself at the head of a huge army, their voices raised in mighty unison as they chanted out his name in the form of a battle song. At his side was Xtlan, smiling at him in confident anticipation of the conquests ahead, and a feeling of power surged through him, sending him dizzy with the realization of total and complete invincibility.

That same night, as Barll's head swam with the scent of victory, Bracca's sleep was dark and disturbed; peopled with shadows and images that flitted through his mind too fast for him to focus on and recognize. No sooner did he begin to recall the place or person that hovered so tantalizingly on the periphery of his mind's eye than it was gone, leaving nothing but a vague uneasy dread lurking in the pit of his stomach. Were they memories of the Bellkindra; the terrible warrior nursery in Xtlan where he had been taken after they had torn him from Melvaig's grasp or were they scenes from the nightmare journey across the scorched and barren wastes of Molobb? Was it these or a myriad other bloated and vicious images from his time in Xtlan that made him toss and turn in his sleep, moaning and whimpering like a child again as Melvaig, lying silent and awake, bled inwardly at the torment of his son.

So the times of peace were gone; at least for the present. Yet Melvaig had hope; hope that, after all, the reign of Ashgaroth would be restored to the world of his vision and the darkness that had come upon them would be banished forever.

CHAPTER VII

The remaining days passed slowly. Early on Nabbeth sought Barll out and told him of the meeting. 'I agree,' had been the willing response. 'We should know how they feel about the new ways; it is good that they should have a chance to tell us.' But even as a smile played around Barll's lips, there had been something about the light in his eyes that had disturbed Nabbeth deeply; a fierce glimmer that sparked and leapt as his gaze met Nabbeth's. The old man had seen that same light when Barll had watched his spear bury itself deep in the flesh of the hunted deer.

Nabbeth, Melvaig and Bracca spent most of the rest of the time together; talking, planning and waiting. The confidence that had buoyed them up before had now almost completely disappeared and they were gripped with a nauseous anxiety. They had to succeed! The consequences of failure were too terrible to think about. Doubts set in again. Were they doing the right thing; was this what Ashgaroth desired? Why did he not come to them; speak to them as he had to Bracca? Some sign; anything to show that he was there, with them.

And then, at Morven's suggestion, it was decided that they would all go to the place of the statues and spend the time that was left cleaning them and tidying them up. The air was mild, the light mellow and comforting in the clearing, as they took away the dead brown bracken, heavy with damp, from the five stone figures. They brought water and washed the mildew and the dirt off them so that they appeared to glow in the rich golden light that filtered through the trees. As they worked, the figures seemed to come to life, transmitting some of their strength to them; some of the vast aura of legend and magic with which the first settlers in Haark had so lovingly and painstakingly fashioned them. The story of their quest for the Faradawn lived again in the spirits of Nabbeth, Shayll, Melvaig, Morven and Bracca and they no longer felt lonely or desolate in their struggle; for this was how Ashgaroth spoke to them so that now at last they felt his presence all about and knew that, whatever might happen in the future, he was with them.

Then, suddenly, it was the last evening. They all shared a meal together outside Melvaig and Morven's hut under a sky that was aflame with great livid gashes of crimson and purple. The dying sun seemed more beautiful than ever as it threw its soft rays down and gilded the clearing with gold before finally descending into the shadow of the far hills. When it had gone it seemed to take with it all the busy daytime sounds; the singing of the birds, the rustling of the branches, so that now silence fell around them like a pall. In the twilight, no one spoke; there was no more for anyone to say and the only sound was the puffing of their pipes. Then after a little while, Melvaig got up, went into the hut and came out with his pan pipes. He sat down a little way away from them, on a flat stone near the stream at the edge of the clearing and began to play. Above him a great silver moon appeared fitfully through jagged rents in the dark clouds so that he appeared in silhouette; his image frozen in dazzling white brilliance against the dark and mysterious background of the forest. The others watched him, hypnotized by the heartstopping beauty of the tune he played. As they listened, all their doubts, fears and worries seemed to fade away; the drama they were facing banished from their minds by the infinite majesty of the sounds that swirled around them like

89

leaves blowing in the wind. And this was all that mattered – ever; this blessed communion with the world of Ashgaroth, for now they felt truly as one with the sky and the trees, the animals, the birds and the grasses; with the sun and the moon, the frost and the rain, the mountains and the valleys and the seas.

Late into the night he played and when at last he stopped, Nabbeth took Shayll by the hand and led her slowly back along the track to their cave where they fell together into each other's arms and made love with such exquisite beauty and tenderness that time stood still and the earth around them seemed to change into an endlessly shimmering vista of golden cloud. For Melvaig and Morven too, comfort was to be found in the warmth and intimacy of each other but Bracca was unable to sleep and he went out for a long walk through the forest, his mind racing with images of what tomorrow would bring, and sought his solace under the majestic canyons of the moonlit sky with the trees and the stars and night creatures for his companions.

The next day dawned, damp and misty with a pale yellow sun blurring the edges of the trees in a soft aura of light. At mid-morning Nabbeth and Shayll joined them again at the hut, with Nabbeth wearing his ceremonial green cloak, and then they set out together towards the five statues. They wanted to get there early, before anyone else arrived, but as they came round a bend to within sight of the clearing they saw, to their disappointment, that there were already a number of people scattered about. As they drew nearer they perceived that there were no women among them and they felt a sharp twinge of uneasiness as they further realized that the men were all from Barll's closest guard. They saw Stigg, standing with a small group at one side of the clearing, and Skatt, another of Barll's lieutenants, a big burly red-haired man, with a different group in the middle. Nabbeth led them towards the steep rock face that rose from the ground a short distance behind the statues. Half way up it, and reached by a narrow track cut into the rock, was the large outcrop which formed the ledge from which they would speak. As they made their way slowly towards it, all heads turned to look at them. Bracca saw them out of the corner of his eye and sensed a furtiveness about their actions that put him on edge. Nabbeth called out a greeting to a few of them. They answered him almost too enthusiastically and then, as he turned away, Bracca saw the sly smirk that spread over their faces.

When they got to the base of the track they turned round and saw Stowna and Nemm making their way slowly across the clearing from the other side. The sun was now high in the sky but the air was still chilly and there were few breaks in the dull grey layer of cloud above their heads. They waited until the two old men had joined them. It seemed to Bracca as if they looked considerably older than they had four days ago and Nemm when he spoke sounded tired and almost listless.

'It is done,' he said, looking at them each in turn. 'The word is round. The village is on its way.'

'And some,' replied Nabbeth, nodding at Stigg and the others, 'are already here. What is the mood of the people? How did they react?'

Neither Nemm nor Stowna answered; their eyes roved along the ground and their heads were downcast.

'Tell me,' said Nabbeth, a note of panic in his voice. 'What do you think? I have to know!'

It was Nemm who spoke. 'It will not be easy. I...' He paused as if searching for the right words. 'I do not think...' and his voice tailed off again.

'We told them nothing of the purpose of the meeting, as we agreed,' said Stowna, speaking urgently now as if he had a lot to say in a short space of time. 'Yet they guessed it was about the new ways. And they welcomed the chance – the chance to praise us for the decision; for its wisdom and the beneficence of its effects, the richness it has bestowed upon their lives. And what surprised us most – Barll seems to be actively encouraging this attitude. Among the ordinary

91

people, those not in his inner circle, you have never been held in higher esteem for your bravery and far-sightedness in leading them forward into a new world.'

No one spoke among the companions; Stowna's words seemed to have stunned them all into silence. Their worst fears had been confirmed and now the enormity of the task ahead seemed to crush them beneath a terrible weight; to stultify them in a morbid torpor of hopelessness. And as they stood there next to the moss-festooned rock face, the clearing suddenly started to fill up with people, ordinary villagers, dressed now in skins and furs, their faces fat and round and their bodies rotund even beneath their garments. When they caught sight of Nabbeth they began to shout and cheer and in a daze he turned to face them, slowly waving his hand in acknowledgement.

'Come on,' said Bracca fiercely. 'We must get up to the ledge, quickly,' and then through the crowd he sensed a current of movement, as a boat makes through water, and looking, he saw the great figure of Barll making his way slowly towards them. A broad smile lit up the darkness of his features yet the light in his eyes was as cold as the heart of a stone and Bracca felt a wave of fear spread upwards from his guts into the rest of his body as a sudden premonition of disaster swept into his mind. But it was too late now! Too late to back out.

Now he was with them, grasping Nabbeth by the shoulders and embracing him as warmly as if he were a long-lost brother, and then on to Melvaig, clasping his hands and delivering a little bow of respect in full view of the crowd so that a great full-throated cheer went up. Nabbeth and Melvaig seemed lost and embarrassed; disorientated by the cheering and bewildered by Barll's behaviour.

It was Bracca's turn now; the mane of dark hair shook as Barll turned towards him. No! He would not let Barll play with him as he was with the others. Quickly he turned to Morven and Shayll who were standing next to him.

'You stay here, next to the wall, at the foot of the path,' he

92

said, and then hurriedly he pushed past Melvaig and, ignoring Barll's attempts at a greeting, grabbed Nabbeth's elbow and with all the force he could muster, began pulling him up the track.

'Come on, hurry.' His words were urgent; his pulse racing with the need to start the meeting as soon as possible before their resolve and their certainty were weakened. This was not how any of them had imagined it and Bracca was afraid of the effect it might have on them. Barll's cunning had been vicious in its ingenuity! He had encouraged this massive show of support (it was his inner circle now who were leading the cheers) knowing how dangerous it would be to speak against it.

Nabbeth stumbled up the narrow rocky track in a daze; his head ringing with the shouts and the almost physical assault on his senses of the adoration that surged up from the crowd. Only the hard, nearly painful grip on his elbow and the desperate tone of Bracca's voice reminded him of their purpose and kept him from being submerged in a euphoric haze of benevolence. He half-turned to look behind him and saw Melvaig following; his eyes wide and staring as if he were in a trance. Barll followed while Stowna and Nemm came last. Beneath them, standing at the base of the cliff, he could see Morven and Shayll; his precious beautiful Shayll. She stood gazing up after him and catching her eye he tried to give her a smile of reassurance but she either did not see it or failed to recognize it for she did not respond and the expression on her face of frantic, yearning anxiety did not change. She and Morven had their arms about each other, clinging together in a gesture of mutual support that was at the same time both beautiful and infinitely heart-rending to Nabbeth.

Now, suddenly, they came out on to the natural rock platform high up above the clearing, from which they could look out and see the scene below them. A dense throng of people milled about, stretching back to the farthest edge. The five statues were completely surrounded by people and

93

Nabbeth could not see the crossroads or the tracks that led to them. They were all there; all the men, women and children of the village, laughing and shouting, their faces individually familiar to him yet all together strangely unknown. Collectively they had become transmuted into a single entity, utterly alien to him and even to themselves, that made him very afraid.

Nabbeth walked, with Bracca at his side and Melvaig close behind, until he was more or less at the centre of the platform. The damp mist had made the rock beneath his feet slippery and he moved slowly for fear of sliding. Cushions of emerald green moss grew out of cracks and fissures in the stone, feeling soft and springy when he walked on them. He moved forward a little so that he was standing at the front, close to the edge with an almost sheer drop beneath him as he looked down to the upturned faces clamouring below. Into his mind there came memories of the last time he had stood here, so many seasons ago as a young man, when his father had announced his son's succession to the village as their leader when he, the old man, died. Behind him now, the others took their seats on the roughly hewn ledges in the rock; Bracca, Melvaig, Barll, Stowna and Nemm. It was time at last, and as he raised his hand to ask for silence, he felt his heart hammering wildly inside his chest, sending him almost giddy, while his bowels rolled and churned as if they had a life of their own.

'Welcome, my friends.' His voice sounded strange and distant, unrecognizable, and he grew acutely aware at the same time of the sound and feel of his own breathing. Gradually the noise subsided, the cheering and the shouting quietened and as it did so, and a wedge of silence came in to take its place, so Nabbeth grew even more nervous, his stomach lurched up into his mouth and he felt as if he would be sick. But he fought down the nausea and said to them again, 'Welcome,' and now the remaining noise receded into utter stillness. The tension, the crushing weight of anticipation was almost unbearable. How! How could he tell them

94

what he had come to say? It seemed unthinkable, inconceivable to betray their adoration and yet ... did he have a choice? And so he started; just as they had all rehearsed so many times before. And the words he used were the same, yet as he spoke them it was as if he was saying them for the first time; clumsy and unwieldy in the pattern of their sounds and the sense of their meaning.

'It is good that we have this chance to talk ... about the new ways ... about the decision we made to depart from the teachings of our forefathers, the spirit of the Faradawn. You are to be praised,' he said, enjoying the security of his words, 'for your ready acceptance of that decision; how you adapted to the revolution that was thrust upon you so suddenly.' He paused and their faces shone up at him in contentment. Now was the moment he had been dreading; no longer to be put off or postponed, imagined or forgotten about. This, at last, was the moment of truth.

'Yet it was not an easy decision to take. I fought long and hard with myself, agonizing over the correct course to follow. And, in the end, believing it to be right, I arrived at the conclusion you know of and have adopted so whole-heartedly; that to kill the animals for food is justifiable if it is done with the least possible pain and suffering, and only when absolutely necessary for our survival. And that the clearing of the forest should be allowed for the growing of crops and for the rearing of creatures for us to eat. We believed that the effect of these momentous decisions could be contained within the narrowest possible limits so that they would never get out of control. We thought that the love and respect and unity with the animals and the forest which is central to our faith, our belief in the spirit of Nab, could survive despite the profound changes we proposed.'

And already the implications of what he was saying had caused a tremor of unease to ripple through the people. There was an intensity of concentration on their faces; their expressions stern and set as they strained to hear every word he spoke and to gather the sense of what he was trying to tell them. Nabbeth felt it and saw also the almost imperceptible change in attitude adopted by the members of Barll's inner cohort as they stood in their positions amongst the other villagers. Then, his heart thumping wildly, he went on.

'I have watched the effects of the decision; seen how things have changed and now I think...' he paused, almost physically incapable of speaking the words, '... I think that my decision was wrong; that if we carry on along this road we shall eventually find ourselves living in a world of shadow and darkness; a world where Ashgaroth is no more and Dréagg reigns supreme. And so, along with all the other members of the Stagg save Barll, I am asking you to have faith in my judgement and to go back on the decision; to revert to our old ways when we lived without killing and destruction.'

He stopped and, for a moment, there was a stunned silence. Then, as if at a signal, there was pandemonium as a great eruption of noise burst out from the crowd. Harsh angry voices clamoured together in a violent cacophony of sound and as he looked out into the sea of upturned shouting faces before him Nabbeth could see Barll's cohorts orchestrating the bedlam from their strategic positions around and amongst the villagers. Desperately summoning together all his reserves of will, he raised both his arms high above his head and called out to them, 'Stop. Stop your shouting. Please listen,' and his voice rang out through the noise with such majesty and authority that they seemed to respond to him and gradually the volume subsided. For a brief moment Nabbeth had flattered himself that it was the re-assertion of his control that had caused them to quieten down but then, from the corner of his eye he caught sight of Barll's signal to his men and his mind lurched suddenly with a terrible awareness of utter debilitating impotence; as if he were a toy, a plaything whose every movement was at Barll's whim. He pushed this feeling to one side and spoke out again.

'I know it will be hard. I know there are many pleasurable

things you will have to forego if we give up the new ways; many luxuries you have grown used to which will be sorely missed. Yet if we carry on with them I believe that our world will swiftly decline to become a place such as none of us could envisage even in our wildest nightmares. Only three amongst us have ever experienced such a world. I beg you therefore, before you reject my request to you, to listen to Melvaig, Melvaig the stranger, who was for many years a member of the Stagg, for he will tell you now of that world, the world of Xtlan.'

The villagers looked at one another, muttering and shuffling restlessly on the damp brown bracken, as Nabbeth stepped back, still shaking from his ordeal and Melvaig came forward to take his place. He was not nervous or frightened; after the horrors he had suffered in Xtlan he had become immune to fear. Yet in his heart there was a dull aching pain at the unthinkable prospect of failure; that they would not succeed in convincing the village of the terrible consequences of the new ways and that the blessed world of his vision would collapse and crumble into a mire of darkness and evil and Ashgaroth would be no more.

He began to speak and to Morven and Sharyll watching and listening to him from the bottom of the rock wall it seemed as if he had been transformed. Shayll had never before seen him like this, yet to Morven it was as if the years had fallen away and he was once again the impassioned warrior who had led her and Bracca and Shuinn through the nightmare of Xtlan fired with a vision so pure and so bright that nothing had been able to stand in its way. Gone now were the gentle ravages of age. He stood tall and strong and proud and in his voice was all the power she remembered from those desperate embattled days. To Bracca too, standing next to Nabbeth and Stowna, it seemed as if he listened to a different man and he saw Melvaig again as he had when a child and the whole world had been encompassed in his father's face. A strange mixture of humility, pride and love coursed through his veins and he went almost dizzy with the intensity of feeling.

Melvaig's words echoed loudly around the clearing, conjuring up images so dreadful that the villagers, restless and aggressive only a few moments before, were now hushed and silent as he took them to the world of Xtlan. Rapt in his words, they listened in stunned horror as he described the desolate barren wastes, parched arid deserts and treeless landscapes of the other world. They were transported with him to the land he knew so well and could never forget, where the sky was always brown and the air dry and acrid, where the sun beat down mercilessly and the rocks burnt if you touched them but worse perhaps even than all of this was the almost total lack of vegetation and the absence of any wild creatures.

Then he described the people; Xtlan's followers, whose life blood was the infliction of pain and suffering on the weak; for whom the degradation and humiliation of others was a religion and whose darkest and most bestial appetites were encouraged as a sign of strength and power. He told of the Lemgorrst; the hinterland wherein dwelt the sick, the infirm and the crippled in a living death, feeding off each other even as the poison in their bodies erupted through their skin. He described the Gravenndra, the brothels where Xtlan's warriors indulged their vile lusts, and he told of the dreaded Gurrtslagg, the mines deep underground from which no man ever emerged to see daylight again. More he spoke of; the vast plain of Molobb and the indescribable horror of the Dammfenn; all of them memories seared forever in his mind and on his spirit so that as his words described them his blood ran cold once more at their recollection. And over everything, dominating the landscape and the people like some gargantuan and loathsome reptile, was the Blaggvald; the Black Palace wherein Xtlan dwelt – the very pinnacle of evil, casting its dark shadow into the souls of all human kind so that none were free of its terrible influence.

Barll, watching the villagers as they listened to the voice of

98

Melvaig, felt his control slipping from him and made a signal to his lieutenant, Stigg, who was standing next to the statues on one side of the crowd. Immediately Stigg raised his fist up in the air and began shouting in a voice that drowned out Melvaig's.

'Enough. We have heard enough. No more from the stranger.' Immediately all the other members of Barll's inner cohort joined in, echoing Stigg's words in an ugly and raucous chant. 'Enough. Enough,' they called. 'No more. No more. How do we know he speaks the truth?' and they chorused, 'No. No.'

'And anyway,' continued Stigg, as the crowd turned their heads to watch him. 'What do his words have to do with us. The world of Xtlan may be as he describes it but what right does he have to tell us that the decision – a decision that was taken by the Stagg – will lead us to such a world, will turn our forest and our people into a place like that?'

'Rubbish, rubbish,' went up the cries. 'Melvaig speaks rubbish,' and this time they did not stop. Instead they grew louder as, to Melvaig's horror, the other villagers began to join in and the chanting spread like ripples from a stone, each infecting the other, their fists punching the air in unison.

Then Barll stepped forward on the ledge and his hand went up in a gesture of quiescence. He was smiling; a quiet placid smile that sent chills of fear through Melvaig, Bracca and Nabbeth. Quickly the row died away but, while there was still a murmur of discontent, Barll began to speak.

'No,' he said, and his voice was heavy with condescension, every nuance laden with barely concealed contempt and scorn. 'My friends! Is this the way to treat our leader and his new-found friends. Let us hear them out, hear what the strangers have to say; why they think we should abandon our new ways.'

He slowly turned his head and looking straight at Bracca, beckoned to him to come forward.

'Do you not want to speak, Bracca?' he said, his words

crackling with sarcasm. 'Surely you have something to say? Come, don't be shy.'

It was a nightmare. Unreal. None of it could really be happening. He would wake up soon, relieved that it had all been a terrible dream. And yet, at the same time that these thoughts reverberated in his head, so, deep down, he knew there was no escape: knew it with a terrible, implacable certainty and he felt sick and faint with fear; his limbs shook and his throat was seized with a dry constricting ache.

Then, as if from outside himself, he felt his body moving in the direction Barll had indicated so that he ended up standing next to Melvaig who had remained where he was, rooted to the spot. There was silence; such utter and complete stillness that even the shuffling of his bark moccasins on the rough stone ledge sounded loud. Then to his dismay he felt his toe knock against a small loose piece of stone. He looked down at it as it rolled slowly away from him towards the edge, eventually dropping over and clattering with awful volume down the steep rocky face, bumping and bouncing for what seemed an age until at last it landed at the bottom with a disconcertingly quiet thud on a bed of damp brown bracken. At that moment, just to one side of where it had landed, his eyes were caught by a sudden movement and, looking, he saw his mother and sister being jostled by some of the villagers standing near. Morven had apparently stumbled and almost fallen but Shayll had caught her and was holding her up. Seeing their faces his guts turned to ice for their eyes were red with tears and panic was etched into every furrow on Morven's brow so that suddenly, and for the first time, she looked very old.

He fought to get a hold of himself. He had to say something, to respond to Barll's challenge; otherwise they had no hope. So he struggled to quell the terror that raged within and he lifted his eyes up so that he was looking out over the heads of the crowd and up into the sky.

'Melvaig's vision,' he began, his voice sounding frail and ragged, so different from how they they had rehearsed it

100

outside the hut, 'was of a place of peace and love. A world where the magic of Ashgaroth still reigned supreme; where the beauty and majesty of the life he created and placed on the earth still glowed and shone as he had intended. And this was that place; blessed with mighty trees and delicate flowers, with lush green grasses and fragrant mysterious fruits of the ground. All around, animals, birds and insects, teeming amongst the vegetation and living peacefully side by side with that most complex and difficult of all creatures, man; who was created with the power of the Three Seeds of Logic and to whom, as it is written, the power of magic was denied. Yet there were some, and you are amongst them, who are called Eldron, or Friends – those amongst men who turned away from the influence of Dréagg, the dreaded Lord of Darkness, and who embraced the spirit of Ashgaroth. And amongst you was the love of Nab and Brock and the other travellers from Silver Wood; the six companions in whose image your ancestors created the statues over there, in the clearing.'

He paused and pointed towards them but as he did so his gaze fell upon the crowd and his mind went blank; suddenly empty of everything, a gaping vacuousness from which he could produce no coherent thought. Barll had done his work well. Bracca had been unnerved by the chanting of the crowd at Melvaig and then Barll, by controlling the crowd and manipulating the situation so that he was seen to introduce Bracca, had completely wrested the initiative from his adversaries. And Bracca now was utterly lost. The more desperately he struggled to co-ordinate his speech, the worse it became; he was unable to utter a word.

The crowd, up until this moment, had been tolerant of Bracca only because of Barll's introduction. Now though, they suddenly felt themselves freed from any restraints, and led by Barll's men they began chanting again.

'No, No, No, No.' The sound surged towards Bracca in waves of anger; they were giving vent now not just to their present feelings but also to all the resentment, dislike and

101

mistrust which they had always felt towards the strangers. And like some repulsive organism the anger seemed to feed upon itself so that the chanting increased in volume and intensity, transforming the crowd into a terrifying monster with an insatiable appetite that only the blood of revenge could appease.

It was then that Barll stepped forward, his face now a mirror of their turbulent slavering rage, and he began to shout; his voice so loud and its tone so resonant with hatred and bile that it could be heard clearly above the crowd.

'You have heard their words, these lovers of Ashgaroth, heard what they have to say.'

At the sound of Barll's voice the mob immediately quietened down and turned to him to listen.

'They would have you go back to the old ways. Abandon your new life of ease and plenty for some vague notion they have that our world will grow barren and treeless; that it is wrong to kill animals and birds, that it is wrong to clear the forest. They think that this will destroy Haark; turn it into a place such as this Xtlan that Melvaig tells us about. Do you believe them? Do you? Do you?'

He barked the words out and they answered him with great shouts of 'No! No!'

'And why do they think this; that there is something evil about killing animals so that we may live a better, easier life. I will tell you. Because of a story; a story that our ancestors believed in and that then this Melvaig, this unknown stranger who arrives on our shores from nowhere with a woman and child, says that he also knows. And he then produces the Book that, he says, the story came from. No one can read it to prove his words; not even Melvaig himself, but he tells us that an old man once read the Book to him. Well . . .' and he leaned forward into the crowd, hands on hips, his face leering in a vicious smile, 'he certainly tells a good story himself!'

Now jeers and laughter started to break out among the villagers, spreading infectiously until it became uproarious;

the laughter and mockery hurting more than the anger.

'We'll show them what we think of their precious book,' he shouted. 'Stigg . . .'

The tall, sandy-haired figure of Barll's lieutenant came forward, the crowd making a way for him as he approached the base of the cliff. Nabbeth started in horror as he saw Stigg holding the casket containing the Book out in front of him as if its possession was a symbol of victory.

'Now, burn it!' yelled Barll, and throwing it on the bracken at his feet Stigg took a large wooden club out of his belt and smashed the stone head down with all his strength on the casket. The top bent but did not break. He brought the club down again and this time there was a tearing sound as it split open to reveal the Book hiding inside. Stigg bent down, put his hand in and pulled it out, holding it up high by the spine so that the crowd, jostling excitedly round him, could all see it.

'Burn it,' snapped out Barll again, and the cry was taken up by the mob. Stigg raised his other hand and shoved it hard in between the covers, scrabbling with his fingers as he did so, and then with a look of triumph, he drew his hand back out and there, crumpled and torn in his gripping fist, their tattered edges protruding out from between his fingers, were some of the pages.

Bracca, numb with shock, rage and fear, was suddenly brought to his senses by a piercing shriek. He looked sharply in the direction it came from and saw Morven struggling desperately to get through the crowd. She was trying to reach the Book, kicking and scratching and biting as she fought against the barrier of bodies that barred her way. Now though, the attention of the villagers was caught by her and they began tossing her from one to the other, the men fondling her crudely as they did so, laughing at her pain.

Barll spoke again. 'Stop,' he said, his tone once again mocking and sardonic. 'Is this the way to treat such an honourable and respected woman. Put her down my friends. Let her go. But as she is so keen to watch the burning of this beloved and precious book take her forward, so that she may have a good view as it disappears into smoke. Then we will have done with the repression these men have kept you under for your lifetimes and the lifetimes of all your ancestors.'

Morven was shoved roughly through the throng, which parted to make a way for her, until she stood on the edge of the space about Stigg who now proceeded to rip the rest of the pages out and throw them down on the bracken, finishing with the cover which he tore in two. He looked up then and someone from the crowd came forward with a lighted brand. They were quiet now and the hissing and crackling of the flames was clearly audible above the slight whisper of the breeze in the trees. Melvaig, watching, was mesmerized with horror and disbelief; unable to comprehend anything that was happening. It could not be his Book down there, the Book he had carried with him all through those terrible days in Xtlan; that not even Xtlan himself had been able to find. No, not his Book that Stigg was now bending down towards, pointing the flaming end of the brand so that it almost touched the crumpled bits of paper that had been ripped from its innards. And then, just as he was about to light it, he stopped and Melvaig saw the spindly figure of Straygoth standing next to Stigg; their heads close together as they whispered conspiratorially among themselves for a few brief moments. Stigg straightened up then, a broad smile smeared over his face, and with a glance up at Barll he began to walk slowly over to Morven who was pinioned between two burly warriors, unable to move.

'Here,' said Stigg, loudly so that his voice carried throughout the clearing. 'You light it. Your book – you light it.'

He thrust the flaming torch towards her, his great hooked nose and jutting chin lit up eerily by the fire. At first she refused to take it, cowering back in fear as he shoved it in front of her face. But then, like a striking snake, his hand whipped out and he struck her hard across the face twice, the sound of the crack and Morven's stifled scream searing their way into Melvaig's brain.

'Take it,' he shouted, and grabbing her wrist he forced her to hold it, dragging her across the clearing until they stood by the book. There was total silence as the crowd revelled in the drama being enacted before their eyes; fascinated by the anguish of Morven's dilemma.

'Now, burn the Book.' It was Barll who spoke now, wallowing in the delicious irony of the situation.

But she could not do it, could not bring herself to light those pages for which, mute and tattered now and moving slightly in the breeze, they had suffered so much. To destroy them would be like destroying herself. And then Stigg hit her again, across the face, and her senses reeled as her head rocked back and the pain spread out from her jaw. Still she could not put the flames to the paper and so once more Stigg took his fist to her, this time smashing her hard across her breasts, first one way then the other. The pain was excruciating and she felt her consciousness slipping but then, through the dizzying haze in her head, she heard a great shout from above, from the platform on the rock face, and knew it to be Melvaig. She tried to look up but everything was a blur and she was unable to focus and then, aware only of a feeling of intense relief, she was consumed in a wave of oblivion.

Melvaig could take no more. As he saw Morven hit for the third time, heard her cry of pain and saw her legs start to collapse under her he lost all control of himself and, bellowing with rage, he began to run down the path in the rock towards the floor of the clearing. Roughly he pushed past Stowna and Nemm, shoving accidentally against Barll who, smiling, gestured to a little troop of his warriors who were standing at the base of the cliff. This signal was what they had been waiting for and, with precision and certainty, they ran to the bottom of the path and then began to walk up it slowly, blocking the way as they did so, so that Melvaig, blind with anger, charged straight into them. Frantically he struggled to get free but it was useless; they had grabbed both arms and were forcing them up behind his back. He tried to kick but one of them swung a heavy wooden club against his shins and the pain made it difficult for him to stand so that it took all his concentration to stay on his feet. And he was old, his sadly flailing body tired and worn out by the years.

Bracca watched as if in a dream. He felt no fear, no remorse, no suffering; all those and a myriad other turbulent emotions were felt by another figure, another Bracca, who he could see standing on a narrow cliff ledge down below, fighting vainly now as the warriors grabbed him also and proceeded to force him, with blows from their clubs on his shoulders and his head, down the path. Just ahead of him was Nabbeth and further in front were Stowna and Nemm; all of them being driven along brutally by those vicious, swinging clubs while Barll, leering at them with a bloated grin of triumph on his face, shouted above the noise of the crowd.

'Burn the Book; destroy the old ways. Now you are free, people of Haark. Free of those who oppressed you by denying you the right to kill. Now you can take your rightful place as masters of the forest. Look at them...' and he pointed to Melvaig, Nabbeth and the others as they tripped and stumbled down the narrow path. 'See how they cringe now beneath the weight of our blows even as they must admit to the truth that they have refused you for so long – that man is master of his world; that all must give way to his strength and might, that all the creatures of the earth and all the green growing things were created solely for his use and enjoyment that he may do with as he pleases.'

He stopped then and, facing the crowd, raised both hands up to the sky.

'So rejoice,' he said, and his voice echoed out amongst the trees, and the animals and the birds froze in terror at the sound. 'Rejoice at the dawn of a new age.' And the people cheered and shouted and danced in happiness that their troubles were over; that times of plenty were ahead and at the prospect of freedom to indulge their true natures, and the satisfaction of cravings that had lain dormant for so long.

They were at the base of the cliff now and Bracca's eye was caught by a swirl of movement to one side. Looking, he saw Shayll wrestling in the grip of three burly men. They were smirking and laughing at her vain attempts to get free, at the way that in the struggle her skirt had been torn up to her waist and that as she threw herself from side to side she exposed herself to both them and the crowd. Her breasts too were revealed; full and milky white they swayed and juddered as she moved. Some of the village women, and the men, began making lewd remarks, wallowing in Shayll's debasement and pawing greedily between her legs as the guards dragged her past them. Melvaig, Bracca and Nabbeth all suffered for her in their own different ways as father, brother and lover; their anguish equally deep and painful and all of them fretted desperately at their helplessness, struggling with their impotence even as she struggled with her captors. Then, suddenly, she was among them, shoved hard towards Nabbeth so that, off balance, she had to throw her arms round his neck to save herself from falling. The crowd cheered uproariously at this involuntary gesture of affection and Nabbeth, numb with grief, held her tightly to him trying to calm her shuddering body, to quieten the tears which, hot, wet and salty, he could feel against his face as he nursed her head. 'All right,' he kept saying over and over again. 'It's all right, I've got you,' though he knew his words were empty, his attempt at reassurance useless and futile.

'Let them watch.' Again Barll's voice quietened the crowd and they stepped away from the captives to make a path towards the spot where Stigg still stood, the burning blood-red brand still poised ready in his hand and Morven lying at his feet. Futile to resist now; Stowna led them passively forward until they came to the edge of the space around Stigg who, when he was certain they could all see clearly, pushed the brand in among the pages. The paper was

107

stubborn at first, smouldering quietly, black with a thin red edging and Melvaig, watching through eyes that were blurred with tears, felt a faint stir of hope fluttering in his heart but then, savagely and cruelly, a gust of wind suddenly caught the red and sent it flaring up with a great crackle of flame. Tongues of vermilion, orange and green flickered and danced and the pages twisted and curled as if they were alive before crumbling into black smuts. It did not last long once the fire had caught and then, suddenly, the Book was gone, its ashes blown away by the evening breeze, and nothing remained, its demise as horribly and irrevocably final as death. Melvaig still stared, unable to believe what his eyes had witnessed, and then Barll's now-familiar mocking tones once more penetrated his befuddled consciousness.

'There, friends of Ashgaroth, there are your dreams; there is your faith. Motes in the winds; more worthless than dust. I have achieved what Xtlan for all his cunning and power could not do. Now we are rid of its stupid ideas for ever.' Then he raised his right arm and, pointing up to the cave where the Stagg was held, Nabbeth's cave, he called out, 'Take them; take them away to the cave. We shall see how fine their words are.'

Stigg sneered at Melvaig. 'Pick her up,' he said. 'She's yours,' pointing to the still figure of Morven.

Bracca moved forward to help Melvaig but just as he was bending down to lift her under her arms he was knocked viciously sideways by a savage blow on the side of his face and he toppled backwards.

'Not you, Bracca. Did I say you? No, your fine and noble father. He can carry her on his own.' Contempt and loathing were smeared all over Stigg's face. They had no choice. Melvaig bent and, putting both arms under her back, slowly lifted her up. A long whining groan came from her throat and her eyelids flickered but she stayed unconscious, her limp body a dead weight in the old man's arms so that for one terrible moment he felt as if he might fall with her but, with an effort, he steadied himself and gritting his teeth against the pain that had already started in his back, he began to walk slowly forward, following Nabbeth in front, who was still clutching Shayll, and with Bracca behind him.

And so this strange, ragged pathetic little procession made its painful way through the narrow corridor that Barll's warriors made for them through the crowd. Their route was lined with jeering faces, shouting out all the envy and mistrust which had smouldered quietly during the years since the strangers had first arrived, their hatred whipped up to fever pitch by Barll's skilful manipulation. For Nabbeth they reserved the special venom a mob has for a leader who has fallen from grace; one who they feel has betrayed them. As he passed them they taunted him, spitting at him and throwing bits of wood and stones that bruised and cut his head and face. And all the while he held Shayll's head away from them, against his shoulder, protecting her face with his hands, wincing with pain when his hand was hit but thankful that it was not Shayll who had been struck.

Above them the sky had turned grey, a drab cold-looking roof of cloud that heralded the winter ahead, though the damp leafy smell of the earth reminded those who noticed it that it was still autumn. Bracca kept his eyes fixed on the sky; it was the one thing that had remained unchanged from before the terrible nightmare of upheaval that had burst upon them; nothing else seemed even remotely familiar. And then, as he looked, a solitary crow flew across his vision, its wings steadily and rhythmically taking it through the air; its blackness stark against the grey. It seemed incredible to him that it did not react in some way to the momentous events on the earth beneath it; that the awful tragedy which had consumed him left the crow completely and utterly unaffected. Then, without hurrying, it was gone as if it had never been and Bracca was left with a feeling of emptiness. All that existed for him now was the motion of walking, his limbs driving themselves forward with a relentless stoicism that seemed to come from outside himself, pushing him on through the torrent of abuse that poured out from the mob.

109

They were nearly at the main path now, that led from Nabbeth's cave through the village to the crossroads and then out to their hut. The five stone statues stood before them, cleaned and cleared in readiness for what was to have been a time of triumph. And now, along with the other swathes of pain that coursed through their spirits, the sight of the statues filled them all with a new and bitter sense of defeat. Then, apparently spontaneously, one of the villagers lifted a great stone headed mallet above his head and brought it down upon Brock's head. The end of his nose chipped off and fell with a soft thud on to the bracken. A cheer went up from those round about and the man swung his mallet again, this time breaking off a large piece of his neck. Others then seemed to come from out of the crowd and began attacking the rest of the statues while the watching mob roared its approval.

The destruction of the statues did not take long; Nab's head fell off and rolled along the ground until, by a vicious twist of fate, it was stopped by Melvaig's feet. Mercifully the old man, who had seen so much, was too absorbed in his own grief and pain to really take notice of what had knocked his toe. He was simply glad of the chance of a rest; the opportunity to put Morven down and earn a brief respite for his back from the pain of carrying her. The others also were too wrapped in their own tragedies to perceive fully what was happening before their eyes. For Bracca though, it was different, for these were his friends with whom he had shared his life; every secret being told to them and listened to by them. He loved them as if they were real; the feel of Brock's smooth round head, the look in his eyes; the gentle beauty that, even in stone, radiated from Beth. He had been sustained by the strength of Nab, fortified by the wisdom of Warrigal the owl, basked in the love of Sam the dog and been heartened by the humour of Perryfoot the hare. And now as he watched them being smashed into pieces the tears finally began to flow and a great racking sob escaped from the innermost depths of his tortured soul.

110

'No,' he yelled, but it was a cry of despair rather than anger. 'Ashgaroth!' He shouted the name so that it sounded even above the breaking of the statues. And again, 'Ashgaroth,' but there was no response: nothing to indicate his presence save the hazy autumn sun filtering down through the golden leaves, the patches of blue sky that showed through the cloud and the feel of the earth beneath the feet. In his torment, Bracca fell to his knees and buried his face in the damp bracken, clutching the fronds to his face and wiping away his tears with them. And it was then, behind the veil of darkness within which he had enclosed himself and with the pungent scent of the bracken drawing his senses, that Ashgaroth came to him for the second time. A silver light appeared before his shut eyelids; a star shimmering so brightly that Bracca felt almost blinded. And at the same time he heard a voice, seeming to come from somewhere just outside himself; the bracken, the earth, he could not say exactly where, but it was clear and calm and he basked in the strength and majesty of its tone.

'I am here. Do not lose your courage or your faith. Simply know that I am with you. So! Be strong and know the peace of my love for you and the others, for I will not desert you.'

Slowly then Bracca took the damp fronds away from his face and opened his eyes. Where the statues had been there was now a heap of rubble, the newly broken surfaces glimmering clean and new in strange and jagged contrast to the old. Yet the pain in Bracca's heart had subsided; the grief, though still a dull ache, had diminished so that he felt able to bear it. The tears had stopped and he sighed long and deeply as he watched a little cloud of dust settling on the stone.

Then from within the crowd came a cry of, 'On. On with them,' and almost at the same time Bracca felt a heavy blow on his back, the force of which pitched him forward so that he fell face-first onto the ground. He got up as quickly as he could with the pain still smarting and, waiting until Melvaig had got Morven settled once more in his arms, he continued on the seemingly endless journey to the cave with the villagers' faces stretched in a violent ugly line down each side of the path for as far ahead as he could see.

CHAPTER VIII

It was early evening. The thick layer of cloud that had dominated the sky all day had broken up, helped by a cold gusty wind that had arisen a little earlier. The sun now cast its warm golden glow over the valley gilding the trees and burnishing the bracken with its light. It glinted off the swords of the guards as they stood outside the entrance to the cave, momentarily dazzling Bracca as he looked past them. He cursed the fragile autumn beauty of the evening for it seemed to accentuate the blackness in his spirit; it both angered and hurt him that it should be so blatantly oblivious to their suffering.

In the gloom of the cave he could see Nabbeth sitting with Shayll, their backs against the far wall and Nabbeth's arm tight about her shoulders. The sound of her quiet weeping tore at his heart and he had to fight the urge to go and comfort her for he knew they wanted to be alone. A little further along, lying huddled up together on the hardpacked earth floor, were Melvaig and Morven. She was conscious now and Bracca heard them talking in low voices, their weariness and pain coming across to him where he sat nursing his own thoughts in a dark spot just on one side of the entrance. Stowna and Nemm sat in silence on the far side, their heads sunk and their shoulders bowed, numbed by despair.

It seemed an age ago since they had first been thrown into the cave yet in fact it had not been long. Nabbeth's home had been unrecognizable; Barll's men had seen to that. The great stone table in the centre, where the Stagg used to sit, with Nabbeth at the head, had been smashed so that it lay in pieces on the floor and the wooden benches had also been broken up. By the light that came in through the natural fissure high up above their heads near the roof, Bracca could see the mess at the far end of the cave, the living area where Nabbeth and Shayll had spent so many precious moments together. Their bedding of meadowsweet and heather had been kicked around the floor and their few treasured possessions, the pieces of wood and stone that Shayll had placed on the natural shelves in the rock wall, lay shattered on the ground. Even the wooden figures Nabbeth had carved for her so long ago had been found and mutilated. Nothing had been left untouched, neither the small delicately carved table that had been in Nabbeth's family for as long as anyone remembered nor the wooden drinking goblets that the members of the Stagg had always used at the end of the meetings. And then, not satisfied, those who had vandalized the cave had fouled the floor and the smell of faeces and urine hung in the air with a revolting pungent sharpness that stuck in Bracca's throat.

Bracca was racked with worry and anxiety and he felt as if he would be sick at any moment. He was dizzy with a kaleidoscope of thoughts; looking back over the events of this tragic day, from the morning, a lifetime ago, when they had left the hut to go to the meeting, until now. What had gone so terribly wrong? Why? Were any of them to blame? And then he thought of how Ashgaroth had spoken to him; the words he had used and the comfort they now gave to him, even in this darkest of times. He wondered, should he tell the others? Did it seem arrogant, self-important? Why had he been picked out rather than any of them? Would it make them jealous, particularly Melvaig; betrayed, over-looked after all that he had done? No. Perhaps it would be better not to say anything. Besides, Ashgaroth might have come to all of them, privately, bringing some comfort to each.

Suddenly the run of his mind was interrupted by the noise of someone coming towards them; heavy footfalls on the ground outside, a short exchange of words and then a blotting out of the light as a man started to walk through the narrow tunnel into the cave. His blood froze in his veins as he saw what he had dreaded; the tangled mane of black hair that was instantly recognizable as belonging to Barll.

When he was through the tunnel he stood up and Bracca felt hatred boiling in his veins as he saw the look of triumph on Barll's face; the smile of contempt and pleasure as he surveyed the misery and pain in the cave. Bracca looked round at the others who were all sitting upright staring back at their captor. Melvaig and Nabbeth were angrily defiant while Shayll, Morven and the others were bravely trying to hide their fear.

'So, you see how it is: you see the way they feel. They would have torn you apart but for my guards.' As he spoke his words shimmered with joy at his victory and Bracca, unable to bear the ignominy of looking up at him, scrambled to his feet and stared him straight in the eyes but Barll was oblivious to Bracca's empty posturing; the futile attempt to salvage some vestige of dignity from the situation, and he smiled.

'Perhaps you would have preferred it like that,' he said, 'but I wanted you alive; you are of more use to me that way, for the moment, than dead.'

He paused now, wallowing in the feeling of power that was filling his head and blowing up his ego till he felt it would burst out of him in a blaze of sparkling light.

'You will all die,' he said slowly, the words dribbling out of his mouth with deep relish as he looked at each of them in turn to gauge their reaction. 'You know that of course. . .' and though they had anticipated it, the confirmation of their worst fears showed in the looks on their faces and to Barll it was as the sweetest of pleasures. 'I cannot let you live. The people would not stand for it; you can see that. They are angry. They want blood; revenge for all the seasons of hardship and suffering endured in the name of your Ashgaroth.' He lunged forward suddenly and grabbing Shayll by her hair, pulled her to her feet and snarled at her. 'And I shall give it to them. It will be my pleasure,' and he twisted her head so that his face was so close to hers that she could smell the fetid stink of his breath.

'My pleasure,' he spat the words out and threw her down again to land in a sprawling heap on top of Nabbeth. 'And with your death the old ways will be lost forever and Ashgaroth will be no more. Then we shall join forces with Xtlan; how does that sound to you! And Dréagg will rule over all things. And yet I can show mercy, for how you die is up to you. I can make it fast and easy or . . .' and their blood froze at his smile, 'I can kill you slowly and with so much pain that you will beg for death as a release. The mob – they want to see you suffer. But if you recant, deny Ashgaroth, admit you've been wrong and that the Book was a lie, then you will die quickly; I assure you of that. Proclaim me the ruler of Haark. It makes no difference; I am already. But if they heard it from your mouth, from you, on your knees hailing me as all powerful, then I would make it quick for you. There are . . . there may be some who doubt me. Your approval of me; that would make my position unassailable.' He stopped, aware that he was saying too much, carried away by his eagerness.

'You have until the sun goes down to decide. I shall come back then to receive your answer. If it is no, then two of you will be taken outside and killed in front of the mob. I leave it to you to choose who is to go first. After that I shall kill one of you at a time, at dawn and dusk each day until you change your mind. So now, for the moment, I leave you. Don't waste your time; the sun is nearly gone.'

Then, as suddenly as he had appeared, he was gone and where he had been was a grim and ominous space; his

116

absence almost more dreadful than his presence. There was silence; no one willing to emerge from the protective cocoon of private misery which they had spun around themselves.

It was Bracca who first spoke, coming forward into the centre of the cave, and, gathering his shattered wits into some semblance of cohesion, tried to draw them out of themselves so that they could at least talk. It was not easy. Apart from Shayll and himself, all the others were old and, though their innate courage and bravery could sustain their bodies, there was no help for their minds and it was heartbreaking for Bracca to watch them struggling to focus their attention on the events that had led them to their present terrible situation. They all looked to him instinctively now for guidance and leadership; Stowna and Nemm, Shayll, Morven, Nabbeth and, most painfully of all, Melvaig – each of them seemed to have lost the will and the identity which before had marked them out so strongly. As Melvaig looked at him with vague wandering eyes, the last embers of his epic fortitude finally quenched beneath the tide of defeat, Bracca realized the truth of Ashgaroth's words, spoken to him on his way back from the last fateful meeting of the Stagg that seemed, now, so long ago. 'The mantle of my light is now upon you,' he had said, and the loneliness and weight of that awesome responsibility now struck him with terrible force. No one was capable of helping him now; neither Nabbeth nor Morven nor Shayll nor Melvaig; he was alone in the final struggle against the forces of Dréagg that were massing to extinguish this last haven of the power of Ashgaroth.

So he gathered them all round him and explained what Barll had said, putting to them the choices they had been presented with as clearly as he could. Outside, the golden rays of the dying autumn sun shone through the evening mists and sent bars of light streaming into the gloom of the cave. The stone walls gave off a damp chill that found its way deep into their bones and their stomachs felt knotted and cramped with fear and the pains of hunger that had begun to gnaw away inside them.

117

Yet, when Bracca had finished, there was no doubt in any of their minds as to how they would decide and when he asked them, quietly and in turn, what they wanted to do each replied, unwaveringly, that they could not deny Ashgaroth. Further, to acclaim Barll as the new leader would be unthinkable whatever the consequences of their refusal to do so. And Bracca marvelled at the courage and pride that still sustained them, despite all the suffering they had already endured, and at the aura of greatness that each still possessed.

Then, suddenly, the light in the cave was gone; the sun had vanished behind the hills and almost before they had realized the terrible relevance of the darkness they heard movement and voices in the tunnel. Bracca had no time to think before Barll was standing in front of them again with three of his men, and his harsh mocking voice was ringing in their ears.

'Well! What is your decision? Are we to have some fun with you or will you deprive the village of its sport by admitting your guilt for the past and hailing me as leader?'

No one spoke. Bracca felt uncertain of his position; wary of the arrogance of assuming the position of leader and spokesman for the others.

'Come on, your answer! Don't play games with me; you've had enough time. We are all impatient, who will tell me? You, my beauty . . .' and he made towards Shayll, 'what do you say to me? Who knows – if you came in with me I might be able to persuade the others you should be spared. They wouldn't like it! The men want your body and the women want your blood but still, with my protection they wouldn't dare harm you. And if you, Nabbeth's woman, were mine then my position would be the stronger.'

He was standing in front of her now; his eyes ranging over her body, the saliva in the corners of his mouth betraying the lust for her that pulsed in his veins.

'You've never had a real man,' he said, looking contemptuously sideways at Nabbeth. 'He's old enough to be your

118

grandfather. Think of it with me; young, strong and powerful. Did he fall asleep in the middle . . . eh? Did he?' and reaching out with both huge hands he clamped them over her breasts and pulled her towards him so that, off balance, she fell against him. The men at either side began laughing. In a flurry of movement she pushed herself back, away from him, while at the same time slashing with one of her hands against his face. Blood began to seep slowly from three livid gashes down the side of his cheek.

'Filth,' she yelled. 'Scum! Never! I'd kill myself first. Keep your foul hands away from me. I'd . . .' but she could say no more for Barll's men had grabbed her and put a hand over her mouth. Desperately she struggled but she could not break free and Bracca fought to control the urge to run forward and try to help her for he knew it would be futile. Barll's face was contorted in pain and fury; his eyes bright and shimmering with a blind rage as he stared in disbelief at the blood on his fingertips where he had touched the wound.

Then, while Bracca's mind still whirled in confusion, Nemm stepped forward and spoke in a loud clear voice that arrested the attention of Barll so that he turned his head away from Shayll to look at the old man.

'We have made our decision,' he said. 'We would all rather die than support or strengthen you. You are evil, Barll; the fires of darkness smoulder deep within you. Dréagg's black misery hangs upon you and will bring nothing but pain and suffering to our land.' And then the tiny figure of Stowna stepped forward, his shock of grey hair quivering slightly as he moved, and he began to speak in his curious high-pitched voice. 'You are indeed as Shayll has said, Barll; filth and scum, fit only to be crushed into the earth beneath the heels of men such as Melvaig. We despise you, scum. . .'

'Enough! Take them! Take them both outside. They shall be the first to taste the wrath of Barll. You, my dear,' turning back to Shayll, 'we shall save for later when my mind has had time to devise a suitable end for you. The rest of you,' and he

119

raised his head to look at the others, 'may still change your minds. Listen to the howling of your friends and see if you still feel as brave. Now! Get them out!'

Brutally he shoved Nemm in the back so that the frail old man collapsed forward onto the stone floor, his thin body seeming to crumple as he fell. But just before Barll pushed them out of the cave Bracca caught the look of triumph in Nemm's eyes and seeing the same smile of victory light up in Stowna's face he realized with a rush of admiration and love that their self-sacrifice had been previously arranged among themselves. Not perhaps in the way that it had actually occurred, drawing Barll's attention and anger away from Shayll, but the speeches, calculated to inflame Barll as they had done were too well prepared and orchestrated to have been spontaneous. So, they had deliberately given up their lives and the reward had been their success in giving the others time; time to try and escape. In a way Bracca envied them, for their trials were nearly over; no more decisions to take, no more struggles, no more suffering to watch of those they loved. It was up to him now, and the others, not to waste the chance that had been given to them. But escape! How? He realized with a shock of guilt and shame that this was the first time the idea had even occurred to him. He had simply accepted that they would all die at the hands of Barll. No. That was being unfair to himself. There had been no time; no chance to think.

Then, without warning, the sound of voices echoed out from the cave entrance again and, suddenly, Stigg was standing in front of them with three men. 'Out,' he said. 'Move! You don't want to miss saying goodbye to your friends do you? Come on,' and he came forward into the cave and started pushing Nabbeth, Melvaig and the others towards the tunnel. Bracca's heart began beating faster in fearful anticipation of what was to come. Had Barll changed his mind and decided to kill them all now, or were they simply going to be forced to witness the deaths of Stowna and Nemm in an attempt to get them to change their minds?

After the cold dank atmosphere of the cave it was good to be out in the open air again. It was a clear night, the sky littered with stars and the moon throwing its white light on the dew-laden grass at their feet. Bracca had come out last, following the others, and the beauty and familiarity of the night made him forget everything for an instant as he lost himself in the blue-black infinity of the skies but then, cruelly, he was brought racing back to the present as he caught sight of the scene in the clearing below. At this distance it was hard to make out exactly what was happening but he could see a great crowd of villagers grouped round in a circle with a large space in the middle. Inside the space he thought he could see, on one side, Stowna and Nemm, while on the other a small group of what appeared, to his astonishment, to be children. His gaze was then wrenched away by a sharp push in the back by Stigg.

'Your friends are waiting for you. Come on. Down the path.'

The rough track down from Nabbeth's cave to the clearing was strewn with rocks and, even in the moonlight, the way was difficult for the aged limbs of Nabbeth, Melvaig and Morven. Often they stumbled and bruised or cut themselves on the stones but Stigg would not let Bracca or Shayll help, delighting in their misery and taunting them as they staggered down.

Once at the bottom it was not far to the clearing where the villagers were waiting. The darkness welded them together into some great black creature from which malevolence oozed like pus and Bracca could smell the pungent stink of its lusts as it parted to make way for them, closing behind them when they had passed as if they had been devoured.

Then, suddenly, there was light and space in front as they reached the edge of the human arena. Bracca looked at the huddled group of small figures standing near them. There was no doubt now; they were children, and the sound of their high-pitched giggling rang out above the murmur of the crowd and sent shivers of horror through Bracca. Opposite the children stood Nemm and Stowna, waiting, their faces in shadow. Their appearance would have struck Bracca, in any

121

other situation, as comical; the one so tall, thin and reed-like and the other, at his side, small and squat like a frog. Now though, there was something horribly pathetic about it as they lurched and swayed together, hardly able to keep on their feet.

Then Barll was talking, his eyes dilated with excitement at the prospect before him.

'This is how we shall teach the children,' he said. 'A good way to learn; do you not think? And watch; see how it comes naturally to them. They have none of our squeamishness; simply an insatiable curiosity. You will find it interesting; the potency of this force, present in all of us, which you and your kind did so much to try and suppress. Now see it unleashed, unrestrained, and realize the enormity of its power.'

He stepped forward into the arena and a tense expectant hush descended on the crowd. His voice was addressed to the children yet was loud enough for everyone to hear.

'Now, my little ones. Let's see what you can do. No weapons; nothing except what Dréagg gave you. Fingers, teeth, thumbs, feet, elbows. And the ingenuity of your minds. So, whenever you're ready you may start.'

He stepped back, raising his arms up to the air in an opening gesture, and then he turned briefly round, smiling broadly, to look at Bracca and the others.

At first there was utter stillness; the villagers watching and waiting and the children uncertain about their first move. And then, slowly, a little boy detached himself from the group and began walking slowly and deliberately across the middle of the space towards the two old men. Bracca recognized him by his mane of tightly curled blond hair, the pert little nose and the thick, slightly fleshy lips – as if the mouth was a little too big for his neat, round face. Spone was his name and Bracca had never liked him despite the initial impression of innocence and purity which had emanated from his angelic countenance; there was a shiftiness in his eyes, a sly, knowing hardness that Bracca had immediately focused upon on the few occasions they had met. His father

Gommsall, one of Barl's warriors, was standing at the very edge of the space, smiling proudly and mouthing words of encouragement to his son.

When he was standing just in front of Stowna, Spone stopped and looked up into the old man's face, his mouth pulled into a grin. Stowna responded uncertainly, automatically, by forcing an answering smile which he held for long agonizing moments, his lips quivering with fear and tension before, with a sudden burst of action, the little boy lashed out with his fist and smashed Stowna in the groin. The old man let out a terrible howl of pain and doubled over, clutching himself pitifully in an attempt to ease the roaring waves of sickness and nausea that sent lights flashing before his eyes and threatened to swallow him up in the yawning chasm of darkness that had opened before him.

Bracca watched, aflame with anger, as the little boy then yanked his knee up sharply so that it crashed into Stowna's thin face. He heard the awful ominous crack as the old man's nose broke and watched as he toppled to the ground, groaning horribly and rolling on the damp grass in agony.

And then the cheering and the chanting started; the mob revelling in the grisly spectacle, urging the boys on as they walked across to join Spone. Nemm had been standing to one side watching mesmerized with horror at what was happening to his friend. Now the boys turned their attention to him, approaching him slowly as he backed away, edging along the circle of spectators, a hand outstretched before him in a pitiable attempt to keep them from him. Suddenly someone in the crowd shoved him in the back and he careered forward into their midst, arms above his head to ward off the expected blows. One of the boys hacked savagely at his shin and Nemm toppled and fell. They were upon him then and Bracca, though violently repelled by what was happening, also found himself unable to tear his eyes away from the scene, gripped by a terrible fascination, as the boys tore at him gouging at his eyes with their fingers; scratching and tearing with their teeth. Sometimes a boy's

123

face emerged from the kicking, struggling mass of limbs and there was blood dripping from its mouth, the moonlight glinting on the snarling white teeth and reflecting the wild maniacal gleam in its eyes. The screaming did not, thankfully, last long and then it subsided, the crowd growing hushed as a steady squelching thumping sound took over, the children grunting with the effort and the occasional sharp crack of a bone seeming a welcome punctuation in the dreadful monotony. Nemm was submerged beneath them, buried somewhere under the jerkily flailing arms and legs, and at first as the tatty, jagged pieces were thrown carelessly back into the open space behind, Bracca failed to realize what they were. When, suddenly, he did, he found a wave of sickness surging up from his guts which he could not quell. Instinctively the top part of his body leant forward and the bilious mess poured out of his mouth onto the ground, the stench of it stinging his nostrils even as he retched.

Eventually they were finished and the dismembered pieces of Nemm's body lay scattered on the grass in the centre of the arena; moonlight reflected darkly against the crimson. His head was barely recognizable, an old man's battered face contorted now into an ugly twisted grimace of pain; the mouth smashed in so it was hard to see an aperture and the cheekbones broken so badly that his whole face appeared lopsided and crooked. But it was the two dark blue-black spaces where his eyes should have been that most affected Bracca and once again sent his stomach churning in a violent fit of revulsion.

Now it was Stowna's turn. Nemm had gone too quickly, affording little sport to the crowd who grew vociferous once more, baying for blood. And so they played with him, taunting and teasing as they chased him round and round, the boys splitting into groups, cornering him, pushing him from one to the other and rejoicing as he whirled and staggered stupidly until he fell. Then two of them leapt upon him and bit off his ears, throwing them to the crowd which clamoured and fought to catch these grisly trophies. They dragged him to his feet again and repeated the macabre ballet, spinning his thin frame so fast that his wisps of long white hair splayed out in a silver fan around his head, and his dreadful screams ebbed and flowed as he revolved. He fell again and this time they took out an eye, giving it to him to hold and forcing his grip tightly upon it before making him throw that too into the mob. When he next collapsed on to the grass and they fetched out his remaining eye, their games acquired a new dimension as the screaming, unseeing creature tried to avoid their savage prodding and poking, veering wildly away from the direction of the blows until, whimpering pitifully, he fell on to the sticky blood-stained grass for the last time. For a little longer he responded to their baiting, squirming and squealing to the raucous delight of the crowd, until the dark clouds of oblivion finally, mercifully, embraced him. As with Nemm before him, Stowna was then torn apart and it was only when this ultimate act of indignity had been completed that the children stopped and, as if waking from a deep trance, raised their faces to the people who roared their approval.

Barll went forward then, smiling hugely, and walked among them patting them on the back, ruffling their blood-streaked hair and clasping them by the shoulders. And they turned their faces to him and he saw the fires of Dréagg raging in their eyes, wild uncontrollable flames of lust that were kept at bay only by their respect and fear of him. They were his now; he knew that. He had given them a taste for blood and violence which would constantly seek release. He could call on them any time, for any purpose, and they would obey him unquestioningly. By catching them as children they would never acquire any of the sensitivities or squeamishness which many of the older villagers possessed; there would be no struggle between darkness and light for them. And the realization of the potential power these children possessed filled him with a burning glow inside his heart; a wild flush of excitement that sent his head spinning and his chest thumping for he, Barll, was their master and

125

they would be the core of his strength.

Suddenly, as if he had just remembered them, he whirled round and looked at his captives.

'See,' he yelled, his voice high and hoarse with tension. 'See what they can do. Limitless! There is no end to what they are capable of. Now you can be afraid, truly afraid, for you have born witness to the sowing of the seeds from which will grow a power so evil that the reign of Ashgaroth will finally crumble into dust even here in Haark, his last stronghold. And then Dréagg will finally rule over all things and the earth, Ashgaroth's precious jewel, will be forever in darkness. Then we shall rule, Xtlan and I together, and our power will be infinite. So go; go back now to the cave and know that the suffering of Stowna and Nemm will be as a thorn in a finger compared to the deaths I have prepared for you if you do not acclaim me as leader and renounce Ashgaroth before my people. Think well on it, for in the morning I shall come again to hear your decision. Take them!'

The guards who had brought them surrounded them now and started to push them back through the crowd which parted reluctantly to let them through. Their senses were reeling as they were led away; terrible images of the horror they had just witnessed kept coming back before their eyes so that they lost all sense of time and place, unable to think of anything else. Each of them was shaking uncontrollably, hardly able to stand, and Stigg and the other guards had difficulty getting them back up the path and into the cave. Beating them failed to work now and anyway more beating might kill them, something which Barll had stressed must not happen; he wanted them alive and well for the next day's sport. So, impotent in the satisfaction of their anger, the guards hauled and dragged and pushed until the captives were finally back. Then, exhausted and relieved, they settled down outside the entrance to watch the celebration below them; the flames of the cooking fires throwing eerie dancing shadows on the trees around the clearing.

Inside the cave, the noise of the festivities formed a bizarre

126

wash of sound, a cruelly antipathetic intrusion into the atmosphere and mood that lay like a black shroud upon Bracca and the others. Now that the immediacy of the nightmare had receded, albeit temporarily, a feeling of guilt emerged from the maelstrom of their emotions to supersede all the others. Guilt in Shayll that her refusal to comply with Barll and her outburst of anger at him had been the prime cause of the suffering of Stowna and Nemm; had they not interpolated as they did what would her fate have been by now? She was alive because of them and the realization of the debt she owed them filled her with an intensely oppressive sadness.

The others too were riven with guilt; gratitude for saving Shayll and in Bracca, Melvaig and Nabbeth the torturing uncertainty as to whether they could have done anything to save them. Who would Barll have chosen if Stowna and Nemm had not so blatantly offered themselves and were they not, with a vicious twist of shame, glad that they were still alive for they would not, they knew, have offered themselves in place of either of the two old men.

And then, along with the guilt there arose in Shayll a livid, burning desire to avenge them; their suffering must not have been in vain. They had volunteered for death so as to give herself and the others a chance; it was up to them now not to squander that chance. So, from the ashes of despair a tiny flame of hope began to flicker. At first wavering and uncertain it grew gradually, fanned by memories of the sacrifice made for them until at last it became too much for her to contain within herself and she began to speak.

'We must escape,' she said, her eyes to the ground, reluctant to break the pall of silence in the cave. Then again, 'We must escape,' looking up this time, her confidence increasing now that she had voiced the current of thought that pulsed in her head like the hammering of rain on a leaf.

For Bracca it was as if a great weight had been taken from him for someone else had now stepped in to share the mantle of responsibility that had lain so heavily upon him, expressing the same idea that had been dominating his own tortured mind. But, and this was why he had not spoken earlier, it was easier said than achieved. How? This was what had been exercising all his intellect during this unreal oasis of calm.

He looked at her; at her tangled mane of red hair falling and tumbling around the delicate oval of her face, her pale tear-stained cheeks, her lips trembling with tension, and thought again how much he loved her, his heart bleeding at the crude indignities she had already suffered and the terrible prospect of what was to come if they did not get away. And when he looked into her eyes he saw there a wild anger and desperate resolve that bolstered his own flagging will so that, to his amazement, he suddenly saw escape as possible.

Melvaig and Morven saw it too; a quiet yet fierce determination, a certain set of the face that brought instant recognition to them both and, in its wake, a host of infinitely poignant memories for, in that tiny instant, it was as if Shuinn himself had been where Shayll was sitting.

'Yes,' it was Bracca who answered her. 'You're right of course. We must try; there's no choice. But how? I can see no way.'

As she replied, all the vague, half-formed notions that had been echoing vaguely around her head seemed to suddenly come together and, almost without thinking, her words formed a coherent and logical plan that surprised herself almost as much as it did the others by its bravery, audacity and most important of all, its chances of success.

'There are no more guards than there are of us,' she began. 'One each. The difficulty is in separating them. I . . .' Here she paused and, taking Nabbeth's face in her hands, she looked him deep in the eyes before continuing. 'I will take two of them, promise them the chance to love me – but not in the cave. I'll lead them away to the oak copse, a little way away – you know where it is Nabbeth – and keep them occupied there. That leaves three guards for the four of you.

128

Perhaps Morven, you could do something to distract them and give the rest of you a chance to kill them. Then you come and get rid of the two who are with me.'

There was silence. 'What do you think?' she said, looking at them eagerly yet with apprehension in her voice. 'Could it work?'

It was Melvaig who spoke first.

'Yes,' he said. 'Yes, it is the best chance we have. But . . . for you . . . it will not be easy for you; and very dangerous. Are you sure you want to go ahead with it?'

Shayll replied, 'Can you think of a better way? We're going to be killed if we stay here. I'd rather die trying to escape than at Barll's convenience and pleasure. Only . . . don't leave me with them too long.'

Bracca spoke then, turning to Morven whose part in the plan was only slightly less hazardous than Shayll's.

'How do you feel about it? Could you do it?' he said, but the sparkle in her eyes gave him the answer he had hoped for.

'Anything,' she replied. 'Anything to get away; to deprive Barll of his victory.'

Now the atmosphere in the cave had changed so dramatically that Bracca almost believed he was dreaming. A feeling of near elation seemed to sweep them up as the idea of escape took hold in their consciousness. At least they were actually doing something; no matter if it failed – they had nothing to lose anyway. They owed it to themselves to try, to Stowna and Nemm, to Nab and the others from Silver Wood and, above all, to Ashgaroth.

And so, while the festivities raged in the clearing below, the moon throwing occasional slivers of silver on to the revellers as they danced and gorged themselves; the five upon whose shoulders rested the destiny of the earth made ready their final preparations, gathering sharp rocks to kill the guards and, for Morven and Shayll, the careful ordering of their clothing and hair – strategically arranging their torn and ragged garments so as to reveal enough to stir the blood of the guards while at the same time concealing the feminine mysteries of their bodies.

Finally they were ready and, her heart beating furiously with tension and fear, Shayll embraced Nabbeth with a fierce passion that brought tears to his eyes. He would not let her go until, gently but firmly, she pushed herself away from him.

'I must go,' she said, her voice breaking with pain. 'Morning is not long away. If ... If I don't see you again, know that our short time together, the love we have known, has made my life worthwhile. Life could hold no greater happiness than we have been blessed with.'

She turned away and after holding Melvaig, Morven and Bracca quickly in turn made her way towards the short tunnel that led outside to the guards.

CHAPTER IX

Stigg, sitting a little apart from the others to one side of the cave entrance, was lost in dreams. Dreams of power and all that went with it; the best food and the best women, the command of absolute obedience from those under him, the glory that would be his in battle. Barll had fuelled his ambition cunningly and now Stigg thirsted for ascendancy with a yearning that surprised even his master.

It was not until a twig cracked just behind him that, swinging round suddenly at the sound, he saw Shayll standing in the shadows. He knew who it was at first sight and his hand relaxed its grip on the handle of his sword. There was no mistaking the cascade of red hair, the exquisitely beautiful face thrown into silhouette by the light and the body that had assailed his senses with its magnificence since he had first grown aware of her, many seasons ago. How often had he longed to take her in his arms and yet he dared not for he knew he would have been an outcast among his own people if he broke the code of the village that forbade mixing with the strangers.

Yet now as she stood before his gaze with the soft moonlight burnishing the exposed flesh of her breasts and thighs with silver, his head swam with a desire which, no matter what the consequences, he knew he was unable to resist. Slowly then she began to move towards him and the shreds of her dress fell apart for an instant to reveal a tantalizing glimpse of the dark shadow at the apex of her thighs. Closer she came and he stood rooted to the spot, mesmerized by the immense power of her sensuality. He was entranced; completely under her spell and he would no more have taken her by force than taken his own life.

She was next to him now, standing with her legs a little apart, her arms hanging loosely by her sides, the steady rhythm of her breathing causing her breasts to rise and fall under the fragile and ragged covering of her dress. The scent of her body made his head spin and she held him with her eyes, drawing him into her so that he no longer had a separate identity. Then she spoke, softly, and the voice seemed to come from inside his head.

'If I am to die tomorrow,' she said, 'then give me one last night of love. Please. You may do with me what you will and I will give you pleasure such as you have never known before and will never know again.' Then she looked down, her eyes cast to the ground in an entrancing play of modesty. 'I would like . . .' she hesitated, 'one other, whoever you care to choose. I enjoy two men . . . together. Would you . . . for me?'

And he was powerless to refuse her. Dazed, he turned away from her and walked across to where the others sat watching him. They had lewd, knowing smiles on their faces as they looked at him but they said nothing. They were slightly afraid of Stigg; wary of his irascibility and his closeness with Barll. He could, they knew, destroy any of them if he so chose. Now his eyes settled on one of them, the youngest; a blond good-looking boy who Stigg had taken a particular liking to. The boy shifted nervously under his imperious gaze.

'Kole,' said Stigg, his voice strange and remote. 'Come! Follow me.'

The boy got up quickly and, aware only of the suppressed sniggers of his older, more experienced, fellows he

132

scrambled after Stigg; his mind in a whirl, his stomach a tight ball of excitement in painfully delicious anticipation of what was to come. As they got near to her, Shayll smiled at them and started to walk slowly away, leading them from the cave mouth and up towards the spot known as Shinntaa, the little copse of oak trees, just as she had planned. Kole's heart beat furiously as he followed her, pounding in his chest so loudly that he felt deafened by the noise. He could not take his eyes from her body; the voluptuousness of her movements set his loins tingling with tantalizing expectations.

They trailed after her, along the stony winding path that led up to the ground behind and above the cave. It had been easy so far; she had even, deep inside herself, felt a thrill of exhilaration at the extent of the power she had been able to exert over them. Never before had she used her body this way and she enjoyed the feeling of absolute power that it gave her. She could sense their eyes upon her as she moved, caressing and exploring the secret places of her body, and despite the revulsion that swam through her mind, she also felt, to her intense shame, a flutter of excitement at the base of her stomach.

Now though, those feelings receded before the growing fear that threatened to banish the coherence of her thoughts. She must stay calm! They entered Shinntaa and the sound of the oak leaves rustling in the breeze gave her comfort with its familiarity. The trees seemed to welcome her, to greet her as their friend; and as she recognized each one from the numerous times she had been here before with Nabbeth, she felt a strength emanate out from them to her. She was in the centre of the copse now, the moonlight painting a silver carpet on the lush green grass. A wave of panic surged over her. Oh, Ashgaroth, let them not be long. She stopped and turned round slowly; willing herself to remain in control. She must make time for the others.

Stigg moved towards her, his eyes yearning and hungry, his arms outstretched. She moved a pace back.

'No,' she said, smiling. 'No, wait,' and slowly, very slowly,

133

she began to undress, lingering coquettishly as she bared each part of herself, teasing them, playing with their emotions until at last she stood, naked apart from a wooden necklace, exposed to their searching gaze. And their eyes feasted on the ripe magnificence of her body, the perfect white roundness of her breasts and thighs. She turned round so that they could see all of her and they caught their breath as she revealed the gorgeous symmetry of her buttocks.

Again Stigg moved towards her and again she put him off.

'Not yet,' she said. 'Let me see you. Take off your clothes.'

And they did, tearing them off frantically until they too stood naked in the moonlight. Now she could put them off no longer. She would have to take Stigg first. She looked at him and it seemed as if she saw him for the first time. There was something pathetic about the yearning expression on his face; his eyes glazed with lust, his mouth open and dribbling slightly from the corners. As he moved towards her the rampant maleness of his body struck her as faintly ludicrous and comical, wobbling as he walked. And thus her fear was tempered with a quite different perception of him so that when he pushed her roughly up against a tree and took her, his hands roaming voraciously over her body, pinching and squeezing as he gorged himself on her flesh, she felt contempt instead of hatred and pity rather than anger. She was aware of his frantic lungings as if from afar; watching from a distance as he tried vainly, again and again, to possess her. She sensed his desperation and revelled in his impotence to break through the spiritual barrier she had erected around herself. He ached for her to want him now, his ego needed that more than anything, and it was just that that she would never give him so that though his body might gain relief his soul would be consumed in an agony of frustration, turning in upon itself in a cannibalistic act of self-destruction.

And all the time Kole watched, paralysed with wonder and excitement, unable to tear his eyes from the scene that was being enacted in front of him.

134

Outside the cave mouth, Morven had succeeded in gathering the three remaining guards together and taking them to a spot a little to one side of the entrance. They stood facing her, with their backs to the opening. The light was kind to her, concealing the wrinkles and lines that the years had etched upon her face and masking the slight filling out of her figure that the seasons of leisure and plenty had endowed upon her. She was still, despite her age, a very desirable woman and now she employed all her wit and guile to ensnare the men in a web of implicit intimacies and sensual innuendo. They were fascinated by her manner and captivated by her sensuousness and, freed from the constraints of Stigg, they fawned upon her as bees around a pollen-laden flower.

She saw Bracca emerge first from the dark cave opening and her heart quickened as she fought the rising tide of panic and fear that threatened to break out in her voice and upon her face. She watched through the space in between the guards' shoulders as he crept furtively towards them, followed by Melvaig and, finally, Nabbeth. She was certain the guards would hear the tension in her voice; she spoke more quickly, desperate to hold every bit of their attention; she flirted, scintillated and glowed with an irresistible power, a charismatic magnetism that had them rapt.

Closer they came, ever closer, and they made not a sound. Their arms were raised now and in each hand she could see the piece of stone, gripped tight, ready to do its work. And then, suddenly, with no warning, Nabbeth stumbled over a root and the harsh rasp of scrunching pebbles rang out in the air as he slipped on the path. Immediately the three guards swung round, drawing their swords and lunging into their attackers. Morven watched, numb with horror, as the three couples grappled with terrible fury. Melvaig and Bracca fought their opponents standing up but Nabbeth had been caught off-balance and he was wrestling on the ground, desperately trying to force his assailant's sword away. Nabbeth was lying underneath, pinioned by the weight of the

135

guard's body, and with both hands clasping the other's wrist was pushing up, twisting and wrenching in an attempt to force him to drop it. The sharp, pointed stone that he had so carefully chosen as his own weapon lay uselessly to one side. He needed help! The guard was young and strong and Nabbeth's ashen face showed the enormous strain he was feeling. Gradually, little by little, the blade turned until it was quivering ominously in the air directly above his neck and then it started almost imperceptibly to descend upon him. He could not hold it away much longer; the veins stood out like exposed tree roots on his forehead and down his neck and the guard's mouth twisted into a leer of triumph. Then, without thinking, Morven ran forward and grabbing the stone up from the ground she raised it above the guard's head ready to smash it down on him but, as she did so, Nabbeth's strength suddenly evaporated and with a violent jerk the sword fell on to the old man's neck and severed it so that through the gush of blood that erupted from the body Morven saw Nabbeth's head slowly roll away down the slope. She leapt back screaming, stunned with horror and the guard, his eyes half blinded with red, rolled over and stood up with his dripping sword raised to strike her down. Dimly then she was aware, through the swirling mists of terror that swam through her mind, of the guard crumpling in a heap before her and of Melvaig and Bracca at each side, taking her by the hand and pulling her away; away from the dead guards, away from the cave and away from Nabbeth.

As they ran up the path towards the Shinntaa, they neither heard nor saw the thin skulking figure of Straygoth the scout slip out from behind the bushes where he had been watching them and make his way quickly and quietly down the steep bank towards the place where Barll and a few of his lieutenants were standing watching the celebrations. The Mouse had suspected that something like this might happen and on his own initiative had stationed himself outside the cave mouth. Now he had, once again, proved himself to be invaluable to Barll; his position in the new order was assured.

Melvaig and Bracca left Morven just outside the entrance to the Shinntaa lying, dazed, with her back against a tree. Her hands lay on the long wet grass at either side and her fingers clutched and clenched at the earth incessantly, of their own volition, as if they had a life of their own. That was the only sign of her terrible inner turmoil for her face was utterly blank. And as she sat, one thought kept pulsing through her mind, over and over again so that she felt she would be driven mad by its intensity. Shayll, how were they going to tell Shayll?

The sounds guided them to the right place. They stopped in the dark shadow of the trees that encircled the clearing in the centre and saw everything. The boy, Kole, had joined Stigg now and they were both venting their lust on her together. They could see her pale anguished face, drenched with sweat, cradled on the tangled skein of her red hair and could hardly bear to look. Yet they had to, for it was vital to try and take them unawares and so, keeping their eyes fixed intently on the naked backs of Kole and Stigg, they began to creep silently forward with their stones, still bloody from the other guards, poised above their heads ready to strike.

Shayll saw them approaching and her heart soared with relief. Soon now, soon, it would be over and as hope and strength flowed through her she concentrated on making sure that the boy and the man were focused on her. And yet, oddly, when Melvaig and Bracca smashed the stones down on their heads and they fell on to her heavily, pinning her down beneath their inert weight, she felt a rush of remorse and pity. Kole, in particular, looked a sad and pitiful figure as, pulling herself out from under him, his fragile body rolled over and lay still, the whiteness of his skin reflecting the moon's light. A small, dark crimson stream flowed from a gash on the top of his head and his long fair hair had been drawn together and matted into spikes by the blood. Despite his inexperience and Stigg's rough aggression as his example, he had been gentle and kind with her, almost loving.

137

Melvaig and Bracca helped her up and gathering her clothes together from the branch where she had left them, she hurriedly put them on. Nabbeth must be outside, with Morven. No one spoke, yet when she was dressed they both embraced her with a fierce passion that she attributed solely to relief at seeing her. Then, with Bracca ahead and Melvaig behind, they walked quickly through the trees to where Morven sat waiting; her heart breaking with the knowledge of what she would have to tell her daughter.

When Shayll saw Morven sitting by herself she said, quite calmly, 'Where's Nabbeth?' still not thinking anything could have gone wrong but as soon as Morven turned her face towards her, she knew. For a terrible endless moment she stood, paralysed with grief, as her consciousness struggled to comprehend the enormity of what had happened; then, suddenly, a great inhuman howl of anguish burst from her and she was convulsed in a mass of tears. Morven went to her then and wrapping her arms about her weeping child, tried to comfort her.

'I'm sorry,' was all she could say, over and over again; pointless, futile words but there was nothing else that seemed either useful or relevant. And Shayll, incarcerated in the agony of her suffering, was impervious to consolation. With her face buried in her hands she wailed uncontrollably until suddenly, without warning, she stopped and grasping Morven by the shoulders held her at arm's length away from herself.

'I must go,' she sobbed. 'Go and see him . . . see him again for one last time. Where is he . . . yes, by the cave entrance. He must be . . . I'll go. . .'

She let go of Morven and turning quickly started to run back down the path.

'No . . . come back. No!' Bracca called, his mind reeling at the thought of her reaction to the terrible sight that she would see. He ran after her and managed to grab her by the wrist but she struck out at him wildly, hitting him in the face and, momentarily stunned, he relaxed his hold and she wrenched herself free.

By the time Bracca had recovered, Shayll was almost out of sight round a bend in the path from which she would have a clear view of the cave entrance and of Nabbeth's severed body. She was sobbing loudly, 'I must see him, I must see him,' and calling his name. Once or twice she fell over a stone on the path and went flying headlong in a heap, but she picked herself up and continued on her way without stopping.

He raced after her again, this time dimly aware of running footsteps behind as Melvaig and Morven followed him.

She had disappeared now round the corner and as he came to the bend some instinct told him to slow down. Keeping well out of sight behind some trees he began walking very quietly and as the sound of his own breathing died down he thought he could hear the sound of voices. Very slowly he turned the corner and, hiding behind the trunk of a huge beech tree, he looked fearfully down on to the scene outside the cave. Shayll was still running blindly forward, oblivious to the mass of warriors who were milling about around the entrance waiting for their comrades to join them. They were staring at her in blank amazement but their initial disbelief soon turned to amusement and they began shouting and jeering as she dashed headlong towards them. Bracca stood rooted to the spot, powerless to save her. Why hadn't she seen them? He willed her to turn back, to at least try to save herself, but she just kept on.

Melvaig and Morven were at his side now, watching, waiting for the inevitable. Then, numb with horror, they heard the shouting of the warriors fade suddenly away and saw the giant figure of Barll walk forward to stand at their head. And still she ran on as, with his face twisted into a horrible grimace of victory, he raised his spear and hurled it at her. It curved in a high graceful arc through the air, shimmering in the moonlight, before crashing through her chest and pinioning her to the earth where she juddered wildly for a few terrible moments before flopping back lifeless in a grotesquely distorted heap around the quivering shaft of the spear, her red hair dancing about her head like flames. A great cheer went up from Barll's men and they immediately began to rush forward, baying with a hideous exultation in their gory hunger to see the body.

With a desolate cry of anguish, Morven collapsed onto the ground and Bracca, wrenching himself free of his shock, lifted her up and carried her back around the corner out of sight of Barll's men. Dazed, Melvaig followed behind them and stood listening, as if in a trance, while Bracca spoke to them, his voice low and urgent, forcing himself to obliterate from his mind the ghastly scene that had just been enacted before their eyes. He had lifted Morven on to her feet and was holding her against his chest in a vain attempt to console her while looking over her shoulder at Melvaig.

'It is better,' he was saying. 'She did not see him. It is better that way. She will suffer no more ... no more now.' His words came to them from a long way away but they listened and they heard and were in some small degree comforted.

'It is over for her now. The pain. All over. She would not have wanted to live without him. But. . .' He paused, his mind baulking at the prospects ahead. 'We must get away. Now. They will soon be coming after us. We can do no more by staying. For their sake, for Shayll and Nabbeth, we must escape. It is what they died for. We must leave the path, go straight up through the forest, and we must go quickly. It will not be long before they start to follow.'

Then, supporting Morven under her shoulders, he helped her up the steep bank at the side of the track and then reached back and, taking hold of Melvaig's hand, pulled him up to join them. The ground was slippery with damp and the old man found it hard to gain a foothold but after falling back twice he succeeded at the third attempt and stood looking back listlessly down the path in the direction of the cave. Only the urgent tug on his arm forced him from his reverie

140

and, turning round, he responded lethargically to Bracca's request to follow himself and Morven as they began to make their way into the forest.

The going was not easy. With no path and only the shadowy light of the moon to illuminate the ground, their feet kept getting tangled in the thick bed of bracken and brambles that lay on the forest floor. Nevertheless the trees and the vegetation were so dense that, despite their slowness, Bracca felt reasonably confident that they had become lost to sight after only a little time. On they went, with Bracca almost dragging Morven along at his side while at the same time he cajoled and encouraged Melvaig who stumbled listlessly along behind them.

But Bracca had not seen Straygoth emerge like a shadow from the stunted hawthorn behind which he had been hiding and run silently back down the track to tell Barll the direction which the fugitives had taken. And Straygoth knew that he would be rewarded well for his foresight and ingenuity by the smile on his leader's face. So simple too! So easy to think a little bit ahead; to anticipate your opponent's moves. Not for him the simple revelries of the others; he scorned such dull and unimaginative pleasures. No! It took just a little thought to gain so much more enjoyment and so much more advancement. His brain was his weapon and already he had inflicted more damage with it than all the others put together, for all their swagger and brash confidence. And now Barll consulted him on everything, had begun to rely on his advice and to make no move without consulting him first. Here was the reward; the feeling of power that gushed through his puny little body and set his nerve-ends tingling with excitement, the bolster to his frail and tattered self-image. Now the others were in awe of him; jealous of his position with Barll yet fearful of incurring his displeasure. All those who in the past had been contemptuous of him, the men who had scorned him and the women who had despised and mocked him; they all fought for his favours now; squabbled and demeaned themselves before him in their attempts to be ingratiating.

Melvaig and Morven soon grew tired, their pace slackening as age took its toll of their weary limbs. They went more and more slowly until, as the sun began to rise above the hills in front and the sky started to grow gradually lighter, they could finally go no further. They had no strength, no energy left. The terrible sequence of events that had begun yesterday – yesterday! it did not seem possible – had left them drained, their will sapped and the last vestiges of their courage frayed and tattered.

And Bracca, who was himself exhausted, was pleased to have an excuse to rest. The day seemed somehow, despite the tragedies that tore at his heart, to be full of promise. The sunshine, full and rich with early morning gold, was diffused by the mist into glistening auroras of light around the huge beech, oak and sycamore trees that towered above their heads, seeming almost to touch the sky. He stopped to listen. Nothing. All around them hummed the distinctive music of the forest, the myriad little noises that came together to make the sound of the forest breathing. He would instantly have recognized one alien note but he could hear nothing to alarm him. All around them the trees and the bushes grew thick and tall, surrounding them in a dense protective wall of vegetation that made him feel secure and safe.

So they collapsed on to the carpet of bracken and, utterly worn out, were soon asleep. The scent of the damp earth and the sunshine playing on their closed eyes soothed their pain and caressed their wounded spirits so that their dreams were untroubled and their minds wandered easily through all the pathways of happiness they had known in the past.

CHAPTER X

Bracca awoke suddenly with a cold prickle of fear stabbing at his heart. He sat up quickly and saw Melvaig and Morven lying near, sleeping, their breath escaping in regular, contented little snuffles. What was it that had woken him? He looked up, his eyes searching the shadows of the forest for any signs of movement. He realized with a shock that it was late afternoon; they must have slept all day. All day! It was too long; Barll could have caught up with them by now. But no, he could not know the way they'd come; he would still be on the main path. They were safe.

Determinedly he tried to still the juddering of his nerves; willing himself to calm his shivering breath. Then he heard it; a long drawn-out rustling noise from somewhere in the undergrowth not far off. It stopped and everything was as before; nothing but the singing of the birds and the heartbeat of the forest. He strained his ears but he could not hear it again. Had he imagined it? Was it an animal; a fox, maybe, or a badger out foraging in the early evening? His instincts told him that it was not. And then he heard it again. The same as before only nearer this time. Suddenly, without knowing how, he knew. It was Barll with his warriors. Somehow he had managed to follow them. Did he know where they were? Was Barll even now looking at him from some shadow deep in the forest and directing his men towards them?

Frantically, his mind racing, he tried to think what they should do. Stay where they were; hope Barll had not seen them and that he would go past them. Or get away, as quickly and quietly as possible. He looked across at Melvaig and Morven, cushioned in their beds of bracken, fast asleep. They were completely worn out; there was no way they could go any further. And if they tried, how far could they get? No. There was no real choice. They had to stay.

The rustling sounded again; it was not far away now. He felt giddy with worry and fear. He had a sickening picture in his mind of Barll, out there, watching and laughing at him; orchestrating his men all around them. He felt paralysed and helpless. All he could do was wait, as a fly caught in a spider's web.

He decided that he should wake them; they had a right to know what was happening, so he leaned across and shook Melvaig very gently by the shoulder. The old man, reluctant to cast off the shroud of sleep, fidgeted restlessly under Bracca's grip; his eyelids fluttering and his lips pursing irritably. Then, under Bracca's relentless shaking, he slowly opened his eyes and woke up. Bracca put his finger to his lips in a gesture of silence and pointing into the forest in the direction the sound had come from, he mouthed the name of Barll. A dark cloud of despair passed over Melvaig's eyes and his body seemed to shrink visibly while Bracca looked at him, as if his soul had been struck a mortal wound.

Their attention was then distracted by the sound of Morven, shifting fitfully in the bracken next to Melvaig. Her dreams had been disturbed. At first sheer exhaustion had blessed her sleep with peace but now terrible images of Shayll and Nabbeth had begun to float across her vision. Shayll, quivering, pinioned by the spear through her chest; Nabbeth's head rolling over the earth; blood pumping from his body. And over all, leering in victory, a face she did not recognize. A face so full of evil that she could not look directly on it and yet neither could she look away so

144

powerful was the aura emanating from its dark and glowering visage.

Suddenly she awoke; jerking bolt upright with her eyes wide and staring and her face deathly pale. She cried out involuntarily, searching around frantically for Melvaig and, finding him, clutched him to her in an embrace of desperate and frightening intensity, sobbing against his shoulder as she did so.

Heavy with pain he tried to soothe and calm her, stroking her hair and whispering the words she wanted to hear, 'It'll be all right,' and 'It'll soon be over,' and 'Try to forget,' horribly aware even as he spoke them of their vacuous futility, fraudulent platitudes whose only effect was to secure a merely temporary abeyance in the never-ending saga of their grief. And even as Melvaig attempted to erase the terrible echoes of her dreams, so he heard the ominous rustling sound of Barll's warriors approaching through the undergrowth.

Mercifully, Morven was too lost in her own trauma to be aware of the noise or of the sense of impending doom that lay upon Melvaig and Bracca. There was little doubt now in Bracca's mind that, even if Barll did not know exactly where they were, he was following a path that would lead straight to them. It had not been possible, nor had he thought it necessary, to cover up their trail, and once Barll knew the general direction of his quarry, it would have been easy to trace their tracks.

Melvaig too, knew that it was only a question of time before Barll found them. Yet he had no energy, no will, to escape. There was no strength left in him any more; his spirit so drained and weary that, strangely, he found a kind of strength and peace in the inevitability of the end. Yet of one thing he was determined; Bracca must remain free. The mantle of Ashgaroth was now cast upon him. In Bracca lay the sum of all their dreams and their prayers; he was the focus of the struggle to wrest the world from the darkness of Dréagg – the legendary struggle that had begun so long ago in Silver Wood, the flame of which had been rekindled and kept alive by Melvaig in the pursuit of his vision through the world of Xtlan and which now was approaching its apocalyptic climax. And it would be Bracca who would see the final conclusion; Bracca around whom Ashgaroth would gather the powers of goodness and light in the ultimate confrontation with Dréagg. The part that he and Morven had played in the conflict had now ended: there was no more for them to do. And he knew what had to be done, for Ashgaroth came to him and brought him comfort and succour. He turned to Bracca and with a new confidence and clarity of purpose that gripped the younger man and held him transfixed with its sublime power, he spoke to him with fierce intensity.

'You must go,' he said. 'Leave Morven and me here. Leave us quickly before they come. We shall be looked after; Ashgaroth will not fail us. You must have faith. It is up to you now; you know that. With you go Stowna and Nemm, Shayll, Nabbeth and Shuinn, Morven and myself. Ashgaroth is at your side always; do not doubt that. The future is with you now, I know you will not fail.'

And Bracca, hearing his father's words and knowing their truth and sense, was nevertheless consumed by a sense of unbearable anguish and loss. He knew Melvaig was right, he had to leave them, yet his whole spirit rebelled against it. Unable to speak, he moved to where Melvaig and Morven were sitting and, with his eyes brimming with tears, held them close to him for long agonizing moments. Morven put her hands up to his face and, cradling him under the chin, held his head so that she could look into his eyes. Bracca could see then that she understood and as she kissed him with infinite gentleness on his cheeks and his forehead, he could feel the power of her love for him filling him with strength and wonder. She smiled at him and his heart ached with a terrible pain yet her smile was not sad. It was her blessing upon him and he knew that he would carry it with him always; the memory of her delicate, beautiful face radiating peace and love would forever be part of his soul, sustaining him through the evil and darkness that lay ahead.

He turned then and embraced Melvaig, unable to let go, unable to face the terrifying prospect that he would never see him again. 'Don't be sad.' Melvaig's voice was calm, soothing and certain. 'We shall always be near you. The love that we three have does not end; it simply changes.' He paused, and Bracca felt his father's grip tighten and a slight tremor come into his words. 'But please, go now. Before it's too late.'

Savagely Bracca tore himself away and, without daring to look back, ran as fast as he could up the hill until, with his breath rasping in his throat and the blood pounding in his veins, he felt he had put a safe distance between himself and the clearing. Then he collapsed down behind a bank of bracken and looked back to where he had come from. The rays of the dying sun shone through the canopy of leaves above Melvaig and Morven and kissed them with a halo of golden light. He could see them, lying together with their arms around each other as if they were asleep. There was about the image a feeling of such peace and serenity that for one crazy moment Bracca wondered if he was dreaming; if it was all a terrible nightmare. But then, suddenly it happened. From the far end of the clearing Barll and a great horde of warriors burst out of the shadows and ran over the grass to the golden blaze of light where Melvaig and Morven lay. Bracca, horrified, turned his head to look at them . . . but they were not there! He strained his eyes but could see nothing; the golden aura of light was completely empty. And then, as Barll and his men rushed towards it, the light seemed to rise from the ground, hover for a moment as if reluctant to leave the earth, and then, slowly and purposefully, rise above the trees and drift off up into the dark autumn evening sky.

Bracca watched, entranced, and his heart seemed to soar up into the sky with it as a wave of delirious relief and joy swept over him. They were gone! They were safe! Ashgaroth had come for them. They had put their faith in him and he

147

had not failed them.

Higher and higher floated the golden cloud of light until at last it merged with the rays of the sun and was lost to sight. And still the power of the miracle held Bracca in its sway. There could be no doubt now! Ashgaroth was with them; he had seen the truth with his own eyes. And the knowledge of that truth filled him with a great strength, a sense of invincibility, so that when he heard the mighty bellow of rage from Barll he was not afraid. A terrible cry it was; a great howl of anger and frustration that sent the birds winging out of the trees and stopped the hearts of all the animals that heard it.

Bracca, watching from the shelter of the bank of bracken that hid him from view, saw Barll raise his hands to the sky as if he was beseeching Dréagg to help him, calling down the wrath of the Dark One to wreak vengeance upon those who had cheated him. It occurred to Bracca then, with a huge sense of relief, that Barll must think that he had been taken along with Melvaig and Morven. He would not now come looking for him. He was safe!

His respite, though, was shortlived for as he looked he saw the thin wheedling body of Straygoth sidle up to Barll and engage him in earnest conversation.

When the discussion ended and Straygoth drew back there was a vicious smirk on Barll's face. Bracca watched then in horror as Barll took the tinder box and flint that Straygoth handed to him and squatted down on his haunches with them for a few brief moments before standing up again and staring in rapt fascination at the spot on the ground where a little red tongue of flame flickered and darted against the blackness of the undergrowth. Suddenly Bracca became aware of the wind blowing towards him, carrying the pungent scent of burning bracken to his nostrils and forcing him to catch his breath. He had not noticed a wind before; now though it seemed to increase in intensity even as, agonizingly, he watched the flames extend their probing fingers, bit by bit, into the blackness of the night. Beneath the

148

autumn dampness the undergrowth was dry and, with the wind fanning the flames, it was only instants before a great wall of fire had sprung up in front of him, lighting up the sky and filling the air with dense clouds of smoke that whirled and eddied in the blazing reds and crimsons of the flames. He heard Barll then, laughing; the manic sounds of his triumphant glee cascading even above the crackle and roar of the fire. Revenge! The taste of it was sweet in Barll's mouth; he could not be cheated so easily. They would pay; the animals, the birds, the trees, the plants; all these reflections of Ashgaroth; odious reminders of the power of the Lord of Good. Their very sight he now found repugnant; their innocence, their beauty and their wildness rankled within him for he could not comprehend nor order them. They were outside his control, beyond the purview of his ability to dominate so he struck at them blindly, revelling in his power to wound, maim and kill and gaining some transient satisfaction from it.

And now it was an inferno, racing up the slope towards Bracca, powered and propelled by that terrible wind that whipped up the flames and blew clouds of burning ash up into the air to scatter and spread the fire. Coughing and choking in the smoke, Bracca staggered from his hiding-place and ran blindly up the hill away from the heat. Barll saw him and let out a great shout of victory. No need to pursue him; the fire would do that, and bring him to his knees in a welter of torment, devouring him utterly so that the last of Ashgaroth's disciples would be nothing but ash to be washed into the earth by the rain or else blown by the wind to be lost forever.

Bracca heard Barll's cry of exultation. It was borne to his ears on the wind and it chilled his blood, dragging at his resolve so that he had to use all his strength to carry on running. His legs felt weak, he could not get his breath – the hot smoky air seared his throat and lungs as he tried to inhale, and his head swam in a dizzy whirling skein of bright flashing lights.

Again and again Barll's cry came to him even above the noise of the fire and every time he heard it, so his will weakened a little more. All around him now the flames danced and the smoke billowed up in dense black acrid clouds as the dead bracken ignited. The heat was terrible, scorching his back as he tried desperately to keep ahead of the blazing tongues of flame. He was dimly aware of an undercurrent of noise beneath the strident crackle of the fire; the thunder and crash of the animals as they smashed through the undergrowth, blind with panic, mad with fear, in their desperate attempts to escape. And, mingling with it in an awful cacophony of sound, their squeals and squeaks of pain, their howls and screams and cries as, oblivious to their natural enemies, the animals all ran together away from the wall of heat that kept licking at them from behind. So they fled, this doomed and tragic fellowship, and Bracca fled with them. Sometimes in their headlong flight the animals would collide with one another or with him and then he would stumble and stagger for a few paces before regaining his equilibrium.

The cloying smell of the burning bracken caught in his throat and his nostrils as he ran; the wind that fuelled the flames and blew past him was dark and redolent with evil. It seemed to have a life and power of its own, brooding and bitter with menace as it stroked and steered the fire towards him, always towards him no matter which way he turned so that there was no escape. It enveloped him, clinging to his legs as he tried to urge them faster up the slope, pulling him back as if he was running through a bog, dragging him relentlessly, remorselessly into the mire. How much further could he go? How much longer could he keep ahead of those vicious tongues of flame, flickering snake-like at his back and legs. His whole body screamed with pain as his mind drove it ever onward, lashing it forward mercilessly with no thought of compassion and paying no heed to the silent pleas for surrender sent out by his tormented limbs, ignoring the overwhelming desire for capitulation, the yearning to submit for which his tortured being cried out.

Then, suddenly, he felt a strange and unfamiliar rush of air against his face and the ground under his feet began to grow level so that he was no longer climbing. A wall of gorse and heather barred his way now and as he pushed his way through, ignoring the gashes in his skin caused by the prickles, he raised his head and saw a great black vista of space ahead of him. The sea! It shimmered darkly in the moonlit reaches of the night, the distant rumble and crash of the waves coming to him as a memory of something long ago.

Overhead the gulls wheeled and cried; angry at being disturbed in their homes by the monstrous creature of fire that flowed over the headland devouring everything in its path.

A breeze, scented with the tang of the salt sea spray, wafted back against the flames but it was as nothing compared to the strength of the evil wind and only seemed to aggravate it, whipping it up in angry spurts and flurries. But still a rush of relief swept over Bracca as he emerged from the scrub on to the flat green expanse of headland. If he could get down on to the beach; clamber out on to a rock and wait there until the fire burnt itself out, then he would be safe. So with hope surging through his veins he urged himself on towards the edge of the cliffs but then his heart sank and despair pulled at his entrails for the drop down to the sea was sheer. There was no way down; just a great chasm of empty space falling away to the inky blackness of the sea below. Slivers of light from the moon fell on the jagged rocks beneath and threw ribbons of silver dancing over the waves as they rolled in and crashed against the bottom of the cliffs.

It was not possible. There must be a way down. Appalled, he ran along the cliff edge first one way and then the other in a desperate attempt to see some gentleness in the falling away of the land; some place where there was a chance, no matter how remote, for him to get down. There was nowhere;

rather the earth seemed to cave away under the ledge.

He stopped and turned round to face the great wall of smoke and flame that was still coming towards him. He was completely trapped now for the fire had pushed forward on each side of him and had reached the cliff edge. There was nowhere to turn to. Nowhere to run. It had all been in vain then; all the deaths, all the suffering. 'The mantle of Ashgaroth is upon you.' The words came back to him and a great tide of bitterness and anger swept through his shattered spirit.

The heat from the inferno now began to attack him, searing his skin with myriad splinters of pain. It seemed to him that the fire was laughing; great guffaws of jubilation roared out of the flames as they pranced and danced in victory. So this was how it was all going to end. Dréagg had won. Where was Ashgaroth now?

'Save me,' he yelled despairingly and then again louder, his lungs bursting with the effort. 'Save me!'

And then the thick black smoke enveloped him and he crumpled to the ground, all strength and will gone, all energy drained away as a final web of hopelessness closed around him and dragged his soul towards the warm and welcoming abyss that lay just before him, ready to embrace him forever in the security and safety of death. Slowly he felt himself edging towards it; his body rolling in slow motion towards the darkness but then, through the red-skeined mist on the outermost periphery of his vision, he perceived a huge winged shape drifting down towards him. He tried to turn his head so as to focus more clearly but he could not, yet still he was able to make out the long straight pointed beak and huge wings of a heron. A great silver heron it was, and round its neck a jagged scar of red where the goblins had severed it long ago in the terrible marshes of Blore; for this was the legendary Golconda. And Bracca felt the iron talons round his waist and sensed his body floating up into the night sky away from the blazing inferno on the cliff edge. He had a last vision of the crimson flames receding into the distance before, with the waves skimming by beneath him, he finally succumbed to the lure of oblivion. And so Golconda carried his precious charge over the sea, his powerful wings bearing Bracca further and further away from Dréagg, even as Ashgaroth had commanded him, for now was the beginning of the final struggle and it was time at last for Bracca to learn of the part that destiny had fitted him for.

CHAPTER XI

The badger, watching from behind the root of a fallen oak tree, saw the heron land with Bracca's limp body and then fly away back over the sea until he was lost to view in the early morning mist. So! At long last the waiting was over; the time had arrived. And now that it had, and the awesome significance of this moment bore into his consciousness, he was so nervous that he could hardly bear to leave his shelter and go down the hill to meet the man in whose hands lay such a terrible responsibility. Bracca the Chosen One; son of Melvaig who had kept the light of Ashgaroth shining through the dark times.

Yet, fearful and apprehensive though he was, he knew what had to be done, so, treading a little warily on the damp slippery leaves, he left his shelter and made his way down the steep winding path that led to the flat grassy ledge next to the waterfall where Bracca lay. The black tip of his nose twitched and wrinkled as the unfamiliar smell of smoke was carried on the sea breeze across from the mainland in the distance which, because of the mist, he could not see today. Soon he was at the side of the inert body, breathing the strange scent of man and studying the hair, the colour of the skin, the face, the head, the shape of the body and all the other unusual and distinctive features of this strange two-legged creature. He was alive; the steady rhythmic rise and fall of the chest showed that he was breathing, but how long would it be before he opened his eyes and was able to walk. There was no way of knowing, he would have to be patient; but it was not easy for he was consumed with excitement and curiosity now that he was so close to Bracca. And so, settling down on the grass next to his head, he began to lick Bracca's face slowly and gently while watching the pale, wintery sun rise up over the horizon and dapple the gently undulating waters of the sea with bands of shimmering primrose petals.

All day he sat there, licking and nuzzling the poor tired face of the young man and, as he did so, he remembered how he had first seen him, not too many seasons ago, when he had arrived on the beach as a little boy with Morven, Melvaig and the dead body of the red-haired giant, Shuinn. How excited he had felt then! and how long he had had to wait since for this moment!

That evening, as a heavy sea mist enveloped them and covered the badger's coat with myriad sparkling drops of crystal, Bracca began to fidget fretfully, lashing the air with his arms and calling out wildly. Sometimes, at the height of his agitation, he sat bolt upright, his eyes wide open, staring unseeing into the distance, and his face was a mask of pain. Then, sobbing, he slumped back down again, curling into a tight little ball as if in an attempt to keep out the invading hordes of memories that were attacking his mind.

And during these times the badger's heart ached for Bracca and he snuggled up closely around his head in an attempt to comfort him.

All that night Bracca tossed and turned and the badger, whose sole focus of attention now was the recovery of his charge, did all that he could to soothe him. In the morning he was rewarded for Bracca grew calm and his breathing returned to a comparatively easy and steady rhythm so that the badger, exhausted by his vigil, fell asleep also and the two of them slept, huddled up together, until the middle of the afternoon when the sun began to descend from its vantage point amongst the great jagged streaks of white cloud that slashed across the pale blue winter sky.

Bracca woke first. He felt strangely refreshed and invigorated but could not think why. Where was he? His first thought was that he was at home; he had fallen asleep in the clearing at the side of the hut. Slowly he raised himself up and, initially, was utterly bemused and confounded by the totally unfamiliar surroundings. He looked around with a growing sense of unease and panic and then, suddenly, realization rushed in upon him in a terrible flood of comprehension. The shock was as if he had been immersed in a river of ice-cold water and nausea dragged at his bowels as the awful memory of what had happened poured over him. Horrific images passed before his eyes; Nabbeth, Shayll, Stowna and Nemm – all gone, killed; and the pictures of their deaths were familiar to him from his recent fevered nightmare. Not Shayll; not his sweet, sweet Shayll! He could see her face clearly now, twisting in pain as her body hung quivering, impaled on Barll's shaft, and the agony of his loss tore at his spirit so that he howled his anguish at the sky.

And then he saw the badger, awake now and sitting upright at his side, and without thinking he flung his arms around the animal's neck and buried his face in the thick fur while the tears ran in rivers down his cheeks. The badger growled low in his throat in sympathetic response to the human's pain and Bracca, aware of the animal's empathy, even through the fog of agony that shrouded his senses, hugged him tighter as if only by so doing could he hang on to life itself.

Then, very slowly, the fog began to clear. He opened his eyes and, through a blur of tears, saw the flat grassy ledge around him, the waterfall at his side that splashed and sparkled in the hazy sunlight and in front the edge of the cliffs, beyond which the pale blue sea stretched off towards the distant mainland. Vaguely he remembered the heron and the flight from the wall of flames, the stench of which still lingered in his nostrils, and then with sudden incredulity he became aware of himself holding, clinging to, the badger. The stone statue! But why here, in this strange and unknown place? And then a vision of it being smashed flew across his mind and he realized the truth that the warmth and feel of what he was touching compelled him to accept; the badger was real. Scarcely daring to breathe lest the truth collapse into a shattered dream, he moved back from the animal while still holding on to it until finally, at arm's length, he was able to look at it carefully and closely, to stroke its head as he had stroked the statue so many times in the days that were now gone forever. The badger looked back at him steadily, snuffling slightly as it rejoiced in the contact it had made at last with Bracca, and as Bracca gazed deep into the eddying brown mists of the badger's eyes he found his pain slipping away beneath the warmth and love he found there and for one shattering moment it seemed as if he was looking straight at Ashgaroth.

Was it Brock? The question roared like a flame in his consciousness, immediately overshadowing everything else. And so he asked the question out loud but there was no easy answer to be found in the mysterious swirling depths of the badger's eyes and suddenly it did not matter; the question became irrelevant, and in a blaze of joy Bracca once again clasped the badger to him and the badger in response gave a little grunt of recognition which sent a thrill through Bracca's spirit.

It was time to go now. Getting up, the badger made his way towards the waterfall where he stopped and, with a gesture of his head, indicated that Bracca should bathe in it. Gingerly Bracca made his way into the pool at the base of the fall, watching his feet as they walked over the sandy bottom. The water felt icy cold around his legs as he went further in and then, holding his breath, he ducked into the cascade of water that arced down from the rocky ledge above his head. It poured over his head and down his face, running over his shoulders and down his stomach and legs, streaming over him in a rush that took his breath away. He stood for a long time under the water, with his face upturned so that it ran across his eyes and through his mouth and, as he did so, he could feel it cleansing him, washing away the weariness in his aching body, banishing the smell and the taste of the smoke, driving out the fear and the horror that had cloaked his mind in darkness.

When he eventually emerged from the waterfall, he felt as if he had cast off an old skin. Refreshed and invigorated, his skin tingling, his whole being seemed possessed of a feeling of energy and power that amazed him. He stepped back out of the pool on to the grass and, to get dry and warm, began to race around; first towards the cliff edge, then up towards the old fallen oak tree from behind which the badger had first watched him and then finally down towards the waterfall. After a while, panting with exertion, he flopped down beside the badger and lay looking up at the sky, watching the streaks of cloud high up move slowly across the pale afternoon sun. A strange feeling of happiness and contentment nestled in his heart for now, he knew, the strands of destiny were coming together at last; now was the beginning of the final struggle and he was at the threshold of taking his position at the forefront of the last conflict, even as Ashgaroth had revealed to him after the fateful meeting of the Stagg in a time that now seemed long ago and far away. And revenge would be there for him; revenge for Nabbeth, Stowna and Nemm, revenge for Shayll and for all the animals that were now suffering even as she had at the hands of Barll; revenge for the gentle and the innocent, for the peaceful and the meek, for all of Ashgaroth's creations whose lives were now being torn asunder as the darkness of Dréagg eclipsed even Haark; the last enclave.

And while he lay there, and the yellow sun sank towards the ice-green sea, he wondered about Melvaig and Morven, about their time on earth and about the manner of their leaving, and as he looked at the sky he seemed to see their faces in the clouds, smiling at him contentedly with all the love he remembered shining from their eyes.

158

The sun had nearly gone before the badger made a move. He got up, looked at Bracca and then started to walk up the path and past the fallen oak. Bracca followed and they were soon making their way through thick undergrowth with great trees on either side. The moon was out now, a full moon, and it threw the shadows of the trees across their path in long thick bands of darkness which gave the illusion of being solid against the silvery white backdrop of dead bracken and old briars through which they were moving. After a while the undergrowth thinned out, eventually giving way to a floor of grassy tussocks that glistened damply in the moonlight while the trees all around them seemed ever taller, their huge trunks green with mildew and festooned with mosses and lichens. Ivy wound around many of them like a protective woven armour, the glossy emerald green foliage hanging down in curtains from the branches so that Bracca had to push a way through with his arms. A feeling of enormous age seemed to emanate from everything around them; the ancient trees, the thick carpet of grasses, even the air itself which was rich and musty, heavy with the scent of decay. Owls hooted, their liquid cries echoing in the stillness, and occasionally a dark shadow would glide across their vision; bats flitted to and fro above their heads and sometimes Bracca saw the shadow of a fox or another badger padding its silent way through the darkness. Once, caught for an instant by a flash of light from the moon, he saw the silhouette of a deer, head raised as it sniffed the air, its antlers proudly awesome in the silver flare. Then it was gone, its bulk melting miraculously back into the night without a sound. Myriad little rustlings on the ground around their feet betrayed the presence of shrews and voles and mice and weasels and stoats in their ceaseless search for food.

They came at last to a valley. The land curved up gently on either side of them and Bracca found himself following the badger along the bank of a delicately meandering little stream which wound its way along the bottom. As they continued, the sides of the valley became steeper and they began to climb. The banks rose up almost sheer and the light from the moon was obscured by the trees that towered above them so that Bracca found the going difficult. It was marshy where they were walking and the trees that grew alongside the stream, alder and willow and oak, had low branches which he was constantly having to avoid. He became cold; the dampness from the earth started to seep into his bones so that he felt himself enmeshed in a chill shroud and he grew aware of the pains of hunger that had begun to gnaw away at his stomach. With a shock he realized that he was unable to remember when he had last eaten; it must have been on that last fateful morning before they all set out together for the clearing . . . to talk to the villagers. As his thoughts returned to that time, so terrible memories began to flood back again and he had to use all his will to banish them and keep them out lest they break back in upon him and submerge him beneath the awful weight of their horror. So too he tried to forget his hunger and to lose himself in the journey; to concentrate on following the badger along the twists and turns of the valley as they continued to climb up the steep winding cleft.

They were nearly at the top now. Bracca could see the lightening dawn sky through the trees and feel a freshness in the air while the breeze that stirred the dead leaves around their feet carried with it the scent of heather and gorse. Suddenly they were out of the forest and walking across a stretch of moorland that swept up and away on both sides of them for as far as they could see. Just ahead, at the top of the slope they were on, was a little rocky crag and it was towards this that the badger walked. The trees whispered behind them as the wind blew through the branches and when Bracca looked round to see where they had come from the forest seemed dark and impenetrable. Until now he had not given a thought to where they were going but now, for the first time, he began to wonder. The badger seemed intent on a definite purpose as he shuffled along in his strange rolling gait, snuffling and grunting as he did so, but what was that

160

purpose and what was their destination? And then, as his mind still wandered in contemplation, he raised his head and saw them. They were silhouetted against the hazy rose-pink morning sky; framed in a delicate aura of mist, they seemed to rise out of the earth in front of the crag while behind them the great jagged slabs of black rock threw tall angular shadows across and around them.

Bracca stopped, awestruck by the realization of what was happening, while the badger continued on and took his place in between the man and the dog. At Nab's other side stood Beth, with the hare sitting next to her. Warrigal the owl sat on top of a low rock just in front, his eyes blinking slowly as he scrutinized Bracca with his intense gaze while the breeze ruffled the brown feathers on his back.

Bracca could not see their faces clearly for they were hidden in shadow yet the reality of their presence was as certain as was the ground beneath his feet and as understanding flooded his consciousness, so his spine seemed to melt with excitement and he had difficulty standing. Then Nab spoke and at the sound of his voice Bracca's spirit soared up to the sky in a great surge of joy.

'Do not be afraid, Bracca,' he said, and his voice was as gentle as a warm spring breeze and as soft as thistledown on the skin. 'Come closer that we may speak with you; there is much that we have to say. We have been waiting for you since you came to Haark with Melvaig and Morven. We have watched you through your childhood and we know of your suffering. We were with you as you embraced our effigies of stone and we heard when you talked to us.'

He came forward then, slowly, and the light fell on his face for an instant, glancing off his long white beard and burnishing his nut-brown skin. He was smiling; his mouth and eyes radiating such love that Bracca felt its warmth embrace him like a cloud. Around his head he wore a woven band of willow and his silver hair fell around his shoulders on to the green cloak that swept down to the ground. As he moved he made no sound nor did his footfalls leave a trace

161

on the dew-soaked grass but it was his eyes that most fascinated Bracca as they looked deep into his own. They were large and as clear as crystal and in them was infinite wisdom; a wisdom that spoke only of kindness and love, of patience and truth and honesty, of selflessness and of the sanctity of all life. Yet so too was there a great cloud of sadness; that terrible sadness that comes with knowledge of the ultimate nature of man. In his eyes was a pall of mourning for all the innocent who have ever suffered because of man; called in the old language the Urkku or Great Enemy. And their pain was his pain as also was their joy so that his spirit was as deep as the bottommost cavern on the ocean floor and as high as the tallest mountain pinnacle; his compassion as encompassing as the sky and his anger as unrelenting as the tide.

He took Bracca in his arms and held him for long moments and Bracca felt the power of magic sweep through his body so that he left his earthbound flesh; his spirit flying up to the sky and racing with the wind. And as he looked down the earth seemed different; he saw the grasses and the trees, the flowers, moss and lichen, the animals, birds and insects as he had never seen them before – each, individual and infinitely precious, worthy of sacred respect. Each with its own identity and character, even as the elves regard them. And his flight through this new enchanted world was a timeless journey of discovery which seemed to last for ever. Eventually though his spirit returned unbidden and he was once again united with his body. Then Nab took Bracca by the hand and led him back into the little circle formed by Beth and the others. He went to each of them in turn and embraced them except for Warrigal and Perryfoot the hare, both of whom he stroked tenderly in response to which they shifted their feet slightly, fidgeted a bit and looked at him with a quizzical interest. He sat down amongst them on a fallen hawthorn branch off an old tree just behind and then Beth bent down and picking up a silver dish she passed it to him, smiling beautifully as she did so. Looking at it Bracca saw that it was delicately engraved with a picture of a badger walking backwards through a snowy wood with a human baby tucked under his forelegs.

'Here,' she said, and her voice sang like water running over pebbles in a brook. 'You will be hungry. Enjoy your food; and here also is a drink to refresh you,' and she placed a silver goblet down on the ground at his side. It was full of a sparkling pale pink liquid and when Bracca lifted it to take a drink, the sweet fragrant scent reminded him of rosehips. It tasted delicious, rushing through his body with a gentle fire that invigorated and calmed and inspired him. When he put it down the goblet was half empty and she refilled it from a silver chalice at her side. He looked at her face. How different it was from the Beth he knew from the statue. Her face in stone had been of the young Beth, beautiful beyond words, her delicate features exquisitely framed with the cascade of long hair whose cold tresses he had so often run his hands down. The years had mellowed her perfect mouth, had shadowed the loveliness of her large round eyes and faded the full bloom of her cheeks. Now her beauty was an inner radiance, shining through her as a flower glows with the love of Ashgaroth, encompassing all within her prospect with gentleness and contentment.

He turned now to the food in the dish, his taste buds tingling in anticipation, fuelled in their expectations by the drink. It was filled with nuts, toadstools and berries, some of which he knew, others that were strange to him. All though tasted impeccable, the flavour perfect, and he savoured each mouthful as if it was his last, feeling it dance in his mouth till he swallowed it and so allowed his body to feel its goodness.

So entranced was he by the food and drink that, in his total involvement with them, he had almost forgotten where he was and it was with a slight quiver of surprise that he heard Nab's voice break in upon him.

'Don't stop eating; it is good to see you enjoying your food. I will talk while you eat for there is much I have to tell you. Some you will already know from Melvaig; from the book of

163

the Faradawn from whence he derived the vision which he pursued till he found Haark. You will know of us and you will know our tale; the story of our journey from Silver Wood to gather the Faradawn, the magical essences of life, from the three elflords who had been entrusted with their care by Ashgaroth. As you will also know, our quest was successful and so we were able to point the way to safety for the animals and the Eldron, those of the human race who followed Ashgaroth, when the time of the holocaust came.'

He paused and looked at Bracca with a wry smile.

'What followed, you know better than I. How when the terrible swath of destruction finally spent itself centuries after, leaving the earth scorched and barren and the skies filled with poison, there arose from the ashes the one called Xtlan and his evil spread like a cancer so that Ashgaroth was crushed beneath the weight of darkness. Viciousness and cruelty; selfishness, arrogance and greed; malice, hate and fear, these flourished and grew while love, gentleness, compassion and kindness withered away and died.

'Of Ashgaroth and Dréagg you will be aware; they are the Efflinch, the Lord of Good and the Ruler of Evil who have struggled with each other since the beginning of time itself. Melvaig will have told you of the first great victory, when Ashgaroth defeated Dréagg and created the earth as his jewel to shine with his light for ever as the symbol of his supremacy. But Dréagg merely used his defeat as a time in which to marshal his energies and he returned with renewed strength and cunning, feeding off his own hate, so that his power waxed mighty and he turned Ashgaroth's creatures one against the other and the air rang with the sounds of their suffering.

'Then it was that Ashgaroth created the elves to aid him in his struggle against the Lord of Darkness. And they are of Magic, which is the first of the Duain Elrondin (or powers of life), and they are born of goodness and light so that they shine like the stars and breathe with the creatures of the earth and the green growing things that spring from its

164

womb. They are the ambassadors of Ashgaroth, his warrior heralds, and their mission was to restore peace and innocence to the earth. Yet though their bravery was immense and their heroes mighty beyond belief, the power of Dréagg was mightier still and the elves succumbed beneath his awesome strength. And so they begged Ashgaroth to grant them the second of the Duain Elrondin which is Logic. But of the Duain Elrondin, Logic is the most dangerous for if used unwisely or in too great measure it would destroy the earth. And he besought the elves only to use it in the time of their greatest need and there was great fear and caution in his heart at his granting of this power. Thus it was that he separated it into three, which are called the Three Seeds of Logic and so that none of the elves should be able to use the power without the others he placed each seed in a casket wrought from the finest copper from the deepest mines of Mixon; and each casket he gave into the possession of one of the three elflords: Malcoff, Lord of the Mountains; Saurelon, Lord of the Seas; and Ammdar who was Lord of the Forests and the Green Growing Things.'

Nab stopped speaking then and turned his head away towards the forest where the rising sun was lighting up the branches of the trees. His mind was far away, in a distant place at a time many worlds ago when the truths that he was now relating to Bracca had been told to him by Wychnor, the Great Elflord of the Forests, in the enchanted woodland of Ellmondrill. He remembered himself in Bracca's place, sitting on the floor of the little room in the huge oak tree that was the home of the wood elves. Wychnor had been framed by the light as he sat in his carved wooden seat in the window and the sun had cast a halo of gold around his head. And the sound of the elflord's voice came back to him as if it were yesterday, the magical words returning with a clarity that amazed him so that much of what he said seemed to come straight from the mouth of Wychnor. With an effort he collected his mind from its journey into the past and looked once more at Bracca before continuing.

165

'But Dréagg thirsted for the power of Logic and in his cravings it came to him to corrupt the mind of Ammdar, the mightiest of the elflords, and so, stealthily in the night, Dréagg came to him and fed him vanity and nurtured pride and arrogance in him so that after a time Ammdar rejected his Lord Ashgaroth and opened his spirit to evil. And the darkness was now in him so that when Dréagg made known his scheme he willingly gave himself to its accomplishment.

'And the scheme was to gather the Three Seeds of Logic together so that, with them, Ammdar would be truly all-powerful. Then Ammdar, with Dréagg always at his side, sought out the weakest of the elves, both of his own and of the other two lords and offered them power if they would accept him as their master and assist him in his search for the Seeds. And these fallen elves are called goblins; loathsome and vile they became when they fell under the influence of Dréagg yet their evil power is awesome for Dréagg rewarded them well.

'So among the sea elves of Saurelon and Malcoff's mountain elves the goblins exercised their new powers to the full using deceit and trickery to insinuate themselves into the highest and most trusted positions so that when Dréagg whispered that the time was right they took the Seeds and all gathered together, rejoicing in their success, in Ammdar's lair in the far forests of Spath.

'And the power of Logic was now in the hands of Ammdar. It could not be granted to the goblins for they were born of Magic and Magic and Logic will not lie together. So Dréagg put it in the mind of Ammdar to offer it to the animals for with them in his control the defeat of Ashgaroth would be certain. So he summoned the leaders of the animals to him in the forest of Spath and offered them Logic in return for their allegiance. But the silver light of Ashgaroth was strong in them and they turned him down. And when Dréagg knew he had been rejected his fury knew no bounds and they fled in terror as the earth erupted around them and the darkness of Spath closed in about them.

'Then it was that Dréagg conceived the idea of creating a race of beings out of pure Logic that would take revenge against the animals for their rejection of him. So Dréagg, with the help of Ammdar, created man, who we call Urkku or the Great Enemy, and man was created to fight Ashgaroth so that in man is the destruction of the earth, the jewel of Ashgaroth. Because he is of Logic, Magic is denied to him so that he does not see the earth as the elves see it. And just as the elves, being born of Ashgaroth, have his qualities so does the evil of Dréagg lurk within the heart of man. Cruelty and selfishness fester there; and a terrible arrogance by which man believes himself to be supreme over all the earth; believes indeed that the earth and the creatures and green growing things on it were created for his benefit and that they only have worth in relation to him. And in his logic this justifies his treatment of the animals.

'With the creation of the Urkku Dréagg had no more use for Ammdar and he destroyed him lest his thirst for power grew too great and interfered with the steady process of destruction which man's existence on the earth had started.

'And Dréagg smiled as he looked down upon the earth for truly his revenge was sweet. Under man's reign the jewel of Ashgaroth was torn asunder; the colours faded and the green growing things withered and died. And terrible was the suffering of the animals as the root of cruelty grew and blossomed in the heart of the Urkku. Mutilated and torn, imprisoned and beaten, tortured and slain, so that the rivers ran red with their blood and the skies rang with the echoes of their pain. None were safe and all were ripe for sacrifice in the cause of the benefit of man.

'Yet some there were among the Urkku who cast out the influence of Dréagg and who, in accepting Ashgaroth, saw the earth even as the elves do; and they are called Eldron, or Friends. They see magic in the mountains and the seas; they are one with the trees and the animals and a great anger was in them as they looked about and saw the devastation that was on the earth and the slaughter wrought among the

167

creatures of Ashgaroth. And they fought the evils of Dréagg and tried to halt the carnage; struggling against the cruelty and blindness in the Urkku. And they were laughed at and abused, vilified and scorned, and their successes were small and of little avail in the steady march of darkness that spread over the jewel of Ashgaroth.

'And the First Holocaust came and the earth was rent asunder and after, there was a terrible desolation upon the land. But Ashgaroth saved the Eldron and the animals and elves so that when the earth recovered the Urkku were no more. But there was that in the Eldron which Dréagg in creating man had planted too deeply to be extinguished even by the light of Ashgaroth and the seeds of cruelty and arrogance began to grow once more among some of the Eldron and again the earth grew despoiled and the animals suffered as the power of Logic asserted itself. And Dréagg came amongst them with infinite stealth so that they should not know he was there and nourished their greed and selfishness so that they rejected Ashgaroth and could no longer see the magic in the mountains and the trees and they lost their oneness with the animals. And they were worse even than the Urkku for the Urkku had no choice in the way they were. But the children of the Eldron had known Ashgaroth; they had seen the light and still they turned away. And the darkness once more spread across the earth and the seeds of self-destruction grew until the time of the Second Holocaust, more terrible still than the First. And this time almost all the earth was laid utterly waste, never to recover and it was this world that you were born into, Bracca, where the sky is always dark and the ground bakes and cracks under a ceaseless heat. So there were survivors of the Second Holocaust and the Third Age of Man began. Some there were like you in your village of Ruann, simple and innocent; Eldron in whom the light of Ashgaroth still burned brightly. Others there were, though, in whom the evil of Dréagg now burst forth and of these Xtlan was the darkest and most vile. And Dréagg was well pleased as he watched this ultimate debasement of the shining jewel of Ashgaroth for truly his victory was a great one. The light of Ashgaroth had finally been extinguished and the earth languished under a blackness so foul that there could be no recovery.

'But some of the Eldron there had been who knew of us; of Nab, Beth, Sam, Perryfoot and Warrigal, of Silver Wood and of the quest for the Faradawn and they lived in the deep forests of Haark. They built the stone statues of us that you knew and loved and there was in them no cruelty or arrogance, only gentleness and love towards all living things. When the Second Holocaust came Ashgaroth used all his magic to protect Haark so that it remained untouched by the horrors that ravaged the rest of the earth. And this was the last enclave of Ashgaroth; where the elves still dwell and where the earth was as it had been in the time of Silver Wood. This was Haark, the place of Melvaig's vision.

'And you know the story of the corruption of Haark better than I. How even among the Eldron the fragments of darkness that Dréagg had woven into man at his creation, were too strong ever to be completely suppressed and how they have risen again so that even this last enclave is now despoiled.

'And so, Bracca, the time has come when man must be no more; his reign on earth must be ended. Yet in him is the power of Dréagg and the task will not be easy for the Lord of Darkness will guard him with all the strength he can muster. And it is for this task that Ashgaroth has guided you; this is the role which you are destined to play in the annals of time and in this the final great struggle between the Efflinch, for with man gone from the earth for ever then Dréagg will be defeated for the power of Logic can never be used again and Magic will rule over all the earth. And over the aeons of time during which man has reigned, so much of himself and his energies has Dréagg invested in man that man's annihilation will leave the Lord of Darkness irretrievably weak; even as a creature with neither limbs nor senses.

'It has been seen that man was created out of the Three

169

Seeds of Logic and just as Ashgaroth divided them so that the power could not be used unless they were brought together, so too did he make it that if the Seeds were ever separated then the power of Logic would likewise divide and be dissipated into the outermost corners of the universe.

'Thus it is that man's existence depends on the Unity of the Three Seeds for the power of Logic exists only so long as they are united. Once separated, the power is no more and man will crumble, for without Logic he cannot exist.

'And Dréagg tried to undo this magic when the Seeds were in the possession of Ammdar but he could not. Yet while the Seeds were in the hands of Ammdar, Dréagg was able to weave a safeguard of his own into the threads of Unity with which Ashgaroth had bound the power of Logic.

'And the nature of Dréagg's safeguard was this; that it was only by the hand of man that the Three Seeds could be separated. Neither elf nor animal nor even Ashgaroth himself could take them one from the other. Thus only a man with the power of Logic was able to destroy the power of Logic and so it is that the man who destroys the power also destroys himself. And Dréagg felt certain this could never happen for the act of destroying oneself, along with all one's fellow creatures, is itself beyond the contemplation of Logic. Melvaig could never have brought an end to you and Morven and Shuinn.

'Beth and myself were granted the immortality of the elves by the grace of Ashgaroth at the time of the First Holocaust so that we too are now of Magic.

'And so, Bracca, it is upon you that this terrible responsibility falls. You who are of Logic, though you are of the Eldron and though in you is the true knowledge of Ashgaroth. It is you, Bracca, who are of the line of Melvaig and Morven, that must perform this final task; the separation of the Seeds of Logic and thereby the destruction of man.'

And now Nab paused for in the eyes of Bracca was a haze of shock and awe. Crushed by the weight of his incredible task his consciousness struggled to absorb and understand all that Nab had just told him and then to fit into it, like the jewel at the top of an infinitely elaborate crown, his own particular role; the part that Ashgaroth had chosen for him and towards which he felt destiny had been guiding him since the moment of his birth so long ago, in Ruann in the land of Xtlan. And as Nab looked at the dazed young man he went back again in time to the room in the elvenoak of Ellmondrill and he remembered so clearly how he had felt when Wychnor, the elflord, had finished telling him of the Efflinch and of his mission in the quest for the Faradawn. And because he remembered his heart went out in sympathy and he took Bracca's face in his hands and turned his head so that they were looking into each other's eyes. They spoke no words but Bracca felt the power of Ashgaroth well up within himself and a hard knot of confidence seemed to form and settle in his spirit.

After a little time, when Nab felt that Bracca's mind was calmer, he smiled and began to speak once again. The sun had risen into the cold grey winter sky, driving away the mist and leaving the day bright and cold, but Bracca hardly noticed it for all his concentration and attention were focused on the figure before him and he was rapt in a spell of wonder and revelation as the words once more reached out and drew him into their web.

'Your task will not be easy. When the Seeds had been used by Dréagg to release the Elrondin of Logic, Ammdar locked them in a silver box which is called the Droon or Casket of Unity and took them to a vault deep underground in a cave in the deepest reaches of the forest of Spath. There, in that most terrible of places, the vault is guarded by the legions of Dréagg's goblins under their vile leader, Degg, and by the hosts of evil creatures that Dréagg has created from the foulnesses of his mind to ensure the preservation of the Unity of the Seeds. Alone you would never reach the forest nor penetrate the vault, for you are solely of Logic, yet you will not be by yourself. The time has now come for you to meet your companion,' and he turned away and called a

171

name which Bracca could not understand. There was silence for a few moments; only the sighings of the breeze in the grasses interrupted the stillness of the air. And then, from a sunlit glade in the forest, there came a deer. Delicately it walked towards them, the light catching its golden flanks and shimmering as it moved. Bracca watched as it approached them, surprised by its purposefulness and mesmerized by its grace. Closer it came, and still closer, until finally it stood between Nab and Beth and faced him. Riveted with fascination Bracca looked into its deep brown eyes and immediately became lost in the vastness of the world he saw there, as if they were somehow the entrance to another universe; a place of eternal truths where nothing was lost and nothing was hidden. And he saw himself reflected in their eternal light and he was frightened.

When Nab spoke, the words came to him as if from a great distance.

'This is our daughter, Tara, named after Brock's sow; my badger-mother in Silver Wood until she was murdered by the Urkku,' and almost before he had finished speaking the words the deer was gone and in its place, standing in a pool of light, was a young woman. So shocked was Bracca by this incredible happening, and so stunned by her beauty, that he was overcome with faintness and leaning forward he buried his face in his hands. Yet the image of her remained even in the darkness and, unable to resist seeing her again, he tore his hands away from his eyes in a fit of rage at his inability to accept the realities of this new world he had entered.

This time he forced himself to keep looking at her. It was no trick of the mind; she was real – as real as he knew the deer had been – and her beauty was as compulsive and fascinating as he had at first thought. She was smiling at him, a genuine smile of warmth and honesty, though tinged, he thought, with a hint of mischievous amusement at the shock she knew she had given him.

'Don't be afraid of her powers,' continued Nab, 'for there is magic in her even as in the elves, yet Ashgaroth blessed

172

her also with the power to change from human form to any animal she chose. She picked out the deer for its grace and speed, its elegance and its beauty. She will travel with you on your journey for without her magic you could never succeed in your task; you would be claimed by the forests of Spath the moment you entered.'

And Nab saw the look in Bracca's eyes as he gazed at Tara and he recognized the desire that blossomed in the young man's heart like a bluebell in spring. And his heart bled with the knowledge he had about them which only Tara could reveal to him if and when the time was right.

'There is much joy and happiness for me in your meeting,' he said, 'yet there is also a great sadness, the reason for which you may learn later from Tara herself. Know only that it was not planned this way. For now, though, let me join your hands in a bond between you for in the times to come you will need each other even as the trees need the earth and the earth needs the rain. Let there be trust and loyalty, compassion and understanding, between you so that the names of Bracca and Tara will echo together through the infinite citadels of time as those who by their faith rescued the earth from darkness.'

As Nab spoke the words the young woman and the young man walked slowly forward towards each other and Nab took their hands and joined them, clasping them firmly in his own. Bracca, utterly mesmerized, felt himself to be floating on a cloud of brilliant white as he looked into her eyes, the eyes of the deer, for though every other part of her had changed into human form the eyes had stayed the same. At the touch of her hand his heart raced with excitement and his head whirled in rapture and when, after only a very little time, Nab released them it seemed to Bracca as if an age had elapsed.

'It is nearly time for us to part now. Yet before we go there are two things I must give to you. Keep them safely for without them you are lost. First, here is a pipe fashioned by Morar, the legendary piper of the mountain elves. In it is an elven enchantment so that when blown it will be heard by all

173

the elves of Ashgaroth. It is to be used only once; to summon
the hosts of the elven armies when you need them. I know
not when that time will be, yet you must know that even now
the forces of Dréagg are mustering to protect the Unity of the
Seeds and he will use all the power at his command to stop
you.'

So saying Nab reached under his cloak and took out from
his belt a dark cylindrical wooden case on which was carved
the magic rune of the elves of the mountains; a new crescent
moon behind a jagged peak around both of which wound a
single blade of grass. Nab then pressed a catch and the top
sprang open to reveal a reed pipe nestling in a cushion of
green moss. It had a single stem that coiled round once and
then opened out into a wide bluebell-like head.

'Here,' Nab said. 'This is now yours,' and he handed it to
Bracca who accepted it reverently and, after closing the top,
placed it on the ground at his feet.

'Now for the second of my gifts,' continued Nab, putting
his hands to the buckles on his belt and unfastening it swiftly.
'The Belt of Ammdar,' he said, passing it to Bracca, 'given to
me in a different age by Wychnor who became Lord of the
Forests and the Green Growing Things after the fall of
Ammdar. Wear it, even as I have worn it, close to your body
under your garments.'

Bracca took the Belt and held it in his hands, spell-bound
with wonderment at the awesome significance of this
moment. Yet it was so simple to look at; green sapling
strands plaited together in a woven mesh with the three
silver lockets in which Nab had held the mystical Faradawn
embedded in the weave.

'Look at the fastenings,' Nab said. They were of burnished
copper, intricately carved into a design that Bracca could not
recognize or understand. Two strange ophidian creatures
enmeshed one with another twisting and turning sinuously
in an endless flow of movement that drew Bracca's gaze
compulsively along the lines until they stopped at what he
guessed was the top of the buckle; two slender serpent-like

174

heads with their thin mouths clamped each onto the body of the other. At the base of the clasp, each creature's single three-toed foot was locked over the other to make the fastening complete.

'Each side of the buckle is a key,' continued Nab. 'A key to the Casket of Unity, the Droon. There is no other way to open it. Turn the key on your left, as you wear the Belt, three times to the left and the right hand key twice to the right. The lid will then open and the Seeds will be inside. What they look like, how you separate them; these matters I cannot help you with: they are for Ashgaroth himself to reveal to you. Cherish the Belt well for nothing else will break the spell that Ammdar cast upon the Droon. At the time of his destruction, when the goblin Degg took over rule of the forests of Spath, Ammdar's rage at his betrayal by Dréagg was such that he gave the Belt to Braewire, an elven spy for Ashgaroth in the camps of the goblins who Ammdar knew as such. And Braewire then escaped from Spath and took the Belt to Wychnor, his lord, who gave it to me in Ellmondrill. But the time was not then right for the destruction of man and so Wychnor did not tell me of the Droon nor of the significance of the Belt and it was only later that I learned of it from him. Now, let me see you fasten the pipe case to the Belt and put it on.'

Bracca did as Nab asked and put the Belt around his waist. It felt amazingly light and as he brought the two buckles together they seemed to draw into one another and fasten almost by themselves. An odd feeling of safety and comfort seemed to flow into him from the gentle pressure round his waist and looking at Nab's face he saw a look of sadness in his eyes and heard a tremor in his voice as he spoke.

'Now there is no more to say. The mantle of Ashgaroth, that was upon me, is now around your shoulders and you must go forward on this, the last great mission, with my precious Tara. I can do no more for you, you are now by yourselves. Yet know that I shall always be with you; I and the others from Silver Wood. Think of us as you journey;

175

keep us in your thoughts as you will be always in ours. And perhaps, when the world is free of darkness forever and sparkles once more under the silver light of Ashgaroth; when cruelty and pain are gone and all living creatures live together in love and peace, then it may be that we shall meet again. Until that time, farewell.'

Then Bracca went forward and embraced Nab and the young man felt a wave of emotion well up from deep within him and his eyes began to sting with the heat of his tears. Afterwards, in turn, he embraced each of the others. Sam; Perryfoot the hare, who laid his long ears down flat as Bracca picked him up; the owl, Warrigal, whose great round eyes shone with power and wisdom; Beth, with a feeling as soft as Morven's; and lastly Brock, the old badger, who snuffled back his sadness at Bracca's leaving, stifling the memories he had of the finding of Nab that snowy night in Silver Wood all those ages ago – memories which had been stirred by his finding of the injured Bracca on the cliff ledge overlooking the sea where Golconda had left him.

Bracca stood back then and waited in the shadows of one of the great standing stones that grew out of the hillside while Tara took her leave of her family; and his heart ached with sympathy for her as he felt the agony and loss of her separation. Yet he could only guess at the depth of her sadness for though, all her life, Tara had known that this moment would come, though Nab and Beth had done their best to prepare her for it, still she found it unbearable and as she clutched at Nab, her fingers entwined in his hair and her face luxuriating in the familiar touch of his skin, she felt the tears erupt from within and she abandoned herself to the racking pain of her grief.

How long she cried she did not know but eventually Nab's warm comforting voice found its way through the turmoil in her head and brought peace to her soul and power and strength to her spirit. Then the agony subsided and she went to the others, holding each with love and tenderness yet free of the anguish she had previously felt. Beth was last and Tara felt the pain starting again until, like Nab's before her, the gentle kindness of Beth's words quenched the flames of torment that had threatened to flare up again.

'Take care, my little one; take care,' she said. 'We shall always be with you though you may not see us.'

Then, swiftly, Tara turned away and walked over to where Bracca was waiting for her.

'Come, I can stay no longer. We must go,' and taking his hand she began to lead him away up the hill. And then Bracca saw, ranged in a line on either side of them, two rows of sparkling silver lights. At first he thought it was an illusion for ahead of them a great orange sunset hung in the sky and the dew was heavy on the grass, yet as he looked more closely he was certain that he could see figures inside the lights. And then he grew aware of a noise that seemed to come from all around them. It had begun almost as a whisper but soon the air was filled with it; a high pitched wall of sound that ebbed and flowed in great lyrical waves of melody, splitting and re-forming, soaring up to the sky and plunging back down to earth, carrying him with it as it surged around him so that he rode on the air, climbing and diving on a limitless flight through space. On and on it went and he lost all track of time and place, utterly content to let himself be carried by the music, until at last he came back down, landing gently on his feet at the brow of the hill. Still the sound echoed all around yet now he was apart from it and as he turned back in the direction it was coming from he saw once again the two rows of lights, shimmering now in the dusk, stretching back down the hill towards the ragged circle of stones where the companions of Silver Wood still stood looking after them. Then Nab and Beth raised their arms in a farewell salute and with a tug at his hand, Tara pulled Bracca over the hill and out of sight of the elves, her mother and father and the animals who had been as her family. The elven song was then no more and only the sound of the wind disturbed the quietness as they walked swiftly down the slope over a thick carpet of heather and dead

177

bracken towards the valley that fell away steeply in front. The cold damp mist from the river at the bottom swept up to envelop them and sent a chill through Bracca that only the warmth of Tara's hand in his could dispel.

CHAPTER XII

And it was as Nab had said; that even as he spoke all the forces of Dréagg were marshalling to protect the unity of the Seeds of Logic. Thus while Bracca and Tara started out on their journey to the forests of Spath, Sienogg, War Chief of Xtlan, was leading the pick of his warriors across the ocean wastes that separated his world from Haark; the land of Melvaig's vision. Long had Xtlan and Sienogg prepared for the crossing; studying the ancient maps and writings that had survived the Second Holocaust and consulting with the Hebbdril – the wise men – who were made to work with him and who alone had preserved the art of reading. And the task was difficult for a way had to be found around the great arc of fire that lay on the surface of the sea between the two lands. Never had Sienogg forgotten the lives of his warriors that had been claimed by this terrible parabola of flame as they had pursued Melvaig on his flight from Xtlan to Haark. His own scars he still carried with him, etched on his back where the fiery tongues had scorched his skin and sent rivers of pain searing through his flesh. He alone among his warriors had survived the fire and he had sworn revenge against Melvaig and all his kin. And Xtlan had elevated him so that he was second only to his lord and took orders from none save he. Mighty were his powers, terrible his cunning and vice, and so it was that he had been chosen by Xtlan to pursue Melvaig into the land of Haark and to crush the last enclave of Ashgaroth beneath the darkness.

And so Sienogg and his lieutenants journeyed for many days round by the islands of Halmeida in the north and down across the black oily wastes of the Farrll, through the corridors of water in between the Neffrick and the Kcaypinn and at last found themselves, as they had planned, on the same stretch of golden beach that Melvaig had landed on so long before. They had travelled for many seasons so that Sienogg grew old in years yet the power of evil burnt so strongly in him that his awesome powers were undimmed by the passing of time.

And he met Barll on the sands of the little cove and was well pleased for he perceived the darkness in Haark and knew that his work had been done for him, while his fury at the escape of Melvaig and Morven was assuaged by the account Barll gave of their deaths. And in Barll he saw a useful ally, a creature of Dréagg who would serve Xtlan well in the final confrontation with the forces of Ashgaroth. So they joined together and for a time they sojourned in the land of Haark and Sienogg's men rested and ate and drank their fill of the plenty that was in Haark. And the forests ran red with the blood of the creatures that were slaughtered to feed the armies; the air rang with their cries and screams and was thick with the rancid stench of burning flesh as the warriors of Xtlan gorged themselves, and the land was despoiled as they rampaged over it and crushed it in their brutal grip.

And the warriors of Xtlan taught the men of Barll all they knew of the ways of fighting and the veins of cruelty that were within them ran thick and heavy so that they became as dark and cruel as their tutors. All compassion and kindness were banished; the buds of goodness that lingered still in these, the last of the Eldron – the people of Ashgaroth – were cauterized away so that it was as if they had always belonged to Xtlan for there was no trace of love left in them.

180

But some there were, a few, who baulked at the brutal savagery of their guests and who winced instinctively as they witnessed the sadistic possession of their women by the men of Sienogg. And even as the great majority revelled in the feast of bloody debauchery that had erupted around them, so these few became disturbed and were made uneasy by the terrible excesses of these dark warriors that they had welcomed into their midst so willingly and accepted so readily. Tentatively then, they began to voice their misgivings and to approach others with their reservations, seeming at first to find receptive ears, but then suddenly they would disappear, these protesters, to be found some little time later horribly dismembered, their parts prominently displayed around the village as a grisly warning to all who would doubt the power and the word of Xtlan. So all those in whom there had been rumblings of discontent quelled their criticisms and, keeping silent, swallowed the bile of their distaste and learnt to live with their sickly and stricken consciences, imprisoned by the cold shackles of terror. And the yoke of fear lay heavy round their necks.

So darkness fell upon Haark and the last enclave of Ashgaroth, the place of Melvaig's vision, was no more. And Dréagg was well pleased; yet even as he gloated over his triumph, the freedom of Bracca and Tara was as a wound in his side, constantly nagging at him and casting a veil over the rich glow of his victory for he guessed their purpose and their destination.

They could never succeed, of that he was certain, for the shroud of evil was now upon all the earth and the power of light well nigh extinguished. And Dréagg perceived Ashgaroth as cowering, defeated, behind the last few remaining vestiges of his kingdom and waiting for banishment even as he, Dréagg, had been banished so many aeons of time ago at the end of the first Efflinch Wars when he had fled to the Halls of Dragorn which are outside the universe. And the taste of revenge was as nectar to him, heightened by a supreme confidence for surely now, at last, the end was in

181

sight. It was impossible to conceive that those few of the ambassadors of Ashgaroth who still survived could possibly prevail against the dreadful might of the goblins, the savagery of the warriors of Xtlan and the dark shadows of the daemonic forces that dwelt in the evil wastes of Spath. Yet he was troubled, for though the power of Ashgaroth was decimated and the few remaining elves lurked in the last forgotten places so far untouched by the new order, still while there was a trace of light left remaining he must be wary lest his lack of caution expose him to defeat.

And he knew what his forces must do. They would march to Spath and there join with the goblins to await the coming of Bracca, Tara and the elves on their mission to wrest the Seeds of Logic one from the other. What a chance then to finally crush Ashgaroth for ever; to annihilate every last trace of him on earth for it was there, on Dréagg's own battleground of Spath, that Ashgaroth would make his last desperate attempt to defeat the forces of darkness, using all the powers he could muster.

And so when Dréagg judged that the time was right he made himself known to Straygoth the scout, who was also called Mouse, as he wandered in the clearing before the hut that had once belonged to Melvaig. He chose Straygoth because he recognized in him a cunning and a noxious intellect as finely developed even as that of Xtlan as he was in the beginning.

And one night while the moon was high and all the warriors were fast asleep Straygoth drew Sienogg and Barll together and told them of the things the Lord of Darkness had made known to him. And they believed him for there was a new authority upon the one they had called Mouse. 'The moment has come,' he said, 'when we should return to Xtlan, all of us, the armies of Sienogg and of Barll. There we shall join up with the rest of Xtlan's forces and together set out to the sacred forests of Spath for he made known to me that it was there, at the chosen place of our lord, that we should meet the followers of Ashgaroth in the last great battle. If we win then the earth will belong to us and those like us completely, but if we lose then it will be the end for us and we shall be no more and the darkness will be forever extinguished.'

While he spoke the night was still, as if even the trees were listening. No bird flew, no creature moved and the grass did not stir as time began to move slowly towards the final confrontation for now was the beginning of the end and for those creatures that were of the light of Ashgaroth and who felt the black shroud of Dréagg descending upon them this time of waiting would be almost unendurable.

It was not many days later that they departed leaving only the very young, the very old, the women and a few of the warriors whose task it was to rule and to keep the colony alive for Xtlan. And so one morning after a final wild orgy of feasting and lechery, those who were not staying set off back to the land of Xtlan; Sienogg's men in the boats they had come in and the men of Barll in their fishing boats. They retraced Sienogg's route and the journey was long and arduous. Many of Barll's men perished of hunger and more yet of disease for they had never before been out of Haark and their bodies succumbed to the strange illnesses that festered outside their erstwhile world.

But Barll survived, and Straygoth, and when they and the rest of the men of Haark who still lived first saw the dead and barren land of Xtlan spread out before them like an open wound they were shocked and dazed by what they saw and some there were among them who wondered as to the wisdom of their actions but they quickly stifled their unease as the fates of the earlier dissenters flashed across their vision. And indeed their doubts were soon forgotten as, upon their arrival in Eggron, the ancient city at the heart of Xtlan's empire, they were fêted and applauded and all manner of sensual delights were lavished upon them so that their memories of the green, and of clear blue skies and pure sweet air and birds singing and animals rustling in the undergrowth, quickly faded and died.

183

They stayed in Eggron just long enough to regather their strength from the journey, training with their weapons during the day and wallowing at night in the delights of the Gravenndra, the houses of women where the physical needs of the warriors were catered for. And Barll grew in stature for his prowess in fighting became renowned throughout Eggron and his reputation for cruelty caused ripples of fear to spread about him wherever he went, the sight of his wild black mane of hair causing those who saw it to turn away lest his gaze should fall upon them and the savagery of his temper explode suddenly and cause him to lash out for no reason. But the women of the Gravenndra where he and the rest of the villagers had been placed had cause to fear him most of all for the vileness of his lechery was unknown even to these, the Elimsorr, whose captive lives were devoted to satisfying every whim of the warriors of Xtlan. For Barll was still smarting from Shayll's rejection of him and he saw her in every woman he took, extracting his revenge upon the hapless substitute with a degree of sadism that shocked even the men of Xtlan though the novelty of his ideas afforded them much amusement.

At last Xtlan judged that they could wait no longer and, summoning Sienogg to him, told him that the time had come. And so one morning, just as the heat began to pour down on the parched and blistered earth, the forces of Xtlan set forth in a mighty tide for the far forests of Spath. Sienogg rode at the head on his great white horse, in appearance not dissimilar to how he had looked those long seasons ago when he had ridden with his raiders into the village of Ruann and taken Morven captive amongst the other women he had snatched to serve in the Gravenndra. How different a mission was this he mused, as he recalled that faraway day and then more recently the talks he had had with Xtlan since his arrival back from Haark. The urgency in his lord's voice as he explained the epic purpose of their journey, the glories of victory and the terrible disaster of defeat. This, at last, was a task truly fitted to his powers – the ultimate defeat of

184

Ashgaroth, the final dousing of the light beneath the black shroud of Dréagg. And the unthinkable consequences of failure, the Separation of the Seeds and the death of man. Yet the cataclysmic results of defeat lent his task an added piquancy for it made the mission truly worthy of him. Sienogg was rumoured by many to be the son of Xtlan himself who had only escaped death, the usual fate of Xtlan's children to prevent rival claimants to his position, by being smuggled away from Eggron by Daikkah, his mother. She had persuaded a friend of hers in the Gravenndra, who was called Fraille and who had been condemned to live in the hinterland as an outcast because her beauty had faded, to take him with her when she went. And so she did, smuggling the tiny baby out under her skirts as she was thrown into the back of a cart and taken away, beyond the gates of Eggron to be dumped in the hinterland, which is known as the Lemgorrst (or living death). Those who dwelt there were those for whom there was no place in the world of Xtlan; the sick, the old, the infirm, the crippled and the mad. A terrible place it was, an open festering sore on the face of the earth. They survived by their wits alone for they were given no food, so they scavenged amongst each other and survived on what little the earth produced by its own labours; rats, grass or the bark of what few trees there were. And they howled out their anguish constantly in a terrible chorus of despair, the Wailing of the Lemgorrst, the memory of which still turned Sienogg's heart to stone when, unbidden, it occasionally flashed across his mind.

And Fraille survived against all the odds, just long enough to see Sienogg begin his long march into manhood in the fifth year of his life. When she died the child's guts gnawed with hunger until he found himself tearing off her flesh where she lay and felt the pangs of starvation fade as the meat settled in his stomach.

And so amongst this shattered wreckage of humanity Sienogg brought himself up, clawing his way through the mire and devoting himself to survival at all costs with a

185

mystical single-mindedness that let nothing stand in his way. And he grew up with the stench of death in his nostrils and the rancid taste of decay on his tongue and he lived through all the horror until at last he captured the horse of a traveller who had had to travel through the Lemgorrst to get to Eggron. He killed the stranger with his bare hands, took his belongings and fled, leaving the body to provide sustenance for those lucky enough to be near at the time.

So it was that, eventually, wearing the clothes of the stranger, he rode into Eggron and made his way to the first Gravenndra he could see, that which catered for the Company of Kegg, the most savage of all Xtlan's warrior troops. The next day he accompanied them on a raid against one of the villages outside Xtlan and showed such skill and savagery that he immediately distinguished himself. More raids followed and on each he climbed one step further in the hierarchy until at last, by a combination of trickery and deceit, he reached the position of Battle Chief of the Company of Kegg. And all the time, running through his spirit like a fire, memories of the Lemgorrst haunted him so that he was driven by an iron resolve to put himself as far away as possible from that awful place; to reach an unassailable position in the world of Xtlan so that he would be safe from it. And there must always be food at his hand and beautiful women to respond to his every whim for he hated the ugly and the sick, the wounded and the weak for the memories they stirred in him.

Then it was that he led the fateful raid on Ruann and the image of Morven's beauty as she had been then still hung in his heart like a golden flame. Time and again he had tried to have her as she and the other captives were taken back to Eggron in the covered wagon and as many times she had fought him off until at last she had given in to him but her submission had been worse for him than her aggression; a bland and patronizing docility that had left him spent but still raging with lust. He had tried no more but a terrible anger had festered inside himself at her rejection of him and a

186

pathological jealousy had planted itself in his soul against her man, the one she called Melvaig.

By then the rumours of his supposed fatherhood had come to the ears of Xtlan and, despite himself, the novelty of the situation appealed to him so that he took a personal interest in Sienogg, elevating him at last to the position of Supreme War Chief over all his forces.

Now, as they rode out of the gates of Eggron with the forces of Xtlan stretching back as far as the eye could see, Barll rode at Sienogg's side at the head of the army, even as it had been in his dream. Sienogg rode his great white horse and Barll rode a magnificent black steed, presented to him as a gift on the orders of Xtlan. He had only learned to ride since he had been in Eggron yet already he sat easily on the horse's back and in training he had shown the promise of a master. He revelled in it, while the black horse followed his every command almost before he knew it himself. Barll's spirit soared with pride and an overwhelming sense of power as the light caught the horse's muscles and shimmered as it moved majestically up the slope. Soon the warriors reached the low ridge that ran along the top of the rise. Each then stopped and turned to look back down on the sprawling brown mass of buildings that was Eggron, baking in the relentless dry heat that poured down from overhead, until eventually every one of the riders sat still on their horses, ranged in a single line that wound its way right around the lip of the ridge. And then, as if at a signal, each man found his gaze drawn upwards, climbing the sheer pinnacle of jagged rock that grew out of the ground beyond Eggron, until it settled on the Blaggvald, the black palace, which seemed to erupt out of the flat apex of the rock; its dark forbidding walls rising up into a cluster of towers and minarets. And it was the tallest of these minarets, capped by a strange conical bulbous dome, that drew the spirits of the warriors towards it for it was there that Xtlan dwelt. They felt the force of his presence now, individually, as if he was standing at each man's side. It emanated out from a small

187

black cavity in the dome in which his image now suddenly appeared before them, striking each of them with a power that left them breathless and dazed. It was a final overpowering display of his strength; a reminder of his omnipotence lest they should dare to forget in the long days ahead for his image was now seared deep into their souls so that they had all become, spiritually, a part of him; imbued with a fragment of the darkness which came through him from Dréagg.

For a long time the great line of warriors stood transfixed by the core of evil that spiralled out from the Blaggvald until suddenly the terrible representation faded and released the watchers from its dreadful hold. For a time they did not move, riveted still to the empty lingering space from which Xtlan had poured forth the full might of his power, starkly and immensely brutal. Then, very gradually, as if reluctant to leave the cocoon of evil which he had woven around them, they turned their horses away from the Blaggvald and, following Sienogg and Barll in front, they rode up the slope till they reached the summit. Behind them Eggron shimmered in a thick mellifluous haze, the boundaries of the buildings merging together in a pulsating blur that lent the city the aspect of a gigantic reptilian creature, brooding malevolently now that its life blood, the warriors, had gone.

Then, as they surmounted the ridge and dropped down the other side, Eggron was gone and there was not one amongst them who did not feel the call of destiny urging him on to his apotheosis in the final conflict with the silver forces of Ashgaroth.

CHAPTER XIII

The icy rain lashed down against Bracca's face as he fought his way up the slope. It drove against him in torrential sheets of water that soaked him to the skin and sent rivulets of water running down his back and legs. His birchbark moccasins were sodden and his toes squelched in them as he walked, paddling his way over the wet earth with his head down and his back bent against the wind. He could hardly feel his face; the freezing drops of rain that had been pelting against it all night had sent it numb so that his head seemed apart from his body.

He felt rather than saw the change in the light that heralded dawn and raising his eyes slightly he perceived a gradual lightening of the sky beyond the dark shadow of the mountains that encircled him. The clouds appeared to be breaking apart and yet as he screwed his eyes up against the rain to look for Tara there was something about the colour of what they revealed that struck a chillingly disturbing note of familiarity within him. Savagely he banished the long-forgotten chords of memory that threatened to break in upon him and focused his attention on the mountains that rose up sheer all around, cradling him as if in the hand of a giant, the jagged peaks like upcurled fingers round the palm of flat marshy bog in which he found himself.

189

She was some distance ahead. He could see her, as a deer, her outline blurred by the rain and her light brown coat difficult to spot against the dead bracken. She was waiting for him, nibbling contentedly at some grass and seemingly oblivious to the torrents of water that deluged down upon them.

He thought back to when they had first set out together, leaving Nab and the others behind with the elves. It seemed a long time ago; an age away. For a while they had walked through a sparse upland area of heather and gorse and bilberry threading their way along little narrow paths between the bushes. As they got higher the vegetation had grown more and more scarce until eventually they reached a plateau of bog and marsh. The ground sagged and gurgled as they put their weight on it and they were forced to go slowly, while the rich dark peaty earth was broken into great irregular cracks and fissures into which he kept stumbling as he grew more tired. She had still been in her human form then and, laughing at his misfortune, would turn and help him out. Then, feeling clumsy and ungainly, he would watch her as she danced ahead once more; gliding over the ground, almost floating, as if her feet never really touched it. She had flitted to and fro like a butterfly; sometimes walking alongside him and at other times some distance away and Bracca had been struck by an aura of restlessness and impatience that seemed to dominate her.

They had drunk together from the streams that ran frequently across their path, cupping the brackish water in their hands and feeling its slightly musty, almost scented taste run down their throats. They had eaten together, gathering roots and shrubs as they went along and, despite their scarceness in this time of early winter, she seemed always, by some unerring instinct, to be able to find some when it was needed.

Yet he was aware of a great space between them; a gulf so wide that he had no conception of how to begin to cross it and his whole being ached with the pain of this chasm that

190

kept them so far apart. The intense attraction, both physical and spiritual, that had swept over him at first sight of her had grown even more overpowering as the days had passed. He had become utterly obsessed with her; her perfect elliptical eyes and the depths that swam in them, her delicate oval mouth, her creamy skin with its gentle rose flush on her cheeks and the great tumbling mass of golden hair that danced on her shoulders as she moved. His eyes were constantly drawn to her, drinking in her beauty as a man would slake a ravening thirst at a cool mountain stream. He longed to take her in his arms and hold her; to wrap her against his body in a great wild flurry of love; to lose himself in her and forget the epic significance of their mission. Yet the distance between them was so immense that to act upon his impulses was unimaginable and so he burned quietly while Tara, seemingly unaware of the turmoil within him, continued on her way talking and smiling in a manner that betrayed no knowledge of his yearning for her.

And then, yesterday evening, while they had been settling down for a rest in the lee of a great flat standing stone that gave them some shelter from the driving mist, he had glanced across at her and been shocked by the look on her face of such intense sadness that he felt for a moment as if he had been struck by a body blow. The barriers of his reserve were shattered then and instinctively he had gone across to her, propelled by a surge of sympathy that would not be checked, and, bending down, had grasped her chin gently in his hands and turned her face towards him.

'What is it?' he had asked her anxiously and, angry with herself for letting her guard slip, she had turned sharply away.

'Nothing,' and her voice had a hard edge to it that Bracca had never heard before. Then as if realizing the obvious lie of her answer she had added. 'I am missing Nab and Beth; all the others. I miss my home; and the elves. I do not...' and she paused, uncertain of how to put what she felt into words. 'I do not feel right. My world, the world of Ashgaroth – we

191

are close to the edge of it. Beyond the mountains we shall enter the realm of Dréagg, and I am frightened.'

It was true; all true. These things had all borne down upon her in the past few days but by the side of the real cause of her pain they were insubstantial for she could accept and cope with them. And her heart turned in upon itself with anguish as she perceived the depth of his love for her, felt his breath against her cheek and his hand on her face and the quickening of her own pulse at his nearness. How dear he had become to her already! She felt all the humanity in her awakening like the rising sun on an early morning in spring, sensed it unfolding within her like the petals of a flower, and, try as she would, was utterly unable to stop it. And she cursed the fates for the terrible trick they had played on her and Bracca, a savage twist of irony that she only now realized the tragedy of.

She looked at his face; at his soft warm brown eyes, the fine line of his nose and the strong set of his chin. She watched the breeze playing with his long auburn hair and longed to hold it in her fingers and pull him to her.

Since the time she had first seen him she had known that this moment would come and had dreaded and feared and fought against it, struggling desperately to crush the seeds of her love before they took root. So she had locked her spirit away and put as much space as possible between them, suffering even as he suffered when she saw the results of her behaviour etched on his face; the bewilderment and confusion that clouded his eyes, the tremor in his voice, the stiffness in his attitude and the sag of his shoulders.

And it was beginning to work. He believed her unattainable. Soon, surely, he would have accepted it, got used to it and put all thoughts of love outside his head. Then they would have learnt to be simple companions and he would have been spared the agony of her knowledge.

Now though he had seen her in that one unguarded moment. How she longed to share with him the burden of her secret; to tell him even as Nab had told her so that they could face it together. No! She must not! She dare not! It would put everything at risk. What if he ignored it; cast it aside as irrelevant beneath the power of his love and took her despite the consequences. Neither was it fair to him to declare her feelings; that would render restraint impossible and jeopardize still further the success of their epic mission. So for the moment she would say nothing and do all she could to distance herself from him. She must change again.

Suddenly then, before Bracca's defeated gaze, Tara became a deer. For a timeless fraction of a moment their eyes had clung to each other and then she had turned slowly from him and walked away. Crushing disappointment and the raging anger of intense frustration had collided with each other and emerged as a great roar of pain that escaped from him and echoed round the mountains as if it was the cry of a wild animal that has just received a mortal blow. 'No-o-o!' he howled, and she had felt her heart about to break with the weight of his grief.

Now, in the cold light of a new day, he had managed to push the pain of last night behind him and was using all his concentration in the effort of keeping up with Tara. When, at last, he had caught up to her, she let him rest for a while as she continued grazing and then, just as he was beginning to feel the weariness fade and his limbs start to relax, she moved off again.

Irritation and anger welled up inside him. He felt utterly worn out, cold and hungry. How could she expect him to keep up with her?

'Stop,' he blurted out; his pride giving way to his anger. 'Stop. Let me rest. Just a little while longer.'

She turned then and looked at him and as he returned her gaze he thought he saw a cloud of confusion pass across the deep brown clarity of her eyes. She was annoyed with herself then, for in truth she had forgotten. She was not tired and so it had not occurred to her that he might be. She had only ever known the elves, whose energy never wanes and who sleep only for the joy of dreaming. Bracca was the only

193

human she had met and though she knew of the frailties of man she had not known of their degree so his need for rest had not impressed itself upon her.

She walked back towards him then and lay down near where he sat so that Bracca knew that she had understood. Feeling a little embarrassed at his outburst yet also grateful for the respite it had brought him, he collapsed back down on to the grass and once more felt his weary body descend towards oblivion.

He awoke to the warm wet feel of her tongue licking his face. It contrasted strikingly with the ice cold numbness that still paralysed the rest of his cheeks and forehead. He opened his eyes. Drifting down from the deep grey sky came snowflakes, tumbling towards his face as if aimed directly at him. He blinked and a flake that had caught on his lash melted immediately and ran into his eye. When she saw that he was awake, she backed away to give him room to get to his feet. The ground was covered in a thick layer of white and his moccasins sank into it above his ankles. There was no wind; everything was utterly quiet and still except for the whisper of the flakes as they settled amongst their companions on the earth. He looked up and around. He could not see very far; the falling snow was like a constantly shifting curtain of silver filigree that flitted across his vision and dissipated the view into myriad tiny moving fragments. The nearby trees, some windswept hawthorn and the occasional ash, were already clothed in their new white garments and each twig and branch stood out against the heavy grey backcloth of the storm-riven sky, thrown into stark silhouette by the pale light of the sun as it tried vainly to throw its rays through the wall of snowflakes that had almost blotted it out.

Tara looked at him and he knew they had to move. So, with her head down, she began to walk slowly up the hill and Bracca followed her. At first they went well; the snow was not deep and, as there was no wind, it fell evenly and they soon got used to it. Bracca even began to enjoy it. The intense silence acted upon him like a soothing balm, muffling the janglings of his mind and healing his wounded spirit. The air was pure and sweet and he became intoxicated by it so that he felt as if he was floating above the ground. Higher and higher they climbed, Tara always just ahead while Bracca strode behind her up the hill, revelling in the new-found energy that seemed to propel him along on the crest of a wave.

But then, quite suddenly, a wind sprang up and began to blow the flakes against him. He bent his head against it and forged ahead, trying to ignore the icy blasts that tore their way through his jerkin and seemed to pierce his flesh like needles. His face ached with the cold and so bad was the pain that it almost blinded him. He could only dimly make out the shape of Tara through the swirl of snowflakes that flung themselves angrily around them. Her head was sunk and she was leaning into the wind, picking her hooves up high and putting them down carefully lest the snow concealed a crevasse into which she might fall. Huge drifts had begun to form against the trees and the outcrops of rock and sometimes, almost without realizing it, Bracca found himself wading up to his thighs through great mounds of snow until, stumbling and threshing about angrily, he realized he could go no further and would turn back, retracing his steps until he found a route where the snow was thinner.

Now his legs began to ache and as the cold and wet penetrated the skin of his jerkin and, enveloping his body, began to attack the fibre and marrow of his bones, so a feeling of the most abject despair and misery came upon him. He could not go much further. The wind had increased until now it howled and whined across the slopes towards them, deafening him but at the same time leaving its terrible wail careering around inside his head so that he felt he would go mad with pain and anger. The wet strands of his hair lashed against his face and sent rivulets of icy water running down around his neck while his hands, tucked away inside his jerkin though they were, had nevertheless lost all

195

sensation or feeling and had become useless appendages on the end of his arms. His feet too were dead with the cold and it was all he could do to stay upright so that he lurched about crazily through the blinding haze of the blizzard.

Now, as the grey light of the sky descended rapidly towards darkness, the cold grew even more intense. The moisture on his moustache and beard froze around his mouth and stuck his lips together yet the effort of prising them apart was almost more than his frozen face could stand. His eyelids too were welded together by the cold so that even sight became a conscious and painful struggle.

He stumbled often now, falling into drifts and dragging his way out clumsily, fuelled by a rage both against himself and the inexorable and merciless fury of the storm. And always, just ahead, was the figure of Tara, forging her way stoically through the swirling flakes. Without her to follow, his spirit would have flagged and collapsed a long time ago and he would have succumbed to the almost irresistible temptation to lie down in the soft white cushion at his feet which beckoned him so enticingly with its promise of oblivion. He tried to recall the momentous nature of their mission so that it would inspire him but beside the immediate struggle to keep up with Tara its epic qualities paled almost into insignificance.

Then, suddenly and unexpectedly, his pride gave way to the demands of his body and it screamed at him for rest.

'Stop,' he yelled. 'Tara! Stop!' but the wind snatched at his voice and threw it away into the air where it was immediately lost. So he called again putting every fibre of his strength into the shout, willing her to listen, and as he opened his mouth wide to form the words, his frozen cheeks were flooded with pain. Again his voice was smothered but this time she seemed to hear for she stopped and waited for him to catch up. Slowly he did so and at the sight of her face he was struck by the almost comical effect of the frozen lines of white around her mouth and eyes and the coat of snow that adorned her back.

He could see it then, in the direction she was looking, just ahead of them. A round pool of blackness set in an enormous rock face. A cave! Shelter! His heart leapt and with a great burst of renewed energy he drove himself towards it, aware of nothing save the need to reach it as quickly as he could.

Suddenly he was there, inside the cave, and it was with a blessed sense of relief that he stood for a moment revelling in the calm. His body relaxed, freed from the constant and relentless buffeting that had pummelled it almost to oblivion out in the blizzard, and he grew aware again of his face, hands and feet as the feeling came back to them and they started to ache painfully.

Then Tara came in, bringing with her a flurry of snow and the cold breath of the storm. She shook herself vigorously and a haze of tiny drops of thawing snow flew out from her in a mist that sprayed Bracca's face. He shouted out in surprise and shock, shaking his head to try and rid himself of the icy water that was running down his hair, but when he stopped and looked at her, meaning to be angry, the deer was no longer there. Instead, laughing at his discomfort, her hair lank and dripping with water, stood Tara as a woman.

'I'm sorry,' she said, smiling at him, and at the familiar sound of her voice and in the delight of seeing her again his anger evaporated and he looked away in confusion and embarrassment.

In silence then they both stood in the cave mouth, side by side, watching the blizzard as it continued to rage outside and enjoying the luxury of not being out in it. They said nothing, each of them immersed in the discomfort of their bodies and their own thoughts. Bracca tried desperately to calm the pounding of his heart as, despite himself, the image of the girl beside him set his nerves quivering with excitement and tension; so much so that he almost wished, for the sake of his peace of mind, that she had not changed. Wet from the snow, her spiky eyelashes framed the liquid beauty of her eyes like frosted ferns around a pool; her long

197

green dress clung closely to the curves of her body and her face shone with a vibrance that seemed to set the air between them alight.

Tara saw all this in its effect upon him and was sorry now that her impetuousness had led her to change. Yet she had felt a desperate need to communicate with Bracca, to make contact with him, and had hoped that his ardour might have been dissipated by the drama of the storm. She could not change back just yet; it would not be fair to him and would breed a bitter divide between them that it might never be possible to bridge. Was she making excuses, she asked herself, risking everything in the face of her longing to be with him as a woman? How selfish was she being in pursuing the dictates of her heart at the cost of his emotions? Yet she was powerless to abstain from her desire even though she might cause him to suffer as a result. Dare she reveal to him the awful consequences were they to express their love in the ways of man? Would that make it easier for him to bear? No! She must keep her secret for as long as possible; must adhere to her original decision.

'It was fortunate,' she said, haltingly; not certain of the words to use or how to intone them. 'The cave ... it's a terrible storm.' As if to emphasize her words the wind suddenly increased outside and the snow slashed through the air with renewed fury. 'As if Dréagg was behind it, trying to stop us. But at least now we're out of the wind, and the snow.'

She would have continued but at that moment Bracca, taut with tension, gave vent to his raging emotions in a cathartic outburst of anger.

'Why,' he shouted, not looking at her, 'didn't you stop? I called. You must have heard me. I was completely worn out. Cold. Hungry. Exhausted. And you just went on.' He stopped, feeling embarrassed and a little foolish at the banality of his words. Clumsy and inadequate, they totally failed in their attempt to communicate even a fragment of the desperation he had felt out there in the storm. But then he continued,

198

voicing the question that was uppermost in his mind.

'And why did you change to a deer? It's difficult for me. . .' but he said no more for fear of revealing more of himself than he wanted to.

But her reply 'It was easier, in the snow,' seemed so logical that he was satisfied by the explanation. 'And back there, in the snow,' she went on. 'I'm sorry. I forgot. I don't get tired; the elves don't.'

So Bracca was appeased but now, with their source of conversation dried up, the awkwardness returned and once more silence towered between them like a mountain. Night was closing in and as they stood watching the blizzard, the white flakes speckling the dark grey backcloth of the lowering sky, the light inside the cave dwindled to darkness so that when they turned back together into it they could see nothing. But then, as Bracca's eyes grew more accustomed to the dense blackness, he noticed a faint shimmering aura of silver light emanating out from Tara's body. She stood next to him and as she moved slowly forward, further into the cave, he followed her until she stopped.

'We can go no further,' she said. 'We've come to the end. We'll sleep here.'

They lay down on the hard earth floor, facing out towards the pale circle of light at the cave entrance. Bracca had thought that sleep would overtake him immediately and he closed his eyes initially under that assumption but to his surprise and annoyance he found that his mind would not be still and sleep did not come. Strange images flickered inside his eyelids. The wild shaggy figure of Barll, charging towards him on a horse with his face contorted into a leering grimace of triumph; Melvaig, whose features seemed to liquify and then re-form as the face of Nab; Melvaig and Nab, Morven and Beth, all shifting in and out of focus and fluctuating in clarity so that he became agitated and disturbed. And then other pictures crowded in, unnameable yet disconcertingly familiar; vast sweeps of dead brown sky stretching off to the horizon in a patchwork of drab and flaccid colour; a sinister black citadel perched on a pinnacle of rock that rose sheer from an arid desert wasteland and whose atmosphere of evil struck a chill of fear into his heart; himself as a young boy fighting others of his own age, with a club, in a kind of arena. Then other images, clearer and more distinct; the faces of Nabbeth and Shayll, frozen in the pain-filled masks of death that had burned themselves into his consciousness; the glimpse he had had of Golconda just after the heron had set him down; and finally the white speckled flicker of snowflakes as they tumbled across his vision, as if he was still outside in the storm.

Then there came into his mind, over and above all these yet somehow intermingled with them, a picture of Tara, naked. It arrived unbidden, this intensely erotic vision, yet while he tried to reject it he found himself powerless to resist its temptation and so for a few brief heart-stopping moments his mental gaze worshipped at the shrine of her imagined sexuality before with a shock of horror he flung his eyes open and sat up suddenly, banging his head on the stone as he did so.

'What's wrong?' she said, her voice cutting through his nightmare and bringing him back to reality with a jolt. 'Bracca. Are you all right?'

As he tried to answer her the image that had so lately been in his head came back to him and a flood of guilt, shame and embarrassment swept over him so that he found it impossible to speak.

'Bracca! What's the matter?' she said again, her voice strained with anxiety, and he felt her hand rest lightly on his arm. For the first time then he realized he was trembling and he forced himself to answer her.

'Yes,' and his words sounded odd and distant, as if they came from a total stranger. 'I'm all right. Just dreaming ... bad dreams.' He paused, waiting for a reaction of some sort but there was none. 'Thank you.'

'I can't sleep either,' she said, as if she had not heard him mention the dreams or, if she had, did not believe him. 'My spirit is racing; it will not be calm. There is too much, too much...' and her voice trailed away for a brief moment before she continued. 'We will talk. I will tell you of myself, and you ... you must describe your life to me; in Xtlan and in Haark.'

So Bracca lay back down with his eyes open, staring into the blackness and let the magic of Tara's voice weave pictures in the air above his head. She described her childhood in the forest; her home with Nab and Beth in the giant grey oak where they played and laughed and sang together. She told him of the others from Silver Wood; of Sam the dog, born and raised among humans, from whom she learnt of the strange ways of man, of Warrigal, the wise old owl, who talked to her of the time before the First Holocaust and who explained the story of Nab to her in the epic quest for the Faradawn. She learnt woodlore from him and he related to her the legends and myths that had once formed the fabric and structure of the world of the animals. And often when he talked, serious and grave, his large round eyes fixed and penetrating, Perryfoot the hare would sit beside him, interjecting occasionally, adding little bits of his own, funny stories, little humorous comments at which she would burst out laughing and Warrigal would look stern and intensely displeased at him.

From Perryfoot she learnt the art of humour, playing with him even as, many ages before, her father Nab had played. Running and catching and rolling and cuffing, chasing each other through the bracken, hiding behind trees and in hollows, leaping out at each other from the undergrowth.

And always there was Brock, solemn yet gentle, his gravity always tinged with a sparkle of mischief. Again and again he would tell her, for she never tired of hearing it, of how he had seen Nab left as a tiny baby by two strange humans on a snowy night in Silver Wood and of how he had dragged the little bundle through the snow to his sett. He told her of his sow Tara, after whom she had been named, and of her first angry reaction to his request that they bring the baby up as their own. But she had quickly grown to love him, more even than her own life, and he in turn had loved her dearly so that when she died, murdered savagely and cruelly by the men with their burning gas which they had pumped into the sett, both he and Brock, neither of whom had then been in Silver Wood, had shared each other's grief and had nursed each other through the horror of their loss. And, as he talked of Tara's death, Brock's grief had brought tears to her namesake's eyes and an ache of sadness to her spirit.

Then Tara told Bracca of Beth, in the way that Beth had described her life to Tara; the years she had spent as a little girl in a human family, learning to read and write, to play music, to dance; her holidays by the sea, her pet cat, her friends, her mother and father and two brothers. And then her meeting with Nab, the love she had felt for this strange wild boy and the destiny that had called her so that she had left with him on his quest. From Beth, Tara had learnt of the ways of humans before the terrible destruction came; of their little ways, of beds and houses, of knives and forks, of cameras and cars and radios and televisions, of shops and books, of fridges and ice cream, of tennis and football, of school and work, of Christmas and parties. And she learnt of their other ways too; of greed and arrogance and cruelty and torture towards both their own kind and the animals as man fulfilled his destiny as the instrument of Dréagg's revenge on the world of Ashgaroth.

And Tara described the summer evenings when they would all go for walks together through the forest with the scent of wild rose and honeysuckle heavy on the breeze and the air filled with the songs of birds; blackbirds and chaffinches, larks and curlews, the cooing of pigeons and the crying of rooks. Down to the river they would walk, to play along the bank or splash in the clear water before wending their way home.

Sometimes they would meet the elves on their wanderings and then they would stay for either a small chat or maybe the whole evening, sharing their food and the marvellous elven wines before wandering back by the light of the moon.

And as she grew, she got to know the elves. At first she only met those who dwelt in the forest, the mighty Wychnor, Lord of the Forests and the Green Growing Things, Reev and many of the others, but later as she wandered outside the woods into the high mountains and amongst the rocks and crags she met the strange and awesome figure of Malcoff, Lord of the Mountains, with Curbar his mystic eagle and others of the mountain elves, Morár the piper, and the battle chiefs, Morbann and Mendokk. She spent much time with the elves and her elven nature developed and grew even as her human nature and her animal nature had.

In the winter, when the snow lay thick in the forest, they would not venture far from the great oak, only walking out during the short days to marvel at the transformation of the forest into a sparkling world of white crystal at those times when the sun shone down from a bright blue sky. At other times, when the icy winds blew through the trees and the snow fell in great droves of flakes then they would stay inside, huddled together for warmth and they would tell tales of the old days, of Silver Wood and of the quest for the Faradawn. So Beth learnt of Sterndale the Fierce, king of the pheasants, and his companion Thirkelow the Swift, leader of the pigeons. She grew to know and love Rufus, the great red fox; Bruin the Brave, Brock's grandfather; and all the other animals of Silver Wood. And she thrilled to the stories they told, sharing their hardships and their pain, their joys and their triumphs, as they journeyed through the land on their quest to gather the three Faradawn or essences of the elven kingdoms; the Forests, the Seas and the Mountains, and so save the world of Ashgaroth from Dréagg's darkness.

She stopped speaking and for a long time there was silence as she mused inwardly on all the evocative memories that had been revived by her narration. Bracca too was quiet, letting the pictures created by her words take root in his mind so that he might feel he had really known her all her life. They were beautiful images and as they filled his head he thought back to his own life and all the darkness and evil that he had witnessed and the terrors he had experienced for while she had basked in the shelter of Ashgaroth he had been exposed to the full glare of Dréagg's black tyranny.

It occurred to him then that he might have to recount his past to her but he was reluctant to start, lacking confidence in his ability to translate his experiences into words and unwilling to inflict his pain upon her. So he said nothing until after a little while she spoke.

'And now you,' she said, and her voice in the darkness was soft and gentle and lilted like music. 'I want to hear about you. Please tell me.'

So he told of his early life in Ruann, barely remembered save through Melvaig's reminiscences, and of how the fragile tranquillity of those days had been torn apart when Xtlan's warriors had descended on his village and captured his mother, Morven. And he related to her as well as he could the frantic search for Morven that Melvaig and he had embarked upon and the horrors that had faced them in the terrible world of Xtlan. Yet always, set amongst the terror of those times, was the faith and love without which his spirit could not have survived; Melvaig's love for him and for Morven, the great and ultimately tragic love of Shuinn, the red-haired giant, the sacrifice of Arkron and, more recently, the depth of his feelings for Shayll. And interwoven with all this was the power and strength of Melvaig's vision.

As Tara listened with mounting revulsion to the catalogue of terrors that Bracca had faced in his short life, both in Eggron and during his struggles with Barll, she found her perception of him changing profoundly. The attraction she had felt for him before, now deepened and broadened in the context of the new light in which she saw him. How perfect, how halcyon had her own life been in contrast. The serene idyll of her experience made her feel ashamed; almost as if it had been achieved at the cost of his suffering. Yet she knew that this was not so and that it was to preserve that serenity and to destroy the evil that Bracca had brought before her that they were now journeying to Spath. Now was the time

204

for her to play her part in the struggle between Ashgaroth and Dréagg. Gone now was the safety and security of her time with Nab and Beth; when she left them she entered the arena of the War; a world where man, Dréagg's disciple and ambassador, reigned supreme over all things and the awesome power of the seeds of cruelty and arrogance flourished unfettered. And she saw now what she had never really understood before when Nab had talked to her of the nature of her destiny; that Bracca and she were to each other as the sun is to the moon or the rain is to the sun; as the sky is to the earth or the land to the sea. Without Bracca's experience under the yoke of Dréagg, forged on the anvil of his epic lineage, she would have been helpless before the awesome powers of the darkness. Yet Bracca, without her elven nature and the purity of her spirit to guide him, would be as a voice raging in the wilderness, a force without direction. Her presence at his side would be a constant reminder of the reality of Ashgaroth, the magic of the elves and the ultimate purpose of their divine mission.

And that she should find herself growing to love him, knowing that he too loved her, was so natural, so perfect a consummation of their alliance that it struck her now more then ever how intensely cruel was the awful blight upon their relationship; the secret which she burned to reveal to Bracca yet was still constrained from doing so by Nab's prohibition to her.

Finally he finished his tale, ending with his flight across the sea with Golconda. As he stopped and the cave was once again plunged into silence, his mind refused to acknowledge the ending and for some time his consciousness remained in the echoing hallways of his horrendous past. And she, sensing his turmoil, stretched out her arm in the darkness and took his hand, caressing it with her fingers in an attempt to convey to him all the love she felt welling up in her heart.

Feeling her gentle touch Bracca's soul was stilled and for a little time they lay quietly, glorying in their contact with each other, until eventually Tara whispered to him, 'Can you sleep?' And her voice caressed his heart like the song of a lark so that upon closing his eyes he immediately drifted away into a deep and dream-free sleep. Tara too, on hearing the steady and rhythmic pace of his breathing, soon fell asleep but her dreams were sprinkled with silver star-dust and took her back to the days of her childhood by the great grey oak, yet now alongside her was Bracca, also as a child, for so much a part of her had he now become that she could not envisage ever having lived without him.

And Ashgaroth looked down upon these two children of the apocalypse and he smiled, for though his heart was heavy with their affliction and the awesome weight of their responsibility, he was gratified at the love they had found for each other.

CHAPTER XIV

All the rest of that night they slept, then the whole of the next day and the following night. Many times Tara woke and seeing him still asleep refrained from waking him, allowing herself to float happily back into the world of her dreams. And each time, before going back to sleep, she gripped his hand a little tighter as if trying to tell him, while he was unconscious, what she could not when he was awake. In that brief moment before she dropped off she was dimly aware of the howl of the wind outside and the wall of driving snow across the cave entrance but they failed to penetrate the blissful cocoon of sleep which had wrapped itself so comfortingly around her.

It was Bracca who woke up to the grim grey light of early dawn. For a brief moment he wondered where he was and then a little thrill of excitement went pulsing through his veins. At first he was unable to locate the source of it but then memories of his talk with Tara came flooding back; the closeness that had developed between them, the thrill of communication and shared understanding, the feel of her hand in his. It was not there now. In sleep it had become limp and fallen out of his grip and lay with the fingers curled like the petals of a half open flower on the dark earth floor at her side.

He looked at her as she slept, wallowing in the luxury of being able to stare at her without embarrassment, and marvelled again at her beauty, aware of his whole being crying out to wrap her in his arms. But she felt the force of his presence through her light covering of sleep and awoke to find his eyes upon her, seeing them cloud over immediately with confusion and shame, as if he had been disturbed in the middle of something indecent or licentious. So feeling guilty at being the unwitting cause of his discomfort and wishing to reassure him as to her feelings she quickly reached out and took his hand in hers again.

'Hello,' she said. 'You've slept well. I woke up but let you sleep on. How do you feel? You look better.'

He looked at her and she knew that his disquiet had subsided. His voice was strong and clear and he looked her straight in the eyes.

'Yes,' he replied. 'Yes, I am, I had a good sleep. We must have slept all night; it's dawn outside. But I think it's still snowing; and I can still hear the wind.'

'We slept all yesterday too.'

'Did we! I didn't think. . .' His voice tailed off as he tried to focus his concentration on whether the wasted day mattered or not and then, as if reading his thoughts, Tara spoke.

'We mustn't waste much longer,' she said. 'The forces of Dréagg will be well on their way, we must reach Spath before them. Come, let's look outside.'

They got up from the cave floor and walked over to the entrance. An awesome sight met their eyes.

A driving wall of snow filled the space between earth and sky with a great grey mass of whirling flakes and as they peered through it they could see a strange and mysterious landscape of white; mountains that stretched up to lose themselves in the heights of the storm and then swept down into plunging valleys and ravines, the surface constantly undulating and shifting as the wind blew the fine white powder into a ceaselessly moving pattern of whorls and eddies.

For some time they stood still and watched in silence, mesmerized by the majestic power of the storm, until Tara spoke.

'We can't go out into that,' she said. 'We wouldn't live till night; let alone find our way.' She was following Roosdyche, the ancient pathways known only to the elves and the animals, and her feeling for them would be lost in the storm. 'We shall have to stay here,' she continued, 'until the storm stops.'

Bracca was not sorry; the prospect of going back out into that awful freezing wind and the relentlessly driving snow had filled him with dread, refreshed though he was by his sleep. He was extremely cold; the air seemed to have penetrated the protective covering of flesh and had incarcerated his bones so that all his joints seemed to be jumping about in a frenzied attempt to calm the restless aching of his limbs. And he was suddenly, overwhelmingly, hungry; his stomach yawning away beneath him in a great empty void that demanded satiety. Where would they find food now; not even Tara could find anything to eat in the cave. Now, as the desperateness of their situation bore down upon him, a feeling of panic began to spread up from his bowels and he fought to control his emotions. Gone now was the cosy anaesthesia of sleep to be replaced by the stark reality of their plight.

And it was at this moment that, turning back into the gloomy half light of the cave, he saw a small round opening in the far wall about the same size as the entrance. The light reflected dully from the space within and moving forward curiously to examine it more closely Bracca saw that, set at about a foot's depth inside, the interior of the opening was completely closed off by a flat expanse of some substance he did not recognize. It was extremely smooth, hard and so cold to the touch that his hand almost stuck to the surface. He realized then, with a rush of excitement, that it must have been made by man.

'What is it?' he said, turning to Tara, and she, equally

fascinated, replied that she did not know. Instinctively he pushed it. He could feel a slight movement. He pushed again, harder this time, and with a groan of protest the door opened and he could see a space on the other side. This time he put his shoulder to it and heaved for all he was worth. The door suddenly swung wide and losing his balance he found himself tumbling down a short flight of what he guessed were steps to land at the bottom with a shock. Dazed, he sat up and saw Tara standing in the opening, framed against the light, laughing. It was a marvellous sound and it filled his heart with joy to hear her.

'I'm glad you think it's funny,' he said, pretending to be offended. 'I could have hurt myself.' In fact he had bruised himself quite badly as his knees and elbows banged against the stone.

'I'm sorry,' she said. 'It's just ... you looked so funny, so clumsy ... and the look on your face!' At her recollection of his shocked expression she started laughing again and he, in a mock show of anger, interrupted by shouting to her to help him up.

She walked down the short flight of steps and, bending down, put her arm round his waist and lifting him to his feet, helped him across to a kind of seat that was next to one of the walls.

'What is this place?' he said, half to himself and half to Tara, as he sat down on the soft padded seat. It was darker in here than where they had come from but some light came from a gap in the rock high above their heads and as their eyes grew accustomed to the gloom they looked around themselves with a growing sense of wonder and excitement. The cave was filled with the paraphernalia of human occupation yet none of it was like anything they had ever seen before. There were a number of beds up against the walls but they were so neat, so perfectly shaped, and they stood one on top of the other. They saw cooking utensils, vessels to drink from and tools to eat with; yet all made with unfamiliar materials and barely recognizable from any they had ever seen before. Oddly shaped tables and seats littered the floor on which were objects that were totally alien to them; flat boards regularly patterned in squares with small round things arranged upon them, other boards strewn with different things, long thin pointed stick-like articles which left a mark when Bracca scratched the point of one on a board.

They walked round in a daze, utterly absorbed in the plethora of mysteries that lay about them. A small rectangular-shaped object with round shiny knobs on that turned and a long thin piece that protruded from the top; a number of articles that he recognized as books, similar to the book of the Faradawn that Melvaig had brought from Xtlan and left with the Stagg, though with different pictures in them. Scattered on the beds were what appeared to be small animals but which, when Tara picked them up and felt them, had obviously never been alive; yet they were very soft and their faces were strangely attractive.

There were oddly shaped shoes on the floor and peculiar clothes. Tentatively they tried them on and laughed at themselves and each other, dressed in this odd attire. At one end of the cave, on a table, they saw a small mirror and they studied their faces minutely in it, amazed by the clarity of the reflection. There was a brush which Tara guessed was for hair, like the carved wooden combs she had been used to using, and she used it to straighten out her tangled mane. And all the time she moved through this bizarre world, the words of her mother came tumbling back through time. Memories of the long descriptions Beth had given her of the time Before-the-War were reawakened by the objects strewn about the cave: for Beth had been concerned that Tara knew as much as possible about the human world, both good and evil, before the First Holocaust. And these unfamiliar objects were like keys unlocking this chest of memories so that she was able to tell Bracca about the toys and pens and books and games, the wash-basin and toilet, toothpaste, soap and flannel, the clock and the radio; so that they were transported back in time to the days of cars and planes, of shops and money and houses, and Bracca lived it even as Tara re-created it.

And then, standing on one of the shelves, Tara suddenly saw a picture. It was of three people, a man, a woman and a little boy, and it was like no other picture she had ever seen before in that it was minutely accurate in every detail, a perfect reproduction, and when Tara had taken it down and wiped the dust off it, it shone out with natural colours.

'They must be the ones who lived here before,' said Bracca, brimming over with curiosity as he stared, fascinated, at the picture. It was the oddness of their clothes that most interested him; that and the strange feeling that these people, from before the holocaust, had used these same chairs and tables and beds and cups that now surrounded him and Tara. There they were, looking out from the picture, smiling happily, their arms around each other, totally carefree. In the background there was a building of some sort which Bracca assumed to be their home. Large, built of stone and perfectly shaped with doors and windows, while in front there lay a great flat expanse of uniformly green grass with precise patterns of colour where flowers grew. And as Tara looked she wondered whether Beth had ever lived in a place such as this.

'Why did they come to this place?' said Bracca, his attention riveted on these three faces from another world.

'I don't know,' replied Tara, and then again, to herself, 'I don't know.' The little boy had captivated her; his perfect face smiling out from the picture with complete innocence and total honesty had struck chords within her that she never knew were there. She wanted desperately to hold him, to protect and cherish him and guard him from harm and the forces of darkness. She ached to share with him all the good things; to show him the fragrant green gentleness of spring with larks and bluebells and curlews and to walk with him through the amber hues of autumn, kicking the leaves and hunting for toadstools in the evening mists.

She put the picture back reluctantly, unnerved by the wave

of unfamiliar emotions that had swept over her. How she envied the mother! And then she found herself growing disturbed and uneasy as she wondered what had happened to them, the suffering they might have endured, and as she thought of the little boy in torment writhing in the terrible throes of the holocaust, she was struck by such an acute and piercing sense of distress that she cried out involuntarily and Bracca asked if she was all right. 'Yes,' she replied, not able to explain her hurt and fighting to clear her mind of the awful images that assailed her.

'Yes,' she said again, and then her eyes focused on a wide wooden ledge that came out from the wall with a seat pushed up against it and she saw a small sheet of something white pinned down to the surface by the weight of a large stone. She moved closer. There were marks on it, moving across from one side to the other. Writing! With hands that trembled in apprehension and excitement she carefully picked it up. Could she read it? How often had Beth tried to teach her to read and to write words, using birch bark or stone on stone, determined that Tara should have some knowledge of the skills of communication used by her people. How she wished now she had paid better attention instead of letting the elven side of her mind dance away with her concentration. Still she had learnt something from Beth's tuition and as she looked at the writing she began slowly and incredulously to read out what had been written so long ago, in that other time. She read the words haltingly, not knowing the meaning of some of them and not certain she had said them correctly, but still the message of the note echoed tragically through time.

'I wonder who you are, reading this?' she began, and Bracca felt an eerie chill run down his spine.

'I wonder how many will survive in the end. Strange that I should write like this to someone I don't know, or maybe to no one, but I want to leave something, just in case. My name is Charles Brent. My wife is Susan and our son is called Tom. We came here straight from the city just before it happened.

213

Luckily I was at home; I'd taken the day off work. A lot did. The jams were terrible but I knew a lot of back ways and we made it. I suppose I thought we were lucky at the time: to get out. This is only the third week. It seems forever. Can anything ever have been normal? It seems impossible to think back to before; it still seems unbelievable.

'The radio stopped last night. The last broadcast. We are to look after ourselves. Those who aren't dead are sick and those who aren't sick are scavenging. We are all sick but Tommy is worse than either of us. I can't bear to watch him. He vomits a lot and has constant diarrhoea. His throat is sore and he has now started to have nosebleeds. He has gone very pale and cries a lot. I tried to play dominoes with him today but he couldn't concentrate. Neither could I, so I was secretly relieved. All of us now just lie on our beds in silence apart from making meals. Thank goodness we had plenty of soya. The trouble now is, the water's run out. I don't know how long we've got – any of us; though Tommy will go first. I'm not going to wait here any longer. None of us can bear it. It feels so closed in, so isolated. Susan and I have decided that anything is better than this so we've decided to go out.' Here the writing began to slope down across the page towards the bottom corner and the letters became badly formed and difficult to read. Still, Tara managed to decipher most of the words though she read them out very slowly.

'We're taking some food with us; chocolate, biscuits and some packets of soya stew in case we find some water. And a pan. And the gun, with the few bullets we've got left. I've got four bottles of wine and three bottles of sleeping pills. When things get hopeless out there we'll get drunk and finish it off with the pills. Thank God Sue had the foresight to get them early on in those strange last few days; before the shops ran out. I'm looking forward to the end now.' Tara turned over to the next, and last page.

'It's a relief to think we shall be getting out of it. It's just not worth the effort. Even if we'd all been well I'd have felt the same. There's a lot more I'd like to say but it all seems

214

pointless now. If you can make use of anything you find please take it. I'm going now; Tommy and Sue are waiting for me by the door. Odd. Now it's come to it I'm reluctant to stop writing. All I can do is wish you luck whoever you are. I don't envy you. Goodbye.

Charles Brent.'

They both continued to look fixedly at the writing for some time after Tara had finished reading, mesmerized by the spell it had cast upon them and hesitant to take their eyes off the paper lest the strangely compelling image formed by the words be dissipated, never to be recaptured again. So neither of them spoke, content to let their minds wander in the mysteries of the tragic drama that had been played out in this place by the three people whose faces still smiled out at them from the picture on the ledge.

'From before the holocaust.' Bracca's whispered words, voicing the incredulity they both felt, finally broke the silence. Only then did Tara look up and with a conscious effort to shake off the poignant shroud of sadness that had descended upon her, she put the writing back where it had lain before and turning to Bracca, spoke in a voice that trembled with tension.

'Come on,' she said. 'Let's look around and see if there is anything left that we can use. He said we should take it.'

A stone shelf ran at waist height. All the way around the walls of the cave and under this there were a series of small doors made of wood. On bending down to look at them, Bracca realized they they opened by sliding them along. Inside were a number of different shapes and sorts of container. Could it be food? Bracca's stomach and his mouth went dry at the prospect. They started to lift the containers out; small round shiny ones, tall thin ones with some kind of a stopper on top and square ones with square lids.

Eagerly they set about trying to open them. Bracca found a knife and resting its point on the top of one of the round silvery containers, he banged the handle with a stone that he had picked up from the floor. It pierced the surface. He

215

moved the point a little way along and made another hole. Then he repeated the operation over and over again until he was able to get the knife under the top and by lifting gently prise it off. Apprehensively they looked inside and saw an orangey-red liquid filled with small ovals, roughly the size of a little finger nail. The smell was pleasant, slightly sweet and it made Bracca's mouth water in anticipation.

'Go on. Try some,' said Tara, laughing at his eagerness, and he needed no more encouragement. Without hesitation he put his fingers inside and scooping out a dollop put it in his mouth and began to chew. The taste was strange at first, quite rich and heavy, but he soon got used to it and started to enjoy it, letting the feel of the food spread through his body. He gestured to Tara to join him and she too, with intense curiosity, scooped some out and delicately began to eat it.

'It's good, isn't it,' he said, and with her mouth full she nodded her agreement.

Very soon they had finished the first container and while Tara wiped out the inside with her finger Bracca set to work opening a second similar container and it was not long before that too was empty. A third container revealed something different altogether; small, uneven white spheres, a lot larger than the others and rather more solid. They were in a clear liquid (it could have been water) and Bracca and Tara ate them by holding one in their fingers and biting pieces off. The taste, rather like a bland nut, went very well with the other stuff and Bracca lost himself in the sensations that flooded his hungry body. And then, suddenly, he was full and with a contented sigh he leant back against the wall.

'That was marvellous,' he said, and Tara, who had watched him guzzling with amusement and pleasure, simply smiled. She did not need food in the same way that he did and she had joined him partly out of curiosity and partly so that he would not feel uncomfortable. 'Strange,' he added, 'to think that that was what they used to eat the whole time. And to have kept for so long. I wonder what they were. And there are quite a few more containers too. We must take them with us

216

when we go. Look, there's a carrier over there,' and he pointed to a large green square container, made of some sort of cloth, on a hard metal frame with lots of straps coming off it. 'I think I could fasten it to my back.' He paused. 'Did you enjoy it?'

'Yes. It tasted lovely. And it's done me good.'

'I'm thirsty now. I wonder what they had to drink. It looks like liquid in that tall thin container. I'll try and take the top off.'

He picked it up and using his knife took the soft covering off the narrow top to expose a small circular opening filled with some substance that felt very soft when Bracca stuck the point into it. He tried to prise it out but only succeeded in cutting it up into little pieces which he then shook out. Eventually it was all gone and he put his nose to the opening and sniffed warily. A wonderful warm smell met his nostrils, smooth and rich with a slightly sharp edge to it that hinted at an exciting taste. He sniffed again, strongly this time, and the smell went straight to his head so that for an instant he felt himself spinning.

'You try it first this time,' he said, handing the container over to Tara. It was surprisingly heavy and when Tara took it she could see the liquid sloshing around through its dark red opalescence. She placed the mouth of the container to her lips and tilted her head back gently until the liquid began to trickle into her mouth and then she lowered the container and swallowed. It seemed to burn her throat as it went down and then when it hit her stomach she felt as if she had suddenly been filled with fire. She coughed and tears came to her eyes yet strangely the feeling was not unpleasant and the sensation reminded her of the wonderful elven drinks that she was used to from before; made from dandelions or elderflowers or clover, camomile, coltsfoot or any of a myriad other plants or flowers that grew in the woods and grasslands. She took another mouthful and passed it to Bracca who was looking with surprise at the reaction it had caused in Tara.

217

'Come on, it'll warm you up,' she said, and her voice sounded strangely rasping and hoarse.

Warily Bracca took a swig and the feel of the liquid in his mouth and throat shocked him at first as it blazed its way down through his gullet but, as with Tara before him, there was something about the feeling that it engendered, the glowing aftermath that warmed every part of his body with a smouldering tingle of satisfaction, that cried out for more and he had another drink before giving it back to her.

Back and forth went the container, from one to the other, and as it gradually became empty so Bracca and Tara found their consciousness expanding until it seemed as if the entire universe was contained within the parameters of their existence. The inhibitions and limitations which had previously formed the boundaries of their separate personalities seemed to fall away like melting snow before the glowing waves of warmth that flowed out from the drink.

Bracca took the last drop and then stood up with the intention of getting another container of the stuff but as he did so his head began to spin and he found himself swaying on his feet. He fought hard to steady himself but try as he might he found it impossible.

'I can't stand up,' he said. 'I can't stand!' and to his surprise he started laughing. He put out a hand to steady himself on the stone ledge but he missed and stumbled and then Tara too began to laugh.

'Here, I'll help you,' she said, and started to get up on to her feet but like Bracca she found herself unable to stay upright and she ended up hanging on to his hand and trying to pull herself straight.

'No,' she said. 'No – you're right. It's not easy,' and she became convulsed in a fit of giggles as he bravely attempted to prevent her from falling back down on to the floor. After a few perilous moments in which they both teetered dangerously on the edge of collapse he succeeded in keeping her up and they set off together around the cave in paroxysms of laughter, lurching and swaying from side to side with their

218

arms around each other.

'It's the drink,' spluttered Bracca, when the chuckling subsided for a moment. 'It must be the drink. Come on, we must find some more,' and he dragged Tara back across to where they had found the lot they had just drunk. Arriving at his destination he bent down without thinking to pick another container up. It was a fatal mistake. He stumbled forward and fell over, knocking his arm on the ledge and pulling Tara down with him. Suddenly then he found himself lying on the floor with the weight of Tara's body pressing down on top of him, just as she had fallen. Her face was barely a hand's length from his; so near that her hair fell down on each side to form curtains and the sweet fragrance of her breath, tinged with the heady aroma of the drink, assailed his senses with an overpowering awareness of her physical closeness. Utterly overawed by the intensely sensuous intimacy he shared with her in the darkness of the curtained room around their faces, the wonderful ragged gaiety of the drink suddenly vanished and his mind became as clear as a starlit night. For a few moments the infinity of time stood between them, suspended by the divinity of love, and then Bracca whispered her name gently, as if it were a prayer, and he felt the pulsing of her breasts quicken where they lay pressed against his heart.

'Tara,' he repeated, and, slowly, almost imperceptibly, her face drew nearer until her mouth was barely a finger's breadth away from his. Then, with his heart beating wildly, he gently lifted his head until he felt the softness of her lips against his own and as they came together and the magical ecstasy of this first delicate contact flooded through their souls so they became lost in the sweetness of each other, aware only of the world that existed between them. For a long time they did not dare to move for fear of disturbing the enchantment but then the hunger for each other grew too great and in a sudden outpouring of passion they wrapped their arms around each other and embraced so fiercely that their bodies seemed to melt together into one while their lips parted to allow their questing tongues to meet in a deliciously sensuous expression of their love.

Wildly they rolled around on the floor of the cave, oblivious to everything save their glorious unity, yet even as they did so Dréagg was looking down at them with euphoric anticipation, urging them to unite in the ultimate consummation of their carnal desires. And it may have been the intensity of his wishes or maybe it was the warning knell that sounded in her spirit that caused the dark shadow of reality to descend upon Tara's inflamed passion. Then, with an icy rush of horror, she realized the terrible danger they were in and, fighting to clear her mind of the clouds of ecstasy which enveloped it, she opened her eyes and, as gently as she was able, tried to extricate herself from Bracca's embrace. Instantly he froze and after a moment's icy stillness he threw open his eyes and pushed himself away from her. At the sight of his wild and angry glare Tara's heart was gripped with pain for she could see the tangled skein of his emotions racing across his vision. Humiliation; the bitter taste of rejection; blind confusion and blazing anger poured out from him to her across the plunging void that had suddenly opened up between them.

'No!' he screamed, and the anguish in his voice was so terrible that Tara was momentarily stunned by his torment. She had to reach him! Make him understand. It would be all right then. It had to be all right. Oh! Why had it happened? She cursed the drink for the effect it had had on them. Perhaps it would have happened anyway, sooner or later. She didn't know. She couldn't think; she had to reach him.

'Bracca. Please listen. You don't understand. Let me explain. I'll have to . . .' but he would not let her finish.

'I understand,' he blurted out. 'I understand too well. You've been playing with me. Playing.'

'No! You're wrong. Wrong!' and the resolve to communicate which had prevented her disintegration suddenly evaporated in the face of his refusal to hear her and, turning her back to him, she burst into tears.

He stopped his ranting then as the sound of her weeping penetrated his grief-befuddled brain. He was puzzled at first, puzzled and confused, but this soon gave way to concern for her since his love was so great that the sight of her distress made him forget his own pain. Forcing himself to be calm he slowly moved towards her feeling clumsy, awkward and embarrassed.

'Tara.' His voice sounded strange, as if it came from far away, and he hardly recognized it. 'Tara. No. Please stop crying. I didn't mean it. I'm sorry I was angry.'

Gently he put his hands on her shoulders; wary now – so different from the ferocity of their · embrace just a few moments before, and turned her around to face him. Somehow her sadness had added a new and greater depth to her beauty; the tears on her cheeks and the glitter around her eyes made her seem strangely fragile for the first time since he had known her. Gone was the veneer of elven calm; now she lay open, vulnerable, her humanity exposed, and his desire to comfort and protect her was so strong that he ached with it. Slowly he drew her closer until he was holding her against him with her head on his chest and she in turn responded by putting her arms around his waist.

They were still for a time and then she shivered a little as if shaking herself free from the last remnants of her tears.

'It's my fault,' she said. 'I should have told you. I didn't want this to happen. I tried to stop it. That's why ... I changed – to stop you from loving me. It's not fair on you...' She broke off and her voice began to quiver with anxiety. Holding him away from her she looked up into his eyes.

'Bracca,' she said. 'There's something I must tell you ... about us... Something we must talk about. Please. You must listen carefully and know that what I have to say causes me just as much pain as it causes you.' She stopped for a moment and then, taking his hand, led him gently towards two wooden stools in the middle of the floor. When they were seated she continued, begging Ashgaroth for the right words to reveal to him the fateful prohibition on their love.

221

'You know,' she said slowly, holding him with her eyes, 'of the two powers of life, Magic and Logic, the Duain Elrondin. Ashgaroth bestowed the first of these upon the elves so that they are of Magic. This power also, which was in Nab from the beginning, he gave to Beth after the time of the First Holocaust and so it was that when I was born, I too was of Magic even as the elves and also of Logic as was in Nab and Beth.' She paused to let her words take root before continuing.

'You Bracca, are of the Eldron, the Friends. Yet the power that is within you is of the second of the Duain Elrondin, Logic, for you are of the race of man created by Dréagg as an instrument of revenge against the earth, the jewel of Ashgaroth's creation, and his creatures, the animals.

'So it is that whereas in me there is both magic and logic, in you there is logic alone. It is for this reason that there can be no union between us for magic and logic will not lie together and if they are joined in that way then one must give way before the other and be extinguished. If you and I made love to each other then either I would lose the power of magic or you would lose the power of logic. Our powers must be intact; without my magic we would be consumed by the darkness of Spath the moment we entered and could never survive: finding the Droon would then be an impossibility. And it is only your hand, Bracca, the hand of logic as it is possessed by man, which can sever the Thread of Unity and Separate the Seeds one from the other, so destroying man. So if you lose the power of logic, your task becomes impossible. Then the light of Ashgaroth will be extinguished forever and the world will languish in torment for all time beneath the heel of man and the dark shadow of Dréagg.'

She stopped talking now for there was no more for her to say. Now he knew it all; the awful trick that fate had played upon them, the bitter irony of a love such as they had for each other which must stay unsatisfied because of the enormity of the task that they had been chosen for. With an

222

aching heart she saw him take his eyes from hers, turn away and bury his head in his hands. A low moan escaped from behind his spreading palms where they covered his face; a sound that was saturated with anguish and that hung in the silence for a long time after it had gone, like the ripples that spread out from a stone long after the splash has died away.

Then at last he took his hands away; slowly, sliding them down his face until they dropped off his chin. Anxiously she looked at him, searching his expression to find his reaction, and was enormously relieved to see him smile; a pale, wan smile that spoke to her of acceptance and understanding, overlaid with a weary sadness.

'It's all right,' he said, in a voice low and choked with emotion. 'I understand. I'm not angry now; now that I know. I wish you'd told me earlier. It's easier when I know it's not you who. . . Tell me though. . . I've got to know . . . if we had not been who we are . . . would you have loved me; like that? Do you love me?'

The words sounded strange to him as they left his lips yet he had formed them quite naturally and they expressed the question that was raging through his mind with an urgency that would give him no peace until he knew the answer. And almost before he had finished speaking she was standing next to him, cradling his head against her breasts as, still sitting, he put his arms around her waist and held her closely to him.

'Oh yes,' she said. 'Yes', and her voice trembled with the relief of telling him. 'You mustn't doubt that. In the time we've been together . . . it seems like always . . . I've felt, somehow, complete. As if a part of me that was missing had come together. I'm pleased, now, that you know. I just hope that I was right to tell you. It won't be easy for us. . .'

She broke off then at the sudden cruel awareness of the warmth that was spreading up through her body at the feel of his hands and the weight of his head against her. Her breathing had got quicker, accelerated by the pumping of her heart and from the sound of his breath, she knew that he was similarly affected. A dark cloud of doubt swept over her at what she had done and then gently she took her hands from behind his neck and, grasping his wrists gently, began to lift them away to free herself from his embrace.

She need not have worried. His hands immediately went wooden and fell away from her body as if she were made of ice. And then, almost before she could blink, he was standing in front of her with a sardonic smile on his face.

'I'm sorry,' he said. 'You're right. It won't be easy. You'll have to keep turning into your deer,' and they both started to chuckle, quietly at first but then, as the bizarre nature of the image grew in their minds, more loudly until soon the cave echoed to the sounds of their laughter and tears ran down their cheeks.

And then the laughter died away and in the strange silence that followed they looked at each other with a deep and lingering warmth until Bracca spoke.

'Come on. Let's see if it's stopped snowing,' he said, and taking her hand he led her up the steps and out of the inner cave until they stood once again just inside the main entrance. The last time they had been here, they had looked out into the full terrifying fury of the storm and Bracca had been riven with fear and hunger. Now, with his stomach full and the warmth of the drink still running through his veins, the scene outside seemed to reflect back the quietness he felt in himself and the new inner strength and serenity which came from his relationship with Tara.

It was late afternoon. The sky was blue and only the occasional wisp of white cloud strewn across the vastness spoiled its uniform clarity. The sun shone down with a watery yellow radiance and set the smooth billowing waves of snow shimmering with an eerie light; a magical incandescence that lifted Bracca's spirit and sent it soaring up into the crystal air. A feeling of enormous power surged through him, as if all the splendour of Ashgaroth's world had focused upon him in a concentration of such strength and purity that he became invincible. The conquest of Dréagg's dark forces then seemed possible; a tangible reality that he could almost taste and, mesmerized by the wonder of it all, he held Tara close as if to reassure himself that it was not just a dream.

'We must go now,' she said. 'The time is right. It is a long way to Spath, many days travelling, and the armies of Xtlan and Barll will be well into their journey. Our greatest chance of success is to reach there before they do; otherwise we shall have to call on the elven armies to fight a way through to find the Droon. I don't know if they would succeed; so much of the earth has been despoiled by man that their strength and their numbers are badly depleted; there are few places left where they can survive. And even those who still remain are weaker than they should be for the powers of the earth from which they derive their strength are diminished in potency, so devastating has been man's destruction.'

They went back into the inner cave and, finding a number of carrying satchels, packed them with as much food and drink as they could carry. Then with a last sad look at the picture of the little boy they went back out and, leaving the big cave, walked into the cold clear snow-bright evening.

CHAPTER XV

Up they climbed, higher and higher, while the daytime whiteness of the moon grew silver in the darkening sky. In the half light of dusk Bracca could see the land falling away behind them; a huge expanse of white broken only by an occasional tree or a dark jagged slab of rock which the wind had cleared of snow. The cave entrance was soon far behind and already, in Bracca's mind, the time spent there with Tara was bathed in the warm and rosy glow of memory. She walked ahead of him following the Roosdyche, the magical routes of energy, rapt in concentration, while he walked behind doing his best to keep up with her. He remembered the anger he had felt before, during their journey through the storm, and was pleased that he felt none of it now. Still, as the night wore on and she continued her relentless pace he found the initial euphoria of their departure from the cave dissipating in the face of his inability to keep up with her. Try as he might, his legs grew more and more weary as he drove them over the snow, forcing them to the limit of their endurance while barely keeping her in sight ahead of him; a distant shadow gliding over the frosted carapace of snow that sparkled silver in the moonlight.

'I mustn't hold us back.' Over and over he mouthed this command to himself while at the same time willing her to slow down. The moon climbed up to its highest point in the deep dark starry sky and then began its slow descent towards dawn. Was it his eyes playing tricks or was it a deer that stood waiting for him in the shelter of a tall clump of trees just ahead? She had changed! Why? And then he understood. She wanted him to ride on her back. His weight would slow her down but it would still be quicker than going at his speed.

And so, gratefully, he climbed on her back and gripping her tightly between his legs leant forward and whispered in her ear that he was ready. Her fur was soft and smelt warm and musky and his mind juddered at the strangeness of this odd new familiarity but he was exhausted and relieved at the chance to rest and the immediacy of having to hang on or fall off as she started to walk forward drove any reservations from his mind.

She moved slowly at first, picking her hooves high out of the snow in a slow staccato rhythm which he found difficult to move with but then she started to run, gliding smoothly over the ground in long curving arcs of motion, and he soon felt able to fly with her over the crisp white carpet beneath them. It was not long then before he felt himself exulting in the feeling of speed; the cold air rushing past his face making his eyes water and his ears tingle, his hair blowing back from his forehead, the blur of grey beneath the hooves and the elemental shadow of Tara and himself that the moon threw against the backcloth of snow as they sped on through the night.

Streaks of pink brought a flush to the livid, blue-black sky and dawn sent its warming rays over the skyline; a dazzling spectrum of turquoise, vermilion and topaz radiating out in a brilliant corolla of colours from the golden core of the sun that still lurked beneath the horizon.

On they raced, as the sun climbed up into the sky and revealed a great flat landscape of white stretching ahead of them for as far as the eye could see and around them on all sides. They had stopped climbing now and seemed to be crossing an enormous plateau unbroken by any rise or fall, hollow or mound; almost, thought Bracca, as if it had once been a sea that had become frozen, for beneath Tara's flying hooves he saw glimmers of ice where the shallow dusting of snow had been kicked away. And the sound of her hooves, clattering and drumming over the surface, echoed off into the stillness to be carried away on the breeze into the shimmering white vastness all round.

Nothing to upset the rhythm, nothing to disturb the unbroken uniformity of the landscape as they surged on through the short bleak afternoon. Bracca's mind grew dazzled by the brilliance so that he rode as if in a dream, suspended above time in a world where nothing existed save the constant flow of Tara's body as it moved beneath him. He was truly at one with her now, fused together in a spiritual and physical unity that grew upon its own momentum.

Then the sun grew pale and the shadow of evening fell upon them as the moon came up to light their way through the second night. And still they did not stop and the leagues fell away behind them like snowflakes in the sun, bringing the malevolent darkness of Spath ever nearer as Tara's flying hooves devoured the distance.

Just before dawn they rested. Tara, still as a deer, wandered off to graze on what sparse vegetation she could find while Bracca, sitting on the snow, ate carefully from the food they had brought with them from the cave. He ate just enough to keep the pangs of hunger at bay and washed it down with a little of the drink; wary this time lest the effects it had had before were repeated. When he had finished he lay back and cradling his head on his arms, fell into a deep and blissful sleep.

He woke to the feel of Tara's tongue on his cheek and when he looked up into her dark brown eyes he knew immediately that something was troubling her. She stepped back and he saw the sky. Only a tiny patch of blue was left, like a sapphire, in a vast expanse of grey. Spumes of dark cloud billowed and raced in from the skyline like waves across the sea, brooding and threatening with a malignance

228

that chilled Bracca's heart so that he tore his eyes away in terror and, grabbing the packs, scrambled to his feet. Quickly then, responding to the feeling of urgency he felt from Tara, he climbed up on to her back and, almost before he was settled, she was racing forward over the ice.

Once more the wind was rushing past his face, fingers of ice pricking his cheeks, but instead of the elation that he had felt before, now he was consumed with panic in what he suddenly perceived as a race against time.

'Run,' he cried out. 'Run,' as the banks of cloud formed into great cavernous cathedrals of darkness overhead, but his voice was whipped away on the icy chariots of air that raced past him. And faster went Tara so that had anyone been watching they would have seen nothing but a dark blur against the grey.

Suddenly Bracca felt a tiny sting of pain against his cheek. It smarted for an instant and then was gone and forgotten in the terrible drama of their flight. He felt it again, then another and another, quickly gathering in number and ferocity until it was as if his face was being dragged through a dense mass of brambles, the thorns pricking and lacerating the skin of his defenceless cheeks. He put his head down so that all he could see was the dark ground rushing along beneath him but the hailstones grew bigger, smashing at his skull and making his head ache blindingly. Rivers of icy water ran down his forehead from his hair and mingled with tears of pain. In an attempt to protect himself he raised an arm and tried to shield his head from the rock-hard chunks of ice that were pounding against him, at the same time hanging on desperately to Tara with his other arm as she lurched and swayed beneath him.

How much further could she go? Surely she could see nothing in this; they would have to stop somewhere. She was slowing down now; he could feel her heart beating wildly and could sense her exhaustion as the pattern of her hoofbeats grew forced and irregular. She began to slip on the wet surface of the ice and once or twice he almost fell off

229

as Tara lost her footing and stumbled. He was completely sodden now; the freezing water had penetrated right through to his skin and much of his body had lost all feeling so that he clung to Tara's back in blind instinct.

Then suddenly there was a great rushing of air and the force and size of the terrible stones of ice increased yet again. The roaring wind now seemed to be hurling the hail straight at them so that it felt as if they were trying to force themselves through a solid wall of rock that was driving against them. Tara reeled and staggered under the impact, pushed herself forward a few paces and then, beaten down by the savage blows that rained down upon her, she gradually buckled beneath him, collapsed on to the snow and sent him tumbling off her back to land at her side. For an instant his face was turned away from her as he rolled over and when he looked back, straining his eyes through the sheets of hail for the familiar brown shape of the deer, he could not see her.

'Tara,' he yelled in panic, his voice sounding feeble and lost in the wind. 'Tara,' and then from close by him, he heard her call his name. Looking towards it he saw her, human again, her frail body lying prostrate on the ice, the white of her face barely visible.

'Tara,' he spoke her name as if it were a blessing and, sick with apprehension, he crawled the few paces across to where she lay.

'Are you all right?' he said, but his words were lost in the storm. 'How are you?' He almost shouted now, with his lips against her ear, but the pain in her eyes gave him the answer he feared.

'The darkness,' she said, but he had to bend his head low to hear her for her voice was faint and barely audible. 'It's Dréagg ... the storm. My spirit ... weak. All around ...' but her words tailed away as her eyes fluttered and closed.

With his heart breaking, Bracca cradled his body over her head to protect her from the bombardment that fell upon them with relentless savagery. And he held her head up

230

against his chest to keep it off the bitter snow, entwining his fingers in the long silken strands of her saturated hair and calling her name over and over as if it was a magical spell that would bring her back to him.

And then, as time rode past him in an empty and meaningless charade, an eerie sensation crept through the incarceration of his grief and pierced his consciousness so that he ceased his lament and froze in fear at the feeling that was stalking through his body. Slowly, very slowly, he raised his head using a hand to shield his face from the hail. Could it be his imagination or was the storm slackening? The light that shone about them seemed to glisten with a deep, ultra-violet iridescence; a brilliant, unnatural light that paralysed his spirit with terrifying apprehension. Something was above them, watching them, relishing its victory. Dréagg?

As the moments passed Bracca felt himself growing weaker; his self-will was being drained out of him. He had to move; just move! That might be enough. If he could only see it! Gathering all his strength he tried to turn his head so that he could look up at the sky. The light blinded him as it poured off the snow and he shut his eyelids tight to keep it out. He stayed like that for a few seconds, feeling its rays burning his eyeballs, and then when he felt the initial shock wearing off he opened them again fractionally and was instantly convulsed with blind terror at the sight that burned itself into his consciousness.

The sky was alive; the clouds had erupted, spewing forth a gigantic black serpent, whose endless tail writhed and twisted into a seething coil that stretched away into infinity, covering the sky with its pulsating mass. Yellow sulphurous eyes protruded in great bulbous mounds from the top of its wide flat head, staring straight down at Bracca and Tara, and its toothless mouth gaped open spasmodically, showing flashes of red from the endlessly flicking tongue, before flapping shut again as if gasping for air.

But what most horrified Bracca, turning his blood to ice and melting the very marrow of his bones, were the tentacles

231

that grew from the front portion of its body. Snaking down from the sky all the way to the earth they slithered slowly towards him, the slender black tips weaving and dancing over the ice, moving to a silent hypnotic rhythm that mesmerized him.

On they came, nearer and nearer, darting out over the surface or else licking upwards into the air. Repulsively lascivious, Bracca could not tear his gaze away from them yet at the same time his soul shrank away in terror. They were within reach of him now; he could see the irregular red pattern of the veins and smell the rancid stench of putrefying flesh.

And then he felt his guts turn to ice and he watched with horror as a black-tipped tentacle retreated back from him; back from where it had reached inside him before he had even seen it. And while his stomach was still churning, another one pounced at his head and shattered his mind, sending it reeling away in tatters into the violet air before he collapsed onto the inert body of Tara.

He opened his eyes to a flood of golden light that poured down upon them from above and bathed them with a warm ochre glow. It came from the serpent's eyes, streaming down in torrents to encircle them in its aura.

Tara was still beneath him; he could feel the rounded symmetry of her body against himself and immediately his senses became overwhelmed by her. He raised himself up slightly so that he could look at her as she lay on the gilded ice. Her mane of tousled blonde hair lay in a wild halo around her head, its dampness reflecting back the light as if it was festooned with gems. The lashes of her closed eyes had been thickened by the wet and framed her eyelids in two sparkling stars. Unconsciousness had ripened the fullness of her lips so that they were pursed half-open in a gesture of such pouting sensuality that his mind reeled with desire.

'Take her.' At first the voice that called out from deep within was soft and quiet so that he almost did not notice it, but as his hungry eyes feasted on her body it repeated itself

232

with growing persistency. The thrusting fullness of her breasts as they pushed up against the filmy wetness of her dress, the gently rounded voluptuousness of her stomach and then, accentuated by the tightly clinging material, the deep vee at the apex of her thighs; all these inflamed his desire until soon the voice was screaming at him.

'Have her! Take her! Bury yourself in the magnificence of her ripe flesh. Feel her softness. Explore her; she will not stop you. Go on. Just look at her! What harm would it do?'

He watched helplessly as his hands moved towards her, powerless to stop them. He strained against them, willing them to stop but it was useless; it was as if his body had lost its autonomy and was being ordered by another. And then, in horrified fascination he saw his fingers clutch at the neckline of her dress and pull it savagely down, ripping the material so that it fell open exposing the milky whiteness of her breasts. And now, numbed by her beauty, he did not even try to resist as his palms tenderly cupped themselves over her nipples and sent exquisite shivers of sensuality coursing through his veins.

And still she did not move. Was it imagination or were her lips smiling in pleasure? Slightly parted they seemed to him, in this oasis of warm springtime light, to be luxuriating in his caresses.

Slowly then, lingering over each new part of her body that revealed itself to his touch, he moved his hands down over her stomach, round the curves of her hips and in to the silky smoothness of her inner thighs. And now the flames of lust roared inside his spirit and set his loins tingling with anticipation as the core of her womanhood lay before his trembling hands as if waiting to be invaded by him. Gone now was all control, swept away in the tidal wave of carnality that surged over him. Suddenly he dived forward and kissed her lips. They were soft and warm and moist and they opened a little to receive him as her fragrance enveloped his senses in an aura of ecstasy.

And the black serpent writhed within him, driving him on

233

in a blind rush towards the consummation of their forbidden union as the blood pounded in his ears and his body gorged itself upon her. But then, suddenly, a great flash of silver light pierced the golden cocoon and for an instant the enchantment was broken. He looked up and saw a great white horse charging across the sky. Its mane and tail streamed out behind it like the spume-tipped crests of waves and silver sparks danced from its flying hooves as it raced towards the serpent, its eyes flashing in the darkness.

Bracca stared, awed by its magnificence, and Tara was forgotten. But then as the horse fell upon the serpent and sank its teeth in the other's neck so Bracca felt his mind being pulled back, his attention drawn towards her as she lay stretched out beneath him. And then once more the white horse would draw him away, stamping out the fires of his lust even as its hooves rained down upon the serpent.

Back and forth went his consciousness, first one way and then the other, ebbing and flowing with the tide of the terrible conflict that raged above him. Sometimes the horse would be on the ascendant, its teeth and hooves cutting and slashing into its adversary as it squirmed beneath the onslaught. Then Bracca's mind was free and he would realize, in a rush of horror, how close had been Dréagg's victory. But at other times the serpent would bury its fangs in the horse's flank and coil its tail around its opponent's body. Then Bracca would feel his spirit crushed and he would have to fight for his breath until, turning to Tara, he found relief, and as the air flooded into his lungs so did her body inflame his passion once more.

Time lost meaning as the battle raged above them but the struggle tore at Bracca's mind, splitting it into two terrible adversaries, each fighting with the other for the control of his mind. His vision grew dim and his spirit sagged as the contest wore on but it could not last and eventually he succumbed to the void that beckoned him on towards the tranquillity of its darkness. Then, with one last desperate flicker of consciousness as he hovered on the edge of the abyss, he was gone.

CHAPTER XVI

For a long time he had been aware of a wall of red and orange that danced and swayed somewhere beyond the dark veil of his eyelids. Subconsciously it had provided a focus for the tattered fragments of his mind, drawing them together slowly until now, at last, he had become whole once again. He felt a warmth fanning out over his cheeks and bringing life back into them with a delicious tingle; gradually thawing out his frozen body until feeling came back into his limbs and the numbness in his bones was driven out.

For a long time he remained in this strange, ethereal state of semi-consciousness, basking in its safety and security and reluctant to open his eyes to reality. As long as he stayed like this, he felt, nothing could harm him. But then, as his body regained its identity, so his mind grew restive and he was unable to suppress the tremors of unease that rippled through it; the images that flashed before him in the darkness of the terrible hailstones as they smashed against him, the serpent and the horse locked together in their savage struggle and, in a way more disturbing than anything else, memories of Tara that still sent shudders of yearning through him.

At last, to escape the torment that battered at his spirit in the darkness, he opened his eyes. Slowly and cautiously he looked; trying to focus his attention through a haze of mist at the scene that appeared before him. At first all he could see was a blur of red; the leaping dancing flames of the fire that had brought him back to life. He heard it too, crackling and hissing as it voraciously consumed a great mound of logs in the huge stone fireplace just in front of him. There was something immensely comforting about it and, as the qualms of apprehension lifted, so he widened his gaze.

The first thing that struck him was the sight of an enormous wolf stretched out on its side in front of the hearth. It had its back to him and he could see its flanks moving slowly and rhythmically up and down in time with the pattern of its breathing. He stared at it for some time, lulled into a state of calm by the aura of peace that emanated out from it, and then he looked around. Directly above him, the ceiling soared up into a high vaulted pinnacle of space but as his eyes moved back they met a dark wooden floor supported by huge wooden beams. The walls were of stone; large uneven blocks of grey and brown and fawn welded together with lines the colour of ash. There was a sense of enormous age about the place, a venerable antiquity that held him in awe as his gaze travelled among the carved stone pillars supporting the floor, across to the curved arch of the doorway in the far wall, up to the black chandelier with six haloed yellow candles that hung from the ceiling, and back to the fireplace.

Tara! Where was Tara? In a sudden fit of panic he tried to raise himself up from the wooden pallet on which he lay. It was then that he saw, getting up from a stone seat built in to the fireplace, an enormous figure of a man. His hair and clothes were of greys and browns as was the stone so that he had been camouflaged and Bracca had not noticed him before.

He walked over slowly, his head barely missing the chandelier and Bracca marvelled at his great size. His face was hidden behind a long beard but his brown eyes were smiling and Bracca felt no fear. As he approached the bed the

237

grey hair that fell about his shoulders moved in waves.

'Hush,' he said. 'Hush, my little one. Don't upset yourself,' and though he spoke quietly and haltingly his voice filled the air with a deep and lyrical resonance.

'Tara,' said Bracca again. 'The girl. . .'

'Lie back. She is asleep. As you were. She will be all right. See. Over there,' and he pointed to a vast bed next to the fire with canopies and curtains festooned around it in folds and drapes of gold which the flickering firelight burnished with the colours of autumn. 'She is inside, resting. Let her be for the moment; she has been through a terrible ordeal. She must regain her power.' He paused and smiled. 'We thought we'd lost you both . . . thought we'd lost you,' and he laid his huge hand on Bracca's head and stroked it as a father caresses his baby. 'I'll get you something to drink.'

He got up from the floor where he had been kneeling and went back to the fireplace. There he unhooked a small black cauldron that hung near the flames and taking a long-stemmed goblet from a nearby shelf poured some liquid into it and put the cauldron back onto its hook.

'Now, drink this,' he said, walking back to Bracca and carefully giving him the goblet. Bracca found it difficult to sit up so the man put one arm round his back to support him and holding Bracca's hand around the goblet helped him to raise it to his lips.

Warily, lest it be too hot, he took a sip of the dark red liquid. The pungency of the vapours it gave off galvanized his senses so that he jerked back sharply with shock and at the same time the warmth of the liquid travelled round every part of his body leaving it refreshed and revitalized, driving out the weariness and oppression in his spirit. He took another sip and then another, losing himself in the aromatic earthiness of its scent and flavour, and, as he did so, his awareness of the old man's physical presence grew and he began to look at him more closely. It was the hands he noticed first; incredibly long bony fingers, the backs of which were covered with a mass of thick orange-coloured hair. The feet too were large and hairy and the toes long and slightly curled, as if constantly gripping the floor.

He looked next at the giant's face. From a distance he had been unable to see through the beard but now, close to, he could make out patches of skin hiding behind the hair. It was dark and very wrinkled; the surface drawn together into an uncountable number of troughs and valleys like the dried-up bottom of a lake. When the old man spoke the deep corrugations of his face leapt and danced in a bizarre choreography of chaos and Bracca became mesmerized by it as the drink loosened his mind.

'Sleep now,' said the giant. 'We will talk when you wake. Sleep well and dream the dreams of the ageless.'

As he spoke the words he laid Bracca gently back down on the pallet and though for an instant he struggled against the wave of oblivion that swept over him he was powerless to resist it and sleep carried him off like thistledown on the wind.

When he woke up he felt wonderfully invigorated and his first thought was of Tara. Propping himself up on one elbow he looked across to the bed by the fire and saw to his surprise that the curtains were drawn back and it was empty. Then his gaze swung towards the fireplace and he saw her talking to the old man. They were sitting on two large solid-backed chairs close together, their profiles bathed in the dark red glow of the flames, and they were talking intently, almost conspiratorially, in voices that carried enough words across to Bracca for him to realize that he could not understand the language.

Tara seemed to be doing most of the talking, animatedly, her fingers and her hands moving expressively in large graceful gestures. He watched for a long time, entranced by her, and then, still under her spell, his mind drifted back over the events of the recent past in an attempt to come to terms with everything that had happened to him since his escape from Haark. At first his consciousness baulked at the strangeness of the memories that filtered through; the

239

terrible deaths of Nabbeth and his beloved Shayll, the pain of his strange and poignant leave-taking from Morven and Melvaig, the flight from Barll, vague memories of his journey over the sea and then the event which seemed now in retrospect to be almost a rebirth; his recovery under the care and love of Brock. His old life seemed to have stopped there and a new one begun. The meeting with Nab and Beth, Warrigal, Perryfoot and Sam; this had been the genesis of his new world, and the words of Nab had given purpose and meaning to his existence.

And then his thoughts returned to Tara and he felt the curse on their love send a rush of poisonous venom coursing into his spirit. Everything else made sense; the journey to Spath, the separation of the Seeds, the conflict with Barll and the timeless confrontation between Ashgaroth and Dréagg. All this was clear to him and he was able to accept his own role in the pattern of these things. But why had fate seen fit to play this cruellest of tricks upon him? Was he not doing enough? It was not fair that along with everything else there was this terrible bane upon him; this breach in his armoury that Dréagg could pick away at like a scab. Why? Over and over the question raged inside his head until, suddenly, as if a flash of lightning had cleaved the darkness, it became clear to him in a way he had not seen before. This dark and evil suppression of their love came from Dréagg; were it not for him they would be free for there would be no need to incarcerate their passion and keep it locked away. Without him their love would fly untrammelled and unlimited, for then the retention of their separate natures would not matter. And it was this that Dréagg was using against him, to defeat him and Tara and so eliminate the only obstacle left in his path before the world belonged to him in its entirety. And as he perceived the struggle within himself to be an integral part of the struggle against Dréagg so a vision of the dark serpent returned and for an instant his soul was turned to ice as he understood the power of the forces that were ranged against him. Yet at the same time this new understanding

240

made the struggle a little easier, for Dréagg was now real to him in a way he had never been before and furthermore had been defeated in the first conflict that Bracca had witnessed.

So completely absorbed had he been in his reverie that the feel of Tara's hand on his face came as a sudden shock for he had not noticed her approach.

'How do you feel?' Her voice was soft and musical, and he turned his attention to her with enormous relief at having been set free from the cloud of darkness that had enshrouded his mind.

'I'm all right,' he said slowly, and his voice sounded strange and distant as if it came from a long way away. 'But I feel...' and he paused, uncertain of how to explain himself, '...lost. I feel lost. How did we get here? Where are we? What are we doing here?' and as he formed the questions that raced through his mind with increasing intensity she gently placed her finger against his lips in a gesture of silence.

'Ssh,' she said. 'Be still. We're safe. Nothing can hurt us here. Come along, come over to the fire and join our host,' and putting an arm around his waist she helped him down from the bed.

'I'm fine. Leave me,' he said irritably, still clogged up with the cobwebs of sleep that refused to leave him, but when his feet met the ground he was, to his surprise, grateful for her support and he leaned on her heavily. He had not known he was so weak; his body felt shaky and feeble and he thought with longing of the delicious drink the old man had given him before. Could he ask for some more? But there was no need, for out of the corner of his eye he saw the giant get up and move across to the cauldron.

Tara helped him down into a high-backed wooden chair and the old man gave him the goblet which he took thankfully. Then Tara sat down on one side of him and their host seated himself on the other so that the three of them formed a semi-circle round the blazing fire. A log suddenly crackled and spat and the wolf jerked upright, his ears erect

241

and his black nose tip twitching to scent out danger. The old man leaned down and patted his head.

'All right, Vane. All right. It's nothing. Calm down. Go back to sleep.'

At the gentle and soothing sound of his master's voice the animal visibly relaxed; his hackles went down and his ears began to flatten again. Languidly now, the alarm over, he turned his head to look at the two newcomers, fixing them each in turn with a look so serene and majestic that Bracca felt both comforted and elevated. It studied them both for a long time until eventually, its curiosity apparently satisfied, it flopped back down again and closed its eyes, breathing a deep sigh as it settled itself to sleep.

'You look better, Bracca. There is colour in your cheeks and a sparkle in your eye.'

Bracca looked across at the old man as he spoke, surprised that he knew his name.

'Tara and I have talked. While you slept she spoke of you and of the sacred journey you are embarked upon. She told me everything. It has been hard on you. Hard for an Eldron, even such a one as you – of the Chosen Line.'

He stopped speaking and there was silence for a time while his eyes stared down at the floor, as if his mind had drifted off to a time and a place far away. And then he looked up and, placing his hand on the young man's shoulder, smiled as he continued.

'Your mind bursts with questions. I know! I know! But you must be patient with me. Vane and I . . .' he looked down lovingly at the wolf, 'we have not spoken much in these last times. I am called Raagon and I am the last of the Old Ones.' He paused for dramatic effect but saw that Bracca was unmoved by this information. 'You do not know? Why should you? Many have thought us gone completely. We would be, all of us, but Ashgaroth would not let us all go. And he needed me . . . needs me.' He stopped, and began to drift as Bracca tried to concentrate on what the old man was saying. Looking across at Tara he could see her eyes bright and sparkling, obviously awestruck by the presence of Raagon.

Waveringly the old man began speaking again, forcing himself with obvious effort to focus his mind on the unfolding of his narrative.

'We were always here. From the first. Ashgaroth made us in the beginning with the animals, after the Efflinch Wars when in the joy of victory over Dréagg he put his creatures on the earth. In the wildest places we lived; way, way up in the mountains or deep in the deepest forests. But we are a quiet and a shy race and when Dréagg created man, who we call Urkku or "the Great Enemy", then we were forced to retreat as this new arrival slowly began to lay waste to our homes. Further and wider he spread as the time passed, cutting, burning and killing, until in the end our numbers dwindled till we were but a few. Occasionally they would see us; catch a glimpse as we fled from them or see a print they could not recognize, and wild tales of our existence spread from those of the Urkku who ventured into the remotest places of the Earth. But we had no magic powers as did the elves. And we are too big. We cannot hide. Not like the elves.

'And so we died for there was not enough space; not enough food.'

There was silence then for a time and Bracca did not want to disturb him. Raagon mumbled quietly to himself, lost in the past, his great shoulders drooping, as he reached down and gently stroked the head of the wolf.

At last Bracca spoke. 'But you,' he said. 'You are still here. You have survived.'

Raagon looked up sharply.

'Ammdar!' he said. 'Ammdar, the Silver Warrior. The mightiest of the elflords. Ammdar before the fall, whose spirit was touched by the hand of Ashgaroth. In his eyes was all the power and gentleness of the great forests and his voice caused the trees to shiver with joy and the birds to sing his praise. Where his shadow fell, there grew the snowdrop and the bluebell; and the earth turned to silver where he walked. Oh Ammdar!' and he raised his eyes up as his voice

243

cried out in anguish. 'Why? Why?' Then he turned and looked at Bracca and Tara and they watched with awed fascination as great glistening tears rolled down his cheeks and got lost in the undergrowth of his beard.

'I knew him you see.' He almost shouted. 'Knew him as he was. We were friends. The two of us so different, yet there was a bond, a kinship that we could not explain. I rode with him and walked with him and fought alongside him as he led the armies of the elves against the forces of Dréagg. But then came the fall, when Dréagg ensnared him with promises and the web of darkness closed around his spirit so that he turned from Ashgaroth and set about gathering the Three Seeds of Logic. I was fearful then and tried to argue against him but the cancers of evil had gnawed too far into the fibres of his mind and he would not listen. So I went with him to Spath when he offered the gift of Logic to the animals in return for their allegiance. I remember his terrible fury and I watched as the animals ran in terror while tongues of fire tore at the sky and the forest erupted around us. And I too fled, for in his anger he turned on me and I ran till I came to this place, which had been his; Operrallmar I called it, which means "refuge" in our tongue.

'Then he and Dréagg created man, and in man was the power of the Three Seeds. So began the reign of terror of which you know when the earth, the chosen jewel of Ashgaroth, was plundered and ravished and a terrible revenge was wrought upon the animals for their rejection of Ammdar.

'But the rule of Ammdar was to be short-lived for it came to me then, from the elves who watched him for Ashgaroth, that Dréagg wanted him destroyed. He had become too powerful and Dréagg relished no rivals to his supremacy.

'The terror of that time is still with me! A goblin, Degg, it was who Dréagg chose for the task. I did not see it but heard from those who were there, that when Degg plunged his sword into Ammdar's heart a great plume of black blood rose up and blotted out the sun. Where it fell the earth grew foul and poisonous so that nothing has grown there since. And the sound; his wailing and his cries ringing through the air so that the leaves and flowers withered and died as they stood and the animals whimpered and cowered in their burrows and their nests.

'And here at Operrallmar I stayed and my spirit twisted in anguish at the sound of his pain. "Ammdar," I cried, "Ammdar, my Silver Lord. Where are you?" for I remembered him as he was and I forgave him for the way he had become for it was the price he paid for his greatness.'

There was silence again, only the hissing and crackling of the logs sounded out to disturb the stillness that lay upon them. Then Raagon reached down and stroked the head of the wolf so that Vane, disturbed from his sleep, got up, stretched and yawned, and went and put his head on the old man's knee. And Raagon spoke again, under his breath so that the words were barely audible yet they clamoured in the minds of Bracca and Tara as if they had been a thunderclap.

'And then you came, my Vane, my Ammdar. And then you came.'

Bracca could find no words to speak; his mind reeled with amazement and disbelief, but Tara immediately knew and understood. Indeed, now that it had been made clear to her she realized that she had known from the moment she had first seen him. Warily she got up and crossed the floor to where the wolf sat by Raagon. Then she put her hands carefully at either side of his neck, letting her fingers bury themselves deep in the luxuriousness of his soft, thick fur and as he felt her touch, his head turned slowly towards her and she met his eyes.

'Ammdar,' she whispered. 'Is it you? Truly? The Silver Warrior. The greatest of the elflords. The fallen. Can it be you?'

And as the eyes of the wolf gazed deep into her soul and spoke to her as only those blessed with the power of magic can, so all doubt vanished.

'Yes, I am,' he said. 'Saved by Ashgaroth who would not let

245

me perish at the hand of Dréagg. He felt the awful pain of my remorse; the terrible burden of guilt for the wrong I had done. To have turned against him; to have embraced the darkness! My treachery was too terrible to contemplate, the stain of my betrayal too vast for the earth to recover. And so he gathered the shattered fragments of my spirit and brought them together and made me as a wolf so that none might recognize me; neither the elves nor the goblins nor Dréagg. All would believe I was no more. And I came to Operrallmar, to my friend Raagon, and we comfort each other in our loneliness and our sorrow. And for every moment of every day since then my soul has ached for the chance of redemption; to erase the darkness that I unleashed upon the earth – the darkness which is man. For I know where the Droon is yet I cannot separate the Seeds for I am of Magic and I do not have my belt, the Belt of Ammdar, the fastenings of which alone will open the Casket of Unity. So I have waited through all the Three Ages of Man, for Ashgaroth promised me that when the time was right, then would the chance come.' He paused a little then before continuing. 'Let me come with you. Without me your task would be well-nigh impossible. You would have to find the Droon and all the forces of darkness would be ranged against you. I still have some powers and you will need all these and more for the times ahead. Above all we must protect Bracca, for only he can open the Droon and separate the Seeds. Take me, and take Raagon for his loyalty and his faith and his wisdom; here on the earth even before the elves. It is only fitting and it is the wish of Ashgaroth. Why else would you be here? And now you must tell Bracca all that I have told you. One last request. Ask him if I can see my Belt – just . . . see it.'

At last Tara felt silence in her mind. It seemed as if she had been locked in conversation with him for an age. Had she imagined it? No! But did this vigorous denial come from her own consciousness and was it Ammdar himself who put it so forcibly into her mind? She looked again at the wolf, their

eyes met, and any last lingering vestiges of doubt disappeared forever.

Ammdar! Her emotions raced wildly around her spirit in a
frantic whirl of confusion. All that she had heard of him had
turned her mind against him. His treachery. His betrayal of
Ashgaroth. The gigantic lust for power which led to the
terrible alliance with Dréagg and the evil that it spawned. He
had been a figure of darkness, worthy only of contempt; yet
now he was here talking to her, requesting forgiveness and
the chance of redemption. This once mighty figure was
standing at her side, as a wolf, and asking to be taken with
them on their sacred mission. Could they trust him? How
could they be sure that, even if what he was saying now was
true, Dréagg would not enslave him once again.

'I know what he said.' It was Raagon, looking directly at
Tara, his brown eyes moist and his voice husky with emotion.
'And I know your fears for I myself had them when he first
came to me. Long ago. So long ago. You must decide for
yourself. You must talk with Bracca. Come. I will take you to
a room where you can be by yourselves.' He turned to
Bracca. 'You must be alone for a while. The two of you.
There is something you must decide.'

While Tara had been talking with the wolf, speaking in the
inner speech of the animals, Bracca had been in a daze. Now,
as Raagon got up and led the way slowly towards a great
wooden door in the far wall, Bracca fought with himself to
accept the idea that the wolf was Ammdar. It stood looking at
them as they crossed the room, its deep mysterious eyes
ranging over them with an immense sadness and yearning
that tore at Bracca's heart. Its ears were down but it held its
head high and proud. Could it be true, what Raagon had called
it? And then that strange episode when Tara had seemed
mesmerized by him, her eyes wide and staring, locked on to his
gaze with an intensity so tangible that Bracca had felt it.

The door opened and they walked out into a huge hallway
that soared above their heads in a vast spherical dome of
open space. Slivers of silver light cut through the darkness at

247

the very top, seeming to come from small openings in the stone wall, and sent an eerie opalescence washing down upon them that threw their grotesquely misshapen shadows onto the grey flags at their feet. Away from the warmth of the fire the air was chill and damp and Bracca was glad for the warmth of Tara's body close to his as, with an arm round his waist, she helped him to walk across to a flight of stone stairs that wound straight upwards from the centre of the floor in a spiral till it lost itself in the shadows above. The sound of their footsteps echoed out into the silence and, as if at a signal, the air was suddenly full of a mass of scrapings and rustlings. The noise rose to a crescendo and then slowly died away until once more stillness fell as the creatures they had disturbed settled back down on their resting places to watch the three intruders as they ascended the stairway.

Raagon went first, then Tara, and lastly Bracca, hauling himself up by the wooden railing that ran up one side. Higher and higher they climbed till the floor below was lost to sight in the gloom and the air was so cold that Bracca's hands grew numb. All around them they could hear little twitterings and squeaks as if every step of their progress was being remarked upon and discussed. Sometimes they would get too close and in a flurry of activity, a winged shape would take off and flap its way through the silver-hued twilight to land on a ledge some distance away. The presence of the creatures had unsettled Bracca at first but now he was used to them and a strange sense of cosiness and security started to spread over him as he became wrapped in the enveloping cocoon of their sounds. All that he could see beneath him was a thin needle of dark orange light escaping through the partly open door of the room where Ammdar still stood.

Suddenly they were at the top of the stairs and ahead of them, stretching away into the depths of the palace, lay a corridor. It was reached by a little bridge that crossed over from the topmost step where they were now standing. It was down now but Bracca could see two lengths of rope that went from the end near him to a drum with a handle on at

248

the far side. Thus, he guessed, the drawbridge could be raised in time of attack and the corridor rendered unreachable by an enemy. Had this been one of the elven strongholds from which Ammdar had led his warriors out to do battle with the goblins in the time before his fall and before the coming of man? Had the defence of this bridge ever had to be used, to retreat into the palace and leave the goblins stranded on the stairway? The stone walls that he could only dimly make out through the murky light seemed to speak back to him of those far distant times; times Before-Man when the jewel of Ashgaroth had still been full and green and pure and the forces of Darkness had only just begun to cast their shadow against the light. The marks on the stone, the chips in the stairs – could these be reminders of the epic struggles that had been waged so very, very long ago – at the beginning. And suddenly, for a brief moment that came and went almost before he knew it, the hall was full of the terrible sounds of battle – the clamour of sword on sword, the whistle of arrows and the hideous baying of the goblins as they fought for their vile and profane cause. And he saw the elves, the silver aura of their bodies shimmering in the gloom as they resisted the waves of evil that Dréagg sent against them.

And at the head of them, in the centre of the fighting, was Ammdar, his sword arm plunging and rearing like some mad serpent as the goblins fell away from him in waves. His cry filled the hall and echoed out around the walls like the ringing of some enormous and divine bell. 'Ashgaroth,' he cried, over and over, investing the name with a rhythmical cadence that stirred Bracca's heart beyond measure and seemed to invest the elven warriors with renewed power.

His ears rang with the tumult and his eyes were mesmerized by the endlessly shifting patterns of the conflict until, as suddenly as it had come, the image faded and Bracca was once again surrounded by the chill silence of the hallway.

They crossed over the bridge and walked down the

corridor. The walls on either side were of a dark wood, burnished so that they shone with a light sheen and cast back their reflections as they moved slowly along towards a large door at the end. There were scenes carved in the walls; pictures of animals and elves, of mountains and rivers and forests, of deep valleys and sharp crags. They teemed with such an abundance of life and energy that, walking past them, both Bracca and Tara felt they were among them, and a wave of nostalgic yearning swept over them for the days of their innocence when Bracca had wandered free and untroubled through the forests of Haark, and Tara had laughed and played and sung with Nab and Beth and the companions of Silver Wood.

Raagon turned the handle of the heavy door and it swung silently open. The room was lit by a dim orange glow that glimmered out from a fireplace in the far wall and Raagon led them towards it, taking care to avoid the dark shapes on the floor – tables and chairs which in silhouette took on a life and a form of their own utterly different from the object that spawned them. The thing that Bracca noticed most strongly was the smell – the delicate, sweet, fragrance of burning pine that went to his head and left him gently intoxicated with its scent. It grew stronger as they got nearer to the hearth and it reminded Bracca of home and of Melvaig and Morven and Shayll and all the evenings they had had round the fire, eating and talking and listening to the sounds of the night. And, suddenly, he could hear the beautiful, plaintive notes of Melvaig's pipes echoing out into the forest and feel again the evocative power of his melodies. And with these memories came the smell of Melvaig's pipe and the sight of the curling blue-green fronds of smoke as they had drifted up into the still summer air.

A sudden blaze from the fireplace interrupted his thoughts and, looking, he saw that Raagon was putting more logs on. The room was now illuminated by the fresh dancing flames that had already begun to lick hungrily at the new wood and Bracca's eyes started to roam around the room. Three of the stone walls were covered with dark wooden panelling almost up to the low ceiling but, unlike in the corridor outside, they had for the most part not been carved upon and had been left plain except for the occasional runic symbol set in the otherwise perfect smoothness of the wood. Yet hanging on them were pictures that appeared to be woven with some sort of material that Bracca could not recognize. They gave out a faint light of their own from the shadows of the walls as if they were somehow vaguely luminous; possessed of a shimmering phosphorescence that contained elements of green and orange and red and purple and blue, all merging and separating out in an endless spectroscopic cycle. They drew him towards them and he found himself walking up to the nearest and looking at it as if in a trance. He could recognize nothing familiar in the patterns and shapes that swirled about inside the limits of the ornate black frame yet he felt a great power emanate out from it; an aura of mystic divinity that filled him with confidence and strength. He seemed to escape the confines of his body and to be swept forward into the world of the picture, a crazily whirling kaleidoscope of colour that carried him into what he perceived to be the realms of the elves so that he saw the earth even as they did – through the eyes of Magic. And at the moment he entered the picture he realized that the textures and colours that before had made no sense were in truth a microcosmic representation of that world. The greens were the grasses and the leaves and the deep plunging sea under an ice-clear winter sky; the oranges and reds and purples were of the fungus in the deepest reaches of the forest or the sunset at the end of an autumn day; the flowers and the berries, the birds and butterflies and beetles, each became clear for an instant before fading back into the flowing colours of the tapestry. And he wandered over the mountains and the moors, along the cliff edge and on the beach, through the valleys and by the side of the tumbling river as it flashed silver in the spring sun. At peace, utterly at peace, for he was at one with the magic of Ashgaroth; indivisible, for he was as much a part of them as they were of him, one and the same, and he felt the limitless majesty of Ashgaroth's creation flow into his spirit as he soared and swooped and dived and flew through the palaces of the earth.

'Come on. By the fire.' As suddenly as the mirage had appeared so it evaporated, and before his eyes was simply the picture as before. It was Tara who had spoken and she was pulling him gently towards the hearth.

Dazed, he tried to speak. 'The picture. . .' he began, but she interrupted.

'I know,' she said. 'The tapestries of Tainoor. I've heard of them before but no one believed in their existence. He was the elven chronicler at the time of Ammdar and it was thought his pictures perished at the time of the fall. But they are too powerful for you now. You need more rest. There'll be enough time to look at them later.'

So he took his eyes away and followed Tara as she led him to a tall wooden seat facing the fire. He sat down and relished again the warmth against his face after the chill of the corridor outside. At his side there was a large carved wooden chest and Tara sat down in a chair just beyond it. For a moment Raagon stood looking down at them, smiling happily, and then he spoke.

'Good,' he said. 'Good. You're comfortable. Now I shall go back down to fetch you something to eat and drink.'

He chuckled and the wrinkles on his face gave a little dance. 'I won't be long,' and he left them.

Exhausted, they sat in silence while the firelight played upon them, throwing their shadows against the walls. Tara had so much to tell him and Bracca so much to ask that the effort for either of them was too great. And then, almost before they realized it, they heard the door open behind them and Raagon reappeared carrying a large wooden tray which he put down on the chest between them.

'There,' he said. 'Now take a fork and warm them by the fire. Honey is in the pot. Help yourselves to the drink.'

In the middle of the tray were two small stacks of flat cakes which Bracca guessed were some sort of bread. He picked up one of the long-handled forks that Raagon had taken down from the side of the fireplace and, following his example, skewered a bread cake on to the prongs and held it so that it was close to the red embers at the bottom of the fire. Tara had pulled a chair up next to him and was doing the same so that all three of them sat in silence with their arms outstretched to the flames concentrating on browning their cakes and changing over as one arm began to ache. The first side was soon done and as Bracca brought his back to change over, a deliciously fragrant, slightly sweet earthy aroma set his taste buds tingling and his mouth ached in anticipation.

When both sides were toasted he took it off the fork. It was very hot and, with his fingers burning, he put it down on one of the rough clay plates that Raagon had brought up on the tray. Tara had just finished spreading hers with honey and she handed him the pot and the wooden spatula.

'I'm going to enjoy this,' she said. 'Put plenty on.'

He watched her for a moment as she raised the cake to her mouth and sank her teeth into it. A little trickle of honey oozed out and ran down her chin and, giggling, she wiped it off with her fingers and licked it clean. Then smiling at him, she nodded as if to tell him to get on with his.

'Come on! Mine's going cold.'

It was Raagon, chuckling at him, his crystal blue eyes glinting with laughter.

So Bracca put his honey on, passed Raagon the pot, and took a bite. A little crisp on the surface, sweetened by the honey and then soft and light inside. His tongue swam in the delicacy of the flavours before he swallowed and the savour seemed to suffuse his whole body. It was delicious! He took another mouthful and then poured himself a drink from a large flagon that was on the tray into one of the ochre-brown earthenware goblets next to it. It was a rich, dark, golden colour and a little cloud of vapour seemed to hang over it, suspended by its heat. He raised the goblet to his lips and,

253

with the fumes making his eyes water, he took a sip. It was a little less heavy than the drink Raagon had given him before and its aromatic dry warmth contrasted beautifully with the sweetness of the honeyed bread cake.

So the three of them sat together eating and drinking until the stack had dwindled to one, by which time they all felt wonderfully full. Then Bracca turned to Raagon and began to ply him with the questions that only weariness and hunger had kept him from asking before. And Raagon told him what he had previously told Tara. He described the vision he had seen in the fire as he had been sitting by it with Vane while the storm raged outside, and he related how he had felt compelled to go and look for the two figures that the flames had drawn for him. Despite the blizzard and the terrible hailstones it had not been difficult to find them for overhead Sylvine, the great white stallion, Guardian of the Pass, had been locked in combat with Krowll, the serpent of darkness, one of the spirits of Dréagg. How the sky had screamed with their struggle, the struggle for his, Bracca's, soul and how awful, at the end, had been Krowll's anger as he tasted defeat.

He told them of Sylvine who was Ammdar's horse in the days before the fall; inseparable whether in the thick of the battle or in the halcyon moments of peace when they would travel together through the forests and the hills regathering their strength. 'And then,' continued Raagon, 'after the fall of Ammdar, Sylvine went back to Ashgaroth. But he would not leave his master so now he drifts among the clouds above Operrallmar watching over Ammdar and waiting for the time that they may ride together once more. And he watches also for the forces of darkness as they fester and lurk in the mire, so that Ashgaroth may know their every movement. So it was that when Dréagg sent Krowll to take you, Sylvine was there to protect you and to beat him off. But the struggle for your spirit sapped your strength and left you weak. You must rest here, with us, until you recover for you will need all your power in the awful struggles that lie ahead.'

He stopped speaking then and for a little time no one

spoke. An aura of great peace and calm lay upon them like a mist and Bracca seemed to lose the awareness of his body so that he felt as if he was floating on a cloud of scented air. He began to look around the room then, almost as if he was seeing it for the first time. On one side of the huge fireplace there was a large, curtained bed, like the one he had seen Tara in downstairs only more elaborate. The wooden base was carved, as were the four posts that supported the drapes, with a dense and intertwining mass of foliage within which Bracca could distinguish various animals all seemingly headed in the same direction. He followed them until his gaze came to rest on the headboard, in the centre of whose dark panel was inlaid in white a tall figure on a horse which Bracca instinctively knew was Ammdar. The figure was riding away from the foot of the bed so that all that was visible was his back yet the skill of the craftsman was such that Bracca could feel the immensity of his power and magic and could imagine himself drawn, like the animals, towards the awesome figure of this, the greatest of all the elflords. And then with a jolt of horror Bracca remembered Ammdar's betrayal of them and into his mind there came a vision of that dark still night all those aeons of time ago in the forests of Spath when he had offered the animals the gift of Logic and after their rejection of it, had exacted his terrible revenge upon them – the creation of man.

Was it possible to forgive him for what he had done? He thought of Ammdar as Vane, the wolf, in the hall downstairs and he remembered the look in his eyes and knew that he had to find it in his heart to do so.

He looked away then, to the other side of the fireplace where, set in the large alcove between the stone chimney breast and the wall, were three wide shelves on each of which stood a scene. From where Bracca sat, all he could make out were crags and bluffs and rocks and islands, carved out of wood or stone and ornamented with greens, oranges, browns and yellows that he guessed were dried lichens and fungi, fashioned and twisted to represent trees, bushes and grass.

255

Raagon must have seen where he was looking for he got up from his chair and, taking Bracca and Tara by the hand, he led them across the floor until they were standing just in front of them.

'The palaces of the three elflords,' he said. 'On the top shelf you can see Rengoll's Tor, home of Malcoff and the mountain elves, where the towering peaks almost scrape the sky. In the middle there is the Isle of Elgol, where the Lord Saurelon met Nab and gave him the Faradawn of the Sea, and then here on the bottom shelf is the elvenoak, deep in the enchanted forest of Ellmondrill, wherein dwell the woodland elves led by the mighty Wychnor, Lord of the Forests and the Green Growing Things.'

As Bracca gazed in wonder at the three wonderfully intricate images, so his mind carried him off to those far away times when Nab, Beth, Brock and the others had made their epic journey to collect the Faradawn, the three essences of the elven kingdoms, in their bid to save the animals and the Eldron (the Friends) from destruction in the First Holocaust. Fragments of the legend returned to him in the words that Melvaig had used and which in turn had come from Arkron, the wise old Hebbdrill, as he read the Book to Melvaig in the terrible desert of Molobb. In his imagination he could see them sailing across the black pond of Ellmondrill to the elvenoak or dancing in the great hall to the magical sounds of the elven pipers; he saw them riding over the sea on the backs of the seals to reach Elgol and he imagined them playing and laughing on the beach, running through the waves, collecting stones and shells with which to decorate their little cave. And when he looked at the strange jagged rocks of Rengoll's Tor there came to him a picture of Malcoff and his giant eagle, Curbar, as they sat behind the rocks and watched the last terrible battle between the elves and the Urkku on the slopes around the foot of the Tor.

His consciousness focused on these images and he became more and more immersed in them, weaving them together

256

so that the story of the Faradawn lived again in his mind. And then he became aware of the sounds of music, dancing among the outer fringes of his thoughts and forming a haunting and evocative accompaniment to the scenes that were playing in his head. Slowly then, for fear of disturbing its flowing lyricism, he turned and looked at Raagon who was cradling a strangely-shaped stringed instrument on his lap and strumming or picking out the notes with a fiercely rhythmic intensity that lifted Bracca's spirit until the blood seemed to sing in his veins and his heart pounded in time. Its clamouring jangle chopped through the air in the room and gripped him with a force so powerful that he almost felt stunned. A wave of exhilaration swept over him, driven on by the extraordinary rhythm; intricate staccato patterns of sound that merged and separated, dipped and soared as if involved in some elaborate game with each other. And in between the surging rhythms Bracca could hear delicate rippling arpeggios that bound them together into an awesome tapestry of music that lifted up his spirit and sent it soaring into the air in a shimmering spume of light to join the travellers of Silver Wood on their strange and mystical odyssey of salvation.

How long the music lasted he could not say for while in its grip he felt the touch of Ashgaroth and time stood still. At last though, he sensed that the music had gone and he realized with a shock that Raagon was no longer with them. Exhausted then, though still swept along on a tide of exaltation, he felt Tara's hand guiding him gently across to the bed. Reaching it, he pulled off his boots and fell on his back onto the deliciously soft expanse of quilt that seemed to stretch away before him in a blur of white. For a moment or two of consciousness he was aware of the fresh tangy scent of mint and then the hungry pull of sleep drew him down into oblivion.

For a little while Tara sat on the edge of the bed, watching him as he slept, stroking his face gently and revelling in the luxury of this private time together in comfort. Poor Bracca!

she thought: caught up in the tangled web of destiny; in the unravelling of events too awesome and momentous for man to understand. How much did he really comprehend? And yet through it all he had remained constant and strong; unwavering in his faith. She began to trace the outline of his chin with her fingertips and then so lightly that all she could feel was the warm mist of his breath, she ran her finger back along his lips.

Looking at him she ached with sympathy and love, a little ball of pain rising from her stomach until it lodged in her chest, constricting her so that she found it difficult to breathe. She longed to hold him, to comfort and protect him with the power of her magic and to invest some of her strength in him, the inherited wisdom of the elvenlore, so that he would be better able to withstand the darkness that lay ahead.

Hardly knowing what she was doing, her conscious mind far away, she began playing with the wooden toggles on his jerkin until, without realizing it she found she had undone two of them and the garment had fallen away to reveal part of his chest. Spurred on then by a strange and intense curiosity she carefully unfastened the others until the top of his body was naked, his skin glowing in the firelight, the contours of his muscles accentuated in the shadows thrown by the flames. Delicately, almost without touching, she ran the palms of her hands slowly down from the symmetry of his shoulders and over the soft curve of his stomach until, suddenly, driven by an overwhelming instinct that she could neither recognize or control, she leant all the way over and kissed the shallow valley between his ribs. For a moment she lingered there, allowing the musky tang of his body to wash over her, and then she moved her kiss a little higher, and a little higher, until her mouth closed over one of his nipples and, ever so gently she began to massage it with her tongue. He stirred then, shifting his legs as if to get more comfortable, and she froze, her heart hammering fearfully lest he should wake up. Then, with a deep and heavy sigh he seemed to settle back down into the depths of oblivion and, unable to resist the emotions that sang in her spirit, she began to move her tongue once again until, to her delight and surprise she felt the little bulb of flesh start to grow. She went to the other one and then, as before, the nipple become swollen in her mouth. A little moan of pleasure escaped his lips and his eyelids flickered but he was buried too deeply in sleep to be able to surface and so she carried on, going from one to the other and as she did so, she continued to stroke her fingers over his skin, enjoying the softness of the surface contrasting with the firm hard feel of the muscles underneath. After a while she felt, quite suddenly, a great wave of exhaustion and she climbed up on to the bed at his side, folding her arms around him and pulling herself against him so that the contours of their bodies came together in a flowing sea of unity, binding them in a way she would never have thought possible. Tightly she squeezed him, hoping he would wake up and respond but at the same time terribly fearful of the consequences if he did. And as she wrapped herself about him there was, in the fierceness of her embrace, a safety and security created by their closeness which warmed her soul. So she lost herself in the cocoon of their physical coalescence and Ashgaroth sweetened her dreams and nursed her wounded spirit.

CHAPTER XVII

When Bracca woke up, he lay for a long time in a euphoric daze, barely conscious, floating on a deliciously isolated cloud which nothing seemed able to reach; no thought, no feeling, no emotion. And then, very gradually, he became aware of little things; the rustle of the embers as they settled in the grate, the lingering, faintly acrid smell of the woodsmoke, and the slivers of light which knifed their way through the join in the curtains and cut swathes of silver in the gloom. Next he felt her, curled up beside him, her body resting heavily against his and her arms entwined around his chest so tightly that he was afraid of waking her if he moved. For a few moments he revelled in their intimacy, feeling her breath against his cheek and the softness of her flesh nestling into his side, and then, quite suddenly, he was awake, his mind racing with curiosity, eager to explore this new environment which he seemed to find himself in for the first time.

So, slowly and reluctantly, he extricated himself from her embrace, taking great care not to wake her, and slipping quietly out of the bed walked over towards the curtains. He paused for a moment then, apprehensive and uncertain, before he pulled them apart just far enough to put his head through.

A blast of cold air struck him and the light was so dazzling that he felt almost physically repelled but then, pulling himself together and shielding his eyes from the glare, he looked outside.

The first thing that impressed him was the height. They appeared to be at the top of a kind of tower which itself was at one corner of the palace. There was a sheer drop beneath him, the hard lines of the stone broken only by a mass of ivy that swarmed all over the walls. The air was cold and crisp and clear and on the ground lay patches of glistening snow interspersed amongst the green in a patchwork mosaic. Just to one side were a number of enormous trees, their bare branches waving gently in the breeze, the intricate tracery of the twigs standing out clearly against the background of opalescent blue sky. Three large rooks flew across the sun towards them and Bracca could see the dense clusters of their nests perched precariously in the topmost boughs. They landed with a clatter, disturbing their companions who began cawing angrily and shattering the stillness with their raucous cries.

Now Bracca's gaze fell to the ground once more. A high stone wall ran out and around from the palace in a huge half circle and opposite him, at the point furthest away, there was a simple wooden gate. Within the wall the ground fell away in random terraces, each little patch of green surrounded by a hedge of fir. Fascinated, he looked more closely and he saw that each little garden had, in its turn, a subtle difference in character. In one there might be a statue of an animal or some other figure while in others there would be a conglomeration of bushes or little trees, seemingly haphazard yet on closer inspection revealing distinct patterns that struck inexplicable chords of familiarity deep within him. In one there was a gentle slope of smooth, even sand in which were a number of boulders. Bracca could not tell whether their positioning was natural or whether they had been placed there. It did not matter: as he looked at them a feeling of peace came over him, a glow of contentment engendered by the absorption of himself into the design. He seemed to lose the sense of his own identity and become one with them, drawn down amongst the rocks until he came back into himself suddenly, with a jolt.

His gaze shifted then to an area a little to one side, a garden completely enclosed by a thick hedge. There was a small pond in the middle in the centre of which a fountain threw a constant spray of water high up into the silvery air and as it fell back down, the sun caught the drops and transformed them into a glistening rainbow arch.

He looked up, his attention dragged away suddenly by a force he could not identify. A cold chill swept through him and he shivered involuntarily. His legs felt shaky and he became aware of a loosening of his bowels so that he had to fight to contain himself. It was to a spot in the middle distance that he found his eyes drawn; beyond the stone wall that surrounded Operrallmar, down across the expanse of woodland that swept away out of sight into a narrow steep-sided ravine, and finally through to a small patch of foliage that was just visible at the end of the deep gorge. He knew what it was even before he heard Tara, suddenly standing at his side, name it in a voice that trembled and shook with fear.

'Spath,' she said, almost whispering it, as if afraid that the very sound of the name could harm them.

A strange yellowish-green light rose up from it and tainted the air with an unnatural luminescent sheen that unsettled him and filled him with a terrible sense of foreboding. The light seemed to come from a thick layer of mist that blanketed everything except for the topmost branches of the trees that floated above it in a multi-hued mass of green like seaweed-covered rocks at low tide. There was something about the leaves that was wrong. Why did they disturb him? He stared hard, squinting his eyes against the harsh light from the mist as he tried to focus on them. It was their colours; red, black, vivid unnatural green, blue, yellow and white, all shining with an eerie bright phosphorescent glow and none of them moving; instead hanging suspended in absolute stillness although the branches of the trees just outside his window were waving in the wind. Then a further thought struck him – why were there any leaves at all? It was winter; late winter, perhaps, but still far too early for the leaves to be out yet.

He became alarmed then, really frightened, for the first time, of the future. He had not given much thought to Spath until now. The vague words of warning that Nab had given him had been pushed to the back of his mind in the immediacy of the problems that had confronted him since then. Now though, the prospect of Spath loomed like an enormous shadow on the horizon and he could evade it no longer. Soon he would be within its awesome presence, armed only with his wits and the magic of Tara.

And then Tara spoke and it was as if she had known the doubts and fears that had begun to sap Bracca's spirit.

'Ammdar asked me,' she said, 'whether we would take him and Raagon with us to Spath. He felt that Ashgaroth had willed it and that without him we would probably fail in our mission. A chance to redeem himself; to put right some of the evil he has wrought upon the earth. Raagon said it was for us to decide.'

For a moment the harsh glare of Spath seemed to beam out through the air towards him, its stagnant phosphorescence numbing his reason, and then with a wrench he turned away, grateful to embrace the strand of hope that Tara's words had provided.

'Yes,' he said, and she could hear the relief in his voice. 'Yes, we must take them. The four of us together; you, me, Raagon and Ammdar; it is right, I know it.'

'Good. I'm pleased. It is what I feel too. We must trust him ... and forgive him.' She paused for a moment before continuing with the second part of Ammdar's request. 'He also wanted to see the Belt,' and as the full significance of the words dawned on Bracca, he felt a tremor of resentment deep within himself. Nab had given it to him and he had been imbued in the magic of its power. Now, though he would still wear it and though it would be he who would use it to open the Droon, he could never again feel that it was really his. The rightful and true owner was Ammdar and it would be impossible for Bracca to forget that. But, of course, he would let Ammdar see it and in a way the fact of his asking was honour enough.

'Yes,' he said, revealing none of his feelings to Tara. 'Of course he can see it.'

They both turned then to the sound of the door opening. It was Raagon, carrying a wooden tray piled high once more with the flat brown cakes they had had last night and a brown earthenware jug full of water.

'Quick, while they're hot,' he said, and hurrying over to the table Bracca and Tara started to eat. They were delicious and, with accompanying sips of the ice-cold, slightly nutty-tasting water, Bracca soon felt wonderfully fortified.

Raagon watched them enjoying their food with obvious pleasure on his face and then, after asking if they had slept well, he put the vital question to Tara.

'What have you decided?' he said, hardly daring to think what her reply might be. She knew what he meant.

'We'd like you with us, both of you. We...' she paused, searching for the right words. 'We would be honoured.'

Raagon got up then and coming round the table embraced first Bracca and then Tara who stood to return his gesture; and his voice, when he spoke, trembled with emotion.

'It is good,' he said. 'It is as it should be. I am very glad. And you will not be sorry. Oh no! We will not let you down. You can have no idea what this means to me and, especially, to Ammdar. When you've finished your food we will go down and tell him.'

So they quickly ate the last of the cakes and followed Raagon out of their room and back down the stairs into the hallway. The Old One kept looking back at them and smiling; his eyes bright and sparkling; his step lighter, almost a youthful spring. There was about him an air of tremendous, scarcely containable, excitement and when he opened the great door into the main room where they had left Vane the night before Bracca could see his hand trembling.

The wolf was on the far side of the room, his coat gilded with the shafts of daylight that poured down from the window spaces high above them so that he appeared to be floating, suspended in a swirling golden nimbus.

Raagon ran across the floor to greet him, arms out-stretched and laughing for joy, so that there could be no doubt as to the good news that he brought. Bracca watched from the other side of the room as the Old One spoke to the wolf in the strange tongue that he could not understand. Vane was silent until Raagon had finished speaking, merely looking at him with a fixed intensity, ears down and mouth closed, and then Bracca heard a long low rumble of contentment in the wolf's throat and saw the pleasure in his eyes as he and Raagon walked back to join them. His whole demeanour emitted an aura of such happpiness, the flatness of the ears, the spring in his stride, that Bracca suddenly felt a great warmth for the wolf – Ammdar – and without thinking he buried his hands under the loose folds of his jerkin and taking a buckle in each hand he unfastened the clasp and took the Belt off. As he held it out in front of him Vane stopped and his gaze locked on to it. He stood there rigidly, without blinking, and only the twitching of his muscles betrayed the impression that he had been turned to stone. And then, impelled by some force that came upon him unbidden, Bracca walked forward slowly and placed the Belt around the wolf's neck, bringing the clasps together so that they hung down in front of him like a medallion, the copper-coloured serpents standing out against the silver grey of his fur.

Proudly he stood then, his head erect and his pointed ears upright like the twin peaks of a crown, as the magic of the Belt, his Belt, poured over him. And through his mind, racing like the waves of a winter tide, came the memories of his reign as the Silver Warrior when he vanquished the forces of darkness with Ashgaroth as his lord, Silvyne carrying him forward and Raagon at his side. And these were were the days when he dwelt in the light before Dréagg ensnared him. Of the darkness he remembered nothing; it was as if the splendour of the Belt around his neck had cauterized his mind of the foulness of those times. Bracca stared, awe-inspired, as Vane's eyes shone with a strange unearthly glow, a light that seemed to come from the beginning of time itself – as clear and pure as the first spring dew on a spider's web. And as Bracca, Tara and Raagon watched, so the outlines of the wolf seemed to grow blurred and hazy and, for a moment it was Ammdar standing before them, tall and powerful, his mane of silver hair shimmering in the sunlight and the gentle beauty of his face transmitting infinite faith to each of them. At the sight of his friend, Raagon's old eyes filled with tears that streamed down his face in rivers of salty warmth.

'Ammdar,' he cried, and then, as quickly as he had come, the Silver Warrior was gone and it was as if he had never been. Yet Vane was still there, with the transcendent light still in his eyes, seemingly unaware of what they had seen. Bracca, dazed and already doubting the truth of what his eyes had revealed, watched mesmerized as the wolf turned to him and with a bow of his head indicated that Bracca should take back the Belt. He did so with trembling hands and replaced it under his jerkin, the serpentine fastenings coming together almost of their own volition. It felt different somehow, as if having been re-united with its original owner it had acquired new strength and greater power, both of which now transmitted themselves to Bracca who felt a ripple of energy pass through his body. He seemed to acquire new presence, to gain in stature and bearing, and a strange aura of power emanated from him almost as if Ammdar had invested him, through the tangible medium of the Belt, with the mantle of leadership. He shifted uncomfortably under the gaze of the others, aware of his new responsibility and of their fresh perception of him. They were looking to him to command them, expecting him to make the decisions from now on. They would advise him and he would listen, either accepting or rejecting what they said, but he was the final arbiter and, whether right or wrong, he had to take sole responsibility for the judgements and choices that were made.

'The time has come,' he said, and his words now carried a sense of authority, 'for us to leave for Spath. We must gather as much food as we can take and carry it with us. Raagon, do you have carriers? And drink? Show us where they're kept and we'll pack everything up.'

So Raagon led them down some steep stone steps to a huge underground pantry and by the light of beeswax candles they filled a number of woven packs with dried fruit, oatcakes, biscuits and other items which Bracca did not recognize. They worked quickly and quietly, the ageless chill of the stones finding its way into the very marrow of their bones and setting each of them thinking about the grim uncharted future that lay ahead, a vision of darkness and uncertainty in which not only their fates but also the fate of earth was enshrined, for this would be the final conflict as Ashgaroth had told Bracca long ago when he was back in the land of Haark, at a time when his world was so different that he could hardly believe the truth of its existence. Bracca recalled the words now. 'You will play a part,' he had said, 'that in the aeons of time to come will be regarded as the Beginning.' Little had he known then of their awesome significance. Now, he was beginning to understand and the power that flowed through him from the Belt of Ammdar seemed to bind him to Ashgaroth in a way he had not known before. He felt a closeness, as if Ashgaroth was at his side watching and guiding him towards this ultimate struggle.

The bags were soon packed and they all went back up into the hallway where Bracca and Raagon attached two panniers to Vane's back, one on either side. Intent on what they were doing while the wolf stood patient and still, they did not notice Tara's change and they were shocked when they turned round and saw the deer standing where she had been only moments before. Raagon was awestruck; mesmerized by this magic that he had witnessed for the first time, and Bracca felt a shock such as he always felt when she changed. He fought against the sense of betrayal that threatened to overwhelm him; as if she had deliberately changed to deprive him of her company. Or was it jealousy that made him angry; jealousy of this symbol of the difference between them, her links with the elves and with Nab and Beth rendering her in some way better than him. Or again was it that this evidence of her magic reminded him of the forbidden nature of their love, exacerbating the pain of their abstinence.

And yet he could see the reason for her transformation as they loaded her with food and drink, and his emotions were soon forgotten in the effort of packing up. Finally, when he and Raagon had put their packs on, it was time to leave.

'Wait here,' said the Old One. 'There is something I must give you,' and he walked over to a carved wooden chest against the wall. Slowly, for the lid was heavy, he opened it and resting the top against the wall he reached in, obviously searching for something. Then, after a few moments he straightened up and, turning round held out a magnificent sword. As he drew it from its scabbard the light caught it and the blade exploded into flashes of liquid silver.

'This belonged to Ammdar. It is yours now; he wants you to have it.' Bracca hesitated and Raagon spoke again. 'Here, take it. Wear it on his Belt; it has lain idle for too long. Fashioned with ore from the sacred mines of Smoo in the east, and woven with the silver light of Ashgaroth, it can only be used against the forces of evil. So it was that after the fall Ammdar was unable to carry it and I put it away, in the chest, till the day should come when it could go into battle again. It is called Tabor; may it light the darkness ahead for us all!'

Bracca walked forward and took the sword. Then, taking the Belt from its place next to his skin, he fastened the scabbard to it and replaced it around his waist. Now though, he wore it over the top of his jerkin and the sword hung down on his left side, its tip almost touching the ground. Yet when he walked he scarcely felt its weight and only the shifting pattern of its rhythm against his thigh reminded him of its presence; that and the feeling of strength that it gave him, flowing through him with each step that he took.

'We must go,' he said, glancing a little apprehensively at Vane as he did so, and finding to his relief that the eyes of the wolf showed nothing but calmness and warmth. For the shadow of a moment each held the other's gaze and a tide of understanding flowed between them before Raagon walked purposefully forward and, after lifting the heavy latch, opened the great wooden door and allowed a stream of pale sunlight to pour through into the hall, momentarily startling them with its brightness.

It was Bracca who led them out with Tara and Vane just behind, leaving Raagon to close the door after them. The excitement Raagon felt at the epic mission they were embarking upon was tempered now with an edge of sadness as a kaleidoscope of memories suddenly rushed through his mind and filled him with a nostalgic ache for all the good times he and Vane had shared together in the safety and comfort of Operrallmar; the long winter evenings by the fire while the snow piled up outside or the lazy days of summer basking outside in the sunshine or working in the vegetable patch. He remembered the delicious smell of oatcakes as they cooked in the oven by the fire and the taste of the wine as they stared into the red embers on the hearth and dreamed of the days gone by. At times too, thoughts of the future had crossed their minds for never had either of them abandoned their faith that Ashgaroth would come to them and give them the chance to play a part in the final struggle. Now, that faith had been rewarded yet Raagon's initial euphoria had begun to evaporate beneath the simmering flames of fear that reached out to him from the eerily shimmering incandescence of Spath. As the door thudded shut, locking away the peace and security of Operrallmar so that it became a mere memory, already remote, so a cobweb

269

of fear started to spread throughout his body, mesmerizing him, paralysing him so that it was only when Bracca, sensing the turmoil that had begun to rage in Raagon's spirit, laid a hand on his arm and gently held the Old One that he tore himself free of his trance-like reverie and remembered where he was.

'Come on,' said Bracca. 'It will do no good to stay. You have your memories; they cannot be taken from you, and we are together – you and Vane, Tara and I.'

So, turning sadly away, they set off across the terraced gardens towards the wooden gate in the high stone wall that encircled them. The brittle brightness of the morning reflected back from the fir hedges and infused each garden with a special magical light. The wind blew through the branches of the elms and the oaks that soared high above their heads, filling the air with a wild elemental rushing sound that seemed to come straight from Ashgaroth, lifting their spirits as they perceived this fragment of his strength; his angry, raging breath shaking the trees with such fury as would cause Dréagg to shrink back in wonder at the might of his opponent.

Down they went, over the grass and along the little winding path that led past the rock garden; then further on past a statue of a heron, hewn from marble, that shimmered with sparkling dewdrops of silver as Bracca and Tara looked at it. Proudly it stood, its long beak pointing out towards Spath as if in defiance of the evil that lay there and in its eyes, though made of stone, they saw the light of Ashgaroth so that Bracca's mind was filled with images of Golconda and the terrible flight from Barll. There were other statues too that they passed, of animals both known and unknown to him and of elven figures which he could not recognize but with which Tara was familiar, knowing them by the runes carved on their pedestals and the stories told of them to her by Nab; the interlaced acorn cups of Wychnor, Lord of the Forests, who succeeded Ammdar after the fall; the three cowries of Saurelon of the Seas and, a little apart from the others with his great eagle Curbar perched on his shoulder, the distinctive face of Lord Malcoff, elf-ruler of the Mountains. There were others too; Morar the piper, Faraid, battle-leader of the sea elves, and Reev who was Wychnor's captain in Ellmondrill; Embo and Urigill; Druin, Moiven and Braewire; Eynort and Ardvasar.

One figure only was missing, Ammdar, the mightiest of them all, the great Silver Warrior. Tara remembered how Wychnor had described him to Nab. 'His power was such,' he had said, 'that the grass turned to silver where he walked and the leaves changed to gold when he wished it.' Yet though there was no statue left now, there could be no doubt that it had been his figure on the plinth where now stood only a heap of rubble. Who had smashed it? Raagon, in a blaze of anger at his friend as he turned against Ashgaroth; or one of the legendary elven warriors who had previously fought at his side – furious now at his betrayal. Or maybe even Ammdar himself, raging against his own image as the Champion of Light. As they filed beside it now, Bracca wondered what thoughts were going through Vane's mind for his head was bowed low and his eyes downcast. Yet he could not resist a sneaking glance to the side and Bracca detected in that skulking look such an attitude of despair and unutterable shame that he wished he had not been witness to it.

Suddenly the wall appeared just in front of them. Strewn with bramble briars and the thorny vines of wild roses and festooned with clinging strands of ivy, it was almost impossible to see. The blocks of stone out of which it had been built were encrusted with layers of grey-green lichens that welded them together into a solid organic mass and there was a timelessness and venerability about it that stirred Bracca's heart. The dark wooden door was set deep inside an archway and Bracca saw Raagon's hand dig deep inside his jerkin and come out holding a large ornate key which he fitted inside the lock.

His hand froze as if reluctant to turn it, and then, as of one

271

mind, they all turned and looked back at Operrallmar basking in the early afternoon sunshine with the majestic backdrop of mountains behind.

The snow on the peaks glistened with twinkling silver lights and Bracca found it hard to imagine the terrible journey across them only two days ago. Two days! Another lifetime away. Strange to think that he had known nothing then of Raagon or Vane and that Ammdar had simply been a mythical name that Melvaig had recounted to him from the book of the Faradawn.

And then his stomach turned over as an image of the black serpent broke over his spirit and with a shudder he turned quickly away. Raagon too had looked forward, this last picture of Operrallmar imprinted indelibly on his mind, and he was turning the key slowly. It grated a little and stuck part way round. Anxiously, his hand shaking, he tried again. How long since it had been opened? When he had brought Ammdar back as the wolf, Vane. How many ages ago was that? And yet now, to his relief, as he turned it in the lock for the second time it swung round easily as if it had been only yesterday. Raagon lifted the iron latch and pushed open the door, holding it back so that Tara, lowering her head to allow her antlers through, could go first.

As they walked out they found themselves in a tall deep-sided ravine. High banks towered above them on either side out of which grew a dense mass of vegetation; the dank smell of wet rotting bracken hung in the air and the massive trunks of ancient elms and oaks blotted out most of the light so that it took their eyes some time to adjust to the gloom. The floor of the ravine was narrow, strewn with boulders and old fallen branches, and a small stream ran down it; the sound of the water amplified and echoing against the banks.

Raagon shut the door behind them and then, pausing only to put the key back in his pocket, he led the way down a little path that wound its way alongside the stream. It was slippery; the dampness covering the stones with a smooth greasy sheen, and, sure-footed though she was, Tara found the going difficult. Raagon was in front, then Vane, then Bracca in front of Tara. They walked in silence, each of them buried in their own thoughts, enjoying the song of the water as it meandered its way over its bed of pebbles and stones.

When the light grew too dim for them to see properly they began to look around for a wide flat area where they could eat and sleep, but there was nowhere near so Vane went ahead to look for a place while the others waited. After a little while he was back, reappearing round a corner just in front and barking softly for them to follow him. He led them forward until, turning a bend, the sides of the ravine suddenly seemed to drop away and they appeared to be out in the open, in a large shallow basin with only a low rise at either side to shelter them. Ahead there was blackness, nothing except an infinite dark void, but as they stared out into it each of them felt the presence of Spath as a black veil drawn over their soul. Tomorrow, they would be there and the evil forces spawned of Dréagg would be unleashed upon them. Tonight they had to sleep, to get some rest for the times ahead, for it could be many days before they would be able to sleep again.

So they settled down on the soft grass, feeling the dampness strike through into their bones, and shut their eyes against the night. But oblivion did not come easily and though the soft tendrils of sleep kept flickering around them, their subconscious struggled against it and fought to maintain its dominion. But they were tired and weariness eventually overtook them, though their rest was not peaceful; punctuated by vague nightmarish visions that welled up behind their eyes and vanished before the image grew clear, exploding slowly into drifting patterns of light, garish globules of colour floating through the core of their minds. Sometimes a face would hover above their heads; a hideous caricature of a man with bulbous eyes and thick protruding lips. As it leered down at them, sinewy gobs of spittle ran down from its gaping mouth and, toss though they might, they were unable to escape its inexorable descent until it fell

273

on their faces, covering them with a nauseous layer of slime that smeared itself across their eyes and clung to their mouths and noses so that they felt as if they were being suffocated. Desperately then they thrashed and shook, struggling to break free, but it was impossible.

CHAPTER XVIII

And they were still flinging themselves wildly about in the middle of the night when the clouds broke up briefly and allowed the moon to cast a brilliant white light down upon them. Then Globb, perched high in his look-out post in the heart of Spath, saw the four sleeping figures and, smiling to himself, signalled down to the goblins waiting at the base of the tree to take the message back to Degg that those they were awaiting had at last been seen. Looking away from them then and turning to the east he gazed into the distance and watched as the massive army with Sienogg and Barll at its head made its slow and ponderous way through the beginnings of the forest. Scouts had already been sent out to meet them and guide them back to the goblins' lair, the place they called Gan, where even now Degg was preparing a welcome. Soon they would be together, man and goblin, the forces of Dréagg united at last for the final struggle. And Globb thought also of the Kwkor, hovering deep in their caves underground, and his black heart quivered with pleasure at the prospect of witnessing their terrible powers again. Let the elves come, as they would, to save the Droon, for they were only hastening to their own destruction. Not since the days Before-Man, during the time of the great wars between the elves and the goblins, had the Kwkor been seen.

275

Then they had wrought a terrible havoc among the elves, only retiring to their caves when the ascendance of Dréagg was assured. But they were to be used sparingly for with each kill they fed off their victims and absorbed their powers so that, let loose for too long, Dréagg feared they would become uncontrollable and turn even against the goblins. Accountable only to him, they were his spiritual children; the physical manifestation of his evil, and though Globb relished the thought of their use against the elves, he could not quell the shiver of fear that ran through him as he recalled their image, blotting out the sky with their huge wings as they sought out their victims, the shadows they cast on the earth redolent with menace.

And even as Globb's thoughts dwelt on the Kwkor so the Halls of Gan rang with the sounds of activity as the goblins scuttled along the corridors, through the rooms, in the kitchens and down the cellars making ready for the arrival of the army, for they were to be made welcome, these human allies, fêted and fed so that they would be at their strongest for the great struggle that lay ahead. For many days now the preparations had been taking place in readiness for this moment. The forest had rung with the sounds of death and the earth was stained black with the blood of the animals that had been slaughtered for the feast, while the vats of wine were tested to ensure their strength and the sleeping quarters laid out in comfort, for the army would be utterly exhausted at the end of their journey. The musicians too had been practising their martial anthems, the strident blasts of sound that seemed to come straight from Dréagg himself to lift the spirits of the goblins and freeze the blood of their enemies as they marched to battle. The armourers had prepared the weapons; sharpening and honing, polishing and tightening, until the vast array of swords and shields and spears and bows and arrows were perfect, glinting in the strange forest light that shone through on to them where they hung on the walls of the corridors.

Through all this hustle and bustle Degg sat impassively in

his little room at the top of the West Tower; watching, listening and commanding through his lieutenants, monitoring every move, every word and every feeling through his network of informers. He planted dissenters among the ranks, to flush out those who were dissatisfied or restive and to bring forth the names of those who could form a challenge to his authority so that they could be destroyed. He encouraged divisiveness and rivalry amongst his captains so that they would be too preoccupied with each other to turn against him.

Thus it was that he reigned supreme, as he had since the day, so long ago, when he had smitten Ammdar with his sword. Each against the other, quarrelling, bickering and fighting amongst themselves, so that his authority would stand above them all. Such was his power and so devastating the aura of fear that he engendered that now, after all these aeons of time, he was still their master, still able to command obedience with a word or a look.

So he sat content in his room, squatting on the high stool by the window and looking out over the courtyard as his minions scampered this way and that, falling over themselves in their frantic rush to carry out his orders. His black eyes gleamed with pleasure and his thick lips frequently drew back from his teeth in a quivering leer of satisfaction as he envisaged the battle that lay ahead; the final epic conflict. And it was all coming together as Dréagg had said it would; that all the forces of darkness would join in one mighty army, man and goblin together, in an alliance that would crush forever the fragmented remains of the once-great elven host; that the elves would be led by those who were of the lines of Nab and of Melvaig and that their mission would be the finding of the Droon and the Separation of the Seeds. This was the bait that Dréagg had placed before them, to lure them to their destruction in a last desperate attempt to reclaim the world for Ashgaroth. And as he thought of the Droon safe within the labyrinthine caves far beneath him, so he turned and looked out of the window and watched the

277

bright silver light of the moon throwing splashes of white on the black surface of the encircling moat. He did not know the depths of those dark waters, nor what creatures dwelt in their subterranean caverns but of one thing he was sure; that, even if the unthinkable were to happen and the one called Bracca was to get through, he would never get across the causeway to violate the sanctity of Gan.

The moon had begun to slide slowly down out of the sky by the time that Straygoth, riding ahead of the others, saw two shadows fluttering towards him out of the forest. He froze where he was, willing his horse to stay still and hardly daring to breathe, while his eyes scoured the trees for the slightest sign of movement. Nothing! Not a breath of wind nor the shiver of a leaf. Had he imagined it? No, that never happened; not even in the state of exhaustion he was in now and had been in for as long as he could recall. No, there had been something ahead; he was certain of it. Patiently he waited and it was not long before he was rewarded with the sight of them again. Nearer now, and moving slowly so that he could see them more clearly. Two shapes silhouetted against the moonlight, their long pointed heads picked out in detail so that Straygoth could see their razor sharp teeth and their large angular ears; their eyes too, thin slits of light in the dark triangle of their faces, shining out across the clearing as they turned towards him. And then a hand darted up into the air, claw-like, and a long thin sinewy forefinger beckoned him towards them.

Mesmerized, Straygoth tapped his horse's flanks and moved out from behind the tree. When it saw the goblins the horse shied and whinnied, almost throwing him off, but it became still as they started to duck and weave with a strange dancing motion, their bodies swaying hypnotically and their long nails raking the sky with patterns of light. On it walked then, as if in a trance, carrying its rider out into the clearing until it stopped just in front of them and he dismounted. And Straygoth was aware of nothing save the two creatures before him, for their presence had taken him over completely. The strange, pungent smell that hung in the air pervaded his senses; the physical shape of them – their hunch-backed stoop, their pot-bellies and the spiky angularity of their arms and legs, the little tail that protruded from the base of the spine and the apparent frailty of the sternum with the ribs exposed like furrows of sand on a beach. Still their bodies undulated, dancing to the rhythm of a pulse that only they could feel, and in the stillness Straygoth could hear the constant rasp of their breathing punctuated by the odd intermittent sibilance of their speech. And all the time, as a hypnotically rhythmic accompaniment, the perpetual clicking of their long fingernails. Barely corporeal, their spirit enveloped him completely and he was at one with them, drawn together by the darkness that united them under a common Creator.

'Go,' they said. 'Take us to the others. Then we will lead you to Degg.'

At once Straygoth turned and began to make his way back up through the trees to the place where Sienogg and Barll waited with the army stretching away behind them into the distance. Only the shuffling of the horses' hooves and the huffing of their breath broke the quiet and Straygoth could feel, almost as a tangible substance into which he rode, the overwhelming weariness and utter exhaustion of the warriors.

Straight to the two commanders he went and, speaking quietly, told them of what had occurred.

It was Sienogg who responded first, his thick lips pulled back from his teeth in a leer of satisfaction. 'At last,' he said. 'I hardly dared believe it. At last our time is come. Xtlan will be well pleased,' and he turned round to one of his captains.

'Send word back. Use Brale – he is our fastest rider. Hurry! Give the order.'

And still, despite the distance between them, the power of Xtlan held them all in its awesome grip. The memory of the Blaggvald, and the image of the master that had seared itself into their souls as they set out so long ago, still burned inside them with a fire as fierce as it had been then. Occasionally Sienogg's mind would stray and he thought of what would happen after the conflict had been won. *His* warriors; under *his* command, who he had held together and led through all the hardships of the journey, who he would lead to final victory. Xtlan; undefended. Was it possible?

But then, as the blasphemy of these ideas began to translate into images in his head, so a sudden recollection of that last terrible vision would crash into him with appalling force and he would be left breathless and stunned, any thoughts of rebellion rendered totally and utterly inconceivable.

Barll too was relieved and excited at the news from Straygoth. The journey had been difficult and there had been times when doubt had descended upon him; a cloud of uncertainty in which he longed for the old times in Haark, when he alone had ruled and where his commands were supreme, where food was abundant and he could have any woman he chose. To have left all that for the abstinence and adversity of these past moons seemed, at these times, to be madness. The visions of glory that had so intoxicated him then, seemed to have been a hollow dream as he rode with Sienogg, exhausted, hungry and bored, through the endless plains of the Daarhill or sailed in the blistering heat over the Runell sea with the sun pouring its heat down upon them as they lay in the boats.

Now though, at last, those precious dreams were beginning to materialize, and as he looked across at Sienogg with the moonlight reflecting off the magnificent white stallion, he once again saw himself as he had been in his vision; riding at the head of the supreme army, a mighty leader whose deeds in battle and whose savagery and brutality were legendary and whose name engendered terror in the hearts of all men.

He looked up then and breathed deeply and all the leaves around him, utterly still, seemed to form a dark and impregnable net, as if Dréagg himself was protecting him. A glorious surge of invincibility suddenly swept him up and,

280

unable to contain his exhilaration he turned his face to the sky and let out a great cry that echoed throughout Spath so that it penetrated even the walls of Gan. Degg, hearing it, was well pleased for he recognized in its tones the blind fanaticism that takes men beyond the bounds of reason and logic so that their strength knows no limitations. It is then that they become truly the tool of Dréagg.

The warriors too heard Barll's cry and its triumphant sound banished their lethargic weariness as glorious images of battle and victory flashed before their eyes and set the blood singing in their veins. And they answered him as one, sending a great shout into the air in response to his call. He dismounted then and climbed up one of the nearby trees so that he could see as much of the army as possible and they could see him. Way back they stretched, winding up through the forest like an enormous snake, and when he had reached as high as he could he let out another enormous yell and they again returned it, raising their arms into the air in a spontaneous gesture of acclaim. Twice more the pattern repeated itself until with a final two-fisted salute he came down and got back upon the black horse that Xtlan had given him.

'Now!' he exclaimed, half to himself and half to Sienogg, and the exhilaration pulsing in his veins gave his voice a harsh and breathy resonance and set his nostrils flaring. 'Now it is starting. Now our time begins. Go, Straygoth. Follow the goblins and let us hurry to Gan.'

CHAPTER XIX

It was morning when the army caught its first sight of Gan. All night they had ridden slowly down the secret ways of Spath; Straygoth in the lead, then just behind him, Sienogg and Barll, and then the warriors. The men of Xtlan were in companies; Sienogg's own, the Company of Kegg, formed the vanguard. They were led by Tshonn, a vicious giant who Sienogg had trained in his own image. Next came the Company of Kil whose leader was Imril, known for his skill as a tactician; small, hatchet-faced and with a mind as cold as stone. After these rode Gemro, who led the Company of Saybok; Bodrax of the Company of Bowk, and Fowman of the Tardrees. Fowman's company brought up the rear for just in front of them came the men of Haark, Barll's men, over whom he had placed Kam who he believed to be his son. With a shaggy mane of black hair, heavy features and a huge frame of a body the two men were remarkably similar in appearance. In their manner also they were alike: stooped shoulders, a heavy shambling gait and a certain way of holding the head; hunched forward aggressively as if about to attack those to whom they spoke. Kam had been presented to Barll as his son by one of his women, Molokk, and the idea had so fascinated him that he had watched the boy grow up with interest, taking pride in the pugnaciousness and arrogance that he began to show early on. When he was old enough Barll had started to teach him the skills of fighting and the use of weapons and had found in the boy a hunger to learn and a natural aptitude that pleased him enormously. During their time in Xtlan Kam had so excelled in all facets of weaponry and warfare that Barll had had no compunction in appointing him leader of the men of Haark and so far had been well pleased with the command and authority he had shown.

The yellow light of dawn was just starting to filter through the overhanging leaves of the forest as the vanguard rode over the brow of a low rise and saw Gan stretching out below them. There was not a breath of wind and the leaves hung suspended in air that seemed almost solid. All around them thin tendrils of mist lay in drifts of greenish-yellow light and coated the capes of the warriors with myriads of tiny droplets of moisture so that they seemed almost to glow in the spectral pallor that reflected back from the leaves.

And there, at the bottom of the slope, lay Gan; the core of evil at the heart of Spath. It shimmered in the strange glow of the mist and at first Sienogg found it hard to identify its different parts but as they descended the hill it became clearer. He could see a large lake, its waters infinitely dark, in the centre of which was an island and on the island stood a long, low squat building, built of a stone so black that it was almost indistinguishable from the lake. Peering through the mist he could see that the building consisted of four round towers joined together by double walls to form a square. Across each of the four pairs of walls was a curved roof but the courtyard in the middle was open. Between the citadel and the shore of the lake was a narrow border of land littered with the stumps of trees, twisted and stunted by their efforts to grow in the perpetual gloom and dankness of the festering atmosphere.

Running across the lake to the island was a narrow causeway, a grass track built on a foundation of rocks that Sienogg could see protruding above the water. As he looked, scores of dark shadowy figures were moving along it, both to and from the citadel, and there was an air of frantic haste about their activities which pleased him for he guessed that it was connected with their arrival.

Now, as they approached still nearer to Gan, the trees became fewer and more sparse. They also noticed a number of conical mounds, roughly as high as a man and as wide as they were high, which increased in number the further down the slope they went. There appeared to be a small opening in each of them and Sienogg could only surmise that they were goblin dwellings for in the ethereal light of the early morning, dark figures could be seen moving around them. Sometimes, when they came close to one of the mounds a pair of yellow eyes would appear in the gloom of the doorway to stare out at these strange newcomers and Sienogg would feel its gaze following him as he passed by and would feel unnerved by the intense scrutiny. He became aware also of an odd smell in the air; heavy and acrid like the smell of rotting flesh, and he found his eyes watering with its pungent sharpness though he did not find it unpleasant. It reminded him of the feasts in Xtlan when they had gorged themselves on meat; stuffing themselves full to bursting until their bloated guts could hold no more.

Now, suddenly, the silence was broken by a succession of high-pitched twitterings and looking across to where the sound came from Sienogg could make out a row of cages inside which was a menagerie of small brown furry animals, none of which he recognized. Heaped one upon the other, packed in so tightly that they were almost indistinguishable from their companions, their agitation had apparently been caused by the arrival of some goblins carrying large clubs. The creatures were being dragged one at a time through a small aperture and battered to death on the ground outside in full view of the others. Sienogg smiled to himself at the display and pausing for a moment allowed himself the luxury of watching as the goblins exercised their sadistic ingenuity on the animals.

So the army carried on, winding its way down the track past an increasing number of the goblin mounds and every so often they would come across another of the cages with more creatures being slaughtered. Then finally they reached the bottom of the hill. Just ahead of them lay the black lake with Degg's citadel in the middle. Between them and the causeway was a short flat stretch of open ground and waiting there were a number of goblins. One, obviously the leader, rode on a large lizard-like creature that stood on two huge hind legs. Its body was covered in dark orange scales that shimmered like liquid gold in the eerie light and it stared at Sienogg and the others as they drew near, fixing them with its red eyes so that for the first time he could remember, Sienogg felt fear trickling down his spine. Here was something utterly beyond the limits of his experience, the light in those terrible eyes revealing a capacity for cruelty, and the power to administer it, that he had never witnessed before. Three large spikes protruded from its forehead and the middle one, longer than the other two, was crowned with a kind of barb from which grew tendrils of red that floated and waved in the air as if with a life of their own. It had two pairs of forearms. The first, in the normal position high up on its shoulders, were short and stubby with huge claws while the second pair seemed to come from its stomach. These were long and sinewy and at the end of them were large pincers that constantly opened and shut; snapping together as they did so with a noise that turned Sienogg's stomach to water.

'I am Zaggdar,' said the goblin, pulling back on the reins as the creature tried to lunge forward, 'and you are welcome in Spath. Do not be afraid of my mount; he will only attack those who displease us. But keep away from these, and these,' pointing to the pincers and the tendrils on the horn, 'for they are deadly and are outside my control.' The goblin's voice, low and rasping, seemed to paralyse Sienogg's thoughts; to dissipate his will so that he was unable to collect his wits together. And then, just as he was about to make his

285

reply, he heard Straygoth speaking.

'We thank you for your welcome,' he said, and the smoothness of his words infuriated both Sienogg and Barll who was equally discomposed. 'We have journeyed long and it is good to finally make our arrival.' He paused then, surprised and pleased by his own show of confidence. He felt truly at home here; at one with the spirit and feel of the place. And he was enjoying too his ascendancy over the others. The Mouse, Barll had called him, humiliating and tormenting him for all those years because he was physically weak and had no aptitude for fighting. Now who was the mouse? So his spirit cleaved to Zaggdar for he saw in him so much more worthy a leader, with all the qualities that he admired, and in his sense of kinship with the goblin he gained in stature.

'I am Straygoth,' he said, his voice strong and without fear, 'and I am called the Scout. This is Barll, leader of my people, the men of Haark, and this,' pointing to Sienogg, 'is our commander, War Chief of Xtlan, of the Company of Kegg – Sienogg.'

Zaggdar's eyes looked at them each in turn and then sitting up high in his crimson saddle, he raised an arm up towards the sky and rasped out a command.

'Go. Bring your commanders here. You and they will meet with Degg and stay in the citadel while the rest of your army remains here to be fed and entertained.'

As he spoke, the goblins at either side of him walked forward.

'Barll,' said Sienogg. 'You go and organize it. I'll stay here.' He paused. 'I think you're meant to take them with you,' and indeed, as Barll turned his horse round and started to make his way back, the goblins followed him.

Sienogg and Straygoth waited uncomfortably with Zaggdar. The goblin ignored them completely and seemed content to talk to the lizard, muttering to it in words they could not understand and stroking it behind the ears with his sinuous fingers. This seemed to have a soothing effect as it stopped its restless shifting about and grew still. Even the pincers stopped their ceaseless snapping, and the red tendrils, though still moving, became almost languid in the way they swayed around its forehead.

A feeling of unease gnawed at Sienogg's gut; he felt he should be talking, saying something, yet he was strangely afraid to open his mouth lest he somehow put himself at a disadvantage with the goblin who so obviously could not care less about him. He swore obscenely to himself. Why did he feel like this? Tongue-tied, insecure, almost – and his mind revolted at even framing the thought – inferior, to the black creature that sat so easily on his awesome mount.

Sienogg's painful musings were interrupted by the return of Barll and the other captains; Tshonn, Imril and Gemro in front, with Bodrax, Fowman and Kam just behind, each in the different colours of their companies; the reds and golds of Kegg and the black of Kil, grey for Saybok and maroon and blue for the Company of Bowk while the warriors of the Tardrees wore yellow. Kam was in green with trimmings of black; the regalia chosen for the men of Haark by Xtlan himself and made up for them by the women of one of the goat farms. The strangely diffuse sunlight wrapped them round in a golden haze, glinting off their halberds and spears and accentuating the cruel lines of their faces; the hook of the nose, the thick bulbous lips, the high cheekbones and deep-set, narrow eyes. Neither were they slovenly or lethargic as they rode up towards Zaggdar. Instead the fires of darkness radiated out from them and their attitude was heavy with menace and the awesome vitality of their epic purpose.

As they approached him Sienogg felt well pleased and his confidence began to return, tentatively but surely. Zaggdar could not ignore the power and authority of these men nor the fact that he, Sienogg, was their commander. Their strength, their power and their allegiance were owed to him, then to Xtlan and then to the Lord Dréagg; there was no place in that chain of command for a goblin. But to his

287

horror, Barll and the others hardly spared him a glance as they rode up to Zaggdar and lined up before him. Then, almost before he could think, Straygoth siezed the initiative and started to introduce them, presenting them in turn by name and company, each one riding forward a little as he did so for the goblin to inspect. And all Sienogg could do was to stand helplessly at one side, fuming inwardly at the humiliation he perceived to have been inflicted on him and watching the dispersal of his army as it broke up into companies, each one being led away into a different part of the forest by one of the goblins that had gone with Barll.

When the introductions were over Zaggdar spoke again.

'Follow me, all of you. It is time for you to enter the Palace of Gan and to meet Degg. But...' he paused and his lips pulled into a thin smile, 'take care as you cross the causeway. The smell of horseflesh...' and his words tailed away into a thin reedy cackling laugh. Then he pulled on the reins and swinging round to face the palace, he started to lead them across, the lizard moving with a strange rocking gait, rolling from side to side so that, to stay on, Zaggdar appeared to have to almost pour himself onto its neck, his long fingers and toes clinging on to its scales.

Sienogg made certain that he was the first to follow, urging his white stallion forward so that he forced Barll and Straygoth to ride behind him. After them came Tshonn and the other commanders and the odd procession made its way over the narrow stone track towards the palace. The still, black water that lay at either side of them seemed depthless as if it fell away to the very core of the earth and the yellow mist hanging over it was heavy with the stench of putrefaction. Frequently the horses baulked and it took all the tricks of persuasion that the riders could muster to force them forward. Sometimes, far out in the middle, a ripple of bubbles would ooze up through the dull sheen on the surface and disturb the smoothness; betraying the presence of something living deep in that awful black void.

Sienogg was half way across when he heard a sudden

288

commotion behind him and he turned round to see Gemro frantically trying to control his horse. The animal was rearing up on its back legs and whinnying madly, refusing to go any further. The more Gemro shouted at it the more it panicked, bucking and plunging so wildly that Fowman in front and Kam behind had to get well back out of the way to avoid being knocked off. Sienogg saw the horse's back hooves smashing down at the ground on the very edge of the causeway and then, powerless to do anything but look on, he watched as the track crumbled away and the horse toppled over into the water carrying Gemro with him. For a few seconds the horse threshed around trying to get back up while Gemro attempted to pull himself on to the path, calling wildly for help. But Fowman and Kam just watched, enjoying the spectacle and laughing at his desperation, until they decided to lend him a hand and started to get down off their horses.

'Leave him!' It was the voice of Zaggdar, rasping out a command that froze them where they were. 'It is the will of Dréagg. Let him be.'

Seeing his comrades refusing to help him Gemro started to whine and beg, his cries growing louder and more frantic as the icy grip of terror gnawed its way into his entrails. And then, suddenly, those watching from the causeway saw the water erupt in a great spume of spray and a terrible scream rent their ears as Gemro's body seemed to fly up into the air. As it came down it was caught by two huge pincers that slowly began to pull him apart and throw the segments back out into the lake where they had seen the bubbles. Something else then broke the surface and caught them before they landed, as if playing a game. Only when Gemro's head was torn off his neck did the screaming stop but then to Sienogg's horror he saw the head flying through the air towards him. Instinctively he put his hands out to catch it and, suddenly, there it was, Gemro's head nestling in his palms, the eyes wild and staring and the mouth still contorted in his last dying scream. Hardened though he was to terrible brutality, he felt the bile rising in his throat but sensing that it would have been seen as a sign of weakness for him to be sick he quelled his feelings. Then he was rescued by a sudden flash of inspiration.

'Here,' he said. 'Catch,' and he tossed the head to Barll who was next to him who caught it and who, in turn, threw it on to Straygoth. So it went to Tshonn and Imril and on down the line and they began laughing as the blood from Gemro's severed neck smeared itself on their hands, their laughter mingling with the terrible cries of the horse as it too was ripped apart and thrown back into the water.

Then, as suddenly as it had appeared, the creature had gone, leaving only the echoes of the dying screams of man and horse and a dark crimson slick on the surface. And Sienogg found to his dismay that somehow he had been left holding the head. The laughter had stopped abruptly when the thing disappeared and it would have appeared foolish and obvious now to try to pass it on.

'So! The prize is yours,' Zaggdar said mockingly. Sienogg looked up and met the goblin's eyes. They seemed to burn right into his mind, seeing through the elaborate charade of a few moments earlier for what it was; an attempt to disguise his weakness. 'Keep it,' the goblin continued. 'Take it to Degg; it will amuse him,' and he began to chuckle; wheezing out his delight in a way that set his shoulders shaking. 'She must have young,' and tossing the reins he pulled the lizard round and carried on across the causeway leaving Sienogg no option but to follow him, cradling the head between his legs where it oozed gore down the flanks of his horse. It was the eyes that most upset him; looking up with a mixture of blind terror and desperate entreaty that Sienogg could not easily shrug off.

Finally, after what seemed an age, they found themselves on the narrow strip of land between the water and the citadel. The mist hung heavily now all around them so that the far shore was lost from sight and the broken and twisted tree stumps seemed clothed in gauzy lace; jewelled with droplets of gold where the sunlight managed to penetrate through. The earth was black and damp and the horses' hooves left deep imprints as they walked towards the long low wall that faced them. As they got nearer Sienogg could see a small arched gate in the centre of it at either side of which was a round tower, and by the time they had reached it a number of goblins had emerged from these towers and were busy removing the bars that locked it.

'The visitors,' called Zaggdar as he went through, and Sienogg and the others felt the eyes of the goblins boring into them with curiosity as they passed. Then the gate slammed shut behind and they found themselves inside a small square courtyard in each corner of which stood a tall tower, bigger than those by the gate, and it was towards one of these on the opposite side that Zaggdar now led them. As they crossed the square they saw, built into the wall at one side, a number of stalls housing more of the lizard-like creatures like Zaggdar's mount and as these saw the horses they began grunting and stamping their feet, their heads rocking from side to side above the half-doors.

'It is their feed time,' said Zaggdar and, dismounting, he handed his reins to one of the host of goblins that had seemingly materialized from nowhere. 'Leave your horses here,' he rasped, 'and they will be fed and watered.'

So Sienogg, Barll and the others got off their horses and, leaving them with the goblins, followed Zaggdar through a low, narrow entrance into the tower. They had to stoop to get under the arch and when they straightened up they found it difficult at first to see in the darkness. The damp chill from the walls was so intense that it seemed to attack them and they shivered as it seeped into their bones. The smell too, that had been with them ever since they entered Gan, now grew more acute. Like badly rotting flesh, it had become tinged with a nauseous fishy stench that gagged in Sienogg's throat as he tried to breathe. Blindly he stumbled along in the gloom after Zaggdar, following the flapping of his feet on the earth floor, until after a while his eyes became

291

acclimatized and he was able to see a little. The passage along which they were walking was only just high enough to stop them scraping their heads; indeed he could hear Barll, the tallest of them all, cursing frequently as he knocked himself on the roof. The walls were made up of large blocks of stone covered with mosses and lichens and they ran with little rivulets of water that formed pools in the uneven floor.

Then, suddenly, they came to a narrow flight of steps that twisted its way upwards into one of the towers. Sienogg had to bend low as he followed Zaggdar and nearly missed his footing on the slippery stone. There were no handholds and in the darkness, holding on to Gemro's head, he had great difficulty keeping his balance, though fear of falling and losing face made him determined not to slip and it was with a great deal of pleasure that he heard the clatter behind him of Barll tumbling against Tshonn and knocking him over. And then the heavy stillness was shattered by the stream of oaths that poured from them until Zaggdar spat out harshly to them to stop.

'Enough! Or Degg will tear your tongues out,' he snapped, and it was then, with a chill of realization, that Sienogg knew what he had felt from the moment they had entered Spath; that of Dréagg's two forces, goblin and man, the goblins automatically assumed the ascendancy. A few more steps and Sienogg found himself standing in front of a door on a small landing with Zaggdar at his side and the others waiting in line behind him on the stairs. There was utter silence except for the nervous breathing of the men and the scraping rasp from the goblin as he drew air in through his teeth. He raised his claw and grasping the end of a length of crimson fibre that hung from the roof he pulled sharply down. There was a slight pause and then, from beyond the door, there came the low dolorous sounds of a gong; muffled but echoing faintly out towards them as if from a long way away.

Sienogg's heart pounded in his chest and he could almost taste the fear that gripped them all; from Barll and Straygoth just behind him right back to Kam at the end of the line. In the deathly silence that followed the last tremors of the gong they heard an ominous slithering from inside the room, accompanied by the strangely rhythmic clicking sound that they all now recognized as the goblins' constant accompaniment. Then came the scraping of a latch and the complaining creak of the door as it was dragged open slowly from the inside to release a widening band of dim light onto the darkness of the landing.

All Sienogg could see at first was a small hunch-backed figure standing silhouetted in the doorway, the diamond shape of the head and the sharp pointed ears etched starkly and dramatically in shadow against the light. And then it turned and moved back inside the room, swaying from side to side and pulling its feet along with it; while its head danced to the clattering music of its fingernails.

Zaggdar looked at Sienogg and motioned to him to go through, whispering fiercely as he passed, 'The head, the head!' and then ushering the others on through the door. The room was long and low and moisture hung in the air like a shroud, dripping from the arched roof with a steady patter on to the dark wooden floor. Degg stood in the pale milky light that filtered through two small window slits at the far end. It had been he who had opened the door and there was no one else in the room. Sienogg stared at him, utterly transfixed. Unlike the other goblins, Degg's body was yellow; a sallow and sickly colour, blotched and nearly translucent in parts, so that the veins and some of the organs showed through, flickering and pumping in a bizarre choreography of life. His head though, was so pale and ashen that it appeared almost white, the bone of his skull stretching the skin taut over his chin but letting it hang down in folds off his cheeks. And from out of this grotesque and pellucid mask Degg's eyes glimmered like burning coals, searing the space between them as he scoured the faces of the humans so that the air seemed to have become ignited and long tongues of fire flickered up and down their backs.

Despite the chill, a rash of sweat broke out on their

foreheads, running down into their eyes and making them smart and sting painfully. Yet they felt nothing, for their consciousness had evaporated beneath the force of the terrible presence before them and all sense of identity had gone. The eyes then fixed on the head that Sienogg carried in his arms and Degg's mouth twisted into a smile.

'For me,' he said. 'For me,' and quickly he scuttled forward, grabbed it by the hair and swung it out of Sienogg's grasp. Then to the horror of the watching humans he gouged an eye from its socket and popping it in his mouth started to chew, salivating as he did so and smacking his lips with obvious enjoyment.

Sienogg stared, petrified with fascination and as the sound of Degg's voice reverberated in his head something stirred in his mind, indefinable threads of memory that nagged at him with frantic desperation and demanded identification. And as he watched Degg; the way he held his head, the eyes – that utterly unique darkness, infinitely deep and unfathomable – a certain set to the mouth so, slowly, did the amazing truth begin to dawn on him and he felt as if the final piece of a puzzle was falling into place.

Then Degg looked up as if sensing the thoughts that were raging within Sienogg's mind, and staring straight into the human's eyes he spoke again. As he did so and the familiar and dreaded cadences of intonation enveloped him, so his blood froze in a sudden chilling rush of recognition.

'Yes, Sienogg. I perceive that you now know the truth. Xtlan and I are one and the same; we are of each other. He is in me and I am in him. In Xtlan you saw me made man; now you see me as I am, the spawn of Dréagg whose spirit dwells within us both.'

That it was Xtlan standing before him, talking to him, there could be no doubt. Yet his mind still found it impossible to accept. They had left him in the Blaggvald, so long ago, and the memory of that last terrible emanation from the black minaret still burned in their hearts. How then could he be here now? How had he travelled to have overtaken them?

How long had he been here in the forest of Spath among the goblins? Or ... and suddenly the truth came to him as an answer to all these questions ... had he never left Xtlan?

Degg had turned his attention back to picking at the face, utterly absorbed now in pecking the flesh off the cheeks with his long nails and, lifting his head up and back, dropping the long slivers down his throat while the blood dripped in streaks over his chin and left a dark trail on his neck. Watching, Sienogg turned the words over in his mind – I am in him and he is in me – and a glimmer of understanding permeated his consciousness. They both existed, together and at the same time; Xtlan in the Blaggvald and Degg in Spath, one and the same.

Then, as if suddenly remembering the weary and ragged band of humans who were watching him, Degg looked sharply up.

'Food!' he spat the word at Zaggdar. 'Food for our guests. They will be hungry.' He turned then to Sienogg, Barll and the others and, holding the head in one hand, gestured expansively with the other towards the wooden benches that were ranged around the walls.

'Sit,' he said. 'Sit and eat while we talk, for there is much for us to plan. Together...' and he looked away, musing half to himself and half to them, '... at last. We have waited a long time. Oh! so long. But now the end is near. Nearly all over. And then ... then the reign of darkness; then the earth shall be ours, to do with as we will.'

And though his words contained nothing that they themselves would not have thought and said, nevertheless Sienogg, Barll and the others felt an icy shiver of apprehension pass through them. All that they had fought for and dreamt of for so long was about to reach its culmination, to be realized at last and become truth. Yet now at the end some last lingering spark of light, a legacy of the Eldron, appeared for a final brief moment from deep within their souls and flared up in the wind of terror that swept through them at the thought of the horror that was about to be unleashed upon the earth. But it did not last long, this faint glimmer of light, before it spluttered and died, extinguished forever in the darkness that Dréagg had wrought upon their spirits.

And so they sat down on the benches while Zaggdar walked across to a corner of the room at the far end where they could see, in the pale milky light from a small window in the wall, a number of cages set out on the floor. As the goblin's footsteps approached, a babble of frightened squeaks suddenly rose up and filled the air with the distinctive sound of fear; a sensation so tangible that they could almost smell and taste it; their throats went dry and a bitterness filled their mouths. With a loud clang the lid was lifted up and, stooping, Zaggdar picked up two handfuls of small green reptiles like nothing any of them had seen before. The goblin then brought them over wriggling and squeaking in his hands and, keeping one for himself, passed the rest round to the humans who took one each and held it gingerly in his grasp, bemused and vaguely repulsed by these peculiar slimy little creatures. Fear had caused them to release a foul-smelling scent which wafted up and caught in the noses of their captors, almost achieving their release as the nauseous stench caused the humans to turn away, a wave of sickness rising up in their throats, and only the venomous glare of Zaggdar prevented them from letting go.

'Like this!' he said sharply, pulling his lips into a grimace of mocking amusement, and, lifting the creature up, he bit one of its back legs off with a sharp snap of his teeth.

He then proceeded to eat the rest of it, limb by limb, the other back leg first, then the front and then, as the creature's agonized screams echoed round the room, he chewed his way slowly up its body until finally it lost consciousness at which point he tossed its head onto the floor, the beak-like mouth still open and its small beady eyes frozen in anguish.

'Now, you!' It was Degg who spoke, his voice bubbling with grim amusement and his mocking gaze fixed on the humans arrayed before him on the benches, their faces betraying the obvious revulsion they felt at having to emulate Zaggdar's performance.

Sienogg knew how important it was to meet the challenge that had been thrown out, both from the point of view of their relationship with the goblins and of his own position amongst Barll, Straygoth and the others. And so, cauterizing his emotions, he lifted the frantic creature to his lips and desperately forcing a smile of anticipated pleasure on to his face he sank his teeth into the smooth slimy skin where the back leg joined the body. Its foot wriggled in the back of his throat so that he automatically gagged but with a huge effort of self-control he kept it down and swallowed the limb whole letting the juices trickle out of his mouth and dribble over his chin. Anxious not to lose face Barll then followed Sienogg's example and the others followed him. The expressions on their faces, showing varying degrees of repulsion, were a source of huge delight to the two watching goblins whose eyes danced in amusement while the humans struggled to force the slippery squealing animals down their throats without being sick.

'Our little delicacy, gathered in your honour,' said Degg. 'We hope they are to your taste. Here! To wash them down with,' and he handed Sienogg a large grey earthenware jug full of a liquid that was immediately recognizable as blood.

'Still warm!' and again it was the harsh sibilance of Degg's voice that sounded out in the long low room and echoed back from the stone walls. 'Fresh from the animals your men are even now feasting on; to build up your strength for the battle ahead.'

It tasted vile, congealing at the back of the throat in a sickly-sweet mass, but if this was the only liquid they were going to receive, it had to be drunk. And so the jug was passed around in turn until it was empty and Kam was left holding it; a look of anger and bewilderment on his heavy, broad features. With obvious embarrassment he stood up and shambled over to where Zaggdar stood to hand back the jug, recoiling in shock as he saw Gemro's skull lying on the floor where Degg had dropped it, eyeless, the remnants of flesh hanging off it in tattered ribbons that stirred slightly as he walked gingerly past.

'Your friend,' said Degg, in a voice so redolent with menace and contempt that the air itself seemed to freeze with fear. 'Take him with you; his presence is no longer required.'

There was a moment of utter silence as his words hung in the room like an axe about to fall. And then, almost as one, Degg and Zaggdar began to laugh; a terrible braying sound that skirled around in the air and rose to a screeching crescendo, draining the humans of any last vestige of dignity that they had hitherto retained. This unworldly caterwauling even found its way out of the window and into the ears of those who were on the other side of the causeway, goblins and humans alike, and they shuddered as the sound sent an icy hand of terror reaching down into their guts.

Watching, Sienogg and the others were nearly as appalled by the grotesque postures struck by the goblins in their fit of mirth as by the awful sound that came from them. Grimacing as if in pain and bent double with their claws clasped against their chests, they rocked wildly to and fro, their heads jerking in a bizarre staccato tattoo that mesmerized the humans. Then, as if they had suddenly become aware of their audience, the laughter died away and the goblins froze as they were, their bodies caught in mid-stance. It was with an obvious effort of will that Degg pulled himself together and addressed himself once more to Sienogg.

'There are more,' he said. 'Many more. As many as you can eat. Go, help yourself,' and he gestured almost derisively towards the cages, his fingernails clicking together carelessly as he flapped his hands.

And so the humans forced themselves to consume more of the hapless little creatures, cramming them into their mouths with blind abomination, not knowing when they would again be able to eat and desperate to build up their strength. As they did so Degg paced up and down, scraping his feet along behind him with a soft slithering noise that formed a strange accompaniment to the sound of their chewing.

After a little while he began to address them, his manner stiff and formal and the tone of his voice harsh.

'We have them,' he said. 'Our time is come, as Dréagg promised. He has delivered them to us even as he said he would for even now they are coming down the path of Ekg towards us. They have been seen; the four of them, the ones who stand between us and the final victory. Bracca the human, who you know from your days in Haark, of the line of Melvaig and Morven, who carries his father's vision in his heart and will not rest until it is reality. Tara, the elven princess, daughter of Nab and Beth, who is of Magic and carries the torch of Ashgaroth deep within her. She travels even now in the form of a deer; her very existence an insult to our Lord Dréagg. Third, there is Raagon the Old One, the faithful servant, dangerous in his devotion to the Silver Warrior, Ammdar, the fallen one, the fourth of the travellers. His thirst for revenge is boundless and his one desire is to make amends to Ashgaroth for his fall. Ammdar, once the mightiest of the elflords, who has taken the form of a wolf; the one they call Vane.'

'And in the hands of these four is the destiny of the earth. They think they travel in secret, in hidden byways and unknown paths, safe from our eyes and away from the knowledge of Dréagg. Fools! We have known where they were from the beginning; watched them approach, lured by the Droon, in the hope of achieving the Separation of the Seeds. Did they think we were so stupid? We could have taken them at any time; destroyed them for ever and put man out of danger; inviolable and supreme over the earth. But what then of the elves? They would have remained; a flicker of light in the darkness, a reminder of the power of Ashgaroth, ready to rise again and take up arms against our master. No; until the kingdoms of the elves are no more the victory will not be won.

'So we let them come to Spath, these four, knowing that when they see the great hordes of men and goblins ranged against them, then they will perceive of the impossibility of their mission. It is at that moment that Bracca will sound the pipe of Morar to summon all the hosts of the elves to his side. There they will be; the tattered remnants of the once mighty armies of Ashgaroth pitched against all the forces of darkness. Terrible and certain will be their destruction and sweet the taste of our final glory. Then the earth will be ours completely, to do with as we will, and man will live for pleasure alone to indulge all his appetites to the utmost. Then the darkness will fall over all the land, the strong and the cruel will inherit the earth and exalted will be the arrogant, the vicious and the vile. All things gentle and beautiful will be crushed and torn out, useful only in so far as they serve to satisfy the desires of those who rule. There will be no justice or fairness; only power. The good, the kind and the compassionate will be spat upon and reviled, and violence worshipped as the one immutable faith. There will be no truth, only deceit; no friendship, only allies of convenience; and no love save the relief of lust and desire. The weak and the fragile, the maimed and the infirm; these will be as tools to use and throw away.

'Then Ashgaroth's green jewel will run with rivers of crimson and the universe ring as it cries out its pain; then will its brightness, which so taunted Dréagg during the time of his exile, be forever extinguished and the revenge he has sought for so long be truly complete.'

Degg stopped speaking and in the oasis of silence that was left it was as if the world shook, a barely perceptible quiver that the humans felt as a vibration rippling out of the earth beneath their feet and the air around them. It seemed to them that, at that moment, the whole of creation was poised on the threshold of a struggle so titanic that the elemental fabric of existence, even to the rocks and the water and the soil and the trees, was awakening from sleep, stretching and

300

feeling the pulse of its own struggle in readiness for the epic conflict that lay ahead.

CHAPTER XX

When Bracca woke up, he guessed that it was some time after the middle of the day. The pale yellow light of the sun had just begun its long slow descent down towards the horizon but its brightness still hurt his eyes. He lay still for a moment, trying to gather himself together and collect his bearings, luxuriating in the little pockets of oblivion that still lingered from his sleep and trying almost to escape back into them. Yet he was also aware of a darker set of images that he could not bring clearly to mind but which hovered just beneath his consciousness, and which were deeply and profoundly disturbing. As these came back to him, his spirit began to dart about inside his body, refusing to settle down, and his nerve-ends jangled as if they were on fire. Willing himself to calm down, he slowly stretched out his legs. They were stiff from the cold and damp and when he tried to straighten them his left knee felt a little twinge of pain from the awkward angle it had been in all night. His side too, was sore from a sharp rock that he must have been sleeping on but the pains were a welcome diversion from the dark images that threatened to loom up out of his subconscious and engulf him in their horror.

As the scales of sleep fell away, he grew increasingly aware of his surroundings; the wide grassy hollow in which he lay, the low banks that surrounded them and the river running down one side, constantly murmuring over its bed of stones. He was lying against the trunk of an old oak tree and as he turned his head to look up, he felt infused by a sense of calmness from the delicately interlocking tracery of the branches outlined against the silver grey of the sky; as if he was in some secret hidden cave where he would be forever safe.

Then, suddenly, with a quick stab of panic, he remembered the others and sitting bolt upright he looked around himself. Raagon lay just to one side facing him, his old face calm and serene and his breathing steadily rhythmic. Then a little further round, sitting in the lee of a large black rock, he saw Vane. His head was up, his eyes open and alert and his ears erect, straining to catch any alien sounds in the stillness of the early afternoon. The hazy rays of the sun fell upon the ruffles of his thick grey coat and created a shimmering aura of silver light around him. It was a divine moment, teeming with undercurrents of magic, and Bracca was mesmerized by it. Then he caught Vane's eyes and there was the light of recognition in them. They looked at each other hard for long moments and in this exchange was much warmth and tenderness as well as the pleasure each felt at the other's presence.

The thought of Tara then cut a swath through his thoughts. Where was she? He looked around with growing unease. No sign! But there was no alarm in the eyes of the wolf, no indication that anything was wrong, so he settled down with his back against the tree once more and waited, gazing up at the branches as they swayed gently in the breeze and letting his mind drift back to the times in Haark with Melvaig, Morven and Shayll. Long ago times which now, looking back, he could remember as clearly as if it had been yesterday. The walks through the great forest with all its smells and sounds; the dampness of the fallen pine needles underfoot after a summer shower, the whispering shadow of an owl against the moonlight, the greenness of the new bracken shoots as they burst through the dark peat of the forest floor, the bark of a dog fox on a warm spring night echoing through the trees, the cold slimy feel of the toadstools that they gathered on autumn evenings and took back to dry for the winter. The sound of Shayll's laughter as she teased him about his appetite; Melvaig's pipes, the notes floating through the still summer night air and carrying him away up towards the distant stars; Morven's voice, warm and soft, telling them stories about Ruann. And he could smell even now the sweet aromatic scent of Melvaig's pipe smoke and see it curling up through the air away from him in billows of delicate blue cloud.

On and on went the chain of his memories, each link leading on to another, and his heart filled to bursting with the heavy ache of deep nostalgia; of precious days lost forever never to be recaptured. It was only when he suddenly became aware of something cold and wet pressing against his cheek that he realized he had fallen back into a sleep from which he now awoke with a start. Before his eyes stood a deer, Tara, her face so close to his that he could feel her breath on his eyelids and smell its sweetness. Their eyes met and held each other for a long time and Bracca's hands came up and caressed her face, gently stroking along her muzzle and over her head. Seized then by a sudden impulse he put both arms around her neck and pulled her close against his face losing himself in her delicate musky scent and the soft furry feel of her coat.

When he let go of her he saw that Raagon was also awake and was busily unpacking the food containers that he had taken off Tara's back before they had all settled down to sleep the previous night. Bracca got up and walked over to him while Tara lay down where he had left her.

'You slept well? You're rested?' asked Raagon, without looking up from his task; and then, 'Good, good,' in answer to his own question. 'Yes, we're all rested now, all rested. And strong. . .' He stopped in the middle of his unpacking and stared straight ahead at the tops of the trees in the distance, the trees of Spath. 'We shall need to be strong. Eh, Vane!' he called suddenly, looking across to the wolf. 'We shall need all our strength, and courage. So come and eat.'

Vane got up and walked across to join them. Raagon handed Bracca one of the large round biscuits spread with honey that he remembered from Operrallmar and then held one out to Vane who took it delicately in his mouth from the Old One's hand. They had three each and then while the wolf padded softly away over the grass to drink at the stream, Bracca and Raagon settled down with their backs against the rock and drank from an earthen jar that contained a delicious golden liquid made, so Raagon said, from the flowers of the elder trees that grew against the walls of Operrallmar. As it went down his throat he felt its gentle fire invigorate his spirit and he became aware again of the presence of Nab's gifts to him; the Belt of Ammdar lying about his waist and, hanging round his neck, the wooden case containing Morar's pipe. How long ago it seemed, since Nab had bestowed upon him the mantle of Ashgaroth and he and Tara had taken their leave of the companions of Silver Wood. Now here they were, on the threshold of the last great adventure; the epic confrontation that Nab had revealed to him and for which he had been uniquely fashioned by the forces of destiny. He shivered inwardly in anticipation of what was to come, yet at the same time there was within him a glow of intense exhilaration sparked by his awareness of the incredible heritage that lay behind him, a heritage of which he was now the guardian. He moved then, only slightly and Tabor, Ammdar's silver sword, rubbed against his left leg as a gentle reminder of its existence. He put his hand down and grasped the hilt, letting its power seep up through his arm and into his body and as it did so the silver-grey clouds overhead dispersed for a moment and the evening sun burst through and bathed him in a pool of liquid gold, dazzling him so that he was forced to look away. As suddenly as it had come, it was gone but the image lingered in his head; the column of light streaming down towards him through the air, the

305

sensation as it drenched him in its aura and the instinctive feeling that somehow this was a sign from Ashgaroth, a reminder of his presence and a symbol of his power. And Bracca felt that it was meant as an inspiration for him to take up the cloak of leadership that had been placed around his young shoulders and to lead the others down into the unknown darkness of Spath to face the enemy.

Side by side they sat in silence, the young and the old, nibbling away at the biscuits and washing them down with sips from the jar, while overhead the sun slowly dropped down out of the sky and the dampness started to seep out of the earth. Banks of dark grey clouds were building up on the horizon and the light was fading fast so that already the trees had lost their detail and turned into patches of black shadow. In front of them, sitting next to each other in the shadow on the rock, were Tara and Vane. They both looked at Bracca intently as if waiting for a signal. Rested and refreshed they both wanted to be on their way and were looking to him to lead them. Recognizing their impatience he turned to Raagon and saw that he too had finished eating and was simply waiting for Bracca to say the word to go. The dying light shone dully on the long ragged beard of the Old One, burnishing the tangle of russet hairs with a crimson sheen that seemed to reflect back up on to his face and fill the myriad wrinkles of his skin with rivers of blood. And his eyes, awash with pain and love, tugged at Bracca's heart for he perceived there twinkling on the surface, the light of hope; a hope that Bracca had kindled and was keeping alive. It was the hope of the world that shone there; the hope of the good and the gentle, the innocent and the brave; the hope that Ashgaroth would finally triumph in the apocalyptic struggle that lay ahead. It was he, Bracca, who was the torchbearer of this hope and upon whom its awesome responsibility lay.

He reached across to the Old One's hand and clasped it, smiling at him as he did so.

'Come on then,' he said. 'It's time for us to go. I'll help you

306

with these,' and he started to pack away the food and drink in the carriers that lay on the ground in front of them. Tara and Vane stood up and came over to them and Bracca fastened the straps around the deer's forelegs until the panniers rested as comfortably as possible, one on each side. He would never get used to this, Tara as a deer, and as he fussed over the fastenings, making sure they were tight enough not to fall off yet not so tight as to cut into her, he was suddenly struck with an impression of how ludicrous it was and to his astonishment he felt a surge of laughter welling up from deep inside himself. And the more out of place the laughter seemed the harder it was to suppress it. Yet there was no one to share it with; Raagon would not understand and the one person who could, Tara, was unable to join with him anyway. Still though, against his will, he found himself sniggering silently as he tied the last of the straps under her stomach and his hand brushed her warm soft underfur. And then the fit of giggling died on his lips and turned into a sudden fierce wave of yearning for her as a woman. Anger then took the place of laughter as the barriers between them reared up in a crushing reminder of their forbidden love. And now he found himself sobbing with rage and frustration as he buried his face against her neck and let his hands roam over the smooth firmness of her limbs. Over and over he repeated her name as hot tears ran over his cheeks and lost themselves on her soft downy skin.

'All right, all right. Be still.' It was Raagon standing at his side, a hand on his shoulder, his voice gentle and comforting as he tried to soothe Bracca's pain. 'I know; it must be terrible for you. But there is a purpose. Have faith. Trust Ashgaroth. And you will be with her; be at least thankful for that. Now, come on. It was you who said we should be on our way. Everything's packed away.'

So, turning gratefully to Raagon, he stifled the hurt that had so suddenly re-surfaced in his spirit and, summoning all his will-power, tore himself away from Tara and banished the sensuous images that had begun to form in his head.

'Yes, thank you. I'm sorry. It's just. . . Sometimes I can't. . .'
His voice tailed off as he fumbled vainly for the words that
would express his torment. But they would not come and
were in any case superfluous for it was clear to Bracca that
Raagon needed no explanation. 'Will Vane lead?' he said.

'Yes, this is familiar country to him,' replied Raagon, and
indeed the wolf was already waiting on the path that wound
its way down the valley alongside the river.

A half-moon had just appeared in the dark grey skies as
they set off towards the distant tree tops of Spath. It was early
evening and there was a damp chill in the air from the earth
and the river. They soon settled into a steady pattern of
walking and Bracca's thoughts grew calm, the frayed and
tattered edges of his mind being soothed by the rhythm of
his footsteps. As night fell and the valley became illumined
by the white light of the moon, so the world of the river
seemed to close in around him; the silhouettes and the
shadows of the rocks and bushes, the winding outline of the
path, the dark green patches of moss on the banks and
always in the background the song of the river, louder now
in the darkness, as it chattered its way over its bed of
pebbles. Vane led the way, his grey coat shimmering in the
glow from the moon. Then came Raagon, followed by Bracca
and, a little way behind, Tara, her hooves ringing out softly as
they knocked against the stones on the path.

All night they travelled while the moon rose high up into
the sky and then began its slow descent towards dawn. They
kept the same steady pace without stopping and without
speaking, their minds focused in upon themselves, wandering through the separate tapestries of their lives as if in an
attempt to draw all the threads together into one cohesive
picture before starting on the final scene. They were neither
cold nor hungry, thirsty nor tired, and though the enormous
burden of their responsibility weighed heavily upon them
each of them felt, in their own way, as ready as they ever
would be for the task ahead.

By the time that the first rosy blush of dawn had begun to

colour the darkness, the river valley had widened out and the high banks on either side had levelled off so that they could see all around at the landscape they were now entering. The lush vegetation of the valley had given way to a desolate wasteland and the only trees they could see were the trees of Spath at the bottom of the long mountain slope that stretched out ahead of them. A dense stillness lay upon the earth, heavy and unyielding as if the air had been sucked out of the atmosphere, and there was no trace of the gentle breeze that had played against their faces all the way down from Operrallmar.

Soon they left the last traces of the green valley behind and started out across the barren expanse that separated them from Spath. The sun had now started its long climb up into the sky but as they descended, a damp hazy mist closed round them so that the light became diffused into a sickly yellow pallor that floated before their eyes in strange shifting patterns. As they walked, the ash grey earth clung to their feet in thick sticky globs of mud and made it hard to move so that they soon grew tired from the effort of freeing themselves from the heavy clinging ooze. The treetops of Spath were now lost to sight and Bracca found himself feeling dizzy and losing his sense of direction as he trudged wearily through the never-ending pall of grey that enveloped them. The shapes that swirled in the mist formed odd images; weird spectral figures that swayed and danced around them unnervingly and resurrected memories in Bracca's mind of the tale Melvaig had told him from the days of the Faradawn when Golconda, the great white heron, had led Nab and the others through the marshes of Blore. How much further in this mud? His legs throbbed and ached as he dragged first one and then the other after him, his whole body screaming with frustration as the effort of walking became almost too great to bear.

Suddenly the sound of a loud splash interrupted his private torment and looking up he saw that Raagon had stumbled and fallen. His arms and legs were spreadeagled in

309

the mud and he was desperately trying to lever his face up out of the slime but he kept slipping and flopping back down. Vane turned round and taking hold of his collar tried to lift him clear while Bracca pulled himself forward and, grabbing the Old One under the stomach, attempted to lift him on to his feet but it was impossible to get a good grip and his feet kept sliding away as he pulled. Once they tried, twice and three times, and at each attempt they got more covered in mud and more exasperated. And then, at the fourth try, they managed to get him upright.

'Can you stand?' Bracca asked, and Raagon nodded his head but when they gently let go of him and he tried to take a step he almost fell again and they only just managed to catch him.

'Just a little tired,' he said, but the tremor of his voice betrayed much more than that. 'A little rest and I'll be fine . . . fine.'

But there was nowhere to rest. The sea of mud lay all around them and the banks of dense drifting mist made it impossible to see more than a few paces ahead. And then Vane gave a little yelp and Raagon, understanding what his friend meant, turned and spoke to Bracca.

'I will ride on his back for a while. He is big and strong enough for both of us. I don't think it's too far to go now; we shall soon be through. If you could just help me up. . .'

So Bracca carefully helped Raagon up so that he was sitting astride the wolf, hanging on to the long fur at the back of his neck to stop him falling, and the little procession set off once again. Bracca had hoped that conditions might start to improve from now on but instead the mud got worse and soon he was up to his knees in it and it constantly pulled and sucked him back as if determined to stop him from going on. So it became a battle between his spirit and his body; the one determined to keep going at all costs, relentlessly pushing its host forward, while the other, aching with pain and weariness, screamed out in mute rebellion that it could go no further.

Then Vane stopped and Bracca, straining his eyes into the mist, saw a wide band of water just ahead. Had the river turned across their paths or was this another river that would converge with the first away off to one side? No matter; it had to be crossed. He moved up alongside Vane and Raagon, who had dismounted and was standing supporting himself on the wolf, and looked at the fast flowing tide of brown water that was rushing past in front of them.

Should they try and find a calmer, quieter place, less deep and less fast, or should they not waste their time and energy looking and simply attempt a crossing here? The thought of traipsing laboriously up and down the bank in a search that would probably prove fruitless was more than Bracca could contemplate.

'What do you think?' he said to Raagon. 'Should we try and get over here?'

'I don't know. I wonder how deep it is.'

'I'll go in and find out,' Bracca replied, and he started to walk into the water. By the time he was halfway across it was up to his chest and he had difficulty in staying upright as the thick brackish liquid pushed against him. It was so dense and murky that he could not see the bottom yet strangely, from the feel of it through his moccasins, it was firmer than the land. Raagon should be able to get across with his help and Vane and Tara could swim.

'It's not too bad,' he called out above the sound of the river. 'Wait there. I'll come back for you.'

He went back to the bank, and reaching out, took Raagon's hand and set out slowly across the water with Vane swimming on one side and Tara wading up to the tops of her legs on the other. With his free hand, the Old One held on to her neck so that the force of the water would not make him lose his balance and gradually, step by step, they saw the other side of the river get nearer until to their relief they felt the level dropping and realized that they were on their way out.

'Come on. Not far now,' said Bracca, as he felt Raagon's

fingers loosening in his grip. 'Hang on!' as a sudden rush of water threatened to knock him off his feet and turning round to look at the Old One for the first time since they had entered the river he froze in horror at what he saw. All the exposed parts of Raagon's skin were covered in masses of little fleshy worm-like creatures that wriggled and danced as if trying to tear lumps of meat off the Old One's body. They must have got inside his jerkin too for it pulsated with the grisly rhythm of their movements; and yet Raagon seemed utterly oblivious to their presence perhaps because, up till now at least, the water had somehow deadened the feel of them.

And then with a sudden, terrible flash of understanding he looked down at himself and involuntarily let out a scream for they were on him too, countless numbers of them squirming all over his chest and stomach, their pellucid little bodies oscillating with a pinkish glow as they drew blood from their victim. Frantically, as a wave of nausea swept over him, he put a hand to his chest and clutching at as many as he could feel, he pulled at them. But they would not move and their tiny black gimlet eyes seemed utterly unperturbed by his tugging; resolute in their mindlessness they were determined to hang on till death. And as he yanked at them their small round sucker-like mouths came away from his skin and revealed the tiny rows of razor teeth which had clamped themselves onto his flesh. He could take no more; the pain as he pulled was excruciating and besides, there was no more time now; wait till they were on the other side.

Looking across at Raagon, Bracca saw that the Old One was now aware of the creatures that were on him for he was looking down at himself aghast.

'We must get to the bank first. Then we'll get them off,' Bracca called out, and the Old One, whose face had turned as white as snow, simply nodded in agreement.

As they made their way across the last part of the river Bracca saw that Vane and Tara were also covered in the creatures; they had burrowed under the fur and were

312

clinging on despite the strength of the current.

At last all four of them got to the far bank but now, without the water to muffle the pain, their bodies felt as if they were on fire. Although they could hardly think, they noticed that the mist was less thick on this side and just a little way ahead they could see patches of green and the first few trees of Spath.

'Wait till we reach firmer ground; then we'll get these things off,' said Bracca, and, still holding Raagon's hand, he pulled himself through the mud as fast as he could. Every step was agony as the revolting creatures swung with the rhythm of the travellers' movements, teeth sinking deeper into the flesh as if to emphasize the determination not to be dislodged. Vane and Tara had already raced ahead and Bracca could see them lying on a patch of grass frantically biting their skins as they tried to rid themselves of their tormentors. Soon he and Raagon had joined them.

'We'll have to try and cut them off. I tried pulling them in the river, and it was no use. Have you got a knife?'

'Yes,' said Raagon, and his voice was thin with shock. 'Yes, I have,' and delving into his robes he drew out a small curved knife with a dark, strangely carved wooden handle.

They started to cut away at the creatures, slicing them through as closely as possible to the skin in the hope that when dead they would release their grip. But to their horror it seemed to have the opposite effect so that rather then relaxing, the teeth seemed to increase their hold.

'No. It's not working,' said Bracca, his arm running with the thick pinkish-coloured matter that seeped out when they were cut. Looking at Vane and Tara he saw that they too were suffering in the same way; they were biting the bodies off but the severed heads remained, clinging tenaciously to their hold on the skin.

'We'll have to try something else. See if you can get the point of the knife in between their teeth and prise them apart.' As Bracca spoke he tried it out, twisting his wrist sharply so that the end of the blade flicked sideways. There

313

was a sharp click and a twinge of pain as the teeth tore out of his skin but it had worked and he felt a great sense of relief as the head fell down onto the grass.

'It'll take a long time but it's the only way. At least it gets them off. Can you do it?' and Bracca looked at Raagon as the Old One tried.

'I think so. Yes! That's it!' as a head dropped off and rolled away down his arm.

How long they worked for Bracca did not know but it seemed an age. There were so many that at first he despaired of ever getting rid of all of them for he seemed to make so little progress but after a time, as the pile of gaping toothy heads on the ground grew higher, he had cleared his chest and arms, leaving only his legs. Where the creatures had been was red and raw, a mass of bloody skin that hung off him in little tattered shreds, but the pain was easily bearable now compared to before.

So, with the end in sight, he carried on with renewed vigour despite the pain in his back from the constant bending and the cramp in his fingers from holding the knife. Fired by his success he took the time to look up and see how Tara and Vane were doing and was pleased to see that they were using their teeth to prise them off and that they too would be finished soon. Only Raagon seemed to be having difficulty. He looked tired already and he had not yet got them all off his chest. And he was so slow! At the rate he was going it would take him days. No. He, Bracca would have to finish his own off quickly, so that he could help the Old One who was growing more and more pale with every moment that passed.

The yellow light of the sun had begun to turn into the dull orange of evening by the time that Bracca got the last creature off. So! It had taken him most of the morning and a whole afternoon. They'd probably have been better off finding a way to walk round the river; and spared themselves this ordeal as well. Still, maybe not; perhaps they would still have been walking. He mustn't let himself think like that.

314

They were across and alive and they had finally made it to Spath. Spath, at last! The end of their journey and the start of the final struggle; the cataclysm that Ashgaroth had told him of all those ages ago in Haark. Looking ahead for a moment Bracca could see the trees of Spath stretching away endlessly into the distance growing more dark and dense the further he looked. Above their heads lay a thick blanket of fog that hid all but the lowest branches from view, and though on the ground the mist was thinner it still moved around the trunks in eerie luminescent wraiths of spectral light, twisting and cavorting to a secret dance that set Bracca's teeth on edge. The atmosphere was damp and chill and seemed to wrap itself round their minds as if trying to quench any lingering flames of hope or belief that still flickered within their battered spirits. The darkness had now begun to fall quickly and the floor of the forest was shrouded in gloom so that Bracca could no longer make out clearly the patches of wet earth and the grasses and rushes that he had seen earlier. They seemed to have merged together beneath his feet to form a sea of emptiness, silent and brooding, waiting to ensnare all who penetrated further into Spath.

His thoughts were interrupted by a stifled gasp of pain from Raagon and he realized with a shock that he had become a little mesmerized by the strange atmosphere of the forest and had forgotten the plight of the Old One, still trying to rid himself of the vile creatures from the river.

'Here. Give me the knife,' he said gently. 'We'll soon have them off,' and he began working on Raagon's arm.

'Yes. Thank you. I. . . I could do with a bit of a rest,' Raagon replied, his voice weak and faltering with exhaustion. 'I. . . I'll just close my eyes,' and leaning back against a hummock of earth behind him, he fell asleep immediately.

Far into the night Bracca worked till his bent back screamed with pain and the weight of his eyelids threatened to force them shut at any moment. The white light of the moon shone fitfully down into the clearing where they sat as ragged streams of black clouds raced across the sky. Vane

315

and Tara had finished long ago and were lying, fast asleep, next to himself and Raagon so that Bracca felt more alone than he had at any time since he had left Operrallmar. It was a strangely personal and private struggle that he waged both against his own weariness and against the creatures that clung so obstinately to the Old One's skin, and as the night wore on his thoughts went back once more to the times with Melvaig and Morven and Shayll. And as the images of their days together came back to him so they too seemed to return, to be here with him now in this moonlit clearing on the outskirts of the legendary forest of Spath. They were sitting down around him looking at his face with pride and hope in their eyes and their features were so clear and distinct that he felt he could reach out and touch them yet when he turned directly to face them they were gone and his spirits plummeted. So after a time he stopped trying to hold them and instead let their presence come at him from the corner of his eye so that he got used to their nearness as a comfort and a reassurance. To know that they were with him now was all that mattered; it gave him the strength and certainty that he needed. 'I know that you will not fail.' Melvaig's last words came back to him; the words of a father whose confidence and faith in his son was unlimited. What an awesome responsibility was a faith such as that, and Bracca's blood ran cold at the thought of failure for it would not be long now before that trust was tested to the limit.

Then at last he finished; Raagon's skin was clear, and with an immense rush of relief Bracca straightened up and stretched his aching back. Sleep! His body cried out for it and with a delicious feeling of abandonment he lay back next to the Old One on the mound of grass behind them and surrendered his body to oblivion.

316

CHAPTER XXI

He awoke next morning as the early sun was sending shafts of pale yellow light through the gaps in the ceiling of leaves above and casting strange dappled patterns on the ground around them. The leaves were clearer now than they had been last night yet still they were partially obscured in the great blanket of mist that hung over their heads just above the level of the lower branches. The air about them was intensely still so that there was not a trace of movement in either the strangely-coloured leaves or the mist that enshrouded them and Bracca felt a stifling sense of oppression bearing down upon him. And there was a total silence except for the steady pattern of drips that fell from the overhanging branches and echoed out into the further reaches of the forest.

Most of his body felt as if it was on fire and it was almost too painful to move as he pushed himself up on to his elbows to look around. Vane and Tara were at the far side of the clearing looking out through the trees while Raagon was delving into the carriers. He glanced up as Bracca stirred.

'You're awake. Good,' he said, and he came towards Bracca holding out a small round green-coloured container. 'Here. This will take away some of the hurt,' and pouring some liquid out into the palm of his hand he knelt down and very gently patted it on to Bracca's inflamed skin. It smelled very strange and had a sharpness that made his eyes water but as soon as it touched him the soreness seemed to melt away leaving only the red marks as a reminder of his suffering.

'There. Is that better?' he said, as Bracca, smiling, got slowly to his feet.

'Yes. Yes, I can hardly feel it. Will the pain come back?'

'No, it shouldn't. I'm pleased I brought the stuff with me. It's a balm I used to make at Operrallmar though there was not much need for it then.'

'Raagon. How do you feel? It was bad for you in the river, with those things.'

The Old One paused and looked down at the ground.

'Better now. But without you. . .' his voice drifted off. 'I don't know whether I'd have got through. I hope I am not too much of a burden. I am old, even for one such as I, and the body grows weak.'

Moved by Raagon's obvious distress Bracca took his hands and looked him in the eyes.

'No!' He almost shouted. 'Please. . . Don't even think like that. We all need each other. Ashgaroth has brought us together, the four of us: I am certain of it. So! No more talk like that.' He let go of Raagon and going over to the carriers fetched out some more of the biscuits and some drink.

'Now. Let's rest and eat. We'll sit down here, on the grass.'

As they ate and the warmth and sustenance of the food and drink banished the horrors of the previous night to a distant place in their memories so Bracca talked to Raagon of the things that were on his mind. From the time he had met Nab and the nature of his destiny had been revealed to him, he had seen his mission in the simplest of terms; to reach Spath, and he had given no thought to anything beyond that. Now, suddenly, he was there and the real purpose of his mission was about to unfold; the search for the Casket of Unity – the Droon, and the Separation of the Seeds. And with their separation man would be no more and he himself would perish along with all his kind. That was all he knew,

318

save that the keys to the Droon were even now on his waist; the buckles on the Belt of Ammdar.

'Where is Vane taking us?' he asked Raagon, 'and how are we to reach the Droon? Do you know? Does Vane know?'

'We are making for a citadel known as Gan,' the Old One replied. 'It is the very centre of the forest, the core of the evil that is this place. It is there that the goblins dwell and it is there, in caves deep under the earth, that we shall find the Droon. They will be well guarded; creatures known as the Kwkor live in the tunnels and alleyways under Gan. They are the custodians of the Droon and we shall have to get past them if we are to succeed. But Vane knows the tunnels well for, as Ammdar, he spent much time here. Follow him; keep your eyes fixed upon him at all times for if you lose him you will fail in your mission. If the goblins are unaware of our presence here then reaching the tunnels should not be too hard but if they know of us; ah, then we shall have problems for they will range their armies against us, even the four of us and we will be forced to try and fight our way through. We could not do it alone and it is then that you will have to summon the elves on the pipe of Morar. But let us hope it will not come to that.'

They talked a little longer; planning and counter-planning, letting ideas come forward to be either adopted or discarded. Tara and Vane sat with them listening and often Raagon would catch the eyes of the wolf and Bracca could sense the thoughts passing between them.

Soon it was time to set off into the forest. It was not far to Gan now, Raagon told Bracca, a day's walk at the most, but they must go carefully for the further in they went the more likely were there to be goblins lurking amongst the trees and they had to reach Gan without being seen. So Bracca put the panniers back on Tara and they started out down the steep slope leaving the clearing behind them.

Deeper and deeper they went and the light grew more and more dim as the canopy of leaves overhead became so thick that only the occasional shaft of light was able to break

319

through into the gloom. The stillness was uncanny; nothing moved and nothing breathed save the four travellers and, careful as they were, their footfalls seemed to crash and echo in the silence. The forest closed in around them, enfolding them in the very fabric of its evil presence, so that as the cold clammy air wrapped their bodies in its arms it drove out the warmth of their blood and froze their veins into tentacles of ice. The trees seemed unreal, the bark as dead and grey as stone and the leaves so perfect and unmoving that it was as if they had been cut out and stuck on for ornament. Yet from the branches hung great curtains of dank vegetation; festoons of creepers and vines that tried to ensnare them in their tendrils as they hacked a way through with their knives.

Time and again, in the perpetual twilight glow, they stumbled into these barriers of foliage and Bracca felt his face being smothered in a web of slimy fronds. Then he would panic for a moment and slash out with his knife until he was through.

For Tara it was not so easy; her antlers kept getting badly entangled and she could not get free so that Raagon and Bracca would have to go back and clear a way for her. It puzzled Bracca why she did not change her form until he realized that she would then be unable to carry the panniers.

Not much grew in the gloom of the forest floor and they found themselves walking on a carpet of sticky grey mud broken only by the occasional patch of green where a clump of grass had managed to germinate and grow. Great flat plates of brown fungus protruded from the trunks of many of the trees while out of the earth grew litters of toadstools of every colour and shape; small round conical ones of a deep shiny green, bulbous orange domes of dark red flecked with white and large flat circles of yellow or brown or crimson or black. They glowed with a weird unearthly sheen, these apostles of decay, as they fed off the putrefaction around them, and they gave off a strange sickly smell that seemed to hang like clouds in the air. Sometimes as the travellers passed by, one of the toadstools would suddenly and quietly explode sending a great shower of spore shooting out which covered them with brown or red or green dust and got into their eyes and mouths and noses.

And all the time, just above the ground, wraiths of mist flowed and twisted around the tree trunks so that they seemed to be floating on a river of white. Disembodied, they hung suspended in mid-air like huge sentinels, malevolently watching the four travellers as they passed amongst them. Prickles of fear broke out at the back of Bracca's neck and his stomach felt shaky and sick as if the dark forces of the forest were already driving their way into his guts. It was hard to even guess at what time of day it was but from the tones of the light it must have been getting towards evening. They felt cold, miserable and dispirited as the initial excitement of their entry into Spath was drawn from them by the perpetual gloom and the dampness that ran down their faces and got inside the clothes of Raagon and Bracca. How much longer now before they saw Gan? Their legs ached from the effort of lifting their feet out of the sticky mud and their eyes were raw from constantly peering through the murk. Surely it could not be much further?

Yet night fell and still they were on the move; Vane plodding along doggedly in front, Raagon some little way behind, rolling a little as his ancient bones protested, and then Bracca and Tara, close together, gaining comfort from each other's company.

There was nearly as much light as there had been during the day for the fungi exuded an eerie luminescent glow that threw their shadows against the trunks of the trees as they moved. For some time now Bracca had walked with his head down, completely absorbed in the effort of keeping himself going, and his eyes had taken in very little around him. So it was that when the dark patches in the mist had first appeared they had simply formed part of the general scene and had failed to make any impression on him. Gradually though, as they increased in number and their movements grew more regular and orderly, so their presence intruded into the

321

privacy of his thoughts until, suddenly, with a rush of fear he looked up and saw them, their outlines vague and indistinct, moving through the mist. Were his eyes playing tricks? He had been staring into the murk for so long that he found it hard to focus on anything precise, and yet as he looked at these dark hazy shapes there was a uniformity to them and an orchestration of movement that left no doubt as to their reality. Sometimes too, one would come a little nearer than the rest and then Bracca could see it more clearly; a strange angular hunch-backed body with a large triangular head, long dangling arms and enormous claw-like hands and feet. When it turned sideways Bracca could see that its head was drawn forward into a point that ended in a hooked beak and that the large ears sat way up on the very top of its skull. But it was the eyes that most startled him when for a brief moment it stared at Bracca and held him in its vision. He was transfixed by the power that came from the two deep dark slashes of orange set in its black face. They mesmerized him, rooting him to the spot as a weasel holds a rabbit, until, as suddenly as it had appeared, it vanished back into the mist and Bracca was released from its grasp. But it had left him feeling shattered, his blood ice-cold and his limbs shaking at the terrible realization that for that instant he had lost all control over his own body.

'Raagon,' he whispered, and then again, a little louder as the Old Man failed to respond, 'Raagon!' This time he must have heard for he stopped and turned round.

'Do you see them? All around us. What are they?'

'Goblins,' he replied. 'Goblins! They know we're here. I don't know how. We couldn't have... Must have been watching for us ... waiting.' His voice was thin and high with tension. 'It's not good, Bracca. They've surrounded us.'

'Why don't they attack?'

'I don't know. We wouldn't have a chance.'

Bracca stopped and looked around him at the arena of circling shadows. Amongst them now he could see, more and more often, the sudden fierce flashes of orange as the

322

goblins scrutinized their quarry.

'They're playing with us,' he said. 'We're doing just what they want; it's as if they're giving us an escort. What are they waiting for?'

'Just keep moving and follow Vane,' Raagon replied. 'We can do nothing else.'

So they continued on their way as Vane led them down through the trees, and all the time the goblins stayed just within sight. At first Bracca's heart had raced at the constant expectation of a sudden devastating attack but as time went on and nothing happened he grew a little calmer. For the moment, at any rate, he believed they were not going to fight. Should he blow Morar's pipe to summon the elves? He had hoped there would be no need. If they had not been seen then perhaps they could have reached the Droon without having to call them. He had hoped that would have been possible. Now though, there was no choice. They would have to fight their way through and without the elves there was no chance of success. But when? Now? Or should he wait a little longer to see what happened? He could only call them once. If he chose the wrong moment tactically and used them too early their powers might be so dissipated that they would not be able to fight when they were really needed. Was that why the goblins had not attacked? Perhaps they knew and were deliberately waiting until the elves had been called.

At the thought that the goblins might know so much about them and their plans, Bracca suddenly felt very vulnerable and frightened. What should he do? His mind raged in a turmoil of confusion; whether to call them now or to wait – the question burned in his head as the arguments ebbed and flowed, first one way and then the other, and he spun in an agonizing whirlpool of indecision.

Then an aura of light started to filter through the leaves and Bracca felt the approach of dawn. And as the grey light forced its way under the canopy of trees so it seemed to drive out the dark shadows of the goblins for now, though he looked hard, Bracca could see no sign of them in the mist. Indeed it was as if they had never existed and had been just a figment of his imagination. But then the memory of those terrible orange eyes came back to him, staring at him again out of the darkness, and he knew that they had been real.

Suddenly Vane, walking a little way ahead, stopped and waited for them to catch up. As they joined him they saw that they were standing on the edge of a very long steep slope upon which the morning sun was just beginning to cast its light. The trees were sparser here and appeared either barely alive, their few remaining leaves drab and insipid, or else dead, their jagged broken trunks adorned with festoons of creepers. And the early sun embellished them with a gauzy film of white that reflected back from the drops of moisture in the mist. The sticky brown earth was littered with lanky tufts of grass and smeared with patches of moss and sphagnum. The occasional bush too grew out of the barren slope, squat hawthorns and spindly gorse, pushing their way reluctantly out of the ground as if trying to form a barrier against outsiders. And in amongst this hostile vegetation, in small groups at irregular intervals, Bracca saw a number of dark conical mounds.

'Goblin dwellings,' said Raagon quietly, as if in answer to Bracca's unspoken question. 'And look! See, there – deep in the mist. There's Gan.'

It lay on an island in the middle of a black lake with a causeway leading across to it. Shrouded in a vaporous green mist, the tops of its ebon towers were hardly visible yet the waft of evil that reached out to him through the putrid atmosphere was deadly and all-embracing. Here was all the vice and cruelty, the horror and pain and madness of the earth distilled into its purest and darkest form.

Bracca's body shook at the memories that came pouring back to him; memories of Xtlan, of his time in the Bellkindra, the warrior nursery where he was forced to learn the art of sadism; of his time in the black palace of the Blaggvald, having to stand by helplessly as Morven was mauled and tortured by Xtlan's warriors. And the strands of horror that he had tried to banish from his mind but that still bound him to that most terrible of times, now reached out over the years and enmeshed him in their grip. Suddenly he was back in the nightmare, attacked by images so awful that they had not recurred till now. A little boy, totally alone, his mother and father both torn from him and reported dead by the matrons of the Bellkindra; the things they had made him watch and had made him do – they all flooded back and submerged him in a sea of anguish. The sick and the lame, the old and the weak – beaten to death as part of his training; the wailing of the outcasts in the hinterland round Xtlan wherein all the cripples and the mutants, the sightless and limbless, were thrown together for the sport of the warriors; the terrible journey across the desert of Molobb in the hands of the Mengoy scavengers; being forced to watch Melvaig killing his horse, Sky, and not understanding that the Mengoy had made him do it.

The visions rushed in upon him, each vying with the other for control of his mind, until he clasped his hands to his eyes and moaning, shook his head in an attempt to rid himself of them. His legs had turned to jelly and his stomach to water as he found himself back in those tormented days yet he could not drive them away for the power of Gan was too strong. Then suddenly two arms were flung around his neck, he felt another's body pressing close against him and knew that it was Tara, changed back. Her head lay on his chest and she shook uncontrollably as tears poured down her face.

'Horrible,' she cried. 'Horrible. This place. The darkness. I'm not strong enough. I couldn't stand any more. I had to . . . break through . . . hold you.'

Bracca pushed his own suffering to one side in the overwhelming need to comfort her as he held her to him and tried to calm her down, and his joy at seeing her again was quickly forgotten as the feel of her shivering body made him sick at the thought of her pain.

'All right, it's all right,' he murmured. 'It'll soon be over.

Then we'll be together.' As he said the words he knew they were meaningless and had no foundation in the truth and yet it helped him to recite them. 'Think how it'll be. We'll walk in the forest on warm spring evenings with the smell of bluebells on the air. And we'll sit and think back on these times and they'll be just a memory. The moon will come out and we'll listen to the owls and watch the stars until the damp from the ground gets too chill and then we'll go back to our hut. We'll watch the rabbits playing and look out for the badger on his evening walk. And we'll hold each other in the night on a bed of pine needles and when dawn comes we'll go out early to eat beech leaves and chickweed while the dew is still on them. All the animals will be our friends. They won't run away from us or be frightened and we'll look after them if they're sick. And nothing will harm them and nothing will harm us. Nothing. Nothing.'

On and on he talked in a magical liturgy whose spell drove away the darkness and brought a glimmer of light back to soothe her wounded spirit. And he gained strength too as the world he was creating took shape in his mind; a world in which the memories of his childhood in Ruann and the later days in Haark with Melvaig and Morven blended with the images that Nab had given him of the days of Silver Wood. And Tara grew calm and her tears stopped flowing as his words took her back to her life with Nab and Beth and forward to a hoped-for time with Bracca.

So she stopped shivering and rested quietly in his arms, letting the power of his words wash over her and build barriers against the lowering clouds of darkness that had threatened to overwhelm her. Holding her, with his lips brushing the gossamer maze of her hair and her body tight against him, Bracca felt a closeness to her that was more than purely physical; rather it was the result of a new awareness of her vulnerability and his pleasure at being able to console her. Always before he had felt her to be inviolate, as if nothing could touch her, with a part of herself deep within that would always remain hidden and unknown to him. This reserve he had ascribed to her elven nature and he had felt it as a barrier between them. Now though, it was gone, blown away in the chill winds of evil that had come up from Gan.

And so they stood together at the top of the slope overlooking Gan, each drawing solace and strength from the other, until Bracca became aware of movement from below. Gently then he held her away from him and looking into her face marvelled again at her beauty even as he had done at their first meeting. The delicacy of her features and the liquid sparkle of her eyes filled his heart and he almost cried with love. And there was more now that bound them to each other; their times together, the suffering and sadness, the joy and the relief that they had shared on the journey; these were the memories that drew their spirits together and joined their souls into one. What the future held was impossible to know but whatever happened, whether defeat or victory, the power of this love could never be taken away from him.

'Better now?' he said, and as she smiled at him he leant forward and kissed the tears from her eyes.

'Look! Down there!' It was Raagon who spoke, his voice low and urgent, and Bracca and Tara turned as one and looked where he was pointing. Emerging from the shadows on either side of Gan was an endless unbroken stream of goblins. They seemed to come almost from the ground itself, oozing their way out of the murk like two great black serpents. They swayed as they walked, rippling over the earth in a hypnotically rhythmic series of undulations, while through the air came a low murmuring chant which rose and fell in time to the pattern of their movements. On and on they came, the two grim processions growing longer and longer as the awful moments passed. Bracca lost all track of time; mesmerized by the sight and sound of this terrible army, his blood had run cold and his heart seemed almost to have stopped beating. The awful dirge, rising and falling, rising and falling, filled his head and his spirit with its dark waves of sound.

Then, as the heads of the two serpents met in front of the causeway, they stopped coming forward and, with smoothly orchestrated precision, broke up their lines to reform in a number of deep serried ranks before Gan; and all the time the drone continued to pulsate as an accompaniment to the unbroken oscillation of their movements. And it was at this moment that, from one side of Gan, the armies of the humans started to march out; first the warriors of Xtlan in the different colours of their companies, greys and maroons and blues, reds and golds and black, making their way out of the drifting swirls of mist until the pale yellow light of the sun caught and burnished them with a dull sheen. Behind them came the men of Haark, some of whom he recognized from what seemed to him now to be a different world and a different age. Yet how their faces had changed! Gone were any lingering traces of innocence or compassion to be replaced by a towering arrogance; their mouths twisted with cruelty and the eyes vicious and unyielding. And the human armies moved as one, with such conformity and unity of purpose that they appeared as a solid mass. Their heads were thrown back and it was their turn now to fill the air with the sound of their battle cry, baying at the sky with a cacophonous roar of sound – a jagged and jarring maelstrom of voices that seemed to make the leaves quiver and the ground tremble beneath their feet. And beneath the human voices was the droning of the goblins as a sinister and evil counterpoint to the raucous savagery of the men; the two sounds now blending together into a rising crescendo of noise that set Bracca's head screaming with pain so that he snatched his arms from around Tara and clasped his hands to his ears in an attempt to blot it out. Tara and Raagon did the same and to his distress he saw Vane whimpering on the ground desperately scratching at his ears with his two front paws.

Then, suddenly, mercifully, it stopped and the silence was broken only by a single high-pitched wail that seemed to come from one of the towers in the citadel of Gan itself. With his head still ringing Bracca looked up and saw two columns emerging from the gates of Gan and starting to cross the causeway. One column consisted of warriors on horseback, the commanders of the men of Xtlan and of Haark; while alongside them, threshing and bucking as if barely under control, came a succession of enormous lizard-like creatures that walked on their back legs. Terrifying and grotesque, these awful beasts lumbered along with a strange rolling gait and Bracca, though initially repelled by them, found his eyes drawn by a strange and lurid fascination. They were like some ghastly apparition from a nightmare with their two sets of forearms and the three great spikes that grew from their foreheads. The vicious crab-like pincers on the end of the arms kept opening and snapping shut with a sound that punctuated the wailing and gave it a bizarre and uneven syncopation, and the red-tendrilled barb at the tip of the central horn shimmered in the grey light as if it was already dripping with blood.

As he looked more closely he could see that they were ridden by goblins sitting high up on their backs in saddles of crimson or gold and that their limbs seemed to be covered with armoured plates of some sort that gleamed with a dull metallic glow. And now the air seemed to have become tainted with a new smell; a heavy fetid stench that clung to the back of Bracca's throat and made him want to retch.

Then, from the great doorway of Gan, rode the familiar figure of Barll. Mounted on a huge black horse with his mane of dark hair hanging beneath his helmet like a curtain, it seemed to Bracca that it might have been only yesterday when they sat facing each other at that historic confrontation in Nabbeth's cave in the hillside overlooking Haark. As he looked at Barll, Bracca wondered if he too was having similar thoughts and, if so, what images of glory must now be surrounding him, for he had journeyed a long, way since those times and had reached the apex of those epic visions that had driven him throughout his life. And Bracca could almost feel the ecstasy of satisfaction that enveloped Barll as

329

he rode out to take his place at the head of all the host of Dréagg; the armies of man and goblin, as they stood waiting for the final battle with the forces of Ashgaroth. This was the moment he must have dreamed of since the time he had first borne arms, the ultimate victory, when the light would be forever extinguished and darkness would reign supreme.

At Barll's side rode Straygoth. For him, perhaps even more than for Barll, this was the fulfilment of a vision that had lain beyond his wildest dreams. In the slanting bands of light that shone fitfully down from the sky Bracca could see his cadaverous features twisted into a vicious and arrogant leer.

Behind Straygoth there came a figure on a great white horse that sent a chord of terror ringing through Bracca as the sight of him struck anguished notes from the memories of his childhood.

Back he went to that terrible day long ago when Xtlan's raiders had ridden into Ruann and smashed his young world into smithereens. He remembered waiting with Morven, hiding from them while Melvaig went over the hill to see what was happening to the village, and then the horror that had engulfed him when the raiders had found them. He could still hear Morven's screams as she had kicked and struggled to get away and he remembered their vile laughter and the vicious smile on the face of their leader, the man on the white horse, as he had watched her frantic efforts to escape. He could see her now being tossed from one to the other, desperately trying to cover her body where they had ripped away her clothes, and he felt again the same terrible ache in his heart that he had felt then, as if his chest would explode with pain. And his eyes filled with tears at the hurt that welled back up inside him as he looked down now upon the face of Sienogg, riding majestically along behind Barll as they crossed the causeway that went over the dark waters surrounding Gan, and the flames of hatred licked hungrily at Bracca's spirit. For what Sienogg had done and for all the crimes that Barll had committed – the terrible deaths of Nabbeth and Shayll, the rape of the forests around Haark and the killing of Stowna and Nemm; for all the pain and suffering that had been perpetrated in their names – Bracca's spirit cried out for revenge.

Finally, on a lizard that was bigger than the others, came Zaggdar. Around his neck he wore a strange black amulet that seemed to glow with an intense, almost liquid darkness so as to cast him in perpetual shadow. He looked straight ahead, swaying slightly in time to the rhythm of his mount, and his lips were drawn back from his teeth in a leering grimace of satisfaction.

As the procession reached the end of the causeway the two armies seemed to divide as on a word of command to form a passage through their midst. The high-pitched drone had stopped now and the only sounds that could be heard were the restless shuffling of the armies and the slapping of horses' hooves on the damp earth as Barll led the other commanders through the hordes of goblins and men to take their place in a line at the front.

Then, suddenly, there was an enormous crash as of a huge gong being struck and the armies turned as one so that they were facing the citadel of Gan and all eyes were drawn to a small black open window at the apex of the tallest tower. A strangely familiar feeling came over the warriors of Sienogg and of Barll, echoing distant memories of the time they had gathered before the Blaggvald and been confronted with the awful power of Xtlan. He had made them a part of him then; had drawn their souls into the black vortex of his evil spirit and now they felt the terrible force of his presence again, surging out towards them from the small figure silhouetted in the window. He began to speak; angular, guttural sounds that crashed together in an explosive torrent of bile and hatred, at one moment rising to a mighty crescendo and at the next diminishing almost to a whisper – a sibilant hiss of menace that licked and curled above their heads.

And the words that Degg spat out were unknown to Bracca yet they dripped with venom and he felt the awful force of their power so that his spirit was caught up in the swirling

331

waves of darkness that they engendered. He became as a leaf in the tide, carried along in its raging currents until, suddenly, with a great surge of release, he was aware of his arm punching the air again and again, his fist clenched in a strange instinctive gesture of salute, while at the same time he heard his voice shouting out in unison with all the host round Gan. 'Dré ... Agg, Dré ... Agg,' they yelled, their fists pumping up towards the sky in time as the second syllable split the air asunder and set the earth shaking beneath their feet.

How long he railed he did not know for he was mesmerized by the terrible rhythm of the chant but suddenly the spell was broken by the feel of Raagon's hands on his shoulder and the warm familiar sound of the Old One's voice calling as from afar. Then, looking up, he thought he could make out the faint image of Sylvine, the white stallion, and the silver glint of his body flashed though the gloom and seemed to strike the scales from his eyes so that he saw clearly what had been happening to him and knew now what he had to do.

Quickly then he put his hand beneath his jacket and found the wooden case on the Belt of Ammdar inside which lay Morar's pipe. Pressing the catch he drew it out from its mossy bed and holding it by the single coil in the middle raised it to his lips and blew. A single clear note soared up to the sky, so pure and sweet that it cleaved its way through the chanting below and the armies of darkness fell silent. Higher and higher it went, gathering in intensity as it climbed so that Bracca thought he could see it as a tiny star of brilliant light racing up into the sky, and on the flat lands below all eyes turned from Degg and followed it. Then, suddenly, there was a crash such as a storm-driven wave makes when it hits the cliffs and the star exploded into a million fragments of silver light that rained down around Bracca and the others as if they were in a shower of snow. And as each glittering flake came to earth it seemed to shimmer for an instant before Bracca saw an elven figure dance out of it. Soon the ground around them was alive with the twinkling lights of the elves as they raced to and fro organizing themselves after their flight; the sea elves in one part, next to them the mountain elves and the wood elves beside them.

Then the shower stopped, there were no more flakes, and the elven armies were gathered together along the ridge overlooking Gan; the forces of light and the forces of darkness facing each other as they had not done since the days Before-Man. Raagon, looking out over the host of elves, found his memory stirred by the sight. So long ago, those times, so long ago, yet he remembered them as if they were yesterday. Where was Ammdar, riding at their head with Tabor raised high above him, leading them to victory against the goblin hordes? Yet his memories were bittersweet for he remembered also Ammdar's fall, and the pain he felt at that terrible betrayal still sent him sick despite all the years since at Oparrallmar with Vane. He looked at the wolf standing beside him and bending down whispered in his ear. 'The time has come, my friend. The time has come at last. Now is our chance,' and the look in Vane's eyes was so powerful and intense that the Old One almost fell back with the sheer physical weight of it, for his memories too had been rekindled and his heart bled with shame for what he had done and burned with a desire to expiate his guilt; to live again, however briefly, as Ammdar the Silver Warrior.

Raagon then became aware of a presence behind him and he saw Vane stiffen with tension before turning round and facing back up the hill. Bracca and Tara also turned and there, walking slowly down the slope towards them, were three figures that Vane had long ago given up hope of ever seeing again. First came Saurelon, Lord of the Seas, his long white hair falling onto the shoulders of his sparkling blue-grey cape. Then came Malcoff, Lord of the Mountains, too weak to walk and so carried in his chair by four elves with Curbar the eagle perched at his side. Behind him was Wychnor, Lord of the Forests and the Green Growing Things, and at the sight of him Vane's spirit was afflicted with

333

poignant memories for it was Wychnor who Ashgaroth had appointed to take his place after the fall. His green and silver cloak fell around his ankles as he walked and a thin green band around his head held a mane of grey-streaked brown hair back from his face.

So the three elflords approached and the darkness of the ground over which they passed was touched with light and the sky opened so that a beam of yellow sunshine bathed them in a radiant golden halo. Heavy were they in age yet their eyes shone with wisdom and wit and their faces were alive with tenderness and love. And so despite their fierce majesty and the feeling of awe in which Bracca watched them come towards him he felt no fear, only warmth and comfort and it took no courage to go forward and meet them.

It was Wychnor who spoke first, his voice soft and gentle and his hands outstretched in greeting.

'You must be Bracca,' he said. 'Son of Melvaig and Morven. It is good to meet you at last for we have heard so much. Your mother and father were true and brave; their courage has become legendary in the palaces of the elves and the story of their epic struggle has passed into our lore. Do not grieve at their departure for they are content with Ashgaroth. Listen and look: you may hear them on the wind and see them in the stars. You have done well, Bracca, it has not been easy; yet the greatest trials are yet to come and we must not fail.

'And Tara. Our little princess. It is a long time ago that I first saw Nab, your father, in the enchanted forest of Ellmondrill. He was with Brock and Warrigal the owl and he was so very young. We talked for a long while and he learnt much and when he finally left on his quest for the Faradawn he was sadder and wiser than when he arrived. Yet he had your mother, Beth, and their love sustained them through the losses and the hardships of their journey. I did not meet her until much later, yet when I did I was moved by her beauty and the gentle tranquillity of her spirit.'

He paused then and took her hands in his, clasping them

334

tightly, and the glimmer of a tear appeared in the corners of his eyes. 'Forgive me,' he said. 'I am a little shaken; there is so much in you that reminds me of them. We should have met in happier times. I was always too far away; too many things to do. The earth has been weeping for so long that we have nearly drowned in its tears. But now, perhaps, at last there will be an end. Here. I am too selfish of your company. I can see that Saurelon and Malcoff are also eager to talk with you.'

So he stood to one side while the other two elflords came forward to greet Bracca and share with Tara their own reminiscences of Nab and Beth. Saurelon spoke of the magical times on the sea-kissed isle of Elgol in the land of Sheigra when they had perhaps been at their happiest since leaving Silver Wood, laughing and playing on the beach with Sam and Perryfoot, talking to Brock and watching Warrigal learn the skills of ocean flying from the gulls.

For Malcoff the memories were less sweet for his time with them had been fraught with tension preparing for the battle with the human Urkku so that Nab could break out from the citadel of the mountain elves in Rengoll's Tor and make his run for Mount Ivett.

'Their sadness afflicted me,' he said, and though his voice was husky and low it possessed a musical resonance that almost turned his words to song. 'Yet I was borne up by the strength and power of their love for each other and their companions.' He paused then and they all turned to face Raagon.

It was Saurelon who spoke first. 'And this,' he said, 'is a joy and a delight. The Three Ages of Man have come and gone and we have seen none like you, Old One. We had thought you were no more; perished with the coming of the Urkku. Would that we had more time to talk for there is much that I am eager to know. Perhaps later when all this...' and he gestured to Dréagg's forces below, 'is over. Yet I feel I know you. Is it possible? There is something in your face that is familiar to me.'

335

'I have it!' Malcoff suddenly exclaimed. 'You used to ride with Ammdar; were always at his side until the fall. The name will come to me in a moment. Don't tell me!' and he looked at Curbar as if for inspiration, his brows beetling in thought. 'Raagon! Am I right?'

'Yes, my Lord Malcoff. That is my name. At one time we knew each other well but it was long ago when the earth was so much younger. We fought the goblins together as it seems we are to do again. I remember those days; you and Saurelon, Embo, Druin and Urigill; Braewire, Eynort and Ardvasar.' He paused and looked down at the ground.

'And Ammdar,' said Saurelon, putting into words what they had all been thinking. 'We never saw you after the fall though we knew you had not gone over with him. It must have been hard on you . . . as it was for us. The unimaginable. Ammdar, the Silver Warrior, the greatest among us. Gone to Dréagg. Our spirits were shattered; it was a blow from which we have never recovered. And then the creation of man. . .'

Raagon winced as the words of retribution fell like knives for he knew that Vane understood and he felt the pain of his friend's anguish as his own. Should he tell them? They presumed Ammdar dead – was it best to leave it that way? And then he realized that Saurelon had stopped talking and he, Wychnor and Malcoff were looking intently at the wolf.

'And what of your companion?' said Malcoff, turning his head and fixing his sharp eyes on Raagon. What should he do? He looked away, unable to meet their gaze; his head on fire, his mind whirling in a blaze of indecision. How would they react if they knew? But could he lie to them? And if he did, how could he explain Vane's knowledge of the location of the Droon? In any case how else could he explain who or what Vane was? No. He had to tell them the truth.

And then, as if to relieve his friend of the terrible burden of divulging his identity, Vane walked quietly up and stood next to Raagon, looking directly at the three elflords. There was no need now for the Old One to speak for they immediately understood.

'It is Ammdar, isn't it?' Saurelon's soft voice trembled as the words left his mouth and his face clouded over with fury and his eyes flashed with a mighty rage.

Then Malcoff spoke and his knuckles were white as they clenched the arms of his seat.

'No!' he said, his voice as cold and hard as stone, 'I do not believe it. You were destroyed by your own black master. What is this! Come back as a wolf! It is a trick; some foul and deceitful ruse that is being employed against us by Dréagg. Raagon! The truth.'

But then Ammdar the wolf spoke to them, and he told them everything. His words were humble and penitent and Ashgaroth blessed them with the power of light for He smiled upon the fallen warrior and knew the part he had to play in the final struggle. And Ammdar craved forgiveness for his blindness and tried to explain the terrible deviousness of his temptation. He told them of the awful horror of living with the knowledge of what he had done and of the pain of his time in the darkness; of the constant grinding torment he had suffered ever since his fall, his soul crushed beneath the unbearable weight of his guilt. And finally he prayed to them that they allow him this one last chance to save himself; to try to bring an end to the reign of terror that he had unleashed upon the earth when he assisted Dréagg in the creation of man and to lift some of the burden of his crime from his spirit. He asked Malcoff and Saurelon to remember him as he had been before Dréagg ensnared him; to think back to their times together when they stood side by side in the fight against the power of darkness and to grant him the mercy of allowing him to fight with them again.

And the magic in his words soothed the wrath in their souls for they recognized the old Ammdar from before the fall, the great Silver Warrior that they had known and loved, and Wychnor saw in him the picture that legend and elvenlore had painted and that Malcoff and Saurelon had told him of so often.

Then Ammdar told them that he knew where the Droon

337

lay hidden, deep in the bowels of the earth beneath Gan, and that he would take Bracca and Tara to it.

And so it was that the elflords buried their anger and allowed themselves the joy of forgiveness. And there was a warmth and a hope in them that they had not felt since that snowy day long ago when Nab had come to them in Silver Wood. But there was no time now to rejoice, for the armies of darkness around Gan were growing restive, their voices raised once again as they chanted Dréagg's name in the familiar chorus of hate. The shock that had stunned them into silence when they had first seen the elves descend had now gone, that advantage had been lost, and they were working themselves up once more into a mad frenzy.

Quickly then they gathered round in the shadow of the broken stump of a tree while the grey light of the midday sun cast their silhouettes on the ground; seven of them, the three elflords, Vane, Raagon, Tara and Bracca, and they devised a plan for their attack and a strategy for getting into Gan, for Vane revealed that the entrance into the tunnels that would take them to the Droon lay inside the citadel itself.

They would have to fight their way through – there was no other way; and there must be no chance of Bracca, Tara or Vane being killed. And Vane it was who suggested that they form a diamond-shaped troop of the very finest warriors and pierce the wall of Degg's armies point first. Bracca, Tara and himself would be in the very centre of the diamond, where there would be least risk and Raagon too would be with them for he would not leave the Old One behind. But they could not hope to break through while their enemy was fresh so the elven armies would attack first along the entire front so as to weaken them and only when it was judged that the time was right would they attempt their breakthrough. Yet all the time as they talked a terrible question hung over them; would the armies of Sienogg and Barll have the power to destroy the elves for if their weapons had been welded with Arnemeze, the infernal metal that Dréagg mined during his exile in the Halls of Dragorn, then they would be able to halt the flow of time within them and so end their immortality. The goblins, they knew, had always possessed this terrible power but they would have to wait until the first blow was struck to discover whether the armies of man had also been granted such an awful capability.

It only remained for the elflords to draw together the flower of their warriors and form them into the troop that would take Bracca and Tara over the causeway into Gan. Among them was Reev, Wychnor's trusted friend from Ellmondrill, Faraid, battle-leader of the sea elves and Malcoff's two battle-chiefs, Morbann and Mendokk, but many others were there also, Saff and Bo-all, Paill, Tego and Vass. Their names were legend in the palaces of the elves and the stories of their adventures rang through the halls on iron-hard winter nights or floated on soft whispers of air in green springtime evenings. But now, as they faced all the armies of darkness, they knew that this was the greatest adventure of all for there would be no second chance; if they failed the light would go out forever and the earth, Ashgaroth's blessed jewel, would lie crushed and bleeding beneath the heel of goblin and man for all the ages of eternity.

When they were ready they drew back to a place a little way up the hill so that they could not be seen by the armies below and were out of sight of Degg, for the enemy must not know of their existence. And it was at this moment that Wychnor revealed the secret of Degg: that he and Xtlan were one and the same, each within the other, so that upon the destruction of Degg so would Xtlan perish. Then Bracca, Tara, Raagon and Vane took their leave of the elflords, for they were to remain behind to direct the battle: when it was time to make their break-through, Curbar the eagle would fly back and give them a sign.

And so, finally, all was ready and the waiting began.

CHAPTER XXII

'Look! Look at the sky!' Tara spoke quietly, her voice almost a whisper, but she could not conceal the shimmer of fear that made her words quiver in the strange, sickly, yellow light that hung over them.

Bracca, standing next to her, looked up. Great banks of black cloud were rolling over each other like waves on a stormy sea; rising, crashing down and racing onwards in a furious surge of motion. And there in amongst the billowing spumes of darkness was Krowll the serpent, his enormous body threshing about wildly, so that the clouds were propelled by the rhythm and pattern of his movements.

'Yes. Yes, I see it' he replied quietly, and held her to him as if to shield her from the nightmare above but they were mesmerized by it and could not turn away, drawn into the dreadful symmetry of its sinuous writhings.

'Don't look! Turn your heads!' It was Faraid who called back to them from the front of the little hollow where they were all standing and with an effort Bracca forced his eyes down and gently moved Tara's head so that she could no longer watch. She shivered and he folded his arms around her.

'Bracca, I'm frightened,' she said. 'I don't know whether I can. . .'

'Yes, I know. So am I. But there's no choice. We have to. We'll be all right. Ashgaroth will guard us. We're going to succeed. We must!' but his heart pounded in his chest with a pain that was almost unbearable and his knees were shivering as if they could hardly support his weight.

The raging clouds threw their shadows onto the ground around their feet. In the hollow there were some old broken tree stumps and, still holding her, he walked over to the nearest one and sank down onto the earth at its base, drawing a strange kind of solace from its brooding melancholic presence and the curtain of creepers that hung down from the branches like a veil. And she turned to him and taking his face gently in her hands looked him in the eyes as she spoke.

'We may never come through this. One or both of us may die and if that happens you must know that I have loved you, and will always love you. If things had been different then. . .'

'No!' he interrupted. 'No. You mustn't talk like that. When all this is over we shall still be together; there will be time then for our love.' And his heart ached at her sadness for her great brown eyes glistened with tears and the thought that he might lose her, that she was thinking of that terrible possibility, was more than he could bear. Yet despite himself his body quickened with desire at her closeness and a flood of bitterness again swept over him at the prohibition on their love. And he leaned forward and gently kissed her lips, as sweet as wild roses and as soft as thistledown, and they embraced with passionate restraint in the gaunt shadow of the old tree trunk.

In bizarre contrast to the wild turbulence of the sky, there was a strange uncanny stillness in the air as if time had been suspended, to stand still while the fate of earth was decided, and in the silence Bracca thought he could hear the earth breathing as all the animals and all the birds, all the insects and all the green growing things waited and watched with grim and terrible anticipation. He looked up again into the sky, drawn by a sudden impulse that he could not resist, and

341

there was Sylvine. The stallion seemed to rear up above the writhing coils of the serpent and shards of silver flashed through the murky yellow light to fall like knives upon Krowll's body. And as they faced each other in the sky, the spirit of darkness and the spirit of light, so Bracca found a new sense of courage and hope within himself for the serpent did not overwhelm him as before.

'We can win,' he whispered, and he felt Tara's arm tighten around his waist. He turned away and saw that the elves too were gazing upwards as if to draw inspiration from the grace and power of the white stallion. And then from just over the ridge came the sounds of Degg's army, chanting Dréagg's name with renewed fervour, a terrible wild chilling sound with a remorseless rhythm and growing volume that became louder and louder until the air itself seemed about to explode. Bracca's head throbbed with a vicious pain that sapped all his strength and he felt himself spiralling upwards, unable to maintain the unity of his body and soul, and drawn only towards the relief of abandoning his suffering flesh. But then he felt his shoulders being shaken and Tara's voice calling to him from a long way off.

'Look at me! Look at me,' she cried, over and over, until he forced his eyes open and saw her face swimming in front of him.

'Now! Listen!' and he heard a joyous skirl of sound coming from just over the ridge. It seemed to cut into the dark savagery of the chant, to rise above and dispel its black power with a delicately interlacing web of notes that twirled and danced with each other to evoke images of sublime beauty and splendour in all who heard it and whose hearts were open to the light. For Bracca and Tara, Raagon and Vane, the poignancy of the scenes that floated before their eyes was almost too painful to bear, bringing back memories of their happiest moments with all those that they had loved; golden autumn evenings with Melvaig, Morven and Shayll, sitting quietly and listening to all the sounds of the forest while the scent of Melvaig's pipe smoke hung in the still air;

342

springtime with Nab and Beth, curlews, larks and bluebells and tales of Silver Wood as they watched the moon go down behind the hill. For Vane and Raagon memories of the times they had shared together in the old days before the fall, feasting and dancing in the halls of the elves, walking quietly through the forests and talking to the animals; foxes, badgers and owls, eagles and bears, elephants, tigers and lions, and so many more, each with his own thoughts and ways, each with his own lore and each with his own place in Ashgaroth's scheme.

'Come forward and see.' It was the voice of the elf they called Reev. He took Bracca's hand and led him with the others towards the brow of the hollow. 'Look there,' he said, and there was a tremor in his words, 'you will never see such a sight again.'

Bracca looked down and was stunned by the sight that met his eyes for there, ranged along the length of the high bluff that overlooked Gan, stood all the armies of the elves. A thick layer of mist floated above the ground and the shimmering spectral figures of the warriors appeared out of it as if frozen in a sea of ice. Each elf held a bow with a silver arrow ready slung in the shaft and pointing upwards into the sky. Quivers lay in the mist at their feet and a scabbard hung from the belt that each elf wore fastened round his tunic. Mesmerized as he was by the awesome majesty of this ethereal vision, still his eyes were drawn to a small mound just to one side and a little in front, at a point where the bluff jutted forward in such a way that the elven army could easily see it. In its centre was the stump of what had once been a magnificent oak tree and it shone with a black viscous glow in the eerie light that flashed intermittently down from the sky, its branches outstretched in a tragic gesture of mute supplication. Next to it in a single straight line stood the elflords, Wychnor, Saurelon and Malcoff, facing their armies as they watched and waited for the moment of attack while to one side of them Bracca could see the elven pipers in their distinctive crimson coats.

343

'That is Morar, the pipe leader,' said Reev, and he pointed to one who stood in front of the others. He held a fluted golden pipe with a single loop to his lips and his head was raised to the sky in an attitude of both prayer and defiance.

'Listen, you will hear his notes above the rest,' and even as Reev spoke Bracca felt his soul captured by a mellifluous cascade of enchantment that soared up into the sky and left him dancing to the vibrations of the light. Any moment now, he knew, the elflords would give the signal and the battle would commence. The tension was unbearable, sending the blood racing round his body so fast that he heard it as a roaring in his ears. His throat became so dry that he could hardly swallow and his chest ached with the pressure from his pounding heart.

And then suddenly there was a brilliant blinding flash from the sky and Bracca covered his eyes instinctively to shield them from the glare, but just before he did so he saw the elflords raise their hands and the look on their faces burned itself into his spirit for never before had he seen such terrible anger. Their hands, as they were lifted skywards, seemed to stretch out as if to draw the spirit of Ashgaroth down to earth to help them in this, their time of greatest need. And they were bathed in the light and their bodies glowed with a silver fire so that all the elves could see clearly that it was time. Immediately then the air seemed to emit a great sigh and become full of a multitude of frantic whisperings and when he drew his hands from his eyes the sky was thick with arrows that drove towards the armies of darkness like a blizzard, the arrows like splinters of ice that fell upon the men of Xtlan and of Haark and sent them crashing to the ground while their horses, free of the burden on their backs, leapt away and raced off to freedom in a wild charge that threw the surviving riders into a frenzy of confusion as they struggled to hold on to their mounts. And then the elves let loose another hail of arrows and once more they came down among the armies of man. None of the horses were hit for an elven arrow will never harm one

344

of Ashgaroth's creatures but Bracca saw Bodrax fall to the ground clutching his chest as a crimson stain spread rapidly over his yellow jerkin. But the warriors had learnt their lessons well during the long training period in Xtlan and they were too well rehearsed to collapse under this first onslaught. The light that had momentarily blinded them had now gone and they could see the elves clearly on the bluff ahead. Sienogg and Barll now rode out in front and began shouting at their men, reorganizing the companies and rekindling the flames of battle that had been temporarily doused by the hail of suffering that had fallen among them. And Bracca saw Imril and Tshonn and Fowman and Kam spurring on their horses as they galloped over the numbers that had fallen and gathered the survivors together into smaller units that at a signal from their leaders began charging up the slope to meet the enemy.

And all this time Zaggdar sat quietly on his lizard steed at the head of the goblin forces, watching and waiting and biding his time, for this had been the plan that he and Degg had evolved; that the humans would bear the brunt of the elven attack, would countercharge to sap the enemy's strength and only then, when the elves had begun to grow weak and tired, would he let loose the full force of his goblin hordes. For were not the humans expendable? Was this not why Dréagg had sent them? Those stupid commanders had not realized what his plans were but the one they called Straygoth, he had guessed, and had threatened to divulge the sacrifice planned for the humans if he was not allowed to join the ranks of the goblins. So now there he was, sitting next to Zaggdar, as his reward for having a mind and a spirit as dark as any of Dréagg's disciples.

Degg also watched with grim satisfaction from his turret room in Gan as he saw the little mobile units of men racing towards the elves. He shivered in vicarious anticipation of the feel of sword in flesh and the tow of resistance as the blade swung into its target and his body weaved furiously from side to side in excitement. He could see the hated elflords

345

standing on the bluff. How long had he thirsted for this moment to see them defeated and crushed for ever! Sweet revenge for his banishment and endless sojourn in Spath; for the strands of goodness and light that their existence had cast upon the world and for all the ignominy and pain that they had caused his master. Now though, now they would pay dearly . . . and his long fingers clicked together frantically as the scent and taste of total victory flooded his senses.

From their hiding place in the hollow on top of the bluff, Bracca, Tara and Reev saw Sienogg and Barll at the head of their human armies, charging up the slope to meet the elves. Their swords were drawn from the scabbards and held ready at their sides and their shields were grasped in the hand that also held the reins, poised to be lifted up in defence. Barll could feel the churning of the damp sticky earth under his horse's hooves and he revelled in the power that surged through its limbs. The rush of the wind pushed his mane of black hair away from his face and exposed his cheek bones like a skull as a tide of elemental darkness consumed his body. This was the moment he had worked for and dreamt of all his life; the vision that had driven him on and given him the power and energy to make it happen. Haark was a long way away now: Nabbeth and Shayll, Nemm and Stowna and the Stagg, Melvaig and Morven; all were gone. But Bracca still survived. Bracca was up there now, beyond the ridge, and he, Barll, would seek him out and drive his sword through him. Think of the glory that would then be his; over and above Sienogg and the wheedling Straygoth, and even above Zaggdar, for surely Degg's reward would be to make him greater than all these.

And then the dull yellow light suddenly clouded over and the air was thick with arrows again. Curse them! Quickly, for his mind was still gorging on dreams of glory, he raised his shield and felt the force of the arrows thudding heavily against it and as he rode into them he turned his head to one side and saw Sienogg leading the men of Xtlan. The great white stallion strode powerfully over the ground and the

346

light glanced off the angles of his helmet. Barll could see the lips drawn into a snarl and the eyes wide and staring in a mad frenzy, caught up in the terrible thrill of the attack. Revenge too, was in Sienogg's mind; revenge against the seed of Melvaig and Morven, for the scars of her contempt still seethed within him like worms inside a corpse and he was still haunted by the shame of their escape from him through the arc of fire. He had paid dearly for that in men and, worse, in prestige but now the score would be made even. Victory would be theirs; he could feel it, and how he relished the prospect of running his sword through the one called Bracca. He would seek him out first and kill him for that was the task Dréagg had chosen him for. And then, almost involuntarily, he began the chant that he had not heard since that fateful day long ago when he and his band of warriors had fallen ' upon the village of Ruann and captured Morven. 'Xtlan,' 'Xtlan,' he began, and almost immediately the riders behind took up the strain and then the ones behind them and so on; the name rippling amongst them like waves until the air shook with it.

Bracca, still watching from the edge of the hollow, felt his guts turn to liquid as the evocative sound of that terrible theme stirred up long-buried memories of that awful time when, as a little boy, he had seen his mother torn from his grasp, beaten and thrown into the back of a cart by Sienogg and his men. He closed his eyes in an attempt to shut out the images that flooded back and putting out his arms, he clasped Tara to him and let her softness ease his pain.

'It's all right,' she said. 'I'm here,' and he forced his eyes open in time to see yet another flurry of arrows loosed into the charging men. Some landed with a clatter on their shields while others succeeded in penetrating the thick hide and, finding their mark, in dealing a mortal blow to the unlucky victim.

Now Bracca watched, mesmerized with tension, as the armies suddenly came together with an enormous crash that resounded through the valley. And the air became full of the

347

sounds of fighting as the humans struggled to gain a foothold on the edge of the bluff but the horses baulked at the nearness of the elves and would not go too close for risk of causing them harm. And they reared up and tossed the riders off their backs so that the humans were left without their mounts as the horses raced away from the scene of the battle.

Malcoff, Lord of the Mountains, looked on grimly and was reminded of the last time that elves and humans had met in battle outside Rengoll's Tor. And then he saw what he had been dreading. One of the humans, a warrior of the Company of Kegg, had lashed out with his sword and caught one of the elves in the chest. Immediately there was a little silver flash and the elf seemed to explode in a shower of sparks leaving only its body behind; perfect and unmarked yet deprived of life. So their worst fears were confirmed; the swords of the humans had been welded with Arnemeze. The other elves too saw what had happened to their companion and hesitated for a moment; long enough for the humans to get up off the ground where the horses had thrown them and organize themselves.

At first the fighting seemed to go the way of the armies of darkness. The elves, though light and nimble on their feet, were outnumbered by the humans and did not have the lust for killing that their opponents had. They had not fought since Rengoll's Tor and their swordsmanship had lost its brilliance. And they were tired; the effort of spiriting themselves through the air in response to the call of Morar's pipe had left many of them drained and in need of time and rest for rejuvenation. In contrast the humans were refreshed and well-fed from their stay in Spath and their blood was up. The scent of victory was in their nostrils and they cut and slashed and hacked their way through the elves, wielding their great heavy swords like clubs and laying waste all about them. And many were the elves who lay lifeless upon the bluff, besmirched and spattered by mud, their vacant eyes staring up at the sky where Krowll and Sylvine battled with each other. Yet there was a look of peace on their faces for with the extinction of their physical presence their spirits had flown to Ashgaroth.

But still the hearts of the elflords were heavy with the pain of their losses and there was a great concern among them for the tide of battle was heavily against them and they could not see how it could be turned their way. The armies of darkness pressed on inexorably, pushing the elves further and further back towards the hollow where Bracca and the others lay in hiding. Then, in the confident luxury that their numbers and their strength gave them, Sienogg looked across at Barll and crossed his sword over his shield in the pre-arranged signal to put their plan for final victory into operation. Let the goblins hang back; they had no need of them! As the human armies took the risk so they would take the glory.

So Barll drew his men together and, attracting as little attention as possible, pulled them back out of the front line and led them away to one side of the battle leaving Sienogg and the warriors of Xtlan to continue harrying the elves. Perfect! It could not have been better. There, just a little way off and running back up from the edge of the bluff, was a steep ravine where the ground fell away sharply. Quickly he led his men towards it and, bent almost double so as to keep well clear of the elves' line of vision, they moved quietly up the little valley – from the rocks and the line of old tree stumps it must once have been the bed of a river – until they came out behind the body of the elven army. When Barll was certain that all his men were ready he gave the signal for them to come out of the ravine and they did so, running along behind and re-forming in such a way that the elves were surrounded. The light was beginning to fade fast now; a dirty yellow haze seemed to hang in the air, to rest on the cushion of white mist that floated just above the ground. Again, Barll thought, Dréagg is with us for he could take the men close up to the elven army without being seen. So, slowly and with infinite stealth, he led them forward in lines abreast, the sound of their advancing steps drowned by the sounds of the battle.

Wychnor, turning suddenly, saw the litter of murky shadows stealing through the gloom and realized the terrible danger, for the elves were now completely encircled by the human armies; their position was hopeless, they would be squeezed and crushed like a snowflake underfoot. And then, with his heart breaking, he saw Barll rise up and give a great shout, to be answered by Sienogg from the other side of the bluff. The elves, weary and sick of fighting, turned round and saw Barll and the dark human hordes bearing down upon them from behind.

This, this was the moment to savour thought Barll and his body seemed to fly over the ground as he charged down the slope. And then, as if Dréagg himself was looking upon them from on high and casting a satanic divinity on their triumph, a brilliant shaft of light suddenly seared down from the sky and there standing in amongst the elves, Barll saw Bracca. Truly Dréagg is smiling upon me he thought, for now is the chance to cast my name in the annals of legend; to kill the hated figure of Bracca, seed of Melvaig and Morven, guardian of the spirit of Nab. He halted for a moment, riveted to the ground by a current of intense excitement, and stared hard at the unmistakable image in front of him, as clear to him now as at that fateful meeting of the Stagg long ago, when the young upstart had first challenged Nabbeth and the old order. Obscured a bit by the light but still there could be no doubt about it.

He took a deep breath, raised his sword arm high above his head and with a great shout launched himself forward over the few paces that separated them, plunging the blade deep into the belly of the figure before him. In! In! he thought as the blood spurted out in a livid crimson gush that spattered his clothes and sprayed the brown earth with a constellation of dark red spots. But the blood was flowing the wrong way; into Bracca's guts rather than out of them. Or was it? And then as he felt the blade turn inside himself he realized with a terrible yawning lurch of despair that the blood was coming from him. Screaming with terror he looked down and saw the hilt protruding from his stomach, clutched by a hand that he somehow seemed to recognize. What was happening?

And then, as if in answer to the terrible questions that were raging through his head, there was a sudden flash of light from the sky and the figure before him was illumined in all its vivid reality. Sienogg! No, it was impossible! But from the light of recognition in Sienogg's eyes and the mask of shock and puzzlement that met his ravening gaze, Barll was forced into a realization of the truth. It was a terrible mistake. Bracca! It should have been Bracca! And then from Sienogg's lips, twisted into a grimace of pain, came the explanation.

'You,' he whispered. 'But I thought. . .' He collapsed into a heap on the earth, the weight of his body pulling Barll's sword down with him so that he was forced to let go of it. Sienogg was shuddering now, his limbs shivering uncontrollably as if he was terribly cold, and his eyes had closed; while from his mouth poured forth a succession of animated, random mutterings, the face changing with them in a rapidly alternating series of expressions. Horrified, Barll watched the quivering of his sword as it stood erect, wedged into Sienogg's chest, while the blood pumped out around it in a steady and regular rhythm. He was gripped with a morbid fascination because that was the way he too was going, his life draining out of him, running over his legs and down on to the ground at his feet. Dazedly his eyes focused on Sienogg's sword hilt in his stomach and he tried to pull it out but he felt empty and cold inside and he could not find the strength. And as his mind grew dizzy and the shocked faces of the warriors who were looking on grew blurred before him so he marvelled at the trick that had been played on them. Brilliant and yet so simple. How it had happened he did not really know but the warrior in him responded with wry admiration. Odd now, that he was hardly aware of any pain; just a numb ache and a feeling of great tiredness. So this was how it was going to end. Strange that just a short time ago he had been invincible. The whole of his life seemed to have been dedicated to those few moments of total glory. The killing of his father, the victorious struggle against Nabbeth, Melvaig and Bracca in Haark, and the time in Xtlan: all these had come together for the short time he had led the battle against the forces of light. He felt himself falling forward, floating as if in space, and was dimly conscious of trying to avoid the body of Sienogg, but he could not and landed with a soft thud on top so that the sword in his belly cut even further into him and caused him to cry out in sudden agony. Not much longer now; he could feel the chill hand of death grabbing at his entrails, and he became consumed with regret that he would not live to see the outcome of the battle. To see Bracca die; how sweet that would have been! Where was he? Watching, laughing? Tormented by these thoughts, the hatred in his body worked as a poison in the wound twisting his spirit up so that it became as a savage, snarling beast gnawing away at the few precious strands of life to which he was still clinging. Sienogg, prostrate beneath him, exuded the fetid stench of death so that his senses were assailed from all sides, pulling him down, down into the darkness. He saw Stowna and Nemm floundering limbless before the children of Haark and he could taste their fear and their pain. Shayll danced naked before his eyes, the voluptuous contours of her body moving with a sensuality so intense that he almost choked with excitement as he reached out to grab her soft white flesh but suddenly, cruelly, she vanished and in her place stood an old, scrawny hag, equally naked. Toothless, she leered at him, her blotched skin hanging down in folds that were stretched and shaped by the bones that poked through from beneath. Revolted he snatched his hand away but, cackling, she grabbed it and held it between her legs in a vice-like grip that he was unable to break. And then a great black wave started to roll over his head. Desperately he fought to escape from it but he was unable to move. Fantasy and reality had merged into one so that he saw himself trying to run away; his limbs threshing about wildly in a fruitless attempt to get out from under the terrible rolling mass of darkness that had begun to smother him but the more he struggled, the less progress he seemed to make. It was as if he was wading through a sea of thick mud that clung to him and refused to let him go. He fought to get his breath and when the expected, life-giving rush of air refused to come he panicked and became gripped with hysteria, clawing at the space about him with awful desperation.

Bracca, watching from behind the ridge, had seen the whole bizarre incident. Now he saw Barll stagger to his feet and, bellowing like a seal, lurch around with the sword sticking out of his belly like some weird appendage and his arms thrashing about wildly. The warriors had gathered round to form an encircling arena within which Barll appeared to be performing a crazy ritualistic dance. Strands of fading sunshine through the tree stumps played upon his whirling limbs, throwing them into alternate light and shade so that the movements seemed to be in slow motion, and Bracca became almost hypnotized by them as he looked on, hardly able to believe his eyes. What had happened to cause this strange incident between Barll and Sienogg? Had Ashgaroth played a part in the deaths of these two and, if so, what would the consequences now be for the battle? As he watched the dying agonies of Barll and heard the awful sufferings evidenced by his screams, he tried to feel compassion but could find none within himself for the figure beneath him that was so stubbornly clinging on to life. Rather, and a little to his disquiet, he felt a joyous sense of relief and satisfaction as the realization came to him that these two ambassadors of darkness, who had caused so much grief to himself and to those he loved, would soon be no more.

Then, as if at a signal, Barll stopped his flailing and stood stock still, rooted to the earth, his head raised to the sky and his arms outstretched. A great howl then rose up from him; unrestrained and primeval it seemed to come from the earth itself, rending the air and turning blood to ice. Bracca felt

353

Tara shiver at his side and he held her close, drawing her to him so that she would feel the warmth of his love. Louder and still louder grew the terrible cry until finally Barll exploded like a rotten fruit. Flesh, blood and bones showered upwards towards the sky, and for one vivid and grisly moment obscured the light from the sun before raining back down upon the astonished warriors. And in the crimson gloom of that moment Bracca saw a small dark winged creature burst out from amidst the debris and soar up towards the gaping mouth of the serpent Krowll. In an instant the jaws had snapped shut and swallowed the creature up, leaving nothing remaining of the one who had been called Barll save the scattered fragments of his flesh that spotted the earth like red snowflakes.

Then, while the men of Xtlan and Haark were still reeling from the shock of seeing their leaders die, the elven warriors seized their chance and attacked the armies of man with renewed vigour. Weary and dispirited though they were, they now fought back with majestic bravery, drawing their courage and their strength out of the elemental forces from which they came. And the elves slowly regained all the ground that had been lost, forcing Barll's army round to join up with the men of Xtlan and pushing them back down the slope towards Gan. With the deaths of Sienogg and Barll the armies of man had become demoralized and now, as they began to suffer losses, their will to fight suddenly evaporated. The chain of command, so painstakingly drilled into them during the long days of training in Xtlan, now fell apart so that their units were fragmented and lost all cohesion. The elves grew more and more deadly, leaping and dancing round their opponents with a speed that rendered them almost invisible, before the final neat thrust through the heart with which they despatched their adversary.

Before long the retreat of the humans turned into a rout as the warriors fled headlong down the slope, frantically trying to escape as the elves pursued them relentlessly back towards Gan where the goblins waited and watched impassively. Then, at a signal from Malcoff, the elven warriors stopped and allowed the remaining humans to get away, scrabbling over the last slippery stretch of mud until they found themselves once more amongst the goblins where they milled about aimlessly, crushed by defeat.

Zaggdar, watching, was filled with contempt for them and turning to Straygoth at his side, he spoke.

'Pathetic rabble,' he said. 'Go! Command them. They are yours.'

Taken by surprise Straygoth did not immediately reply and after a few moments Zaggdar's voice rasped out again.

'Well!' and the stridence of his tone sliced into Straygoth's mind.

'Leadership,' he thought. 'This, now, is my chance. At the head of the men of Haark and of Xtlan. Barll dead, and Sienogg; and now I, Straygoth, have been chosen to command all the armies of man. Yes, I will take it,' and he nodded affirmation to Zaggdar.

'Very well then. Order them to form up at the side of my goblins for we await the attack of the elves. Inspire them, Straygoth, with your courage,' he sneered, but the object of his scorn barely perceived the barbed sarcasm in his voice for as he rode out towards the humans his ego swelled till he felt ablaze with the fires of omnipotence. He had come a long way from the days of the Mouse. A shame Barll was not here to see him now; stupid hulk that he had been. Still, no matter. There were others here from Haark; faces he recognized from the past with their jibes and taunts about his stature and his bearing. Now it was his turn. What he lacked in strength and skill with weapons he would make up for with cunning. He would mould them into a force so potent that the goblins would be unable to ignore it. And he, as their commander, would then have a power base on which to stand next to Zaggdar, for without a position of strength his survival among the goblins could only be temporary.

So he spurred his horse out across the black earth as the faint rays of the dying sun threw his iron grey shadow on to the ground. Then, in a voice that he barely recognized as his own, he started to harangue the hapless remnants of the human army. Dazed and bewildered they responded to the vicious tone of his words as he ordered the surviving commanders to form the men up into squads; and they moved as if in their sleep, with eyes wide and staring and blank with fear.

Upon the bluff, in the shadow of the ancient oak, Saurelon turned to the Lords of the Mountains and the Forests and as he spoke his voice was slow and heavy with sadness at all the killing.

'We must regain our strength and our power before the final attack. Let us rest tonight. What say you?' Gravely they nodded their affirmation and Malcoff gave a sign to Morar upon which the pipe-master blew the signal to fall back.

At the sound of the pipe the elven leaders turned their companies round and led the weary warriors back up the hill. Now that the rush of battle was over they felt infinitely tired and as they walked up the slope past the bodies of the men they had killed and the starburst remains of their fallen comrades so their spirits grew heavy and the light within them faded and grew dim.

The elflords walked down to meet them and, gathering their own elves together, spoke, and told them that they were to rest till morning. So they sat where they were, in three assemblies, each group addressed by its lord who spoke to them of home and told again the legends and stories that they knew but never tired of hearing. Perhaps the greatest of these was the story of the quest for the Faradawn; of Brock and Perryfoot and Sam, of Warrigal and Nab and Beth. There were some of the elves who had known them; Morar the piper and Faraid, battle-leader of the sea elves. Others who had glimpsed them from afar in the Halls of the elvenoak in the forest of Ellmondrill, on the enchanted beaches of Elgol or else in the mountain chambers of Rengoll's Tor. Many there were who heard the tale who had their own memories of the quest and to them it was a living story for they saw themselves as they had been in those far-distant times. Others had not been alive then and for these it was legend; a fabulous extravaganza that lifted their spirits with its images of the world as it used to be and the heroism, bravery and love of the companions from Silver Wood.

It was this tale that the elflords told now, seated on the dead black earth amidst the mockery of life that was Spath. Here was the presence of Dréagg more than anywhere else on earth; in the brash, unnatural colours of the leaves, the ugly mutant shapes of the trees and in the dank clammy atmosphere that hung everywhere like a shroud. The stench of evil was in the very air they breathed and the ground beneath them; putrefaction and decay stung their senses and weighed upon the quicksilver brilliance of their elven nature so that their spirits faded and grew dark. Yet, as they listened once more to the story of Nab and Brock and the others, the light of Ashgaroth seemed to penetrate the darkness and to revive and rejuvenate them despite their desolation.

The elves who had been waiting in the hollow now broke up and, for the moment, went to join their own companies. Bracca, Tara, Raagon and Vane sat amongst the woodland elves and listened to Wychnor, letting his words flow over them and the magic of his images fill their hearts. For Vane though, parts of the story came as a revelation. There was much Raagon had told him but much also that he did not know and as he heard Wychnor's soft and gentle voice recounting the whole story, his heart ached once more with a terrible sadness and guilt, the elflord's words falling upon him like a hail of retribution. It was only the thought of the part he was determined to play in the dangerous times ahead that kept him from being so consumed with shame as to lose all his dignity and self-respect. The prospect of atonement shone before him like a beacon of hope and salvation.

Raagon, sitting next to him, knew and felt his friend's pain and, reaching out, put a hand on his shoulder to try and comfort him. The wolf's fur was wet from the dampness in the air, myriads of tiny droplets of moisture that shone dully

357

in the light from the sky like a coating of black diamonds. Their eyes met; Ammdar and Raagon, friends from the beginning, and a wave of love flowed from one to the other so that each was buoyed up by its strength and power. So much between them; so many worlds, from the ancient days Before-Man through the terrible time of the fall up until the days in the wilderness at Operrallmar. Now, they both knew, it was the end of the journey.

CHAPTER XXIII

And all through that long night, while the elves sat and listened to the voices of their lords and golden flasks were passed round of the precious amber drink from the dandelion and the elderflower, the sky thundered and cracked in a tumultuous bedlam of sound as the ambassador of light and the ambassador of darkness fought each other for supremacy of the air. Locked together in a savage and deadly embrace, the stallion and the serpent writhed and thrashed amidst the dark swirls of cloud that raged across the vivid orange moon. As the corridors of time waxed and waned in that endless night, so first one and then the other gained the ascendancy; either Krowll, his sinuous body wrapped around Sylvine, squeezing the life out of him while stabbing at his head with the twin barbs of his tongue, or else it was that the serpent lay beneath Sylvine's flashing hooves with the stallion's teeth rending and tearing at its flesh.

And then around dawn, as the sky began to lighten and the first pale yellow rays of the sun started to appear through gaps in the clouds, there was a sudden eruption overhead. So massive and violent was it that the earth seemed to shudder beneath its onslaught and the attention of the elves was torn away from their lords as they looked up to see the serpent floundering on its back with Sylvine's teeth clamped onto its neck. Wild and desperate, it thrashed at the air and at the white flanks of its oppressor, screaming out its fury and its pain until finally, with a last anguished cry so dreadful that the elves were rendered dumb by it, the creature ceased its struggle.

For a moment there was utter stillness while the sky was flooded with a brilliant blaze of white light as if in triumphant celebration of Sylvine's victory, but the joy of the elves was short-lived for suddenly, even as they looked up, the serpent seemed to disintegrate before their eyes, its body liquifying into an infinite number of tiny drops of black moisture which dispersed slowly outwards into the air and cast a great dark shadow across the light.

And this was Krowll's revenge, that in abstraction he would be as dangerous as in existence for then, to the dismay and horror of the elves, this foul liquescence started to fall to earth in a torrent of black rain. Bracca, his mind in a daze of confusion, felt the heavy drops pummelling his face so that he bent his head down and covered it with his arms in an attempt to protect himself. He could feel the fluid running down his neck; slimy and warm, it stung him where it met his skin and his stomach shrank in repulsion.

'Tara,' he called, his voice almost drowned in the noise of the downpour, and reaching out he felt her to one side. 'Here, come to me,' and, taking her hand, he pulled her towards him. Already though, the earth had become drenched, turning it into a quagmire of mud so slippery that she almost fell twice in the short space over to him.

For what seemed endless moments they huddled together with their heads down, watching the drops of rain spatter thousands of tiny craters in the shiny black ooze and form puddles at their feet. Only a short time before things had been so different, thought Bracca bitterly. The weary elves, victorious against the armies of man, had been refreshed and rejuvenated by the night, their spirits high after their sojourn in the times of legend and the feeling of buoyant optimism sealed by Sylvine's victory. Now though, all that had gone.

Cautiously he raised his head. Little groups stood dejectedly about beneath the unrelenting torrent; heads bowed, sodden and utterly miserable. Using his hands as a shield over his eyes he looked up into the sky and saw flashes of silver behind the swathes of blackness as if the white stallion was still vainly trying to fight Krowll, lashing out against nothingness, impotent against an enemy that had no substance.

Then, high and clear above the sound of the rain, a voice suddenly boomed out and all eyes turned towards it. It seemed to come from the bluff where the three elflords were standing side by side, bathed in a column of golden light that shone down through a gap in the dark sky. And the light seemed to be playing some sort of trick on them for they appeared as giants, their bodies towering above the oak tree and reaching way up into the swirling heights of the storm. Yet where they stood, framed in their aura of gold, seemed to be an oasis of tranquillity and as they looked down upon the elves a feeling of great strength radiated out from them. Its source was the power of Ashgaroth; the power of the seas and the skies, the mountains and the forests and of all the creatures he made that dwelt therein. And behind and above all this was the power of love for it was out of love that he created all these things.

Wychnor it was who had spoken, standing in the middle of the other two. His great green and silver cloak stretched down to earth and the moons and stars around its edges seemed to shiver with life.

'Boahim na ess graill,' he said, and Raagon thrilled with excitement at hearing the language of the Old Ones again. 'Be not afraid,' were the words he had spoken, and then, in a voice that sounded out as pure and sweet as a spring morning, he went on. 'Shaleen y Ashgaroth, naim a vol tumis gan,' 'children of Ashgaroth, now is your greatest moment,' 'Ta heen, et mowlaa sheesh Ebonn,' 'Rise up and throw back the forces of darkness.'

Though Bracca did not know the words, his heart was

361

buoyed up by their sound and all around him he could feel the spirits of the elves surge upwards like a tidal wave as they lifted their heads and raised their sword-arms to the sky. 'Y Ashgaroth,' they shouted, 'Y Ashgaroth,' and as the chanting grew louder the three elflords reached up into the blackness with their hands outstretched. Then, as one, they let out a mighty cry and immediately great tongues of silver flame leapt down on to the ends of their fingertips, crackling and dancing amidst the torrents of rain that poured down from above.

Now the elflords looked down to the earth from on high and there was fire in their eyes; a blazing inferno so intense that the elves could not look directly at them.

Bracca, though, was mesmerized; unable to turn away he looked on as Wychnor, Malcoff and Saurelon swept their gaze over the ground. Within moments the saturated earth had started to hiss and little wisps of steam were drifting up into the air leaving the ground parched and cracked with dryness. And then the air was filled with a mighty roar as Bracca saw the elflords bring their arms down from the sky, drawing the pillars of flame on the ends of their fingertips with them so that the swirling darkness of the storm was sliced by six great arcs of silver fire.

Now there was a feeling of expectancy amongst the elves so fierce that Bracca became infected with it and found it hard to breathe; a huge lump seemed to have risen up into his chest and was hammering to get out. Looking along the six corridors of light he could see the goblins waiting at the far end, Zaggdar and the other leaders on their lizard mounts, while the rest were formed up behind in columns that stretched back to the bridge and away into the distance at either side. And there, in front of the remnants of the armies of Barll and Sienogg, Bracca, to his immense surprise, recognized Straygoth. Suddenly everywhere seemed to be alive with movement as the elves scurried about to form themselves up into their battle formations.

'Here! Come back with me. The attack will start at any moment.'

362

It was Faraid who spoke, the silver light flickering off his tunic and helmet; and, grabbing Tara's hand, Bracca found himself following the elf back up the hill to the hollow from which he had previously watched the rout of the humans. Just ahead of him he could see Raagon and Vane walking side by side over the steaming ground with the rest of the elves.

Just as they clambered down the bank into their shelter a huge cry went up once again: 'Y Ashgaroth, Y Ashgaroth,' and almost at once the elves started racing down the paths of light with their swords raised. Bracca felt his eyes filling with tears at the poignant majesty of this awe-inspiring spectacle. How many would come back? The terrible question gnawed away at him with an awful nagging ache in his stomach. They looked like six rivers of ice glimmering in the sun as they flowed through the blackness of the storm towards the goblin hordes.

They watched from the hollow for what seemed an age. The rain was still lashing down outside the tunnels of flame and the ground had become sodden again after its temporary drying out by the elflords but Bracca and the others were now oblivious to the wet, their eyes focused once more on the fortunes of the elven army as it went in to the attack for the second time in two days. This time though, they knew it would not be like it had been against the humans and this time also there was the awful knowledge that when the signal was given, the moment would have come upon which everything depended; the breakthrough into Gan. If they failed, then the light would go out forever and the world would plunge into darkness.

The two armies met with a great crash; the elven swords colliding with the shields of the goblins in a terrible clamour that jarred Bracca's nerves. Seemingly rejuvenated by their journey through the flames the elves fought with a brilliance and courage that caused the elflords to marvel and Ammdar, every muscle tensed, felt himself to be there among them, his sword arm itching and his body ducking and weaving in sympathy with every duel he watched. And yet despite the bravery of the elves they made little progress for the giant lizards wreaked a mighty havoc amongst them, sweeping up numbers at a time in their snapping mouths or crushing them beneath their feet. The elflords cried in their hearts as they saw the carnage that was unfolding beneath their eyes. They could do no more. They had cleared paths through the storm that still raged all around and they had used up much of their energy in drying up the earth. How much longer they could keep this going they did not know for it was the power of Ashgaroth that helped them now; the elemental power of light that blazed from their fingertips.

All day the battle raged with neither side gaining any sort of ascendancy. The air grew rancid and foul from the stench of the goblins' blood and the earth became putrid as the black slime from their wounds seeped out and spread in pools around their bodies. As the day wore on the elves managed to kill a number of the goblin mounts, attacking in groups and using their speed and agility to infuriate them and then bring them down by hacking at their legs. But the cost was high both in the numbers of elves lost and the spiritual upheaval caused by this particularly gruesome sort of death. The goblins, superior in numbers and brimming with energy and strength, made up in their lust for killing all that they lacked in skill and courage. Savagely they wielded their heavy two-handed broadswords, always working in threes so that they could single out one of the elves and so minimize the risk of defeat. Others used a ball and chain, swinging it around the head to get a good speed up and then bringing its arc low to lash out at the elves and knock them down so that others could deal the fatal blow. And all the while there was Zaggdar moving amongst his warriors on his enormous steed, organizing, cajoling and exhorting them in their fight. Straygoth too was relishing his new-found power, pushing the men forward with threats while he rode along behind them. They responded too; now that the goblins were at their side and the elves were being pushed back, their courage had revived. The dreams of glory that had been dashed by their previous defeat now seemed real once more and they fought with a savagery that surprised even the goblins. Degg, watching the scene of battle from the darkness of his tower room, skittered and jumped with excitement as he saw the elves floundering in the mud and with every elf that fell a rush of pleasure coursed through his body.

From just under the rim of the hollow Faraid too was looking down on the awful conflict. It was towards evening now; he could just sense the change in the light, and since the fight had started early on that morning the elves had hardly made an impression into the goblin army, ranged as it was like a solid wall around Gan. By now the ground was thick with bodies, slumped one against the other. The elves were tranquil in death, their bodies shimmering slightly as they lost their substance and slowly metamorphosed into the air, while the goblin corpses still seemed to be in turmoil, their ugly bloated features twisted into masks of hatred and their limbs arranged in grotesque patterns round grossly distended bellies.

As he watched, threads of panic started to pull at Faraid's mind. Would they ever achieve the breakthrough that Malcoff had said was so necessary to enable them to push through into Gan; and as time went on things seemed to be getting even worse. The continual rain had turned the ground into a quagmire in which the agility and speed of the elves were rendered more and more impotent and he could tell that they were now wearying of the terrible struggle. Then, out of the corner of his eye, he caught a movement at his side. It was Tara, and as he turned slightly to look at her he was reminded of her mother, Beth, and of the last time he had led his warriors against the goblins. Long, long ago now, and yet he remembered it so clearly; the rescue of the travellers from Silver Wood from the goblins in the marshes of Blore. He could still recall the look of shocked surprise and wonder on the face of Beth when she saw the elves for the first time and an image of that moment came back to him as if it were yesterday; the blue sea glistening in the bright spring sunshine, the crying of the gulls as they wheeled overhead and, just a little way off the shore, the beautiful barnacle-encrusted island of Elgol, his home, washed by rolling white-tipped waves that crashed against its rocky beaches.

He was brought abruptly back to the present by the interminable clamour of the battle and by the sensation, vague at first but quickly becoming clearer and more defined, of a voice deep inside himself. He looked up to where the figures of the elflords towered high above, their faces almost disembodied in the sheets of water that fell from the sky.

'Go! Go now. And may Ashgaroth go with you,' said the voice, and he recognized it as the three elflords speaking to him all together, their eyes bearing down upon him with an intensity that could not be denied.

He hesitated for only a moment before turning round to face the host of elves in the hollow. Then, raising his sword in the air, he addressed them in a voice that was as pure and sweet as the song of a mountain stream.

'Now is our moment,' he said, and his words sounded out clearly above the sounds of fighting.

'We will not fail; for we are fighting for justice and goodness, for love and compassion and beauty, for gentle-ness and innocence and truth. These are our battle standards and their power is illimitable.'

And then the darkness overhead was split by a shaft of silver light and all the elves looked up.

'Ashgaroth smiles upon us,' said Faraid. 'Now take your formation.'

He turned then to Bracca and spoke to him gently.

'Go with Reev. You and Tara and Raagon will stay with him in the centre. Vane too, I think will go with you. Keep away from the fighting for as long as you can; you must take no chances.'

And so, clutching Tara's hand, Bracca followed Reev down

366

into the middle of the hollow. The elves made a passage through for them and Bracca could feel the force of their gaze upon him. He was not nervous any more. Instead he moved automatically, numbed by the pressure of the task before him and the awesome responsibility that lay upon his shoulders. On the way down he accidentally knocked a small bush and a shower of drops fell onto his leg and wet his skin. It was something so ordinary and so resonant with evocative images from the past of rainy walks through the forest of Haark that he felt suddenly very humble and mortal again. And it was a good feeling, sending a sensation of substance and reality through him that, strangely, filled him with a new confidence. He felt the rhythm of the sword, Tabor, at his side as he walked, the great scabbard bumping against his thigh and he became aware again of the Belt of Ammdar round his waist.

Finally, they stood in the centre of the hollow; the four of them with Reev just in front, the greens and browns of his jerkin making him at times difficult to see in the murky light. Around them stood the ranks of the elves, their swords raised ready for the command from Faraid who had now taken his place at their head. A strange unreal stillness settled upon them; a breathless apprehension that was almost too painful to bear. And all the time, high in the sky, the brilliant silver glow shone through the dark storm clouds as if Ashgaroth himself was watching them while just ahead the six corridors of light stretched down to the scene of the fighting.

Bracca's tongue was dry and he had difficulty in breathing but he forced himself to whisper to Tara.

'Stay with me. Above all else stay with me,' he said, and then, just as the words had left his lips, Faraid brought his sword down and immediately Bracca felt a great surge forward as the elves raced towards the avenues of light. The air was full of the sound of their battle cries, each one different, handed down from the beginning of time itself and from the bluff came the sound of Morar's pipes, their pure wild notes seeming to enter Bracca's soul so that he was buoyed up by them and carried along on their rolling waves of sound. He seemed to have stepped outside himself and to be watching from above. He saw himself racing along through the driving rain, squelching and slipping in the mud yelling, 'Ashgaroth, Ashgaroth,' till his lungs felt like bursting, hanging on to Tara's wrist with one hand while with the other he held Tabor above his head, the water pouring off the blade and running down his arm into his jerkin.

Then, suddenly, he was brought back to himself by a blinding flash of light and he realized that they had entered one of the corridors. He seemed to be totally enveloped in a shimmering blaze of silver; tongues of white flame leaping and dancing around them as they raced along, and he became infused with their power and strength. On and on he ran for what seemed an eternity; his body bursting with energy and his feet almost throwing him forward over the dried-out earth so that he felt he could go on forever. Out of the corner of an eye he saw Tara and was caught by her loveliness; her stream of honey-coloured hair fanning out behind her and her face imbued with a magical radiance from the light. She moved with a gentle liquid grace, the rhythms of her body reminding him of the deer in whose form he had so often seen her.

And then, as suddenly as they had left the gloom of the storm, they were once again in its throes, only now their time in the corridor had so rejuvenated them that they hardly noticed the mud and the rain. The other elves, weary though they were, felt inspired by the sight of their comrades and fought with renewed vigour, pushing the goblins back on either side of the wedge of warriors containing Bracca.

This new onslaught and the arrival of a fresh body of elves took Zaggdar by surprise and by the time he realized what was happening, Faraid, Bracca and the others were close to the causeway that led across to Gan. Furiously the goblin shouted to his commanders to come back and seal it off but there was so much noise and confusion that they either did not hear the order or were unable to carry it out. Indeed the goblins had started a number of fights amongst themselves as different groups tried to carry out Zaggdar's orders while those who were mounted drove their lizards through the mass of flesh that was in their way not caring whether it was composed of their own kind or the elves. The sight of these terrible beasts lurching violently towards them was almost too much for Bracca and it took all his will-power to make himself go forward. They were a grisly and terrifying sight; impaled figures, still alive, wriggled on the spikes on their foreheads; the snapping pincers at the end of their forearms were littered with the severed remains of other victims while their razor sharp teeth cut a swath through those that stood in their way.

But as the lizards grew ever closer to Faraid's elves, so the others redoubled their efforts to bring down the goblin steeds. Terrible were the elven losses but for every moment of time that they bought, Bracca and the others got a vital few paces nearer the causeway. Now Bracca could see it just ahead, stretching out over the dark waters to where Gan stood framed against the purple-black sky, its pinnacles, turrets and towers reaching upwards like fingers in prayer. Desperately the goblins tried to cut them off from the bridge. All about, Bracca could see their hideous faces and was almost suffocated by the nauseating smell of their breath yet still the elves were thronged around him so that, though Tabor was drawn and ready, he had not yet had to use it. The clash of sword against sword was deafening and the cries of the wounded railed at his mind so that his head started to spin. Zaggdar, mad with fury, was stuck in the middle of a thick wedge of goblins and his lizard was unable to move either forward or back. Impotent with rage he stood up in the stirrups and screamed at those in front, frantically urging his steed forward through the helpless mass of bodies in which it had got bogged down.

Then, suddenly, almost without knowing it, Bracca found himself standing just at the end of the causeway. The elves had managed to push the goblins back and hold them there leaving, as Faraid had planned, a narrow passageway through which Reev could lead Bracca and the others.

'We're through. We've made it,' shouted the wood elf. 'Come on, before the wall breaks.'

The jubilation that Bracca momentarily felt had now become tinged with panic as Faraid and the others fought a desperate action to hold the line of goblins back. They raced forward, Reev in the lead, followed by Vane and Raagon and then, hard on their heels, Bracca and Tara. The causeway was narrow and the constant damp had coated the stone with a layer of green slime so that they had to be careful not to slip and fall into the dark waters. In parts the stone foundation on which it was built showed through and they were unable to avoid stepping on the jagged exposed rocks, hurting their feet on the sharp edges.

They were nearly halfway across now and their lungs were aching with the effort but still Reev urged them forward. Raagon was painfully aware of his age; taking in great gulps of air he felt his muscles screaming out in protest and his eyes burning from the heat of his exertions. Yet they dare not stop for the clamour of the goblins behind them was rising in a crescendo of fury as their quarry slipped from their grasp.

Suddenly they were brought to a halt, quivering with fear, by a sound that came from the direction of Gan and looking up they saw Degg with a long spiral horn-shaped cone held to his mouth. He stood there, a tiny figure framed in the open window of the turret, and as he blew on the horn so the noise grew louder and louder, swelling up until it eclipsed everything else, piercing the air with a droning whine that battered at their ears and curdled the blood in their veins. And then they became aware of a second answering drone coming from much nearer at hand and looking down to the dark waters at the edge of the causeway they saw the surface start to bubble and froth. Transfixed with horror they stared as the commotion grew ever greater, the water boiling with fury as its black surface shimmered with gashes of crimson light.

Then out of the depths it erupted and Degg, watching from the safety of his room in the tower, felt a thrill of horror as it broke the surface. 'Now my beauty. Now. . .' he mouthed to himself in a voice that was tremulous with excitement, and as if it heard him the creature started to rise up out of the darkness of the moat. As it emerged the water broke in torrents over the shiny blue-green carapace of its back and ran down between the jointed segments as they moved to a juddering and macabre rhythm in their efforts to propel it upwards. The air was filled with the sound of its breathing; a stentorian liquid wheezing that bubbled up through the water, and Bracca felt himself turning faint at the overpowering stench of fish that emanated from it. The terrified onlookers could see it clearly now as it lay facing them partly submerged, its jet-black eyes staring out at them from under the great rim of curved armour that lay across the first part of its body. Its eight hairy segmented legs moved in unison just under the surface and from each side of its savage beak-like mouth there were long red feelers some of which curved away over its back till they reached a fluted fan-like tail while other, shorter, ones grew out at the front, waving sinuously above the water. But it was the pair of huge and terrible pincers that froze their blood and rooted them to the ground in terror; floating menacingly in the air at the end of two short, stocky, jointed arms, they opened and closed purposefully with dreadful and malignant intent.

Then suddenly, with a swiftness that was astonishing for a creature of its size, it sped over the water and threw one of its pincers forward towards Bracca in a rapid thrust. Instinctively he fell to the ground flinging his arm round Tara as he did so, and as it passed by just overhead he could feel the rush of air and smell the sharp acrid pungency of fish. He turned his head to one side and saw that the others were also lying flat but that the creature had moved nearer, its eyes and mouth clearly visible just a few paces away and was

371

preparing to strike again, its pincers poised just above them.

'Run when I say. It's our only chance,' he said to Tara, grabbing her chin roughly and turning it so that she was forced to look at him. She didn't hear at first, staring back at him with terrified bewilderment and so he had to repeat it, shouting to make himself heard above the creature's breathing.

'I can't. . . I can't leave you. I won't,' she said.

Seething with frustration at her refusal, he yelled out to Raagon. 'Take her! Wait for us in Gan,' and almost as soon as the words had left his lips he saw the grey shadow of the wolf, Vane, leap up off the edge of the causeway to land, snarling, on the creature's face and bury his fangs under its eye.

'Now! Go!' he yelled, for the creature was bucking and writhing in its attempt to shake the wolf off. She was gone then, suddenly, torn away from his side by Raagon's strong arms.

'Look after her,' he called out, but the Old One's answering response was lost as the two of them raced away over the bridge towards Gan.

Then, horrified, he saw the creature's attention drawn by their movement and, ignoring the pain on its face, it lunged out wildly towards them with its nearest claw and he was forced to press himself flat to the ground as it swung over him again. Now he knew what he had to do. Willing himself to be brave he gripped Tabor tightly with both hands and then, the moment the claw had gone by, he leapt up and summoning all his faith and strength he swung the sword down as hard as he could. It seemed to be possessed almost of a will of its own, drawing his aim until the blade came down against the knuckled joint in the creature's elbow. He felt the cutting edge connect with the piece of hard shell and a jarring shock went through his whole body but then it slid off and cut deep into the flesh, slicing easily through the gristle and sinews. He experienced a strange thrill of triumph until suddenly with a loud crack the lower half of the pincer swung violently back towards him at the same time as the creature let out a terrible howl of pain. He ducked quickly and almost managed to avoid it altogether but it just caught him on his knee and he fell down in agony as a mist of pain swam before his eyes. The pincer was hanging loosely, swinging from side to side and scraping the earth as it did so. He had apparently severed one of the tendons that controlled it and it was now useless. As he lay on the ground clutching his knee, he saw Raagon and Tara just leaving the far end of the bridge and he was relieved to see that the creature was so enraged that it had forgotten all about them, turning instead to its human attacker while still trying to get rid of the wolf. It fixed its black gaze upon him and he felt the cold chill of terror spread through his body as its gimlet eyes bored into the depths of his soul and sucked at his spirit.

It was near the causeway now, its blood-red feelers sweeping the ground in a strange elliptical motion and its shattered elbow dragging the pincer behind it. The good pincer was poised in the air to one side, the jaws opening and shutting in an ominous and relentless rhythm. Soon they would crash down upon him and snap him in two, and he had a sudden terrible vision of his body crushed and broken between them. He had to move now; to get under and inside its reach. But how? And then, seeing the feelers waving about just in front of him, he knew. Without thinking he leapt to his feet, willing himself to ignore the flash of pain in his knee, and ran across the short stretch of earth that separated him from the creature. This close, the stench was sickening but he fought back the waves of nausea that broke against him and, waiting until the feeler was almost touching him, he made a sudden leap forwards and found himself hanging on to its thick, slightly feathery surface. To his relief it was not slippery and he was able to hang on more easily than he had imagined though the serrated edges were sharp and he had to be careful not to cut his hand. Now he had to climb up so as to get nearer to its eye for that he guessed would be its most vulnerable spot. Then he heard a cry and looking across at where it had come from he saw that Reev had followed his example and was hanging from the other feeler.

'The eyes. Go for the eyes,' he shouted, but whether the elf heard he could not tell for the creature was snorting and whining in pain and rage. But still he was immensely heartened by the sight of Reev for now, with Vane still tearing at its face, they must have a chance.

And so, hand over hand, Bracca climbed his slow and painful way upwards. Luckily the creature did not seem able to control the feelers well but it tried to get them off by bucking and shaking its huge body so that in his efforts to hang on, his hands began to hurt, bleeding and becoming sore. He was on a level with its mouth now and it kept trying to lunge forward, snapping its teeth together so close to him that he could feel its foul breath on his face. But it could not hold the feelers still and every time it tried to get him he swung tantalizingly out of reach.

Up and up he went until the black waters of the moat seemed a long way below and the battle between the elves and the goblins seemed to belong to a different world. All he was aware of now was the terrible and awesome presence of the monster, the pain in his knee and his hands and Tabor swinging in its scabbard at his side. Almost there now; and looking across he saw that Vane was level with him, the sound of his snarling stirring Bracca's blood with the reassuring thought that they were on the same side. He could see the wounds on the monster's face; great ragged patches of purple-green flesh that hung down loosely and dripped a dark blue liquid into the water. Reev too was as far up as he was and exchanging glances they each drew strength from the other's success.

And then suddenly there it was, a shimmering black pool of darkness out of which poured a current of malevolence with such powerful force that it almost knocked him physically off his precarious hand hold. And there in the centre, infinitely disconcerting, was a reflection of himself

374

looking back out with fearful bewilderment. For a few momentous heartbeats he stared at his image, paralysed into immobility, and then the clear pure voice of Reev broke the spell and clinging to the feeler with one hand he grasped Tabor's hilt with the other, drew it from its scabbard and raising it high above his head brought it slashing down in an arc against his reflected body. He felt the blade judder slightly as it met the resistance of the eye's gelatinous surface and then he watched as his own body crumpled up before his eyes folding in upon itself until it suddenly split open and a jet of stinking black ooze streamed out towards him. He shut his eyes instinctively, waiting for it to hit him, and in that dreadful moment the air was rent by a mighty scream at the same time as the creature, with a great flap of its tail, reared up out of the water and began thrashing around frantically in the throes of its agonized blindness.

Bracca hung on desperately for as long as he could but when the spume of slime slammed into him, his grasp was wrenched away and to his horror he found himself falling backwards into space. Down and down he plunged with the black stuff all over his face; sticking his eyelids together and making it difficult to open his mouth to breathe. Twisting round in mid-air he put Tabor back into the scabbard and then set about scraping off the slime but no sooner had he cleared it away from his lips than he hit the water with a force that thumped the air from his chest and sent a haze of stars floating crazily across his vision. And now he felt the water close in around him as his body rapidly became immersed in its clammy, oily weight. Fingers of coldness felt their way up under his jerkin and down his neck and he felt his hair floating up from his head and tugging gently at his scalp. Wiping the ooze from his eyes he forced them open and looking up was horrified to see a mass of darkness broken only by the occasional glimmer of grey light from the surface.

Further and further he sank and suddenly he became aware of a cluster of sharp stabbing pains in his lungs like searing tongues of fire. He had no breath left, the impact of his fall had expelled it all and he saw no way now of getting up to the surface in time. The whole of his chest ached; as if it was being crushed by the weight of the water and he had the most terrible temptation to open his mouth wide and gulp in great mouthfuls of what should have been air, glorious lifegiving air, instead of what he knew would be a fatal last breath.

He struck out now with his arms and legs, kicking and flapping wildly in a desperate attempt to get up, but the pain was becoming unbearable, pounding outwards against his rib cage in wave after wave of pressure that sent his head spinning and caused his vision to shatter into a whirling kaleidoscope of colours. He felt himself going then, his spirit turning in upon itself as his consciousness floated away, but through the drifting maze of images that passed across his mind he was aware of one above all the others; his arm was being pulled upwards by something just above him in the water and forcing himself to concentrate he thought he could just make out the outlines of an elf, its body glinting with silver light through the murky water, and catching a glimpse of its face he knew that it was not Reev but Ammdar. And then oblivion claimed him.

CHAPTER XXIV

He was jolted to his senses by a sensation of being dragged over a series of bumps and then, left to lie still, he was suddenly stung into wakefulness by a flurry of hard slaps on his face and the sound of a voice frantically calling his name from far away. With an enormous effort of will he tried to fight his way through the shrouds of fog that swirled around in his head to get to whoever it was that was calling him. His body ached terribly; his back and his ribs felt bruised and sore as if he had been in a fight and his legs were heavily laden with a great tiredness.

It was Tara's voice. Forcing his eyes open he could see her face swimming before him, the outlines blurred and distorted but unmistakable. And the tone of her voice, nearer now, was frantic with anxiety.

'Bracca,' she kept saying. 'Hurry. Hurry.'

He had to get up. Crazily he lurched forward in an effort to stand and felt himself gripped by strong hands and hauled to his feet where he staggered and swayed for a moment before being held and steadied upright. Then a sudden anguished howl jolted him to his senses and with his nostrils assailed by the terrible and familiar stench his memory flooded back in a rush of horror. He swung round then and looked back over the causeway to where the monster, blinded and maddened with pain and rage, was turning towards the mass of goblins who had been standing on the edge of the water. Drawn by their scent it flapped its way rapidly across the moat and with a wild and savage sweep of its one good pincer it grabbed a number of them and bringing them across to its mouth began placing them, almost delicately, into its beak until Bracca saw their screaming, wriggling, bodies disappear inside. Furiously, Zaggdar was trying to force them across the bridge after Bracca and the others but, witnessing the terrible fate of their comrades who got too close, they refused to go, preferring to face his wrath than the monster.

Straygoth too was unable to drive the humans forward and they ran around in frantic circles, panic-stricken by the sight of the creature, lost in a waking nightmare from which there was no escape.

So as the creature lumbered its way forward, the armies of the goblins and the humans scattered like seeds in the wind, running desperately back up the slope and out into the trees of the forest, blind to everything save the overwhelming need to get away. Zaggdar managed to control his mount and the lizard carried him off after the others but Straygoth's horse reared up in fear, bucking and tossing crazily, and he was thrown off in the monster's path. He scrambled to his feet and, screaming for help, tried to run up the muddy bank but time and again he slipped and soon the creature was upon him. Bracca, watching, felt almost sorry for the wretched figure as it flapped about in the slime in a pathetic attempt to get away. With a shock he realized that if he succeeded in the task that Ashgaroth had set for him, then this would be the last time he would see another human and at this thought something inside him cried out in protest. He must try to rescue Straygoth.

'I'm going after him,' he shouted, and launched himself forward but as he did so he felt two strong arms wrap themselves around his waist and though he struggled to get away, he was unable to move. And now it was too late, for the monster had scooped Straygoth up and, pausing only to locate its mouth, it fed him into its black pointed beak and snapped it shut on his neck leaving the head, with its mouth still gaping open in its last dying scream, to roll out and fall down into the mud.

Bracca relaxed then, all the tension that had built up inside him suddenly vanishing, and he became aware for the first time of the arms that had been holding him. They lessened their grip now and as the arms fell away from his waist he saw to his surprise that he did not recognize them; and in that same instant he knew whose they were. He recalled then the vision that he had seen under the water pulling him up from the foul depths of the moat just before he passed out. So he had not been wrong! He became frightened now to turn round and face him. A whirlwind of thoughts and emotions raged inside his head; the power and intensity of the legend brought to life; humility and jealousy; the sword, sheathed now inside its scabbard but with its weight and feel still in his hand; fear and apprehension, relief and joy.

'Bracca.' The voice was as gentle as the rustle of leaves in the breeze and had with it all the music of the woods in spring. 'Bracca. Don't be afraid, please. It is I who am grateful to you and it is for you to forgive me if you can find it in your heart to do so.'

Slowly Bracca turned around, drawn by the magic of the voice and the humility of the words until at last Ammdar stood before him and he was even as Bracca had imagined him, with the light shining off his helmet and breastplate and his face so infinitely soft and gentle that Bracca felt the force of his love almost as a physical blow. His long mane of silver hair fell down around his shoulders stirring slightly in the breeze that blew across the water and as Bracca looked into his eyes he saw the familiar unmistakable light that he recognized from Vane wherein was not only gentleness and nobility but also a mighty strength and a resolution that knew no bounds.

'Come, Bracca, let us be comrades and friends,' he said. 'Ashgaroth has indeed chosen well,' and he held his arms

379

open so that the young man instinctively stepped forward and embraced him.

It was a moment of intense poignancy and the weight of its significance was lost on none of that small band who were part of it. Neither on Raagon who had dreamt of a moment like this ever since Ammdar's temptation and fall, nor on Tara who was still struck with wonder by the transformation. Bracca too marvelled at what was happening; hardly able to believe its reality, he felt it must all be a dream from which he would wake at any moment and all the peace and certainty that he now felt would shatter and blow away like thistledown in the wind. And Reev, mesmerized at the sight of the earliest and greatest of all the elflords, found the silver alleys of his mind suddenly crowded with myriad legends of Ammdar before the fall, all now rushing in upon him in an overwhelming kaleidoscope of magical images.

For Ammdar himself the moment was so exquisite as to be almost painful; that Ashgaroth had not forgotten him and had granted him the chance of redemption, that he had been given back his elven form and that he was here now on the threshold of the final victory – these were what he had prayed for during all the long days of darkness. He had not known of the change until he came out of the water with Bracca and had only realized the miracle of his transformation by the reaction of the others and only now, as he had the young one in his arms, was he able to fully believe it. And then, in his mind, he heard the silent call of the other elflords and looking up he saw them in the distance, high up on the bluff in the shadows of the ancient oak, and with them, at Saurelon's side, to his joy and relief he saw Faraid. He thanked them for their trust and their faith and mourned with them for the loss of so many of the elves. They had paid a high price and it would be few indeed who would make the journey back but they had succeeded; the armies of the humans and the goblins were now scattered and Gan had been penetrated. They had fought with great skill and immeasurable courage against overwhelming odds and the battle for Gan would live for ever in the annals of elvenlore. It was up to him now to guide Bracca and the others on the last stage of their journey.

And they all turned then to look towards the elflords. The shattered remains of the elven army had gathered around them and for a moment they all stood still together, gazing down upon the arena of the battle as if in memory of all those who had fallen. Then Wychnor, Saurelon and Malcoff raised their hands and in a great flash of silver light, all were gone. Some there would be whose magic had been so weakened by the fighting that it would not carry them home but most would get back, saddened by the absence of their friends but content in the victory they had wrought from the forces of darkness.

'Look!' It was Tara who first spotted them, a large number of goblins running out from an entrance across on the other side of the courtyard.

'Degg's bodyguard. The cream of his warriors,' said Ammdar, and as they looked up they could see Degg's shadow in the topmost window of the tower. Then suddenly while they watched he let out a great cry of rage that reverberated round the walls of the square and seemed to echo his anger, so that they were surrounded on all sides by the awesome sound of his fury.

'I feared he would keep them away from the battle,' continued the elflord. 'Now look at them, strong and fresh and with his passion to spur them on. Come on. Follow me. We must move fast.'

With Ammdar in the lead they raced away from the causeway across the stone flags of the yard until they reached a small arched doorway set deep in the opposite wall. Already the goblins were half-way over as Ammdar turned a large iron ring in the stone door and it opened before them to reveal a dark passageway leading off on either side. When they were inside Ammdar pushed the door shut and leaned against it.

'Try and find something to wedge it,' he said. 'Bracca, you

and I will try to hold them back.'

It was dark and musty in the passage and the nauseating stench of goblin was heavy in the air. Bracca's knee still hurt and the jolting across the yard had revived the pain but it was tolerable. In a moment the others had come back carrying a small stone bench and just as they put it down they heard shouts from the other side and saw the handle being turned.

'Quick. Put your end against the opposite wall,' said Ammdar, and he and Bracca pushed it down against the door so that it was jammed tight. 'That should hold them for a bit,' he added, as they stood up straight.

'Are there no other ways in?' asked Bracca.

'Yes, one; but it's right at the other end of the square so it will give us some time. Now, we turn down here. How is your leg?'

'It's all right,' replied Bracca.

'Here,' said Tara. 'I'll help you. Lean on me,' and he did so, gripping her round the shoulder, as they set off after Ammdar whose armour exuded a faint sheen of silver light which helped them to see their way along in the gloom. Behind him came Raagon and finally Reev, who was thinking a little wistfully of his friends on their way back to the elvenoak in the enchanted forest of Ellmondrill.

They walked along in silence. The thick stone walls allowed no trace of noise inside and it was almost as if the nightmare of such a short time ago had existed only in their imagination. The only sounds were the steady rhythms of their breathing and the padding of their feet on the stone floor; there was no indication yet of any pursuit. Now they came to a corner but instead of carrying on round, Ammdar opened a door that led off it and they found themselves in a large circular room littered with tables and benches. There was a different smell in here that reminded Bracca of rotting fungus and as they went in there was a chorus of frightened squeaks and the patter of lots of tiny feet scampering away into the corners. Bracca tried to see what was making the noise but all he could make out was the flicker of movement in the gloom.

'Don't be afraid. They won't harm you; they're more frightened of you than you are of them. Now, we must wedge this door again,' and they hurriedly piled benches and tables up against it. While they were doing so Ammdar walked across to the opposite wall and Bracca saw him moving along it very slowly, feeling over its surface with his fingers outstretched, all the while talking quietly to himself. Then he stopped at one particular place and with obvious excitement began tracing the outline of a door in what appeared to be a solid stone wall.

'Yes,' he called across to them. 'It's here. I've found it. Come over!'

They did as he asked and when they were all together he turned to Bracca.

'Unsheath Tabor,' he said. His tone was gentle for he did not want to usurp Bracca's authority over the sword and this gentleness dispelled the young man's first reaction to the request which had been, as Ammdar had feared, antagonistic.

So he grasped Tabor and pulled it slowly out of its scabbard. It was still wet from the moat and water dripped down from the point to form a little pool on the floor.

'Unscrew the end and inside the hilt you will find a small phial made of blue stone. Take it out.'

Bracca looked up at the elflord. 'Do you want. . .' he began, but Ammdar cut him short.

'No! Tabor is yours. Now, please. Do as I ask.'

When Bracca had extracted the phial Ammdar told him to pull out a small bung from the top of it and then to lick his hand and pour some of the powder inside on to it.

The powder was very fine and silvery and shone with a sparkling phosphorescent brilliance so that Bracca could not look directly at it. A fountain of light seemed to be erupting from his hand throwing the room into intense brightness while from the dark shadows that still lingered in the corners, he could see an army of tiny yellow eyes staring out at them.

Ammdar spoke again. 'Here. Let me take your hand,' he said, and, proffering it to him, Bracca felt the elflord's fingers intertwine with his and his hand was lifted up so that his palm faced outward towards the wall. Where the beam of light shone on it the faint outline of a doorway appeared at the same place that Ammdar had been looking earlier.

The elflord then took Bracca forward till they were standing just in front of it and putting his hand against the rock traced the line of the door carefully all the way round. As Bracca's hand passed over it the line grew much more distinct and acquired a depth so that the door began to look real. Again and again Ammdar repeated the process until finally there was no doubt; there was a door in the wall.

'Good,' he said, partly to himself and partly to the others. 'Now, Bracca, open it. Open the door. Just push and it should swing free,' but Bracca hesitated, unable to believe the evidence before his eyes. 'Go on!' he said again. 'Push.'

Gingerly Bracca put his hand flat against the stone door and to his amazement he found that it moved even under the slight pressure he applied to it. Excitedly he pushed harder and so easily did it give way that he almost fell forward.

'Go through,' said Ammdar. 'I'll close it behind us.'

So Bracca led the way through the open doorway onto a small stone ledge the other side. The light from his hand glimmered against the rock walls of what appeared to be a small cave but just in front of him the floor seemed to fall away in a sheer drop into blackness. He felt Tara against his side and taking her hand squeezed it gently. The air was dank and musty and the walls exuded a cold chill that struck through into their bones.

When they were all through Ammdar called to Bracca and, taking his hand again, played the light over the doorway. After a few moments the space in the wall became crisscrossed with lines as if a large web had been spun across it and then the lines grew thicker until eventually the doorway was completely filled in and there was no trace of where the opening had been. By this time the light from his hand had

384

faded so that it gave off no more than a slight glow but it left him with a strange and irritating tingling feeling.

'It will soon go,' said Ammdar, reading Bracca's concern from the look on his face.

The only light now was a faint reddish glow that they had not noticed before. It seemed to come from somewhere beneath them and flickered against the stone as if from flames, illuminating their faces in a way that was strangely comical and grotesque, and casting their shadows in weird elongated caricatures against the walls.

'Now we are safe for the moment,' said Ammdar. 'It will take a long time for Degg to penetrate the wall though he must have a good idea of where to look. Still, the goblins are not now our main concern.' He paused and looked at the little band around him. How much more could they take? Exhausted and emotionally drained they could not be far from the end of their endurance, and yet now they were to embark on perhaps the most perilous part of their whole mission. He looked around at them in turn and marvelled at the fortitude of each one. Reev, worn out by the battle against the goblins, alone and desperately homesick for the enchanted forest, was visibly fading as the tentacles of darkness insinuated their way into his elven spirit. Raagon, his friend, who had borne so much for him and whose faith had sustained him during the seemingly endless time of his spiritual exile at Operrallmar. But now he was old, he looked tired and drawn and his initial joy at taking part in this epic final conflict had become fractured as the physical and mental limitations imposed upon him by his great age took their toll.

Tara too, he felt, was suffering as the evil of Spath tore at the fabric of her magical nature. She had been travelling for so long now that her time with Nab and Beth must seem to belong to a different age. Her long hair was tangled into a wild confusion of golden curls, her clothes had grown ragged and torn and the delicacy of her features had become blunted by the black smudges smeared across her face. The shimmer in her eyes too had grown dim and she looked more and more to Bracca for strength and support while he in turn seemed to draw much of his faith and courage from her need for him. Yet there was something else also he knew that drove Bracca and sustained him through all these dark times; the faith that had first led him so long ago into conflict with Barll and the knowledge that the mantle of Ashgaroth now lay upon him. And there was also in Bracca, Ammdar felt, a powerful and stirring sense of lineage as if Melvaig and Morven were constantly at his side, and through them the guardianship of knowledge of the Faradawn. He looked at the young man now, dishevelled and unkempt, his long tousled hair falling about his shoulders and his face encrusted with grime and dirt, and wondered at his resolution and courage. The dark eyes were tired and a little wild but the fire of battle still burned brightly in them and there was an eagerness about him that inspired Ammdar with hope for the trials that lay ahead.

'At the moment,' he said, his voice echoing slightly against the stone walls 'we are standing on a ledge at the start of a long tunnel and we are going to walk down it towards the opening you see in the distance.' They looked to where he pointed and saw the faint red glow far ahead and beneath them. 'Take care, for the ledge is not wide and falls away into nothingness on the other side. For any who slip, it will be the end. When we reach the farthest point of the tunnel then we shall be at the entrance to the network of caves beneath Spath in one of which, long ago, I hid the Droon. May Ashgaroth aid my memory of those dark times for the caves are many and the routes to them devious and complicated. But...' and here he paused to make sure they were all concentrating on his words, 'we are nearly there. We are on the threshold of the ending of our mission.'

And Ammdar saw that they had listened and had heard for there was a lightness in their bearing. 'Bracca,' he said, 'you and Tara lead the way – and keep close to the wall.'

So they set off down the tunnel. Nobody spoke for they

were each lost in their own thoughts and there was silence
except for the footfalls and a peculiar kind of rushing noise
in the background which seemed to grow louder as they
descended. Also, the air grew less chill the further down they
went and gave way now to a rather pleasant dry warmth.

After they had walked for a while Ammdar, who was last in
their little procession, called to Bracca to stop.

'We'll rest here,' he said. 'I think Reev has something for
us.'

Gratefully they sat down and rested their backs against the
stone wall. Only now did they realize how tired they were
and how much their limbs ached. As he wallowed in the
luxury of being able to relax Bracca reflected for a moment
on his feelings about Ammdar. He felt he should be resentful
of the role of leader which the elflord had taken upon
himself; something in his vanity and pride told him he ought
to be offended. And yet he was genuinely not in the least
upset; rather he was relieved that the burden had been taken
from his shoulders. If Ammdar had been less gracious or
warm towards him then maybe he would have felt hurt but
Ammdar was almost deferential and there was no trace of the
arrogance and pride that had once led him into the hands of
Dréagg. So Bracca was content to let the elflord guide them
and in truth with the passing over of ultimate responsibility
he felt as if a great burden had been taken from him.

Reev now opened the large satchel that was slung around
his shoulders and took out some round flat cakes wrapped in
leaves and a rounded silvery container which he passed to
Raagon.

'Here,' he said. 'Drink this. And enjoy it. I've carried it far
enough!' Then he laid two of the cakes on the ground at
Raagon's side and walking round to the others gave them
each the same. At the thought of food and drink Bracca's
mouth began to water and his stomach rumbled in eager
anticipation of the delights to come. Delicately he
unwrapped the leaf from around one of his cakes and took a
bite. It was delicious. It had a warm, slightly tangy flavour that

burst upon his taste buds and sent little ripples of pleasure through the whole of his body while the slightly rough crunchy texture and spicy smell compouded the overwhelming sense of satisfaction that it gave him. Now Tara passed him the container to drink from and raising it to his lips he saw that etched into its smooth surface were a number of pictures drawn with fine delicate lines: pictures of a badger and an owl, a hare, a dog and a boy and girl; and he thrilled to the realization that the carvings were of Nab and the other travellers from Silver Wood. Then he placed the mouth of the container against his lips and tilting his head back let the cool liquid flow down his throat, refreshing and revitalizing him. It had a beautifully fragrant flavour that reminded Bracca of elderflowers and dandelions and honey and conjured up wonderful visions of the times he had known walking in the forests of Haark with Melvaig and Morven and Shayll.

And so they ate and drank slowly and carefully, savouring the exquisiteness of the elf cakes and the wine, and feeling energy and strength come back into their weary bodies. When they had finished Reev told them of that time, long ago and lost in the mists of legend, when Nab, Brock and Warrigal the owl had journeyed from Silver Wood to the enchanted forest of Ellmondrill, the home of the wood elves, to meet and talk to Lord Wychnor. They listened enchanted as he recounted the trip over the dark pond to get to the elvenoak where he dwelt and they laughed inwardly at Brock's apprehension as he realized he would have to travel across on a leaf. Reev's words conjured up wonderful visions of those magic times which shimmered before their eyes in the gloom of the tunnel and brought lightness and joy to their spirits as they drifted off into the sleep which their bodies yearned for.

'Let them rest,' said Ammdar to Reev finally when only the two of them were left awake. 'They have surely earned it, and it will be a long time before they get another chance. But would you carry on your tale for me? There is so much I would like to know, so much I have missed.'

So while Raagon, Bracca and Tara lay sleeping, Reev told Ammdar of Silver Wood and of the quest for the Faradawn; of the First Holocaust and the survival of the Eldron, and then the Second Holocaust and the line of Melvaig and Morven. And as he listened his spirit wept for all the sadness in the world; all the pain and suffering, pestilence and ruin unleashed by the creation of man and once again he felt the terrible scourge of his shame.

At last he got to the moment when the sound of Morar's pipe was heard in Ellmondrill summoning them, with all the other elves, to leave their homes and answer its call. He stopped then and they both fell silent wandering through the hills and valleys of their own different thoughts; Reev sadly nostalgic for the deep green wonders of his home in the enchanted forest while Ammdar let his mind drift for a while among all that Reev had told him before turning his attention to the perilous times that lay ahead.

Tara woke first, her sleepy gaze travelling slowly and with growing awareness around the stone walls of the tunnel. Bracca lay at her side, curled up with his head resting on his arms, his face calm and beautiful in the flickering shadows that danced around them. She looked at him for a time, wondering at the mystery of their relationship and at the strange inexplicable depth of her love for him. He awoke then, as if aware of the intensity of her study, and holding her hands out she helped him to sit up.

'I feel better,' he said. 'Food, drink and sleep; now I'm ready for anything,' and he smiled at the levity of his words for in truth there was a lightness and a confidence about him that he had not felt for a long time. They had been through so much together, fought, struggled and survived; surely Ashgaroth would guide them through to the end of their mission. And it could not be much longer now. What had Ammdar said? At the end of the tunnel they would be at the threshold of the caves where the Droon lay hidden.

'Look at Raagon,' said Tara. The Old One lay flat on his

back with his mouth open and his arms folded across his chest, snoring with great long rasps of noise; breathing in with a high pitched whine through his nose and out through his mouth with a juddering and explosive snort. And in between snores they could see his lips fluttering delicately, muttering silent and secret words that only his dream self knew, while his fingers clasped and unclasped each other in little flurries of activity.

It was Tara who started giggling first, her humour caught by the comic sight of Raagon, and then, as the waves of laughter built up inside her, she let them go in a joyous release of tension, great peals of mirth escaping from her lips to echo round the walls.

Soon the others were infected by her laughter and they too joined in so that the whole tunnel rang to the sound of their hilarity; and the more Raagon snored on, utterly oblivious to the amusement he was causing, the funnier did the whole episode seem until finally the noise must have got through to him for he began tossing and turning from side to side.

'Hush,' said Ammdar, raising one hand in the air while wiping the tears from his eyes with the other. 'Let him wake up now in his own time.'

Gradually then he came to, his eyelids flickering open in fits and starts, until at last he sat up with a sudden jerk and looked at them bemusedly, wondering at their red faces and tear-stained cheeks.

'What. . .' he started to say, and his voice was thick and heavy with sleep, but Ammdar interrupted him, coming across and putting a hand on his shoulder.

'It's all right, old friend. You were snoring. We couldn't help . . . laughing. I'm sorry. We didn't mean to wake you. Did you sleep well? Are you rested?'

'Laughing! Oh. At my snoring?' and then a smile spread slowly over his face as he saw the twinkle of merriment in their eyes. 'Well, I think I deserve another drink. Come on, Reev. Pass it over.'

So Reev handed the container over to Raagon who took a long deep draught of the golden liquid before passing it round to the others and at last, when they had drunk their fill, Ammdar uttered the words that, in one form or another, they had all been dreading.

'It is time we went,' he said. 'I'll take over the lead now. If I remember correctly the path gets narrower from here on so we must stay close together and you must keep in line with me.'

So they set off once again carried forward by a new feeling of buoyancy: being well-rested and fed gave them a confidence that was only intermittently shaken by the strange rushing noise that grew ominously louder as they neared the red glow at the end of the tunnel and by a sharp acrid sulphurous smell that occasionally wafted up and caught them at the back of the throat. Soon it became uncomfortably hot; great waves of heat rolling up towards them and hitting them with a force that took their breath away. They had to go very carefully now for, as Ammdar had predicted, the ledge had become so small in parts that there was barely room for one person to walk. As they shuffled precariously along with their backs to the wall, feeling with their fingertips for whatever handholds in the stone they could find, they could see over the edge into the sheer drop that fell away beneath them. They saw now where the rushing noise was coming from, far at the bottom of the deep chasm there was a huge river. But it was not water that hurtled along the gorge for it was red and black and seemed to boil with a terrible anger as it surged furiously round the twists and turns of its narrow bed.

'It is molten rock,' Ammdar told them when the ledge got wider again and they were able to walk more easily. 'Legend says that deep in the very heart of the earth there lives an army of Dréagg's creatures whose task is to stoke up great fires that will render the core of Ashgaroth's jewel into liquid. And then, at times and places that none can foretell, they eject this terrible liquid on to the surface of the earth in

391

rivers of fire to cut swathes of death and destruction through everything that lies in their path. And this as a reminder of the terrifying powers of the Lord of Darkness. Terrible are these times, for the earth groans and shudders and great cracks appear in its crust and the sea rolls up into enormous waves the size of mountains that crash down upon the land and sweep all before them.'

They wondered at Ammdar's words as they carried on along the ridge, feeling the heat from the river of molten rock on their faces. They made slow progress now for the path had narrowed again and soon they lost all track of time, existing in a private battlefield where fear and courage were locked together in a desperate struggle with each other as the prospect of falling into the abyss beneath their feet loomed as a terrible and ever-present danger.

And then suddenly, before they realized it, the end of the tunnel was just ahead and the path had widened out so that they were able to walk the last few paces up to it with ease.

Now that they were close they could see that it was not so much a doorway as another, much smaller, tunnel at the end of which the red glow was almost dazzlingly bright. There was only room for one of them to go through at a time and even then they would have to stoop.

'We are finally here,' said Ammdar, turning to address them all, 'at the entrance to the Halls of Fire. Bracca, you have earned the right. Will you go before us?'

So Bracca led the way through the roughly hewn entrance into the small tunnel, bending low and feeling the stone walls close in around him. The heat was now intense and the noise of the fire echoed and bounced round the sides so that he felt as if he was being physically assaulted. He became disorientated and seized by a desperate longing to straighten his back, stand up and look around but he had to go on, heading into the noise and the brightness that lay ahead.

Soon he came to the middle of the tunnel. He put his hands on his knees and rested for a moment, trying to gather his wits together before continuing and then, hardly daring to think about what lay ahead, he carried on. The distance between himself and the end of the tunnel grew shorter and shorter until finally, suddenly, he emerged from it into a blinding glare that forced him to turn his head away and cover his eyes with his hands. Cautiously he opened his fingers and looked out carefully at what lay around them. Through a shimmering haze of red he saw a vast underground cavern that stretched away ahead of him, its limits obscured by drifting clouds of fumes. The floor of the cavern was covered by a sea of molten rock that was fed by other rivers like the one they had followed pouring into it from all directions so that it raced and swirled in constantly moving eddies. It rose and fell like the breathing of a huge beast, its surface pock-marked by myriads of bubbles that boiled up from its depths and every so often erupted explosively into a huge geyser of flame, slashing up towards the cavern roof and sending showers of liquid fire cascading all around it.

His face was already beginning to burn and when he breathed, the fumes caught in the back of his throat and set his lungs gasping, seared by their pungent sharpness. And all the time the noise; rushing and roaring through the air as the rivers crashed against one another so that his mind seemed unable to focus on anything. He turned and saw that Ammdar was just behind him. His lips were moving, he was obviously shouting something, but Bracca could hear nothing above the sound. And then he looked in the direction that Ammdar was pointing and saw a long narrow spine of rock winding its way across from the small shelf on which he was standing and out over the cavern floor till it disappeared into an archway in the opposite wall.

'We have to go across.' The words came to Bracca faintly as Ammdar put his mouth close to his ear. 'It's the only way.'

He could see Tara's face behind the elflord, thrown half into shadow by the soaring columns of flame. She was looking at him intently, urging him to go on, trusting him to lead her across. And so, with her faith in him as a spur, he cautiously began to edge his way out on to the ridge, willing himself to be brave despite the fear that clawed away at his stomach and sent his head dizzy. There was just enough room for his feet to move next to each other and he was forced to look down to keep them away from the edge. The rock fell steeply away on either side, plunging down to the morass of seething lava beneath, which with its constantly rolling movement seemed to mesmerize him, beckoning him down towards the security of its perpetual rhythm. And the path was so awkward! Sharp and craggy so that his feet seemed to be constantly on the verge of slipping. Every geyser that erupted set his heart beating wildly until he saw where it came from and realized he was safe for the moment. Sometimes though he hung back when one had blown up close to the path and then he waited till its fury was fully spent before carrying on.

And so, very slowly, picking their footholds with infinite care, they made their way across, but the further they got into the cavern the hotter it became. The atmosphere now was almost unbearably oppressive; the combination of scorching heat and suffocating fumes was beginning to take its toll of them, undoing all the good that their rest back in the tunnel had done. Bracca's limbs became leaden and heavy and every movement required the most enormous effort. He was drenched in sweat and he felt as if all the moisture in his body was being drawn to the surface; it ran in torrents down his back and under his arms; it soaked his scalp and trickled down over his forehead till it got in his eyes and made them sting. His breathing grew laboured and painful; when he took a deep breath it was as if something was scraping at his throat and so he began to dread even the act of inhaling.

And yet somehow they continued on until at last, to Bracca's relief, they had passed what he judged to be the half-way point and the archway on the far side did not seem so far away. It was then that he became aware of the presence of something above him. At first it was no more than the flickering pattern of a shadow that interrupted the steady glare of the flames and he ascribed it to his imagination but, suddenly, above the noise of the fire, he heard a strange sinister flapping sound which increased in volume until it seemed to be all around him. He turned then and saw them and his blood chilled to the bone.

'The Kwkor,' yelled Ammdar, over the appalling resonance of their huge black wings and, terrified, he watched as they swept down towards them from their lair under the roof of the cavern. Halfway along their wings were two great talons which were extended and poised ready to attack while from inside beak-like mouths the flames reflected crimson splinters of light off rows of savagely pointed teeth. And then to his astonishment he saw puffs of flame coming out of their wide puckered nostrils; tongues of fire that flickered and curled menacingly for a few moments before being sucked back in again. Red eyes glared out fiercely from deep black sockets that were surrounded by concentric folds of skin and as they flew through the flames Bracca had the uncanny impression that they were feeding off the fire and transmitting it through their bodies for their black skin seemed strangely incandescent.

Then, almost before Bracca realized what was happening, the Kwkor were among them and his senses were assailed by the sulphurous stench of their breath and the horrible rasping sound of their cries. It was over in an instant leaving him dazed and numb with shock and he watched them flying back up to their holes with a feeling of relief. Then, to his surprise, he realized that he was lying down on the path and looking behind him at the others he saw that they too must have fallen or been knocked down. Ammdar was helping Tara up while behind her Raagon was slowly getting back on to his feet. But where was Reev? Frantically he looked for him but there was no sign. His stomach seemed to turn to liquid and with his heart pounding he scrambled onto his feet and quickly crossed the few steps to Ammdar.

'Where is he? Reev! Where is he?' he blurted out, knowing and dreading the answer before he heard it.

'They've taken him,' said Ammdar, in a voice that was

heavy with grief. 'We were unprepared. My fault. I should have remembered – should have known.'

Then Bracca looked up and saw the Kwkor folding their wings and landing on what he now perceived to be a network of ledges and caves up near the roof of the cavern. Suddenly there was a flash of silver from one of their talons. It shone through the swirling smoke and flame for only the briefest of moments yet it was so intensely fierce and pure that there could be no mistaking it. 'Do not be sad,' it said, 'for I have gone to Ashgaroth. Only be true and have faith and you will conquer the darkness.' Then it was gone and Reev was no more but there was no time for grief as the Kwkor spread their wings and took off once again; only this time Bracca and the others heard the terrible wailing screech that rang out even over the noise of their wings and the roaring of the fires beneath them and they trembled in fear. Down they swooped, filling the air with their stench, and their eyes burned a path through the pall of flame to pierce their victims as a moth is caught in light so that they lost all self-will and became paralysed with fear.

Then Tara, desperately trying to free herself from their hold over her and struggling against her physical immobility, lost her footing and slipped just as the Kwkor crashed down upon them. Her frantic scream echoed through the cavern as Bracca, numb with horror, saw her fall over the edge. His guts collapsed and his heart swayed and lurched inside his body as he lunged wildly towards her. He could just see her hand on the very edge of the path; the fingers, hooked into a tiny outcrop of jagged rock, were already starting to slide off as he threw himself forward with his arm outstretched and just managed to grab her wrist.

'Hold on,' he yelled, as he saw her fingers slip, the sinews taut and straining as they tried to hang on to their precarious grip, until finally her hand burst open and she was left swinging in open space with only his hold stopping her from falling into the inferno beneath them. Already his shoulder was hurting from the sudden jolt as she had fallen and from the weight of her body as it swung like a pendulum from the end of his arm. And then he was enveloped in a searing blast of heat from one of the Kwkor as it swooped over him snorting smoke and flame out of its nostrils and sending tongues of fire licking down his arm. He cried out in pain and felt the strength and will ebbing out of him. Now his fingers and wrist developed sharp agonizing cramps that were almost too excruciating to bear but he held on for he knew that he could not let go and through the clouds of torment that swirled through his consciousness the image of Tara's face was fixed before his eyes so that his love for her gave him a power and a strength that he would not otherwise have possessed. But surely it could not be long now. Looking up quickly he could see the Kwkor circling round in the middle of the cave as if waiting for a signal. And then he saw the figure of Degg standing on a ledge just under the roof holding a long black rod straight up into the air; he had a vision of the rod flashing down and an eerie whistling sound filled the cavern. This was the sign the Kwkor had been waiting for. Instantly they flocked together and flew straight down at them in a terrifying blur of speed. But as he waited for the end that he knew was inevitable he felt Ammdar at his side, pulling Tabor out of its scabbard, and he heard Raagon shout to him above the noise.

'Keep hold. I'll keep a grip on your legs as you wriggle backwards.' His ankles were immediately clasped in the Old One's hands and he felt Raagon trying to pull him back over the rough stone path. And then he became aware of a bright light to one side of him and glancing quickly up he was dazzled by what he saw. It was Ammdar, of that there could be no doubt, but he had become so massive that he towered high above the path and he was immersed in a brilliant silver glow that shone out into the flaming darkness of the cavern. In his right hand was Tabor and he wielded the sword in such a blur of speed that Bracca could feel the wind against his face; huge arcs of light that slashed through the air and left trails of glittering stars in its wake. And Ammdar, the

397

Silver Warrior, sang in a voice that soared up to the roof in great majestic curves of melody and seemed to push back the frontiers of darkness; shimmering cadences of rhythm that rose and fell in time with the pattern of his sword play so that there was a deadly synchronization between them that gave his movements a terrible power and beauty as he kept the Kwkor at bay.

And all the time with his stomach scraping painfully across the jagged stone of the path he crawled backwards pulling Tara further and further away from the edge. His worst fear was that she would slip from his grasp for his hand was dripping with sweat but at least now there was hope and Tara's spirits had begun to revive. She pulled herself up so that her fingers were able to grab hold of Bracca's wrist and she gave him all the help she could by finding little footholds in the rock face so as to relieve the weight on his arm.

Suddenly the air was filled with a terrible scream and looking up Bracca saw one of the Kwkor plummeting down past his eyes towards the inferno beneath. One of its wings was flapping uselessly where Ammdar had severed it and as it spiralled helplessly into the blaze Bracca caught a fleeting glimpse of its wild crimson eyes. It glared at him as it fell, fixing him with a look of such dark and malicious hatred that his heart seemed to stop beating for a moment, and then it was gone and he could see the flames licking hungrily over its skeletal black body until it was devoured by them leaving no trace, except that where it had fallen the flames seemed to dance a little higher and to burn with a little more intensity than before.

And then another fell and another and another as Ammdar wreaked his revenge against the forces of darkness until the stink of their roasting bodies rose up like a cloud and Bracca found himself coughing as he fought to get his breath. But he kept dragging himself and Tara relentlessly back until now with a surge of relief he could see her face. They would do it! Not much further to go. She smiled at him with eyes that glistened with tears and, overcome with joy and relief, he smiled back at her.

Suddenly she was up and standing precariously on the edge of that terrible drop. He scrambled to his feet and pulled her, almost savagely, into his arms; wrapping himself around her as if to shield her from any further harm. And the tears ran down his cheeks with happiness as he felt the softness of her hair against his face and the truth of her body pressing against him, shuddering convulsively as she cried away the terrible nightmare of what she had been through. And they would have stayed like that forever, enshrined in the sacred world of each other, had not Ammdar's voice shattered their isolation.

'Go,' he shouted. 'Go while there is time. I cannot hold them forever.'

So they broke apart and, with Raagon following after them, they ran as fast as they could along the causeway. Pausing once to look back Bracca saw Ammdar still beset by the Kwkor, cutting and slicing with dazzling and brilliant skill to keep them away. When finally they got to the end of the path they found themselves in the small arched entrance to a tunnel and there they stopped to wait for the elflord. There were only two Kwkor left now and soon they met the same fate as the others, crashing down into the fire to join the ashes of their comrades. But, no sooner had Tabor despatched them than a terrible shriek echoed out around the cavern and looking up to where it came from they saw Degg high up on his ledge, stamping and waving his arms in a mad fit of rage. Again and again he screamed but they could not understand the words and these repulsive torrents of sound fell upon them like a hail of blows, assaulting their spirits so that they reeled before the onslaught. Horrified they watched as he grew before their eyes and then, when it seemed the ledge could no longer hold him, he spread his arms wide and launched himself forward with a huge leap through the air towards Ammdar who turned to face his new opponent with Tabor held high above his head.

With a mighty crash the two adversaries met, Degg smashing into Ammdar with such force that the elflord staggered backwards and toppled off the path into the flames beneath pulling Degg with him. As they fell, locked in terrible combat, Bracca saw Ammdar trying to wield Tabor but the angle was wrong and he was only able to use the hilt, driving it in hard against Degg's back. At the same time the goblin's fingers were clamped round Ammdar's neck and his legs were locked about his body.

Twice they twisted round in mid-air before they were lost to sight in the blaze but as they hit the fire a great column of flames erupted towards the cavern roof. And now the inferno heaved and boiled in time to the rhythms of their struggle as Tara, Bracca and Raagon looked on with dreadful apprehension. Time seemed to stand still as they watched breathlessly and the tension was almost more than they could bear, yet they were unable to take their eyes away as the struggle went on and on. And they had no way of knowing who was winning, for the crimson waves of fire were impenetrable. Again and again they would see a sudden surge of flame above the rest and they would hold their breath for terrible moments before it subsided.

'How can they survive in all that?' Bracca spoke the words quietly, almost to himself, but Raagon heard him and answered.

'Because they are protected,' he said. 'Dréagg and Ashgaroth are guarding their own.'

They could not say how long the fight went on. It seemed an eternity. The thunder and crack of battle resounded round the walls till they were deafened and the constant movement of the fires exerted a mesmeric grip upon them. They forgot where they were, forgot the black mouth of the tunnel that loomed behind them and even forgot the purpose of their mission. Their entire concentration was focused on the epic conflict that was being enacted before their eyes.

And then, at long last, when time had ceased to have a meaning for them, a glittering silver vision rose up out of the inferno and in its right hand was Tabor while its other was clenched into the fist of victory. Festooned with little tongues of fire, the figure emerged from the blazing sea around it with a glorious shout of triumph and as the flames fell away they saw that it was Ammdar and rejoiced. With the knowledge of Ammdar's victory came the realization that Degg was no more and they were seized with wild elation. For Bracca the defeat of Degg was doubly sweet for it meant also the end of Xtlan, the disciple of darkness at whose foul hands Melvaig and Morven had endured such terrible suffering. And far away, in the empire to which he had given his name, in a small room at the top of the tallest turret in the Blaggvald, Xtlan was dying, slain by the sacred sword of Tabor against whose shimmering power the guardians of evil were impotent. His followers, looking on, rejoiced in their hearts for this at last was the end of their leader whose omnipotence had been unquestioned for as long as they could remember. Now they could take their rightful place in the succession to the mantle of darkness. How long they had waited for this moment; a time they thought would never come. Each looked at his neighbour and wondered at his intentions; already they were plotting each other's ruin for the germs of greed were so strong that there could be no sharing of power.

Bracca watched joyfully as Ammdar seemed to float up through the air towards the path and when he landed he seemed no different than before. He walked forward slowly, as if unable to trust his legs, and once or twice as the others watched he seemed to stumble. Raagon went forward then and putting his arms round his friend, helped him along till they were all together once again. Then, smiling, Ammdar held Tabor out to Bracca and gestured to him to take it. 'Here,' he said. 'Take it back. It is still your sword,' and after Bracca had sheathed it Ammdar embraced both him and Tara in turn. No one spoke, for their sorrow at Reev's death and the weight of the emotions they were feeling were too great to find expression in words. For Ammdar the exquisite

401

beauty of this moment was something that he had dreamt about for the aeons of time since the fall. He had destroyed the one who had destroyed him, Degg; chosen by Dréagg as his successor to rule the forests of Spath. Now, with the destruction of Degg, his redemption was almost complete; until the final act was committed his salvation could not be achieved for only when man was no more would he know true peace.

CHAPTER XXV

They rested for a while in the small cave-like chamber at the end of the path. They were all immensely weary in their bodies and their hearts and they needed time to recover. They would dearly have loved some of the food and drink that Reev had been carrying and their hunger and thirst were a constant reminder of the pain of his loss.

Bracca sat with his back to the stone wall and looked out on to the flames as they flickered and danced in the cavern, throwing eerie patterns onto the walls and roof. Tara lay at his side with her head on his lap and he played gently with her hair as he tried to gather himself together. It could not be much longer now before they found the Droon. And then what? With the separation of the Seeds, man would cease to exist. Would he also be destroyed along with the rest of his race? That was what he had always expected and until now he had accepted the inevitability of his fate without question. But now that the moment was coming nearer he found it difficult to believe that his death could be so certain. And what of Tara; would he never see her again? Could she and Raagon and Ammdar stand by and let him die? Surely Ashgaroth would save him; it must be within his power. But if he was created from the Seeds of Logic and they were parted from each other how could he exist? No! He must prepare himself to face the end, although the thought of leaving Tara cut into him like a knife. And what kind of death would it be; slow and painful or over before he knew it? How would the destruction of man happen? What did the Seeds look like? How would they be separated?

Suddenly the flood gates opened and a host of questions began to race through his mind till his head spun. But there were no answers. He was tormenting himself and it was futile; there was no choice in what had to be done, so he tried to calm his restless mind for he was tired and he needed sleep. He listened to Tara's steady breathing and soothed by its rhythm he soon dozed off.

When he awoke some time later it was to a curiously restless and empty feeling which at first he found hard to trace. And then the pain and the doubts he had suffered before he had gone to sleep returned in a rush and he was overcome with a feeling of hopelessness and lack of purpose. He felt that the future held nothing for him and this left him empty and disconsolate.

Ammdar had woken up a little earlier and lay watching Bracca. He saw the look on his face; the sharpness of anger and the vacuousness of despair and knew what was happening in his mind. It was what he had feared most. Now, on the last stage of their journey, Dréagg was starting to use his most potent weapon. He had expected and dreaded it but still now that it had begun he felt more afraid for the success of their mission than at any other time for this would be the most difficult adversary they had yet faced. What Dréagg was doing, in the subtlest and most insidious of ways, was to plant in Bracca's mind the seeds of paranoia and mistrust which would eventually grow into such a feeling of abandonment and disillusion that he would refuse to unlock the Droon.

Ammdar got up then and walking across to Bracca put his arm round the young man's shoulders.

'How long have you been awake?' he said gently.

Bracca looked startled and a little taken aback at the

404

elflord's presence, almost shrinking away from his touch.

'Not long,' he replied, and there was a tremor of nervousness in his voice.

'Did you sleep well?'

'Yes, yes. I was exhausted. We were all exhausted.' And then some of the tension seemed to leave him and he became more relaxed.

'But you,' he went on, turning to look Ammdar in the eyes. 'Are you. . .?' and he could not find the words as the image of Ammdar emerging from the flames after his victory came before his eyes.

'I am recovering,' he said smiling. 'It was not easy. Years ago it would not have been so difficult but now. . . Still, I survived.'

'And is Degg. . .? Xtlan. . .? Are they really. . .?' but then Ammdar interrupted him.

'They will trouble us no more. They have returned to Dréagg. We are rid of them.'

And somehow only now, hearing Ammdar say it, was Bracca fully able to believe that it was true and to accept the evidence of his eyes. And then the elflord continued in a voice that willed Bracca to listen.

'But we must not relax our vigilance for it is now that Dréagg will be at his most dangerous. He will come to us in the quietest and stealthiest of ways when we least expect him. He will talk to us in such a manner that it will be impossible for us not to listen. He will lure and tempt us with promises that will set our hearts aflame and he will try to turn us against each other. I do not talk idly of such things, Bracca. He spoke to me once before and I listened.'

He paused then for a moment so that his words should be fully understood. He could tell by the confusion and pain in Bracca's eyes that the young man was wrestling within himself against the thoughts of only a few moments before and was trying to put them into the context of what Ammdar had just told him. Was the elflord telling him the truth? Did his feeling of betrayal really come from Dréagg? He could

405

hardly believe it; there was a cold logic in those thoughts that could not easily be explained away. And Ammdar had not answered the question that had now become uppermost in his mind. He would ask it; now. But he could not find the right words; they seemed to block in his throat as he tried to speak. Then Ammdar looked into his eyes and Bracca was drawn into such a world of infinite kindness and wisdom that all his uneasiness and anxiety seemed to float away. He felt as if he was suspended on a sea of cloud, weightless and ageless, while all around him billowing out in every direction a carpet of white rolled away in gently undulating rhythms of movement. Such a great sense of peace had now come over him that the question he had been going to ask seemed to lose all meaning for this was a world of total trust and faith and love where the dark splinters of betrayal, disloyalty, selfishness and greed did not exist.

Bracca's immersion in this euphoric world seemed to last a lifetime yet it could not have been more than moments for when finally the touch of a hand on his arm brought him back the others were still asleep and Ammdar was still at his side. They were silent then for some time; so much had passed between them that there was no need to speak. For the time being, Ammdar knew, he had beaten back the powers of darkness yet this was only the first skirmish: Dréagg would try again and again and again, and each time Bracca's ability to overcome him would grow weaker. They would have to move fast now for the more time that elapsed the greater would be Dréagg's chances of success; Bracca could not survive many such encounters within himself. Then at last Ammdar spoke.

'Come,' he said. 'Let's wake the others,' and standing up he walked across to Raagon.

The Old One was deeply asleep and did not take kindly to the gentle shaking of his elbow. He mumbled and grumbled and flicked his wrist as if to get rid of a fly that was annoying him. When that did not work and this disturbance to his state of blissful oblivion persisted he flung himself wildly over on

406

to his other side catching Ammdar's face with his arm as he did so. Bracca caught the elflord's eye and they both laughed.

'It will not be easy. He loves his sleep,' said Ammdar, and this time, bending low over Raagon's head, he blew in his friend's ear. The Old One immediately opened both eyes wide and then shut them again until Ammdar repeated the process. This time the eyes stayed open a little longer and Bracca could see him trying to take in his surroundings. For a moment or two he stayed stock still and then he seemed to relax for he stretched and yawned and putting both hands out to Ammdar said, in a voice that was still choked with sleep, 'Here, if you want me up you'll have to help me up.'

Tara had slept through all this. Her tangle of long golden hair was spread out over Bracca's lap like autumn mist and her beautiful face was still and calm, the lips slightly parted as she breathed. It had been a long time, thought Bracca, since he had had a chance to really look at her. How lovely she was and how much he longed for some peace in their lives so that they could enjoy each other. He tried to imagine what it would have been like in Haark with her; walking through the forest, going to the beach, taking her to all his favourite places, talking and laughing and sharing their lives. What a shame that Melvaig and Morven would never meet her and that she would never know them. And he wondered how she would have got on with Shayll, both strikingly lovely, both wilful and both obstinate. Would they have been jealous of each other or of Bracca's affection? How he wished that they had met for he felt in his heart that there would have been a lot of love between them.

Gently he put his hand down and stroked her cheek, marvelling at the smoothness of the skin, and then ran a finger delicately along her fine high cheekbones and round under her chin. In the strange red half-light from the fires her face was partly in shadow so that she appeared ethereal and almost unreal and he was more aware of her elven nature than at any time since he had first seen her. She stirred then just a little, settling herself more comfortably into his lap, so that he was terribly reluctant to wake her. His eyes were drawn then to the sensuous fullness of her lips and giving way to an impulse that welled up from deep inside himself he drew the tip of his finger around them, moistening them with the saliva which he got from her tongue. And in her sleep she responded by pursing her mouth and kissing this gentle invader, arousing such flames of sensuality in Bracca that he felt his head start to spin with excitement. Then she opened her eyes and holding him in her gaze drew her lips away and smiled with a radiance that filled his heart. As he moved his hand away she took it in hers and holding it to her mouth pressed her lips and teeth so hard against the fleshy base of his thumb that it almost hurt.

'Soon it will be our time,' she said, and before he could ask what she meant she had put a hand on his shoulder and was pushing herself up off the floor.

And now the four of them stood in the cavern waiting to embark on the search for the Droon. They were reluctant to leave, partly because at the back of their minds they could not get used to the absence of Reev and were waiting for him to join them, and partly because of the short moments of peace they had known here. The red glow from the fires had somehow given the cavern a sense of home for all of them and they felt a warmth of spirit for the place that they had felt for nowhere in a long time. The uncertainties of the future lay before them in a terrible black void and they instinctively knew that once they left the cavern, the security they had felt with each other would be lost forever. Dréagg lay waiting for them in the darkness of the labyrinthine tunnels that stretched away into the bowels of the earth, determined to use all the terrible powers left to him to defend the creation of which he had been most proud and through whom he had reigned on earth for so long: man.

Then Ammdar spoke to them and they all turned towards him to hear his words.

'The time ahead will not be easy,' he said, and his voice

was grave. 'Our love and trust will be tried to the utmost. It is upon us that the ultimate and final responsibility to save the earth has been placed. We must not fail or it will languish forever in the darkness; this you know. I say only this to you. Keep to your faith; hold in your hearts the images of those in whose footsteps we follow; Nab and Beth and Brock, Melvaig, Morven and Shuinn for it is their work which we have been called upon to finish and it is their vision for which we are fighting. And do not forget that Ashgaroth is with us; trust to your instincts for they are his way of speaking to you.' He stopped speaking then and looking around at them saw their fearful apprehension at the task ahead. Yet he saw also the reserves of courage and strength that still burned through in their eyes and their eagerness to set out on this last stage of their epic mission. And then he smiled at them for their hearts should not be heavy on such a momentous occasion.

'Come then, let us go,' he said, and started walking towards a small tunnel entrance at the back of the cavern. Once inside, the floor of the tunnel seemed to slope sharply down and to become so narrow that they were only able to walk in single file. The roof also dipped and they had to bend low to avoid banging their heads. Tara had followed Ammdar, then came Bracca, with Raagon last, and for the first few steps they could see each other quite clearly by the glow from the fires but soon they were enveloped in total darkness and started walking into one another. And now the size of the tunnel became a huge problem for not only were they forced to walk in a back-breaking stoop the whole time but they also had to feel the walls ahead with their hands in an attempt to avoid scraping themselves on the rock as they moved along. They started to feel an acute sense of claustrophobia, as if the rock was closing in on them, and their distress was intensified by the frequency with which they knocked themselves on the jagged stone. Soon their heads, arms and shoulders were ablaze with lacerations, grazes and bruises and they began to dread every step they took for fear of a

409

further injury. The dense, impenetrable blackness incarcerated them like a prison and even the stillness, deafening in its unbroken silence, seemed to lie upon and smother them like a shroud. They lost all sense of space and time and their heads began to spin in the awful vacuousness that swirled around them. Utterly directionless, their minds began to play terrible tricks. They imagined they were walking upside down and backwards. Colours started to appear in the dark – whirls and flashes of green and red and blue and silver that danced and sparkled before their eyes. The walls and roof seemed to be moving; great lumps of rock suddenly billowing out in front of them so that they either ducked or swerved to avoid them and bumped into the person in front or behind.

At first the constant collisions between them had been regarded as a joke and this had helped to keep their spirits up but now they felt great surges of irrational irritation each time it happened and this had begun to turn to anger.

It was Bracca who succumbed first when Tara's head banged, once again, into his back.

'Stop it,' he snapped. 'You did that on purpose.'

Normally Tara would have been able to control her response, but her own back was throbbing painfully from bending; hunger and thirst were gnawing away at her insides and her head ached where she had knocked it against the stone.

'Don't be stupid,' she retorted angrily. 'It's the same for all of us. You should be more careful.'

Bracca stopped walking and, forgetting the narrowness of the tunnel, tried to turn round so that he could face her and in doing so scraped his knee.

'That was your fault,' he shouted. 'Don't ever call me stupid.'

'All humans are stupid.' The words came from her mouth before she realized it. Afterwards she would never remember consciously forming them in her mind but now it was too late; they hung almost visibly in the air, stark and terrible.

'Melvaig wasn't stupid. Nor was Morven.' He spoke quietly now, brimming with rage yet confident in the knowledge that she had made an awful mistake and determined to press home and enjoy his victory. 'And nor was Beth.'

She could say nothing. She knew that what she had said was not only wrong but foolish. She knew that she had hurt him deeply. Yet somehow she could not bring herself to apologize; she tried but the words would not come.

They had all stopped now and the tension in the dark airless tunnel was almost unbearable. And somehow the fact that they could not turn round to face each other added immeasurably to the horror of the situation. And then Bracca spoke the words that Ammdar had been dreading.

'And without this human, the Seeds will never be separated and the reign of Dréagg will last forever.'

'Tara,' said Ammdar, his voice tremulous with anxiety. 'You know it was wrong to say that and you know it is untrue. You owe Bracca an apology. Please, say you are sorry: for the sake of all of us but more especially for Nab and for Beth.' And the elflord cursed the powers of Dréagg which had begun their evil work already. How quickly his words of warning had been forgotten. Why could they not see it?

'No.' It was Bracca who spoke. 'She need not apologize. It is too late for that now. The damage has been done. Now I know the truth of how she regards me. It is not your fault, Ammdar; nor yours, Raagon. She forgets all those good and brave humans who struggled and fought against Dréagg's influence and who suffered to preserve the world of Ashgaroth. Many there were who railed against cruelty, arrogance and greed; who preached love and respect for all living things and who suffered for their beliefs. They did the best they could. Such humans were not stupid.'

And Tara wept inside herself with anguish for she knew the truth of his words and she realized the irreparable harm she had caused.

'I'm sorry,' she said, but the words sounded limp and

useless and it would almost have been better to have left them unspoken. She must say it again; convince him that she meant it. 'I'm sorry,' but though she begged him inwardly for forgiveness her voice still sounded flippant and uncaring.

Now Ammdar spoke again, desperate to try and heal this dreadful wound that had arisen.

'Bracca. Tara. Listen. This is the work of Dréagg. It is he who makes it impossible for you to forgive, Bracca, and it was his words that Tara spoke. Please. Stop.'

But Dréagg had done his work well.

'I thought you might try and find his hand in all this; to blame him for Tara's thoughts. It all fits in so perfectly. It's too easy, Ammdar, too easy. Now, are you going to move on or are we to stay here forever?'

There was an arrogance in Bracca's voice, a harsh abrasive edge that none of the others had heard in him before, and they found it deeply disturbing but there was nothing that could be done now. They had to go on.

So they walked slowly forwards and, without the easy friendship of before, their feet seemed to drag and their limbs ached with a grinding weariness. The joy in their mission had gone and they were left with a sense of desolation. In Bracca there was a blind anger that allowed no room for reason. Deep down, in the far reaches of his subconscious, he knew Ammdar was right. He knew also that Tara was sorry, but somehow he could find no room in himself for forgiveness and so he emptied his mind of everything save the need to go forward and to concentrate on avoiding the jagged edges of rock that seemed to constantly close in around him. He waited with almost a gleeful apprehension for Tara's head to bump into him again but it never did for she kept herself a long way after him, listening to the sound of his footsteps to help her to keep her distance. And then from behind came the sound of Raagon singing. It broke in on the darkness of his thoughts with a shock for it was a strange and beautiful sound and his mind tried to fight against it but the power of the melody was too strong and soon it overcame him, lifting his spirit and cleansing it of the poison with which it had become infected. It reminded him of Melvaig and the times he used to play on his pipes as they sat outside the hut in the evenings and he pictured himself there again with Melvaig and Morven and Shayll and felt the magic and peace of those times flow through him.

For Tara too, Raagon's tune conjured up halcyon memories of her life with Nab and Beth for she heard in it fragments of the songs that her father and mother had sung and played in the forest and as with Bracca the recollection of those golden times banished the darkness and gloom that had settled upon her. Once more she walked through the deep green paths of summer and listened to the hum of insects on still balmy evenings or else played and laughed with the animals during the silver days of spring. And she heard again the staccato liquid trill of a skylark and the sweeping cries of curlews in the clear blue sky.

For Ammdar the ancient elven melody that Raagon was singing stirred up memories of Operrallmar and their lives together since the fall and he wondered once again at the blessing of his friendship with the Old One. And he joined in for he knew the words and the tune so that the darkness of the tunnel was filled with light as their voices rose and fell together to the cadence of the music. How many times had he heard Raagon sing it as they sat together by the fire and how he had yearned to lend his voice to the refrain, raging with frustration that the only sound issuing forth would be the bark of a wolf. Now at last he was able to join with his friend; and how marvellous they sounded.

Soon the others too joined in and their hearts were light and the walking was easy. They forgot the pain in their backs and the knocks and scrapes from the rock and time lost its meaning for them. Tara forgot to keep her distance and they were all bunched together, bumping and jostling each other but now it did not matter for they joked and laughed about it.

Then, suddenly, Ammdar stopped for they had come to the

413

first junction. The song died in the still air and they waited silently in the darkness. Ammdar tried to remember the pattern of the tunnels as he had last seen them, aeons of time ago, when he had come down with the Droon. Then he had carried a flaming torch to light his way and the tunnels had seemed so different. If only he had carved a mark or left a sign of some kind, but not for a moment then had he thought he would ever be returning. He tried to clear his mind so that the deepest part of his subconscious could show him the way. It was the direction of his sword arm! Or was it? He could feel tentacles of confusion start to pull at his certainty and he was forced to think again. No, he had been correct first time, and without any further thought he set off to the right.

They seemed to descend for a while now and then when the tunnel levelled out, there began a series of twists and turns that left them almost giddy when finally they came to another junction. They had stopped singing some way back; the tortuousness of the last part of the journey had required all their concentration. This time Ammdar turned left, though the decision was not as easy as before as he had become disorientated and the more he tried to think the more unsure he became so that in the end he relied on his first instinctive decision.

After a little way they came to another junction and then, after only a short stretch, the tunnel appeared to diverge into three different openings; left and right as before but this time straight on as well. Ammdar had nearly missed the side tunnels and it was only when he stumbled over a rock and fell over that he realized that they existed. Now where? Straight on, to the left or to the right? Desperately he tried to recall the route he had taken before but it was hopeless; there was not even the faintest hint of an impulse to guide him. Now, Ashgaroth, he thought. Now is when I need you. Show me the way!

But nothing happened. Try as he might the choice remained impossible to make and he became no clearer.

And then suddenly his head began to ache; a terrible grinding pain that started behind his eyes and spread till it felt as if his head would split open. It throbbed mercilessly, pulsing with a cruel and pitiless rhythm that drew his whole body up into it so that the muscles of his legs, arms and back stiffened into columns of excruciating agony.

'Ammdar! What is it? What's wrong?'

Bracca's words seemed to come from a great distance away; from another world. He heard them but could neither understand nor answer; something was happening to him over which he had no control.

Bracca and the others, watching in amazement, saw the elflord's body start to shimmer with a weird pulsating yellow light; circles of colour radiating outwards like ripples of gold in a black lake, and then before their eyes his image seemed to divide into three, each of which began walking in a different direction. After a few steps they turned round and the three Ammdars began beckoning to Bracca and the others to follow them into a different tunnel.

'What shall we do?' said Bracca, his voice sharp with tension. 'They're exactly the same but only one of them can be true. Which is it? Tara, Raagon, which is it?'

'I don't know; but if we take the wrong tunnel we shall be lost for ever in this darkness.' It was Tara who replied first and Bracca could hear the panic in her voice. In himself too there was a rising tide of desperation for he could see no solution to the problem.

And now the three separate visions of the elflord became ever more frantic in their attempts to convince Bracca and the others that they were genuine, each of them waving and calling out in a bewildering barrage of entreaties. Then the image in the left-hand tunnel raised its voice so that it sounded out clearly above the rest.

'Bracca,' it shouted. 'I am the true Ammdar but there is only one way to prove it.'

'He lies. I am the true Ammdar,' was the chorus that echoed from the other two.

'Now we shall see,' replied the first. 'There may be three of us but there is only one Tabor and Tabor will only respond to whichever of us is telling the truth. Lay it on the ground, Bracca, and let whoever is genuine pick it up and destroy the others with it.'

'Don't listen to him. He only wants the sword for himself: he will use it to kill you. It is Dréagg speaking. Can you not see what he plans?'

Bracca turned to Raagon and Tara.

'What do you think? Do we do as he says?'

'We have no choice,' said Raagon. 'What else can we do?'

'But is it true?' asked Tara. 'Can Tabor only be used by Ammdar?'

'I don't know, but we have to take that risk.' Bracca waited for a moment before lifting up his head and calling out their reply. 'We accept what you say. I will walk forward a little way and lay Tabor down. Do not move until I am back with Raagon and Tara.'

'Bracca. Are you sure? It may just be a way to get hold of the sword so he can use it against us.' Tara's hands were on his arm, holding him back.

'I have to go,' but as he moved out into the shimmering amber light his heart was hammering inside his chest and a terrible uncertainty gnawed at his stomach while the other two images of Ammdar voiced his fears and threw them at him like hammer blows in voices that were grave and dignified in their concern.

It was not far that he walked but it seemed to take for ever for each step was dogged and heavy with doubt. Finally he came to a spot at the centre of the cross formed by the tunnels and he put his hand to Tabor's hilt. Was it imagination or did it seem to shy away from his grip? It was not too late to change his mind. And then a sudden surge of resolution came upon him and pulling out the sword in one swift easy movement he bent down and placed it on the rock floor. Straightening up he noticed that all three images had fallen silent and there was total quiet. Slowly he retraced his steps backwards until

416

he felt Tara reach out and take his hand. Without Tabor he felt naked and vulnerable and the silence intensified his nagging sense of unease.

Then the image on the left spoke out.

'Now, will either of you move forward and take the sword. I am here, defenceless. Let us see you prove your claim to be the true Ammdar.' Neither of them moved. 'Come on. If you speak the truth you have nothing to fear,' and still there was no response.

'Very well, then.' He walked out of the tunnel to the spot where Tabor lay and quickly bent down to pick it up but before he reached it the hilt seemed to rise up off the ground and guide itself into his hand. Then he raised it high into the air in a gesture of victory. 'Now you see the true Ammdar,' he shouted, and he moved towards the images in the tunnel ahead but he had not gone more than a few paces when the tunnel was shaken by a mighty explosion and the golden light suddenly faded back into the darkness. For a few moments there was total stillness and Bracca could hear his heart beating in the silence. Tara's hand gripped his so tightly that he felt afraid her fingers might break. 'It's all right,' he said quietly. 'It's all right,' for he did not know what else to say.

'Raagon. What's happening?'

'I don't know.' The Old One's voice trembled with fear. The darkness was awful. 'If only...'

Then they heard it; a strange rushing noise coming from way back in the depths of the tunnel. And then a voice came out of the darkness just in front of them.

'Quickly. Hold hands and get down. Here, Bracca. Take my hand.'

'Ammdar! It's you.'

'Of course. Who else?' and there was a chuckle in his voice as he said it that lightened their hearts. 'Get ready. Hold on,' but his last words were whipped from his mouth by the awful blast of wind that had suddenly fallen upon them. It whined and moaned about their ears like some huge and

417

terrible creature in agony, pulling and tearing at their bodies as they clung to each other and the floor in its efforts to prise them away and hurl them off down the tunnels into oblivion. It dragged at their hair till the roots hurt and tugged at their limbs till the muscles throbbed with pain; it ripped their clothes into shreds and lashed them against their bodies till they bled and all the time it howled with a savage ferocity that froze the blood in their veins and turned their stomachs to water.

How much longer would it last? How long could they withstand its awful power? Ammdar felt Bracca's hand slowly being torn away from his grip and wondered about the others. It could only be a matter of time before the wind sapped all their strength and will, snatched them away from their precarious handholds and tossed them up to play with them in the tunnels, smashing their bodies against the walls till their lives were driven from them. He had to try and do something to stop it.

Bracca, his eyes shut tight against the wind and all his concentration focused on resisting its awesome power, suddenly felt Ammdar's hand loosen in his. It was not the wind, more a deliberate untangling of their fingers. Was the elflord abandoning him? Had they after all made the wrong choice?

'No! Don't,' he yelled, but though he shouted as loudly as he could and Ammdar could not have been more than two arms' lengths away his words were rendered soundless by the noise of the wind.

Frantically he tried to keep hold of the hand, to hang onto it so tightly that it would be impossible to let go, but it was useless; the elflord was determined and their fingers were soon separated. And then as if Ammdar had read his fears Bracca felt the elflord give his hand two gentle reassuring pats.

Forcing his eyes open he looked into the darkness and to his amazement and joy saw Ammdar standing in the tunnel facing the wind. His body exuded a gentle white glow and

418

Bracca could see his face set in a mask of grim determination as he braced himself against its force. He could feel Tara's grip slowly growing weaker and her hand being slowly pulled away from his. And then Ammdar held Tabor up diagonally across his body and shouted something into the wind. Immediately the sword began to emit a piercingly brilliant silver light and simultaneously to jump out of Ammdar's grip, fly through the air to the other side of Raagon and start to perform a series of movements in the air that were too quick for Bracca to follow.

After a moment or two a dense patten of intricate silver lines began to form across the tunnel like a web. Raagon saw it and recognized in it myriad ancient runes that he had not seen used since the elven wars, all woven together into a force so powerful that this terrible wind of darkness was unable to break through it. Gradually then the wind began to diminish but as the space left for it to blow through grew smaller so it began to shriek and screech in fury until they were deafened by the noise and their ears ached with pain. Higher and higher went the awful sound as the web grew more impenetrable, till they felt they could stand no more. And then suddenly it stopped and they were bathed in blessed stillness.

For a while they continued to lie on the ground, numb with exhaustion. Their ears still rang from the dying screams of the wind but their bodies rejoiced in the luxury of peace, stretched out and relaxed in the darkness that enveloped them once more. Perhaps they would have lain there for ever had not Ammdar gently talked them back into awareness by trying to explain what had happened. He told them how Dréagg had attacked him in his moment of uncertainty at the junction of the tunnels and split his body into three, the other two of which existed only in form and not in substance. Then when he, Ammdar, had used Tabor to defeat Dréagg's plan, the Lord of Darkness had converted their form into energy and hurled it at Bracca and the others as that terrible wind. The rest they knew, except that he was now

419

certain that the left-hand tunnel was the correct one to follow and that was the way they would go.

Then, after he had given Tabor back to Bracca, he gave each of them a small round pebble-like object and told them to put it in their mouths to suck.

'They will ease the pangs of hunger and thirst,' he said. 'It is lucky I kept them with me and did not give them to poor Reev to look after. They will last a good long time. Do not lose them; they are all we have left.'

'How much longer, Ammdar?' said Tara, putting it on her tongue and letting its strange, slightly sweet taste wash around inside her mouth.

'I am not certain, but it cannot be much further now. Are you ready? Shall we go?'

Weary though they were and drained by memories of the wind, the thought that they would soon reach the Droon spurred them on, and the relief of the pains in their stomachs gave them a glow of well-being and energy. So, a little shakily, they stood up and, with Ammdar once again leading, they set off down the left hand tunnel into the darkness.

Now, with a strange new confidence, Ammdar found himself remembering this last part of the way almost as if it had been yesterday that he had made the journey. At each fork or junction he would stop for a few moments with his eyes shut, empty his mind of all thought and let his subconscious make the decision. And they sang again as they had before, with Raagon's voice leading them, Ammdar taking up the refrain and Bracca and Tara joining in when they had learnt the tune. As if to further ease their travel the tunnel had become wider and taller so that they made good progress, walking with long easy strides down the gently sloping floor at a pace they would never have imagined possible further back. But all the time, as they descended further and deeper into the earth, the temperature grew hotter so that they became drenched in sweat.

On and on they went, and time once again lost all meaning

for them. Indeed since they had first entered the tunnel beneath Gan they had seemed to exist in a strange vacuum where time stood still so that it was impossible to say how many days, moons or even seasons had passed; if any. They had stopped singing some way back and had been growing steadily more tired when Bracca suddenly broke the silence with a question that broke upon them like a thunderclap.

'Are you sure we're going the right way?' he said. 'You told us it would not be far.'

The question had troubled him for some time, coming into his head from nowhere and niggling away at him with a persistence that would not be ignored. And now he felt he had to ask it, and the easy rhythm of their journey was shattered.

'I am as certain as I can be,' replied Ammdar, with a lightness in his voice that he did not feel.

So they carried on, but there was a crackle of tension about them now that weighed like a shroud upon their shoulders. Raagon tried to break into song once more to dispel the atmosphere but, though Ammdar joined in, neither Bracca nor Tara took it up and the tune died on Raagon's lips.

At the next junction, the easy certainty of before had gone and Ammdar once more suffered agonies of indecision before deciding to go straight ahead. Was it the hand of Dréagg that was guiding Bracca's thoughts or was it just the young man's own innocent and perfectly understandable doubts. Ammdar did not know any more; he only cursed the words for having been spoken. When they came to another turning and, after considerable debate inside himself, Ammdar chose to go right, Bracca spoke up loudly and confidently and said that he felt they should turn left.

'What brings you to that conclusion?' the elflord asked gently.

'I'm guessing, the same as you are,' came the reply.

'You have not been here before. I have.'

'So long ago you can't possibly remember,' and so steeped

in venom was Bracca's reply that Ammdar had no doubt now that Dréagg was behind it.

'Very well, then. We shall have to vote. Raagon, which way do you think?'

The Old One's voice was flawed with the pain of their dissension.

'I shall go right with you, Ammdar,' he said.

'And you, Tara?'

But Bracca did not let her reply.

'Oh, she'll go with you too, I'm sure. She wouldn't believe what I say. Would you, Tara?'

There was silence.

'Would you, Tara? Come on, you think Raagon's right, don't you?'

'Bracca. Don't. . .' she said. 'Please. Don't!'

'Ah, you see,' and his voice was bright with triumph as his paranoia was confirmed. 'I told you. Of course she'll follow you. I'm only a stupid human. My word counts for nothing.' There was a pause then as he revelled in his victimization. 'And don't try to find Dréagg in my words. I speak for myself. Come on, then. I'll go along with you. What choice have I got? But don't blame me when we get lost, wandering around these cursed tunnels for ever.'

Ammdar's heart was heavy but there was nothing he could do. He had to obey his first instincts and hold to his decision, so he set off up the right hand tunnel with the others following.

Further and deeper they went and still they did not reach the cave where he had hidden the Droon. And the seeds of mistrust and doubt that had been sown grew in all of them so that Raagon and Tara began to wonder whether Bracca had not been right after all. At the thought that they might be lost a terrible knot of panic formed in their stomachs, constricting their throats so that breathing became difficult and turning their legs to jelly. Ammdar too was beset with a lack of faith in his decisions and an awareness of the growing unease of the others that turned every step into a grim toil.

How much longer now? Surely it could not be far.

And then, for some strange inexplicable reason, the feeling started to grow on him that the cave was very close. Now, just as he remembered, the roof started to dip and the tunnel became much narrower. This was how it had been but was it a false alarm? There must be many such places in the tunnels and without a light he could not be sure. If he was right the passageway would get much smaller still so that they would end up having to crawl. He would say nothing yet in case he was wrong, but his heart beat wildly with excitement at the prospect that at last they were nearing their destination.

On they went and as he had hoped the tunnel got smaller and smaller until they were forced on to their hands and knees. He was certain now.

'Stop for a moment and listen,' he said. As they knelt on the hard stone their knees seemed to hurt even more than when they had been moving and irrational flashes of anger flickered across the minds of the others at Ammdar for stopping them like this.

'We have finally reached the entrance to the cave,' he went on, anxious not to allow the joy and relief he was feeling come through in his voice for fear that Bracca would think he was gloating.

For Raagon and Tara this was marvellous news and they felt as if a great weight had been lifted from their shoulders but it was not so for Bracca. He felt as if a battle was going on inside himself; part of him felt vindictive and cheated that he had been proved wrong, and somehow very frightened that the moment he had been struggling and fighting to reach for so long had finally come. The other part of him was elated and relieved that soon it would all be over and the destiny marked out for him by Ashgaroth had come to pass at last.

'From now on the opening is so small that we shall have to crawl on our stomachs until we come out in the cave itself. It is a tight squeeze in there, we must be careful. Are you ready to go in?'

Raagon and Tara replied that they were but there was silence from Bracca.

'Bracca?' The elflord's voice was gentle.

'Oh, yes! I'm ready. I'd follow you anywhere, Ammdar. You're always right.' Bracca's voice was strained and brittle and Ammdar could hear both resentment and fear in the heavy sarcasm of the words. It was worrying for it meant that Dréagg was still very close to Bracca, nurturing his isolation and feeding his apprehensions.

'All right, then, you'll have to get down flat,' and so they pressed themselves down onto the floor of the tunnel and started to crawl forwards into the space ahead.

At first it was not too tight and they moved fairly easily, shuffling along with their arms at their sides and pushing themselves forward with their toes. But then the rock seemed to close in upon them and they were forced to put their arms out in front. Time and again they had to wriggle through the tiniest of openings, scraping themselves as they did so till they could feel little rivulets of blood running down their arms and legs. But it was the tops of their shoulders that bore the brunt of the pain, constantly rubbing against the roof as they forced their bodies forward.

Suddenly Bracca was stuck; his shoulders wedged tightly in a narrow fissure that Ammdar, before him, had only just managed to get through. Desperately he pushed himself forward with his feet but the rock just bit deeper into his flesh.

'Wait,' he shouted. 'I can't get through. I'm stuck.'

He could feel a wave of panic welling up inside himself as he became aware for the first time of the enormity of the weight that was pressing down upon him. He thought he could feel it moving, slowly and imperceptibly lowering itself onto his back till the life was crushed out of him. Galvanized into action by the mounting horror that was crashing into his brain he started to flail about wildly, throwing himself from side to side and screaming, but he was unable to move either forwards or backwards.

The others waited in the darkness, horrified, as the awful

424

struggle was enacted until finally with a terrible sob he collapsed with exhaustion and there was silence. They felt so utterly useless. Ammdar could not turn round and all Tara could do was push.

'Bracca.' Tara's voice was tremulous with anxiety. She had felt his pain as if it were her own and her heart had wept for his suffering. She was wary too of his reaction to her. There was no reply.

'Bracca.' She called his name again, a little more loudly this time, and to her relief he answered her but his voice sounded desolate and weary.

'Please, listen,' she said. 'There is something we must try. It may only be a small piece of rock that's stopping you. We must try and knock it off. We can use the hilt of Tabor. If I reach my hand forward I'm sure I can get to it. What do you think?'

'Yes,' he said, his words muffled by the rock. 'Yes, anything's worth trying. It won't work though; you can be certain of that. It would be too easy.' And then, conscious that his self-pitying had gone too far he tried to inject some optimism into his voice. 'But you're right. We must try.'

Tara found it impossible to manoeuvre Tabor out of its scabbard so eventually, after a lot of twisting and turning, Bracca agreed a little reluctantly to let her unfasten the scabbard and take it off. It was then relatively easy, even in the cramped space of the tunnel, to draw out the sword and turn it so that the hilt was pointing forwards. However getting herself into a position from which she could knock at the stone around Bracca's shoulders proved extremely difficult. She had to squeeze herself in between him and the roof and in trying to do so she kept scraping her back on the rock till it throbbed with pain. Then at last she was on top of him and she could feel the hard outline of his muscles pressing against her breasts and stomach.

'Bracca. Are you all right?' she said, and though he answered that he was she could tell that he was in some discomfort. Light though she was, her weight forcing his

425

body down onto the rough uneven stone of the floor must be hurting him considerably. Then, lying on her side with one arm tucked underneath, she began hitting at the stone with all her strength. From the sound that came back she did not think it was too thick and this hope gave her fresh energy. After a little while though, when her arm and wrist were aching and still she had failed to remove any of the stone, her initial enthusiasm had almost evaporated.

'I'm having a rest,' she said and, lowering Tabor till it lay on top of Bracca, she let her body flop down in delicious relief.

'How's it going?' asked Raagon anxiously from behind.

'Not too badly,' she replied, but Raagon could hear the weariness in her voice.

All too soon she felt she ought to carry on and so raising herself up she lifted Tabor and began thumping away at the stone, feeling once again the jar in her shoulder and cramp in her hand that had become so familiar to her from before.

Thump ... thump ... thump ... she tried to keep a steady rhythm because that let her forget about the pains in her body and allowed no room for thoughts of failure to enter her head. On and on it went and every time she heard the sound she prayed that it would be followed by the sound of splintering stone.

When the muscles in her arm were knotted in agony she rewarded herself with another rest, before continuing on again. For Bracca, trapped and immobile, the feel of Tara's body on top of his had stirred a host of lascivious thoughts that almost banished the web of panic that had gripped him earlier and helped him to forget the pains in his shoulders and stomach. They had never before been so physically close and the steady rhythm of her movements had inflamed his body to such a height of sensuality that he could think of little else. For Tara also, despite the hurt and the pain, there was a delicious excitement in the touch of his body under hers that set her heart pounding and the blood tingling in her veins. Now that their task was nearly over the prohibition

426

on their love was almost ended and the thought that they would then be free to know and explore the joys of each other's passion sent her almost giddy with apprehenson.

And then suddenly while her mind was lost in a whirl of intoxicating images there was a sharp crack and a shout from Bracca as a piece of rock broke away and fell onto his shoulder and down against his neck. A flood of relief swept through her and there was a spontaneous cheer from all the others.

'Can you move?' she said, and she felt his body shift and turn beneath her as he pushed against the rock.

'Nearly,' he answered. 'Just a bit more.' So she set to again with a burst of enthusiasm that lent her new strength. Soon there was another crack and another shout from Bracca as a piece, larger this time, fell away and hit him on the head.

'Be careful. You nearly killed me.' The abrasiveness of his words shattered the euphoria of her success and she forced herself to stay silent so that they hung in the air as a grim reminder of Dréagg's closeness to Bracca. He moved again and this time she felt his body move forward through the tunnel. So, he was free. She had done it.

'Right. If you get off me we can get moving. And I want Tabor back.'

Holding back the rage that threatened to break out from her, she wriggled off him and, putting Tabor back in its scabbard, passed it forward and felt his hand snatch it sharply from her. There was not even a thank you. Damn him; damn him! And now the lascivious thoughts of a few moments ago were gone as if they had never been. Impossible that they could ever have existed. It was too easy to blame Dréagg; and yet she had to believe that that was the reason for his behaviour otherwise she would lose her faith and her will to carry on. But her pride would not let the incident pass without comment.

'Aren't you even going to thank me?' The silence that followed seemed to last an age, as if Bracca was struggling within himself to find the right words. Once or twice she thought he was going to speak but nothing came until finally he blurted out.

'Thank you! What for? If you hadn't freed me we'd all have been stuck. Come on! Don't try and pretend you did it for me. You had no choice. You were just. . .' but then Ammdar interrupted him.

'We'd better make a move. Come on.' And in the effort of moving forward again through the narrow tunnel there was no energy left for the poison of his words. Tara too lost the incentive to reply as she crawled after Bracca in the darkness.

Bracca was now in a state of torment; his personality torn in half and each half in constant bitter struggle with the other. He heard what he had said to Tara with horror, the words coming out of his mouth almost of their own volition, and yet once they had been spoken they seemed to acquire a truth that he could not argue with. And try as he might, he could not rid himself of the paranoia that so afflicted him. More and more now, as they neared the cave, he found himself seeing the other three as conspirators in some secret plot to make use of him and in the end to sacrifice him for some great and mighty purpose that had become so vague and obscure he could not really remember what it was. Tara's role in this plot seemed now to him to be the most insidious and the sensuous images that still floated across his mind only seemed to confirm it. He saw her now as using the promise of her body to so inflame his desires and cloud his reason that he would follow her slavishly in the hope of eventually possessing her. But if, as she had told him, they could only consummate their love after they had accomplished their mission and mankind would then be no more, then he also would have ceased to exist. And so he would never be able to love her. It was all clear to him now. It was as if, suddenly, someone had drawn away a veil and he was seeing everything as if for the first time. And, as he followed Ammdar through the twists and turns of the tunnel, he resolved what he would do to thwart her plot. He would force her to love him before the Droon was opened. She would protest, of course, that he thereby ran the risk of losing his humanity and acquiring her elven nature but he would not listen. That was the price they had to pay for him agreeing to open the casket. Yes, that would do it. She would see then that he was not so easily taken in. 'All humans are stupid.' Her words seemed to echo in his head and to confirm his mistrust of her.

He felt very calm, almost joyous, now that he had seen through the elaborate machinations of her plan. All the frustrations of their time together came back as if to haunt him. He could see each occasion so clearly: how she must have laughed at him! Well, he would have his revenge for all that humiliation, and how sweet it would be.

They moved along in silence now; no one spoke and there was a tension in the air that was almost tangible. And then to Ammdar's relief a tiny crack of orange light appeared in front of them and he knew that the cave was just ahead. Now that they were almost there he felt dizzy with nervousness. After so long and so much!

The orange light grew larger and more bright as they got closer until suddenly Ammdar found himself awash with it and realized that he was in the entrance to the cave. He felt a glorious sense of space around him as he slowly stood up, easing the cramp from his muscles and rubbing his knees gingerly as they straightened out. Turning he bent down to give Bracca a hand up but his offer was brusquely ignored so he waited for Tara and Raagon.

'Well, old friend,' he said, as Raagon emerged, blinking, into the light. 'What do you think? We've made it!'

'Yes. I never thought. . .' and the Old One's voice drifted off on a wave of emotion as his memory took him back to the long days of Operrallmar and way back beyond those to the first elven wars when he had ridden with Ammdar against the goblins. All those times of waiting and hoping and dreaming and in the end despair that the Silver Warrior would ever fight again. And now, here they were – on the threshold of victory.'

Then Ammdar saw a large tear seep out of the corner of one of Raagon's eyes and start to run, glistening, down the folds of his cheek.

'I know,' he said, putting his arm round the Old One's shoulders, 'I know. Come on, we're almost there.'

For a few moments they all stood still just inside the cave, shielding their eyes and letting them get slowly used to the light. It was Tara who first raised her head and took a long clear look at what was around her. She had imagined that the cave would be quite small and was surprised to find that it soared way up high above her so that she could not see to the top. It was not long though, maybe thirty or forty paces at its widest, and the walls were festooned with enormous stalactites that hung down from the rock like huge icicles. It was these that gave off the light for they glowed with a shimmering golden-ochre brightness that pushed back the darkness and threw strange spiky silhouettes against the walls. The floor too was littered with large stalagmites and these great pillars of stone stood like giant sentries glowing eerily in the orange gloom. Feeling very frightened and apprehensive she put out her hand to reach for Bracca's but checked herself just in time. It was this above all that made her feel so uneasy; this awful estrangement between them, the walls that had suddenly appeared to drive them apart and the isolation that he had retreated into. She perceived him now as a total stranger and yet when she glanced quickly sideways to see him in the light for the first time in so long he was still the Bracca that she had always known. Unsettlingly disorientated she looked up again and felt as if the space above her head was a huge spiral, sucking her upwards into its black empty void. And then she heard Raagon's loud exclamation. 'Look, there it is!' and she turned to see the direction in which he was pointing. At the far side of the cavern the wall shelved sharply back as it neared the floor so that a deep grotto had been formed. Here were a host of smaller stalactites and stalagmites, many of them meeting together in the middle to make solid columns and behind these, resting on a natural raised stone dais, stood a small silver casket. It glinted dully in the light and Tara could see a black lock on the front and intricately worked inlays of black tracery that wound around it like a web. So, that was the Droon! It looked so innocent and pretty sitting there bathed in the golden glow of the grotto that it was almost impossible to think that they had travelled so far and been through so much to reach it. And as she looked, the shapes of the rock seemed to change in the light; to become strange unknown creatures that stared out at her with chilling malevolence. Were they moving or was it just the shimmering of the stalactites that made them appear so? She closed her eyes and rubbed them as if to banish their images and when she opened them and looked again they had gone but she could not forget them and the memory of them added to her sense of foreboding.

And then, in terrible confirmation of all her worst fears, she glimpsed Bracca out of the corner of her eye as he suddenly leapt behind her and she felt his arm lock around her neck in a savage choking hold.

She stumbled and fell against him as he swung her round to face the others and, in a daze, she realized that she had almost been expecting something like this. His voice, guttural and harsh, echoed out into the cavern.

'Now! Now, I have you. And if you want to use me to open the Droon you will do as I say. Listen to me, Ammdar and Raagon. I have seen through Tara's plan. She has had me as a fool for too long but I will have her now before the Droon is opened and if I have then lost the power; well, so be it.'

Tara squirmed wildly in his arms as she tried to break free but he only laughed at her efforts and tightened his grip on her neck.

'See! See how desperate she is. She never thought she would have to give in to me and now she's panicking. She can't bear the thought. Well, I've lived on her promises for too long. But no more; now is the time I take my reward. Then we'll see about opening your precious Droon, though why I should sacrifice myself I don't know.'

The elflord and the Old One looked on in disbelief and horror.

'Bracca. Don't ... please. Not this. Not now...' Raagon's voice was pleading and gentle. He remembered the young man as he had first seen him in the snows outside Operrallmar; how innocent and good he had seemed. And though he knew it was the force of Dréagg that had turned him, still the situation was too horrible to contemplate.

Ammdar too was reeling with the shock of seeing Bracca this way. How finely now the success of their mission was balanced. Even Bracca's face had changed; the cheeks gaunt and hollow, the forehead elongated and the eyes empty and black. So this was how much Dréagg had taken control. And there was nothing he could do. Powerless he merely stood and watched, praying that Ashgaroth would somehow show himself.

'What, Ammdar! You're saying nothing. Not going to try and persuade me it's all Dréagg saying and doing this. Perhaps you've realized the truth – that you can't trick me any more. I've seen through it all. All right, then. You can either turn away or stand and watch us – it makes no difference to me. You might enjoy it though,' and his laugh was as brittle as ice.

He swung Tara round to face him and she felt his eyes boring into her soul.

'Now,' he said. 'Our time has come. Are you not quivering with excitement? After all that waiting too. Oh...' he paused and grabbing her by the hair pulled her head forward so that her ear was next to his mouth. 'Don't think of changing, will you? Like all those times before. If you do the Droon will never be opened. It's up to you.' His voice, low and hoarse and quivering with lecherous expectation, filled her with terror and she hurled herself forward in an attempt to break out of his grip, lunging from side to side, but it was hopeless and she soon wore herself out and was left hanging limply in his arms. She still could not really believe that any of this was happening. It had to be a nightmare. It was Bracca! He could not be doing this; it was impossible to think of – she must wake up ... wake up. If she could talk to him, make him listen, make him understand that she really did love him; how hard it had been for her as well not to give in to her desires and join her body with his. But they must not do it now and risk him losing his human nature. To have come so far and then to lose, like this. There had to be a way to show him.

'Bracca! Please listen. I...' but roughly he swung her round to face him and slapping a hand over her mouth pushed his face so close to hers that she could feel his breath.

'No,' he rasped. 'No, you listen. You thought I wouldn't realize that once the Droon is open and the Seeds are separated then I too will be destroyed with the rest of man. You three are all right. You'll survive; but I shall be gone. Then where are your promises of love? Broken! Do you hear me? Broken! So don't try and trick me any more. I'm going to have you now,' and savagely he began to maul her down until she was lying flat on the rough stone floor of the cave.

Desperately Raagon turned to Ammdar.

'What can we do?' he said, and there were tears in his voice. 'We must do something. We cannot just...'

'No. There is nothing. If we stop him we shall never separate the Seeds and we shall never defeat Dréagg. Yet if we don't stop him and he loses his humanity we are again defeated. We cannot win. It is as I feared. He has succumbed to Dréagg even as I did and we are rendered powerless against him.' Raagon's heart ached at the despair in the elflord's voice and his eyes looked back at the terrible scene being played out in front of them.

Bracca was sitting astride the prostrate body of Tara with his hands clamped on her wrists to keep her down for still she was wriggling wildly in a vain attempt to throw him off.

'Lie still,' he barked, and brought a hand down hard against her face with a slap that echoed loudly against the walls of the cavern.

'Now, let me kiss you,' and, gripping her hair to hold her head in position, he bent down and placed his lips against hers, crushing them against her mouth in an effort to get some response from her for she was as still and cold as stone. But there was nothing; not a flicker of warmth came from her and so, raging with frustration, he lifted up his head and yelled.

'Love me, damn you, love me,' before placing both his hands around the neck of her gown and pulling down with all his strength.

There was an ominous ripping sound as the gown split open from the top. For an instant he was blinded by a vision of such dazzling white beauty that his heart seemed to stop beating but then, as he looked on in wonder, her body seemed to dissolve into a cloud of twinkling silver stars and was gone leaving only a dark and empty space where she had been. For a few terrible moments there was silence and then Bracca's face contorted into an image of such abject horror and pain that Raagon could not bear to look. He lifted up his head and screamed and the sound was such as Ammdar had never heard before; a terrible wailing cry that soared up into the heights of the cavern and came from the bowels of the earth itself. And the stone upon which they stood seemed to quiver and shake beneath their feet and the walls moaned with grief. Then the screams began to die and words grew out of the formless cries of remorse. 'Where are you? What have I done?' he cried, in a voice that sobbed with remorse, and Ammdar's heart was glad for he knew that the struggle was over; Dréagg had been finally expelled from Bracca's soul and Ashgaroth had claimed him back.

Stumbling blindly through a dense whirling fog of despair Bracca looked down at the crumpled pile of clothes where she had been and wept, and tears rained down his cheeks till he could not see. And, finally, when Ammdar felt the time was right he went up to the young man and put an arm on his shoulder so that Bracca raised his face to look up at him.

'What have I done?' he said again, and Ammdar's spirit

434

bled for Bracca's suffering. He raised him up then and gently wiped the tears from his eyes with his hands. His voice was soft as he spoke.

'She does not exist in hate, only in love,' he said, 'and she could not live for you in hatred.'

'I destroyed her.'

'No. You didn't destroy her. Dréagg destroyed her. You must not blame yourself; you could do nothing.'

'How can I go on, without her? I can't ... there is nothing.'

'Bracca. If you give in now Dréagg has won. You must go on, for Tara's sake. For her memory. You cannot let her down.'

'Ammdar. I don't know ... I'm so tired. I feel so weak. Please, can I just lie down. I can't stand.'

'No. If you lie down now you may never get up again,' for Ammdar was worried that the struggle had taken such a toll on Bracca's spirit that once asleep he would never wake up. 'Here, put your arm round my shoulder and the other around Raagon.'

So the three of them, the elflord, the Old One and the human, walked slowly across to the grotto at the far wall of the cavern wherein lay the Droon. And Bracca's heart was sick and the tears would not stop flowing as the image of Tara reverberated through his head. He saw her as he had first seen her with Nab and Beth; he saw her silver shadow as they had battled through the snow and he remembered their laughter in the cave where they had taken shelter. He could taste again the anger as she became a deer and his happiness when she turned back. He remembered her at Operrallmar and saw her beside him at the battle outside Gan. Her eyes, her nose, her ears, her voice, the tilt of her head, the fall of her hair – all were etched into his mind so sharply that they were part of his soul. But already, when he tried to summon up the image of her face before his eyes he could not do it and it was then that the anguish of her loss cut into him again and the ache in his throat almost choked him.

How dearly he would have loved to rest now, to lie down

and wander through the maze of memories of his time with Tara; to savour each one at his leisure and be with her again, but there was no time for Ammdar and Raagon kept pulling him forward, stumbling with exhaustion, until they were bathed in the golden light of the grotto where the Droon lay.

'Stay here with Raagon,' said Ammdar. 'I'll go in and bring it out.'

He had to bend quite low to get to it for the roof sloped sharply down and Bracca watched as he picked his way among the stalactites and stalagmites until at last the elflord laid his hands on the casket. Strange, thought Ammdar, as he felt its familiar shape once again, that he had been the last person to touch it. How different things had been then; concerned to hide the Droon where none should ever find it so that the reign of man would last forever on the earth. He could never have guessed that aeons of time later it would be he who would be destroying the very creature he had helped to create. Gently he picked it up, surprised at how small it was and how easy it was to hold. It was easier to back out with it so very slowly and carefully he walked backwards with the Droon cradled in his arms. He was worried about Bracca; the loss of Tara had affected him terribly and he was very weak. Would he have the will and the strength to sever the Seeds?

Now he found he could straighten his back and he knew he was out of the grotto. Turning he found himself facing Bracca and he placed the Droon down in front of him. Bracca looked up at him and smiled. How long had he dreamt of this moment; the fulfilment of his destiny, the reality behind the voice that had long ago come to him and told him that the mantle of light was now upon him. He remembered those times as if they were yesterday: Shayll's laughter, Melvaig's pipe, Morven's gentleness; the beautiful stone statues of Nab and Beth, Brock, Warrigal and the others; his endless walks through the lush green depths of the forest; the terrible argument at the Stagg and his falling out with Melvaig. His life in Haark flashed before him in a

436

series of disconnected images and he felt a terrible yearning to see again the ones he had loved and to relive those faraway days.

Almost unconsciously he found that his hands had gone to the clasps on the Belt of Ammdar; that he was fingering them gently and feeling the pattern of the serpents' bodies as they wove into and around one another. Then with a sudden movement he had snapped them open and the Belt was off and hanging loosely in his hand. Oh, why was Tara not here with him now to share this moment? What had he done? And as memories of Tara flooded back in upon him he seemed to see the face of Nab as clearly as those of Ammdar and Raagon. But where Bracca would have expected anger there was only compassion and love. 'Do not punish yourself,' he said. 'Tara does not blame you.' There was a pause before he went on. 'Do you remember my words? Each side of the buckle is a key to the Droon. Turn the key on your left three times to the left and the right hand key twice to the right.'

'Yes,' Bracca answered. 'Yes, I remember,' for it was as if Nab was standing speaking to him. And then he turned to Raagon who was still holding him up. 'I'll be all right now. I need both hands free. Thank you.'

'Well, if you're sure,' he said, and took his arm away. Bracca swayed for a moment or two, unsupported, and then clasping the serpentine head of the left hand buckle in both hands he inserted it quickly into the lock. It went in easily and he turned it round three times as Nab had said, finding to his satisfaction that it clicked each time. Despite his weariness his heart was pounding with excitement and his hand shook as he got hold of the other key and put it in the lock. This did not seem to fit as well as the other and he had to try it a number of times before it finally slid home. Just two turns and it would be open. What would they find inside? What would the Seeds be like and how would they separate them? The ending of the reign of man was just two turns away. He turned it once quickly until it clicked but then he hesitated and the key seemed to turn heavy in his hand. He

437

looked up into the eyes of Raagon the Old One, who had seen so much, and then he turned to Ammdar, and they both smiled at him for they knew the turmoil that was in him and were sorry. And his mind raced back to Xtlan and to the darkness in man; the horrors of a world dominated by arrogance and cruelty, where compassion and kindness have no place and love is weakness. He remembered Haark before the fateful decision of the Stagg, and Barll's vicious slavering face appeared again before him. But what of all the goodness in man? What would happen to that? Was that also to perish?

He could think no more. He was tired. It had to be done for the sake of all those whose mantle he had inherited; for Nab and Beth, for Brock and Warrigal, Perryfoot and Sam. He had to do it for Melvaig and Morven and Shuinn, for Shayll and for Tara and for all those who had followed the light of Ashgaroth and fought against the darkness. And so he gave the key its final turn and lifting up the lid let it fall carefully back till the hinges caught it and the Droon was open.

As they looked inside all they could see was a dark swirling mist drifting around the inside of the casket in eerie billowing clouds. It was icy cold and Bracca felt the chill seep through into his bones. This was not how Ammdar remembered it; the box had been clear and empty save for the three Seeds lying at the bottom of the box. Where were they? Cautiously he put his head closer and peered in. There was something moving in there, waving about in the mist. It looked like a plant of some sort growing from the bottom with three long single stalks; and at the end of each there hung a bright red, oval pod. There was something infinitely sinister and frightening about them and he was just about to tell the others to move back when, suddenly, without any warning, the three tendrils snaked like lightning out of the box and fastened themselves around the necks of the intruders.

Bracca, hardly able to breathe, felt it growing tighter and tighter and as he struggled to free himself he saw the veins on the pod next to his face start to pulse and glow with a steady, regular rhythm. With each beat the constriction around his neck grew tighter until a black starry mist started to float across his vision and he knew that he was losing consciousness. Desperately he twisted his head so that he could see the others. Raagon was already hanging limply while Ammdar, threshing about wildly, was clutching at the vicious thongs around his neck and trying vainly to pull them away.

How he longed to give in to the soft dark depths of oblivion that beckoned him! If he stopped struggling the pain in his throat seemed less terrible; how easy it would be to abandon himself to death. His head was spinning now and the stars before his eyes were whirling round his head in myriads of interweaving circles. He felt himself slipping backwards as if he was falling off a cliff.

And then through the dark swirling mists of his pain he saw a brilliant silver star. It drew him towards itself effortlessly, onwards and upwards, until he was consumed by a mighty resolution and he knew what he had to do. There was a strength and a will in him now that he could never have imagined as he reached his hand down for Tabor and drew it out. Tighter still grew the noose around his neck yet it did not seem to matter as he raised Tabor high above the casket and saw the root from which grew the stalks of the Three Seeds of Logic. He looked across at Ammdar and Raagon and saw to his horror that the elflord was now as still as the Old One. Were they dead? No! Please no! and his tortured soul screamed out in protest as he brought the sword plunging down into the very heart of the root. There was a terrible shriek as if the thing were in pain and a thick jet of foul black liquid spouted upwards. Again and again the silver blade of Tabor came slashing down into the Droon until at last the tendril round his neck had fallen away and the root lay in a thousand pieces. All his rage and anger spilled out through the flashing curves of the sword as he turned now to the Seeds and sliced them so finely that they were as dust. Only then did he stop and look for the bodies of his two friends but it was too late for there was nothing left of them but a faint shadow against the stone.

Then suddenly a column of silver light came down from somewhere high above and as it enfolded him in its brilliance he felt a soft warm breeze start to blow against his face. At first it was only gentle but within moments it had grown into a mighty wind that swept him off his feet and sent him soaring upwards towards the roof of the cavern. Higher and higher he floated, spinning slowly through a never ending series of shafts in the rock until at last he was carried out through a small cave in the ground and found himself drifting through daylight. Still the column of silver light drew him up and now he saw Gan and the forest of Spath falling away beneath him, the garish multi-coloured leaves of its trees blending together into a bizarre patchwork. And there, away in the distance up in the mountains, was the citadel of Operrallmar where he had first met Raagon and Ammdar with Tara. Now they were all gone. Yet he had severed the Seeds; he had succeeded in the task that Ashgaroth had set for him and he felt certain that somewhere, somehow, they would know and be content.

And he wondered about himself for, oddly, he felt no different except that there was a glorious euphoric calm deep within him. He tried to divine what effect the Separation of the Seeds had had on him but he was unable to and then, as he watched the land beneath him slip further and further away, he caught sight of a figure just ahead waiting for him and he was consumed with joy for he knew immediately that it was Tara. With outstretched arms she caught and held him and he felt the tears of happiness wet against his face as their two bodies joined with one another in love at last.

CHAPTER XXVI

On earth it was as has been written; that when the Seeds of
Logic were separated and the power of Logic dissipated into
the farthest reaches of space, so man could not exist. Some
there were who died of starvation, others of the heat or cold
or of disease and illness, while still more met their end at the
hands of their fellows. In Xtlan the evil that had been
harnessed and directed by their lord now rampaged
unhindered throughout the land as man fell against man,
raging and slobbering with lust and greed until all had
perished.

Some there were, the innocent, the pure and the good,
whose spirits were taken by Ashgaroth; and he made them as
elves for without Logic they could exist in the realms of
Magic. And the roots of cruelty and arrogance which Dréagg
had planted deep within the nature of man, were no more in
them.

And slowly, as the moons came and went and season
succeeded season, the skies above the earth cleared and the
seas became wild and pure and shone like silver in the
sunshine, and all the creatures rejoiced for the Great Enemy
had gone. So it was that gradually the earth healed itself and
the scars left by man grew over and became green and it was
as if man had never been.

441

Now, once again, the three elflords ruled over all the three vastnesses of creation; Malcoff over the mountains whose majesty and strength were as testaments to the power of Ashgaroth, Saurelon over the seas and Wychnor over all the forests and the green growing things. And in the halls of the elves the name of Ammdar was praised and sung and his memory rang out through the great ages of forever for he had been redeemed and had undone the terrible wrong he had wrought upon the earth.

In the long dark nights of autumn and winter and on the gentle pastel evenings of spring and summer those who had been there told stories of the terrible battle of Gan, of Sienogg and Barll and Degg and the mighty goblin armies with their fearsome lizard steeds. They thrilled with excitement as they heard of the bravery of the elves and listened spellbound to the history of Bracca, Tara, Raagon and Ammdar and the epic saga of their journey to the Droon.

And so the earth lived in harmony for with the extinction of man it was as Nab had said; that Dréagg was truly defeated and was without limbs or senses. And there was peace amongst all the creatures of the earth and they were at ease with one another, neither fighting nor feeding off the flesh of their fellows.

Magic ruled over all the life on earth for the elves were the guardians of the spirit of Ashgaroth and he was well pleased for the earth shone out once again as his jewel and glory; testament to his final victory over Dréagg and the forces of darkness.

And those who had been human wondered at the marvels of the earth in harmony and all their suffering and pain were forgotten in the beauty wherein they dwelt.

Bracca and Tara rode through aeons of time and space in the corridors of the universe, floating in the silver-tiered void of eternity with their spirits bound together as one, and Ashgaroth smiled upon the wild ecstasy of their love and blessed it so that in Tara's womb there grew the seed of a

442

new life and it was a boy.

From her the child took the elven part of its nature, which was of Magic and from him the human part, which was of Logic, so that their son was truly of the Duain Elrondin (or powers of life) for in him lay both Magic and Logic.

And now it was that Bracca felt a change in himself for that in him which was of Logic had now been passed on and was gone.

Ashgaroth guided their path through space until he brought them to a planet at the very farthest end of the universe and this planet is also known as earth for he had chosen it as a mirror to the original though it was further back in time so that it had not been touched by the defeat of Dréagg.

And he brought them down through the clouds until at last they alighted on this other earth. They found themselves in the middle of a field and it was here that Tara gave birth to her baby; and the snow was falling heavily so that she wrapped it in her shawl to keep it warm.

Then Ashgaroth led their footsteps through the fields until they came to a stile and beyond the stile was a wood. The wood was strangely familiar to them so that they seemed to know where lay the Great Oak under whose mighty boughs Ashgaroth had told them to leave their baby.

And all the time as Bracca dug away in the snow to make a place in which the baby would be safe they felt the presence of a creature watching them.

So it was that at last they laid the baby down and covered it over with leaves and peat moss to keep it warm.

Then Bracca bent and kissed it goodbye and as Tara lowered her head to do the same she caught sight of a badger watching her from the cover of some nearby rhododendron bushes.

She smiled then and having looked long and hard at her baby she kissed it and, standing up, held Bracca for a few moments before they started to wander back across the fields.

And then Ashgaroth took Bracca and Tara away from this other earth and led them back through the infinite vastnesses of space until they came down once more on the place they had always known as earth and in front of them lay Silver Wood.

It was a spring evening and the air caressed their faces with a sweet softness that was heavy with the scent of bluebells. Hand in hand they walked across the grass towards it listening in wonder to the songs of the blackbirds in the rhododendrons and the larks high above them in the clear blue sky.

As they got nearer to the Old Beech they saw Nab and Beth standing waiting for them. At their side stood Brock and Sam and Perryfoot while Warrigal sat perched on a large root at the base of the tree. Melvaig too was there, standing smiling with Morven holding his arm, and next to them stood Shuinn and Shayll and Nabbeth. Then finally, in the shade of the tree, they saw Raagon and Ammdar.

And as they walked towards their friends, the evening sun cast their long shadows against the trees at the front of the wood. And they smiled at each other and their hearts were full to bursting with happiness for they were all home at last.